RAGDOLL

RAGDOLL

DANIEL COLE

First published in Great Britain in 2017
by Orion Books,
an imprint of The Orion Publishing Group Ltd
Carmelite House, 50 Victoria Embankment,
London EC4Y 0DZ

An Hachette UK company

1 3 5 7 9 10 8 6 4 2

A CIP catalogue record for this book
is available from the British Library.

ISBN (Hardback) 978 1 4091 6874 4
ISBN (Export Trade Paperback) 978 1 4091 6875 1

Typeset by Born Group

Printed and bound in Great Britain by CPI Group (UK) Ltd, Croydon, CR0 4YY

www.orionbooks.co.uk

'So tell me, if you're the Devil, what does that make me?'

PROLOGUE

Monday 24 May 2010

Samantha Boyd ducked under the wobbly police barrier and glanced up at the statue of Lady Justice perched atop London's infamous Old Bailey courtrooms. Intended as a symbol of strength and integrity, Samantha now saw her for what she really was: a disillusioned and despairing woman on the verge of pitching herself off the rooftop and into the pavement below. Appropriately, the blindfold carved into her likenesses the world over had been omitted; for 'blind justice' was a naive concept, especially when issues such as racism and police corruption become involved.

The surrounding roads and Tube stations had all been closed again due to the swarm of journalists that had settled there, transforming a busy area of central London into an absurdly middle-class shanty town. Empty food packaging flaunted Marks & Spencer and Pret A Manger logos up from the litter-strewn floor. Designer sleeping bags were being folded away to the buzz of electric razors, while one man's underwhelming travel iron failed to disguise the fact that he had slept in his only shirt and tie.

Samantha felt self-conscious as she wove through the crowds. Running late, she had worked up a sweat during her six-minute march from Chancery Lane, and her platinum-blonde hair pulled where she had pinned it up in an unsuccessful attempt to alter her appearance. The press had identified those attached to the trial on day one. Now, by day forty-six, Samantha had probably featured in every major newspaper in the world. She had even been forced to call the police when one particularly persistent reporter followed her back home to Kensington and refused to leave. Determined to avoid any further unwelcome attention, she kept her head down and strode on.

Two meandering lines stretched across the Newgate Street cross-roads, originating from the insufficient set of Portaloos on one side and the pop-up Starbucks on the other. Caught in the current circling perpetually between the two, she broke away towards the police officers guarding the quieter side entrance to the court-rooms. When she accidentally stepped into shot of one of the dozens of recordings taking place, a small woman snapped at her angrily in Japanese.

'Last day,' Samantha reminded herself, leaving the incompre-hensible torrent of abuse behind; just eight more hours until her life could return to normal.

At the doors, an unfamiliar police officer scrutinised Samantha's ID before leading her through the now very familiar routine: locking away personal possessions, explaining that she physically could not remove her engagement ring when the metal detectors went off, worrying about sweat marks while being frisked, and then making her way down the featureless corridors to join the other eleven jurors for a cup of lukewarm instant coffee.

Due to the overwhelming worldwide media attention and the incident at Samantha's house, the unprecedented decision had been made to sequester the jury, sparking public outrage as the hotel bill spiralled into the tens of thousands of taxpayers' money. After almost two months, the morning's small talk predominantly consisted of bad backs caused by the hotel beds, the monotony of the nightly menu and lamenting the things that people were missing most: wives, children, the *Lost* season finale.

When the court usher finally came to collect the jury, the tense silence that the trivial chatter had been masking was liberated.

The foreman, an elderly man named Stanley, who the others had appointed – seemingly for no better reason than that he bore an uncanny resemblance to Gandalf – slowly got to his feet and led them out of the room.

Arguably one of the most famous courtrooms in the world, Court One was reserved only for the most serious criminal cases; the room where such macabre celebrities as Crippen, Sutcliffe and Dennis Nilsen took centre stage to answer for their considerable sins. Artificial light flooded in through a large frosted window overhead, illuminating the room's dark wood panelling and green leather upholstery.

As Samantha took her usual seat on the front row of the jury, closest to the dock, she was conscious that her white dress, one of her own designs, was perhaps a little short. She placed her jury bundle over her lap, much to the disappointment of the lecherous old man who had almost trampled someone on the first day in his haste to claim the seat beside her.

Unlike the familiar courtrooms depicted in American movies, where the smartly dressed defendant would sit at a table alongside their lawyers, the accused at the Old Bailey faced the intimidating room alone. The small but prominent glass screens surrounding the raised dock only further adding to the notion that those inside were of considerable danger to the rest of the room.

Guilty until proven innocent.

Directly opposite the dock, to Samantha's left, was the judge's bench. A gold-hilted sword hung from the Royal Coat of Arms behind the chair in the centre, which had remained the only vacant seat throughout the entire trial. The court clerk, defence, and prosecution teams occupied the centre of the room, while the elevated public viewing gallery, against the far wall, was packed with the ardent and bleary-eyed spectators who had been camping out on the street to secure their place for the conclusion of this extraordinary trial. At the back of the room, on the forgotten benches below the gallery, sat an assortment of superfluous people vaguely involved in the proceedings: experts that the lawyers might wish to, but probably would not, call upon; various court officials; and, of course, the arresting officer at the centre of all of the controversy, the detective nicknamed Wolf: William Oliver Layton-Fawkes.

Wolf had attended every one of the forty-six days of the trial. He spent the countless hours staring into the dock with a cold expression from his undistinguished seat beside the exit. Solidly built, with a weathered face and deep blue eyes, he looked to be in his early forties. Samantha thought he might have been quite attractive if he hadn't looked as though he had been awake for months and had the weight of the world bearing down on him – although, to be fair, he did.

'The Cremation Killer', as the press had dubbed him, had become London's most prolific serial killer in its history. Twenty-seven victims in twenty-seven days, each a female prostitute between the ages of fourteen and sixteen, attracting even more attention to the case by exposing the ill-informed masses to the harsh realities happening on their own street corners. The majority of the victims had been found still ablaze, heavily sedated and burned alive, the inferno incinerating any potential evidence. And then the murders abruptly stopped, leaving the police floundering, with no significant suspects. The Metropolitan Police Service was criticised heavily throughout the investigation for failing to act while innocent young girls were dying, but then, eighteen days after the final murder, Wolf made his arrest.

The man in the dock was Naguib Khalid, a British Sunni Muslim of Pakistani origin, working as a taxi driver in the capital. He lived alone and had a prior history of minor arson offences. When DNA evidence, linking three of the victims to the back of his taxi, was presented to the court alongside Wolf's damning testimony, the case had appeared straightforward. And then it all started falling apart.

Alibis came forward contradicting surveillance reports gathered by the detective and his team. Accusations of assault and intimidation while Khalid was being held in custody, emerged. Conflicting forensic evidence suggested that the charred DNA could not be considered reliable evidence and then, to the delight of the defence lawyers, the directorate of professional standards within the MPS came forward with a letter that had been brought to their attention. From an anonymous colleague and dated just days before the final murder, the letter expressed concerns over Wolf's handling of the case and state of mind, suggesting that he had become 'obsessed', 'desperate' and went on to recommend his immediate reassignment.

The biggest story in the world suddenly got bigger. The police were accused of using Khalid as a convenient scapegoat to disguise their own failings. Both the commissioner and the Specialist Crime and Operations assistant commissioner were pressured into resigning due to the blatant corruption occurring on their watch, while the tabloids were awash with scandalous stories about the disgraced detective: his alleged problems with alcohol, his possibly violent tendencies leading to the breakdown of his marriage. At one stage, Khalid's smug defence lawyer had been reprimanded for suggesting that Wolf and her client swap seats. Throughout, Naguib Khalid watched the circus unfold before him in bewilderment, never showing so much as a glimpse of satisfaction at his transformation from demon to victim.

The concluding day of the trial played out as expected. Both the defence and prosecution made their closing speeches before the judge gave his directions to the jury: a brief summing-up of the limited evidence still considered valid and advice regarding the intricacies of the law. The jury were then excused to consider their verdict and were led out behind the witness stand into a private room unimaginatively decorated in the familiar wood and green leather theme. For over four and a half hours, the twelve jurors sat round the large wooden table debating their verdict.

Samantha had decided how she would vote weeks earlier and was surprised to find the rest of her peers so split. She would never have let public opinion influence her decision, she assured herself, although she was glad that her vote would not add any more fuel to the PR bonfire that her shop, her livelihood, and her happiness now sat upon. The same arguments were repeated time and time again. Someone would then bring up an aspect of the detective's testimony and become irritable when told, for the umpteenth time, that it was inadmissible and to be ignored.

Periodically Stanley would call for a vote, after which a note was passed, via the usher, to the judge advising that they still had not come to a unanimous verdict. With each vote another person would crack under the pressure of the growing majority until, minutes before the fifth hour, a majority of ten to two had been reached. Stanley grudgingly passed the usher a note to this effect and ten minutes later, the man returned to escort the jury back into the courtroom.

Samantha could feel every set of eyes on her as she returned to her seat beside the dock. The room was silent and she felt irrationally embarrassed as every step in her high heels echoed around the room. Fortunately the awful creaks and scrapes that followed, as all twelve jurors simultaneously took their seats, rendered her minor disturbance reassuringly trivial in comparison.

She could see people attempting to decipher her expression, too impatient to wait another minute for the official verdict, and she enjoyed it. This room of 'learned' people had been strutting about in their wigs and gowns, treating her and the other jurors with a condescending pleasantness; now however, they all found themselves at the mercy of the jury. Samantha had to fight a grin; she felt like a child with a secret she was not supposed to tell.

'Will the defendant please stand?' the clerk barked over the silence.

In the dock, Naguib Khalid tentatively got to his feet.

'Will the foreman please stand?'

At the end of Samantha's row, Stanley stood up.

'Have you reached a verdict upon which you have all agreed?'

'No.' Stanley's voice cracked, rendering his reply almost inaudible.

Samantha rolled her eyes as he cleared his throat with three rattling coughs.

'No,' Stanley almost shouted.

'Have you reached a verdict upon which a sufficient majority have agreed?'

'We have,' Stanley winced, having blown his line. 'Sorry . . . Yes.'

The clerk looked up at the judge, who nodded his acceptance of the majority vote.

'Do you, the jury, find the defendant Naguib Khalid, guilty or not guilty of twenty-seven counts of murder?'

Samantha found herself holding her breath despite already knowing the answer. Several chairs creaked in unison as eager ears leaned closer in anticipation . . .

'Not guilty.'

Samantha glanced up at Khalid, fascinated to see his reaction. He was trembling in relief, his face in his hands.

But then the first shouts of panic started.

Wolf had covered the short distance to the dock, dragging Khalid head first over the glass partition before any of the security officers even had time to react. Khalid landed badly, his winded cry muffled as the ruthless assault began. Ribs cracked beneath Wolf's foot, the skin liberated from his own knuckles with the intensity of the attack.

An alarm sounded somewhere.

Wolf was struck across the face and could taste blood as he stumbled backwards into the jury, knocking the woman nearest to him off her feet. During the few seconds it took to steady himself, several officers had flooded the space between him and the broken body lying at the base of the dock.

Wolf lashed out as he staggered forward, feeling strong hands grasping to restrain his failing body, forcing him onto his knees and then finally to the floor. He took an exhausted breath, laced with the scents of sweat and polish, watching one of the injured officers' discarded batons roll with a hollow thud into the wood panelling beside Khalid.

He looked dead, but Wolf needed to be sure.

With a final surge of adrenaline, he kicked out and crawled towards the lifeless man decorated in dark brown stains where blood had already soaked into the fabric of his cheap navy suit. Wolf reached for the heavy weapon, wrapping his fingers round the cold metal. He had brought it up above his head when a devastating impact knocked him onto his back. Disorientated, he could only watch as the dock security officer swung again, crushing his wrist with a second vicious blow.

Barely twenty seconds had passed since the 'not guilty' verdict, but when he heard metal clattering against wood, Wolf knew that it was over. He only prayed that he had done enough.

People were screaming and rushing for the exits but a flood of police officers drove them back inside; Samantha just sat on the floor, dazed, staring into space despite the events taking place only metres away. Finally someone took her by the arm, pulled her to her feet, and rushed her out of the room. The person leading Samantha away was shouting something, but the words were not reaching her. A muted alarm barely registered at all. She slipped on the floor of the Great Hall and felt a knee connect with the side of her head. The pain failed to come, but she fell back onto the black-and-white Sicilian marble, staring up in confusion at the ornate dome, sixty-seven feet above, the statues, stained-glass windows, and murals.

Her rescuer pulled her back up once the crowd had passed and led her as far as the disused main entrance before running back in the direction of the courtroom. The immense wooden doors and black gates stood wide open, the overcast sky beyond beckoning her outside. Now alone, Samantha stumbled out onto the street.

The photograph could not have been more perfect had she posed for it: the beautiful blood-spattered juror, dressed all in white, standing traumatised beneath the stone sculptures of Fortitude, Truth and the ominous Recording Angel, cloaked from head to toe in a heavy robe, imitating death, preparing to report an endless list of sins back to heaven.

Samantha turned her back to the ravenous pack of journalists and their blinding lights. In the flicker of a thousand photographs, she noticed words carved into the stone high above, resting upon four separate stone pillars, as if to support their metaphorical weight:

DEFEND THE CHILDREN OF THE POOR & PUNISH THE WRONGDOER.

As she read the words, she was overcome with a sense that she had failed in some way; could she honestly say that she was as unequivocally certain of Khalid's innocence as the detective had been of his guilt? When her gaze eventually fell back to the hooded angel, Samantha knew that she had made the list.

She had just been judged.

4 years later . . .

CHAPTER 1

Saturday 28 June 2014

3.50 a.m.

Wolf groped blindly for his mobile phone, which was edging further across the laminate floor with every vibration. Slowly the darkness began to disassemble itself into the unfamiliar shapes of his new apartment. The sweat-sodden sheet clung to his skin as he crawled off the mattress and over to the buzzing annoyance.

'Wolf,' he answered, relieved that he had at least got that right as he searched the wall for a light switch.

'It's Simmons.'

Wolf flicked a switch and sighed heavily when the weak yellow light reminded him where he was; he was tempted to turn it off again. The tiny bedroom consisted of four walls, a worn double mattress on the floor and a solitary light bulb. The claustrophobic box was sweltering thanks to his landlord, who still had not chased the previous tenant up for a window key. Normally this would not have been such an issue in London; however, Wolf had managed to coincide his move with one of England's uncharacteristic heatwaves, which had been dragging on for almost two weeks.

'Don't sound so pleased,' said Simmons.

'What time is it?' yawned Wolf.

'Ten to four.'

'Aren't I off this weekend?'

'Not any more. I need you to join me at a crime scene.'

'Next to your desk?' asked Wolf, only half-joking as he hadn't seen his boss leave the office in years.

'Funny. They let me out for this one.'

'That bad, huh?'

There was a pause on the other end of the line before Simmons answered: 'It's pretty bad. Got a pen?'

Wolf rummaged through one of the stacked boxes in the doorway and found a biro to scribble on the back of his hand with.

'OK. Go ahead.'

Out of the corner of his eye, he noticed a light flickering across his kitchen cupboard.

'Flat 108 . . .' started Simmons.

As Wolf walked into his ill-equipped kitchenette, he was dazzled by blue flashing lights strobing through the small window.

'. . . Trinity Towers—'

'Hibbard Road, Kentish Town?' Wolf interrupted, peering down over dozens of police cars, reporters, and the evacuated residents of the block opposite.

'How the hell did you know that?'

'I *am* a detective.'

'Well, you can also be our number one suspect then. Get down here.'

'Will do. I just need to . . .' Wolf trailed off, realising that Simmons had already hung up.

Between the intermittent flashes, he noticed the steady orange light coming from the washing machine and remembered that he had put his work clothes in before going to bed. He looked around at the dozens of identical cardboard boxes lining the walls:

'Bollocks.'

Five minutes later Wolf was pushing his way through the crowd of spectators that had congregated outside his building. He approached a police officer and flashed his warrant card, expecting to stroll straight through the cordon; however, the young constable snatched the card out of his hand and examined it closely, glancing up sceptically at the imposing figure dressed in swimming shorts and a faded '93 Bon Jovi: *Keep the Faith* tour T-shirt.

'Officer Layton-Fawkes?' the constable asked doubtfully.

Wolf winced at the sound of his own pretentious name: 'Detective Sergeant Fawkes, yes.'

'As in – Courtroom-Massacre Fawkes?'

'It's pronounced William . . . May I?' Wolf gestured towards the apartment building.

The young man handed Wolf's warrant card back and held the tape up for him to pass under.

'Need me to show you up?' he asked.

Wolf glanced down at his floral shorts, bare knees and work shoes.

'You know what? I think I'm doing pretty well by myself.'

The officer grinned.

'Fourth floor,' he told Wolf. 'And be careful heading up there alone; it's a shitty neighbourhood.'

Wolf sighed heavily once more, entered through the bleach-fragranced hallway, and stepped into the lift. The buttons for the second and fifth floors were missing and a brown liquid had dried over the remainder of the control panel. Using all of his detective skills to ascertain that it was either poo, rust or Coca-Cola, he used the bottom of his T-shirt, Richie Sambora's face, to push the button.

He had been in hundreds of identical lifts in his time: a seamless metal box, installed by councils all over the country. It had no floor covering, no mirrors and no protruding lights or fixtures. There was absolutely nothing for the underprivileged residents to destroy or steal from their own life-enriching piece of equipment, so they had settled for spray-painting obscenities all over the walls instead. Wolf only had time to learn that Johnny Ratcliff was both 'ere' and 'a gay' before the doors scraped open at the fourth floor.

Over a dozen people were scattered along the silent corridor. Most looked a little shaken and eyed Wolf's outfit disapprovingly, except for one scruffy man wearing a forensics badge, who nodded in approval and gave him a thumbs up as he passed. A very faint but familiar smell intensified as Wolf approached the open doorway at the end of the hallway. It was the unmistakable smell of death. People who work around such things quickly become attuned to the unique mix of stale air, shit, piss and putrefying flesh.

Wolf took a step back from the door when he heard running footsteps from inside. A young woman burst out through the open doorway, dropped to her knees and then vomited in the corridor in front of him. He waited politely for an opportune moment to ask her to move when another set of footsteps approached. He instinctively took another step back before Detective Sergeant Emily Baxter came skidding into the corridor.

'Wolf! I thought I saw you lurking out here,' she roared across the hushed hallway. 'Seriously, how cool is this?'

She glanced down at the woman retching on the floor between them.

'Could you puke somewhere else, please?'

The woman sheepishly crawled out of their way. Baxter grabbed Wolf by the arm and excitedly led him into the apartment. Nearly a decade his junior, Baxter was almost as tall as him. Her dark brown hair turned black under the gloom of the unimpressive entrance hall and, as always, she wore dark make-up that made her attractive eyes appear abnormally large. Dressed in a fitted shirt and smart trousers, she looked him up and down with a mischievous grin.

'No one told me it was a mufti day.'

Wolf refused to rise to the bait, knowing that she would quickly lose interest if he only remained quiet.

'How pissed is Chambers gonna be he's missed this?' she beamed.

'Personally I'd take the Caribbean cruise over a dead body too,' said Wolf, bored.

Baxter's huge eyes widened in surprise: 'Simmons didn't tell you?'

'Tell me what?'

She led him through the crowded apartment, which had been dimly lit in the glow of a dozen strategically placed torches. Although not overpowering, the smell grew steadily stronger. Wolf could tell that the fetid source was close by because of the number of flies zipping about feverishly above his head.

The flat had high ceilings, contained no furniture, and was considerably larger than Wolf's own, but was no more pleasant. The yellowed walls were peppered with holes through which the antiquated wiring and dusty insulation bled freely onto the bare floor. Neither the bathroom suite nor the kitchen looked to have been updated since the 1960s.

'Tell me what?' he asked her again.

'This is the *one*, Wolf,' said Baxter, ignoring the question, 'a once-in-a-career case.'

Wolf was distracted, mentally sizing up the second bedroom and wondering whether he was being overcharged for his poxy box of a flat across the road. They rounded the corner into the crowded main room and he automatically scanned the floor, between the assorted equipment and pairs of legs, for a body.

'Baxter!'

She stopped and turned to him impatiently.

'What didn't Simmons tell me?'

Behind her, a group of people, standing in front of the large floor-to-ceiling window that dominated the room, moved aside. Before she could answer, Wolf had stumbled away, his eyes fixed on a point somewhere above them: the one light source that the police had not brought with them: a spotlight on a dark stage . . .

The naked body, contorted into an unnatural pose, appeared to be floating a foot above the uneven floorboards. It had its back to the room, looking out through the enormous window. Hundreds of almost invisible threads held the figure in place, which, in turn, were anchored by two industrial metal hooks.

It took Wolf a moment to identify the most unnerving feature of the surreal scene before him: the black leg attached to the white torso. Unable to comprehend what he was seeing, he pushed his way further into the room. As he drew closer, he noticed the huge stitches binding the mismatched body parts together, the skin tented where the material punctured through: one black male leg, one white; a large male hand on one side, a tanned female counterpart on the other; tangled jet-black hair hanging unsettlingly over a pale, freckled, slender, female torso.

Baxter was back at his side, clearly relishing the look of revulsion on his face:

'He didn't tell you . . . One dead body – six victims!' she whispered gleefully in his ear.

Wolf's gaze dropped to the floor. He was standing on the shadow cast by the grotesque corpse and, in this simplified state, the proportions appeared even more jarring, gaps of light distorting the joins between the limbs and body.

'What the hell are the press doing out there already?' Wolf heard his chief shout at no one in particular. 'I swear, this department has got more leaks than the *Titanic*. If I find anyone talking to them, they'll be suspended!'

Wolf smiled, knowing full well that Simmons was only play-acting the part of the stereotypical boss. They had known one another for over a decade and, until the Khalid incident, Wolf had considered him a friend. Beneath the forced bravado, Simmons was in fact an intelligent, caring, and competent police officer.

'Fawkes!' Simmons strode over to them. He often struggled not to address his staff by their nicknames. He was almost a foot shorter than Wolf, was now in his fifties, and had developed a managerial belly. 'Nobody told me it was a mufti day.'

Wolf heard Baxter snigger. He decided to adopt the same tactic that he had used on her by ignoring the comment. After an uncomfortable silence, Simmons turned to Baxter.

'Where's Adams?' he asked.

'Who?'

'Adams. Your new protégé.'

'Edmunds?'

'Right. Edmunds.'

'How am I supposed to know?'

'Edmunds!' Simmons bellowed across the busy room.

'Work with him a lot now?' asked Wolf quietly, unable to hide the hint of jealousy in his voice, which made Baxter smile.

'Babysitting duty,' she whispered. 'He's the transfer from Fraud, only seen a few dead bodies. He might even cry later on.'

The young man bumbling through the crowd towards them was only twenty-five years old, stick-thin and immaculately presented, apart from his scruffy strawberry-blond hair. He was holding a notebook at the ready and smiled eagerly at the chief inspector.

'Where are forensics up to?' asked Simmons.

Edmunds flicked back a few pages in his book.

'Helen said that her team still haven't found a single drop of blood anywhere in the apartment. They have confirmed that all six body parts are from different victims and were roughly amputated, probably with a hacksaw.'

'Did *Helen* mention anything we didn't already know?' spat Simmons.

'Actually, yes. Due to the absence of blood and lack of constriction of the blood vessels around the amputation wounds . . .'

Simmons rolled his eyes and checked his watch.

'. . . we can be certain that the parts were removed post-mortem,' finished Edmunds, looking pleased with himself.

'That's some fantastic police work, Edmunds,' said Simmons sarcastically before shouting out: 'Could someone please cancel the milk carton ad for the man missing a head? Thank you!'

Edmunds' smile vanished. Wolf caught Simmons' eye and smirked. They had both been on the receiving end of similar putdowns in their time. It was all part of the training.

'I just meant that whoever the arms and legs belonged to are definitely dead as well. They will know more once they get the body back to the lab,' Edmunds mumbled self-consciously.

Wolf noticed the reflection of the body in the dark windows. Realising that he had not yet seen it from the front, he moved round to look.

'What have *you* got, Baxter?' asked Simmons.

'Not a lot. Slight damage to the keyhole, possibly picked. We've got officers questioning the neighbours outside, but so far no one's seen or heard a thing. Oh, and there's nothing wrong with the electrics – every bulb in the apartment's been removed except for the one above the victim . . . s, like it's on show or something.'

'What about you Fawkes, any ideas? Fawkes?'

Wolf was gazing up at the body's dark-skinned face.

'I'm sorry, are we boring you?'

'No. Sorry. Even in this heat, this thing's only just beginning to stink, which means the killer either murdered all six victims last night, which seems unlikely, or he's had the bodies on ice.'

'Agreed. We'll get someone to look into recent break-ins at cold-storage units, supermarkets, restaurants, anywhere with an industrial-sized freezer room,' said Simmons.

'And see if any of the neighbours heard drilling,' said Wolf.

'Drilling is a reasonably common sound,' blurted Edmunds, who regretted the outburst when three pairs of angry eyes turned on him.

'If this is the killer's masterpiece,' continued Wolf, 'there's no way they would risk it dropping out of the ceiling and just being a pile of bits by the time we got here. Those hooks will be drilled into load-bearing metal beams. Someone should have heard it.'

Simmons nodded: 'Baxter, get someone on it.'

'Chief, could I borrow you a moment?' asked Wolf as Baxter and Edmunds moved away. He pulled on a pair of disposable gloves and lifted a handful of knotted black hair away from the gruesome figure's face. It was male. The eyes were open, the expression unnervingly calm considering the victim's clearly violent end. 'Look familiar?'

Simmons walked round to join Wolf by the chilly window and crouched down to better examine the dark face. After a few moments, he shrugged.

'It's Khalid,' said Wolf.

'That's impossible.'

'Is it?'

Simmons looked up again at the lifeless face. Gradually his expression of scepticism transformed into one of deep concern.

'Baxter!' he shouted. 'I need you and Adams—'

'*Edmunds*.'

'. . . over at Belmarsh Prison. Ask the governor to take you directly to Naguib Khalid.'

'Khalid?' Baxter asked in shock, involuntarily glancing at Wolf.

'Yes, Khalid. Phone me the moment you've seen him alive. Go!'

Wolf looked out towards his block opposite. Many of the windows remained dark, others contained excited faces filming the spectacle below on their mobile phones, presumably hoping to capture something grisly to entertain their friends with in the morning. Apparently they were unable to see into the dimly lit murder scene that they would otherwise have had front row seats for.

Wolf was able to see into his own flat, a few windows over. In his hurry, he had left all of the lights on. He spotted a cardboard box, at the bottom of a pile, with the words 'Trousers and Shirts' scrawled across it.

'*Aha*!'

Simmons walked back over to Wolf and rubbed his tired eyes. They stood quietly, either side of the suspended body, watching the first signs of morning pollute the dark sky. Even over the noise of the room, they could hear the peaceful sound of bird-song outside.

'So, most disturbing thing you've ever seen then?' Simmons joked wearily.

'A close second,' replied Wolf without taking his eyes off the growing patch of deep blue sky.

'Second? Do I even want to know what tops this – this thing?' Simmons took another reluctant look at the hanging collection of dismemberments.

Wolf gently tapped the figure's outstretched right arm. The palm looked pale in comparison to the rest of the tanned skin and the perfectly manicured purple nails. Dozens of silk-like threads supported the outstretched hand and a dozen more held the extended index finger in place.

He checked that no one was listening in to their conversation and then leaned across to whisper to Simmons.

'It's pointing into my apartment window.'

CHAPTER 2

Saturday 28 June 2014

4.32 a.m.

Baxter had left Edmunds waiting for the juddering lift. She stormed through a fire door and into the dismal stairwell, where a seemingly endless procession of cold and irritable people had finally been permitted to return to their homes. Halfway down she put her warrant card away, realising that, if anything, it was hindering her progress against the steady flow. The initial novelty of the night's events had worn off hours earlier, leaving the sleep-starved residents with only resentment and ill feeling towards the police.

When she eventually barged out into the foyer, Edmunds was already waiting patiently by the main doors. She marched past without acknowledging him and stepped out into the chilly morning. The sun was yet to make an appearance, but the perfect clear skies overhead suggested that the persistent heatwave was set to continue. She swore when she saw that the growing crowd of spectators and journalists had swelled around the police tape, cutting her off from her black Audi A1.

'Not a word,' she snapped at Edmunds, who ignored the tone of the unnecessary order with his usual good grace.

They approached the cordon to a barrage of questions and camera flashes, ducked under the tape and started pushing through the crush. Baxter gritted her teeth on hearing Edmunds apologise repeatedly behind her. Just as she turned to shoot him a glare, she collided with a heavyset man, whose bulky television camera fell to the floor with an expensive-sounding crack.

'Shite! Sorry,' she said, automatically producing a Met Police business card from her pocket. She had gone through hundreds over the years, handing them out like IOUs before immediately forgetting the chaos that she had left in her wake.

The large man was still on the floor, kneeling over the scattered remains of his camera as if it were a fallen loved one. A woman's hand snatched the card from Baxter's grip. Baxter looked up angrily to find an unfriendly face staring back at her. Despite the early hour, the woman was immaculately made-up for television; any trace of the exhaustion that had marked everybody else with heavy bags beneath their eyes had been concealed. She had long curly red hair and was wearing a smart skirt and top. The two women stood in tense silence for a moment as Edmunds watched in awe. He had never imagined that his mentor could look so ill at ease.

The red-headed woman glanced fleetingly at Edmunds:

'I see you found someone your own age, at last,' she said to Baxter, who scowled back at Edmunds as though he had wronged her simply by existing. 'Has she tried to have her wicked way with you yet?' the woman asked him sympathetically.

Edmunds froze, genuinely wondering whether he was experiencing the worst moment of his entire life.

'No?' she continued, checking her watch. 'Well, the day is still young.'

'I'm getting married,' mumbled Edmunds, unsure why words were coming out of him.

The redhead smiled triumphantly and opened her mouth to say something.

'We're leaving!' Baxter snapped at him before recovering her usual indifferent demeanour: 'Andrea.'

'Emily,' the woman replied.

Baxter turned her back on her, stepped over the guts of the camera and continued with Edmunds in tow. He triple-checked his seat belt as Baxter revved the engine and reversed suddenly, bouncing up and over two kerbs before speeding off, letting the flashing blue lights shrink in the rear-view mirror.

Baxter had not said a word since leaving the crime scene and Edmunds was struggling to keep his eyes open as they raced through the almost deserted streets of the capital. The Audi's heater was blowing a gentle warm breeze into the luxurious interior, which Baxter had littered with CDs, half-used make-up and empty fast-food packaging. As they crossed Waterloo Bridge, the sunrise burned behind the city, the dome of St Paul's Cathedral a featureless silhouette against the golden sky.

Edmunds surrendered to his heavy eyes and headbutted the passenger window painfully. He immediately sat upright, furious with himself for showing weakness, yet again, in front of his superior officer.

'So, that was him?' he blurted out. He was desperate to spark a conversation to distract him from the drowsiness.

'Who?'

'Fawkes. *The* William Fawkes.'

Edmunds had, in fact, seen Wolf in passing several times before. He had noticed the way in which his colleagues treated the seasoned detective, ever conscious of the clearly unwelcome air of celebrity that surrounded him.

'*The* William Fawkes,' Baxter scoffed under her breath.

'I've heard so many stories about what happened . . .' He paused, waiting for a sign that he should abandon the topic. 'You were on his team around that time, weren't you?'

Baxter continued driving in silence as if Edmunds had not even spoken. He felt foolish for thinking that she would ever want to discuss such a significant topic with a trainee. He was about to get his phone out for something to do when, unexpectedly, she answered.

'Yes. I was.'

'So, did he do all of those things that he was accused of?' Edmunds knew that he was on dangerous ground, but his genuine interest outweighed the risk of provoking Baxter's wrath. 'Planting evidence, assaulting the prisoner—'

'Some of them.'

Edmunds made an unconscious tut-tut sound, jabbing at Baxter's temper.

'Don't you dare judge him! You have absolutely no idea what this job is like,' she snapped. 'Wolf knew Khalid was the Cremation Killer. He *knew* it. And he knew he would do it again.'

'There must have been legitimate evidence.'

Baxter laughed bitterly.

'You just wait until you've been in a few more years, watching these pieces of shit wriggle themselves out of trouble time and time again.' She paused, feeling herself getting worked up. 'Everything's not black and white. What Wolf did was wrong, but he did it in desperation for all the right reasons.'

'Even brutally attacking a man in front of a packed courtroom?' Edmunds asked challengingly.

'Especially that,' replied Baxter. She was too distracted to pick up on his tone. 'He cracked under the pressure. One day you will, I will – *everybody* does. Just pray that when you do, you have people there standing by you. No one stood by Wolf when it happened, not even me . . .'

Edmunds kept quiet, hearing the regret in her voice.

'He was going to be sent down for it. They wanted blood. They were going to make such an example of their "disgraced detective" and then, one chilly February morning, guess who they find standing over the barbecued corpse of a schoolgirl? She'd still be alive today if they'd only listened to Wolf.'

'Jesus,' said Edmunds. 'Do you think it's him – the head?'

'Naguib Khalid is a child killer. Even criminals have standards. For his own safety, he's locked up in permanent solitary confinement in the High Security Unit of a maximum security prison.

He doesn't see *anybody*, let alone anyone who could walk out of there with his head. It's ridiculous.'

Another strained silence grew between them following Baxter's definitive conclusion that they were wasting their time. Aware that this had been by far the most successful conversation that they had shared during their sporadic three and a half months together, Edmunds reverted back to the previous unresolved topic.

'It's amazing Fawkes' – sorry, Wolf's – back at all.'

'Never underestimate the power of public opinion and the eagerness of the people in charge to bow to it,' said Baxter with disdain.

'You sound like you don't think he should be back.'

Baxter did not respond.

'It's not much of an advert for the police, is it?' said Edmunds. 'Letting him off scot-free.'

'Scot-free?' said Baxter in disbelief.

'Well, he didn't go to prison.'

'It would've been better for him if he had. The lawyers, saving face, pushed for the hospital order. Easier mess to clean up, I guess. They said the stress of the case had triggered a response "completely out of character"—'

'And how many times does someone have to do something out of character before people finally accept that it's not?' Edmunds interrupted.

Baxter ignored the remark.

'They said that he needed ongoing treatment for, what his defence lawyer diagnosed as, an underlying Antipersonality – no, Antisocial Personality Disorder.'

'Which you don't believe he had?'

'Not when he went in, at least. But if enough people keep telling you you're crazy and stuff you full of enough pills, in the end, you can't help but wonder,' sighed Baxter. 'So, in response to your question: one year in St Ann's Hospital, demoted, reputation in tatters and divorce papers waiting on the doormat. Wolf most certainly did not get off "scot-free".'

'His wife left him even after he was proved right all along?'

'What can I say? She's a bitch.'

'You knew her then?'

'That red-headed reporter back at the crime scene?'

'That was her?'

'Andrea. She got some stupid ideas into her head about us.'

'Sleeping together?'

'What else?'

'So . . . you weren't?'

Edmunds held his breath. He knew he had just blundered right over the delicate line that he had been treading and the conversation was over. Baxter ignored the intrusive question and the engine growled as she accelerated along the tree-lined dual carriageway that led up to the prison.

'What the hell do you mean he's dead?' Baxter yelled at Prison Governor Davies.

She was back on her feet while Edmunds and the governor remained seated at the large desk that dominated his bland office. The man winced as he sipped his scalding coffee. He tended to arrive early for work, but the lost half-hour had completely disrupted his day.

'Sergeant Baxter, the local authorities are responsible for relaying information such as this to your department. We do not routinely—'

'But—' Baxter tried to interject.

The governor continued more firmly:

'Inmate Khalid was taken ill in his solitary cell and moved to the medical room. He was then transferred to the Queen Elizabeth Hospital.'

'Ill how?'

The governor took out a pair of reading glasses and opened up the file on his desk.

'The report states: "shortness of breath and nausea". He was moved to the QE's Intensive Care Unit at approximately 8 p.m. due to "becoming unresponsive and oxygen saturation falling despite O_2 therapy", if that means anything to either of you?'

The governor glanced up to see Baxter and Edmunds nodding along knowingly. The moment his eyes dropped back to the report, they shared a bemused shrug.

'Local police were on twenty-four-hour guard outside his room, which turned out to be twenty-one hours overly optimistic, seeing as he was dead by 11 p.m.' The governor closed the report and removed his glasses. 'That, I'm afraid, is all that I have for you. You will have to speak to the hospital directly should you require anything further. Now, if there is nothing else?'

He took another painful sip of boiling coffee and then pushed it out of reach before he could hurt himself. Baxter and Edmunds got up to leave. Edmunds smiled and held his hand out to the governor.

'Thank you for taking the time to—' he started.

'That'll do for now,' Baxter snapped as she left the room.

Edmunds awkwardly took back his hand and followed her out, letting the door swing closed behind him. Just before it clicked shut, Baxter burst back into the room with one final question.

'Shit. I almost forgot. When Khalid left the prison, we're absolutely positive he still had a head?'

The governor gave a bewildered nod.

'Ta.'

The Homicide and Serious Crime meeting room was filled with the sound of 'Good Vibrations' by the Beach Boys. Wolf had always found it easier to work with music on, and it was still early enough to get away with it without disturbing too many other people.

He was now dressed in a crumpled white shirt, dark blue chinos and his only pair of shoes. The handmade Loake oxfords had been both an uncharacteristically extravagant purchase and the most sensible that he had ever made. He vaguely remembered the times before them, almost crippled by the end of a nineteen-hour shift, only to slide his feet back into the same ill-fitting footwear after a few hours' sleep.

He turned up the volume, failing to notice his mobile phone lighting up on the table beside him. He was alone in the room that could comfortably seat thirty people and was so infrequently used that it still smelled of new carpet over a year after being refitted. A frosted-glass window ran the length of the wall, obscuring the main office behind.

He picked another photograph up off the desk, tunelessly singing along to the music and danced over to the large board at the front of the room. Once he had pinned the final picture in place, he stood back to admire his work: enlarged photographs of the various body parts overlapped to create two enormous versions of the terrifying figure, one the front view, one rear. He stared again at the waxy face, hoping that he was right, that he could sleep a little easier in the knowledge that Khalid was finally dead. Unfortunately Baxter still hadn't phoned in to confirm his suspicions.

'Morning,' said a familiar voice behind him in a coarse Scottish accent.

Wolf instantly stopped dancing and turned the radio down as Detective Sergeant Finlay Shaw, the unit's longest-serving officer, entered the room. He was a quiet yet intimidating man who smelled persistently of cigarette smoke. He was fifty-nine years old with a weather-beaten face and a nose that had been broken on more than one occasion and never set quite right.

Much like Baxter had inherited Edmunds, babysitting Wolf since his return to the service had become Finlay's primary duty. They had an unspoken agreement that Finlay, who was on the gentle wind-down to retirement, would let the younger man take the lead on the majority of the work, as long as he signed off Wolf's monitoring paperwork each week.

'You've got two left feet lad,' rasped Finlay.

'Well, I'm more of a singer,' said Wolf defensively, 'you know that.'

'No, you're not. But what I meant is . . .' Finlay walked up to the wall and tapped the photograph that Wolf had just pinned up, '. . . you've got two left feet.'

'Huh.' Wolf flicked through the pile of photos from the crime scene and eventually found the correct one. 'You know, I do stuff like this from time to time, just to make you feel like I still need you.'

Finlay smiled: 'Sure you do.'

Wolf swapped the photographs over and the two men stared up at the horrific collage.

'Back in the seventies I worked on a case a wee bit like this: Charles Tenyson,' said Finlay.

Wolf shrugged.

'He'd leave us bits of bodies: a leg here, a hand there. To start with, it seemed random but it wasn't. Each of the parts had an identifying feature. He wanted us to know who he'd killed.'

Wolf stepped closer to point up at the wall.

'We've got a ring on the left hand and an operation scar on the right leg. It's not a lot to go off.'

'There'll be more,' said Finlay matter-of-factly. 'Someone who doesn't leave a single drop of blood at a massacre doesn't leave a ring behind by accident.'

Wolf rewarded Finlay for his thought-provoking insights by yawning loudly in his face.

'Coffee run? I need a smoke anyway,' said Finlay. 'White and two?'

'How have you still not learnt this?' asked Wolf as Finlay hurried to the door. 'An extra-hot, double-shot skinny macchiato with sugar-free caramel syrup.'

'White and two,' shouted Finlay as he left the meeting room, almost colliding with Commander Vanita on his way out.

Wolf recognised the diminutive Indian woman from her regular appearances on television. She had also attended one of the countless interviews and evaluations that he'd had to endure to secure his reinstatement. From what he remembered, she had been against the idea.

He really should have spotted her approaching, seeing as she perpetually looked to have stepped out of a cartoon, that morning's ensemble consisting of a vivid purple blazer inexplicably matched with garish orange trousers.

He retreated behind the flip chart too late and she paused in the doorway to speak with him.

'Good morning, Detective Sergeant.'

'Morning.'

'It looks like a florist in here,' she said.

Wolf glanced at the hideous montages dominating the wall behind him in confusion. When he looked back, he realised that she was gesturing into the main office, where dozens of extravagant bouquets were scattered over desks and filing cabinets.

'Oh. They've been arriving all week. I think they're from the Muniz case. Pretty much the entire community sent flowers in from the looks of it,' he explained.

'Nice to be appreciated for a change,' said Vanita. 'I'm looking for your boss. He isn't in his office.'

Wolf's phone started buzzing loudly on the table. He glanced at the caller ID and hung up.

'Anything I can help you with?' he asked half-heartedly.

Vanita smiled weakly.

'I'm afraid not. The press are tearing us apart out there. The commissioner wants it handled.'

'I thought that was your job,' said Wolf.

Vanita laughed: 'I'm not going out there today.'

They both spotted Simmons heading back towards his office.

'Shit rolls downhill, Fawkes – you know that.'

'As you can see, I'm completely tied up here. I need you to go out there and speak to the vultures for me,' said Simmons with almost believable sincerity.

Within two minutes of the commander leaving, Wolf had been summoned to the chief inspector's poky office. The room was barely four square metres. It contained a desk, a tiny television, a rusty filing cabinet, two swivel chairs and a plastic stool (in case of a crowd piling into the tiny space). Wolf found it a depressing incentive to flaunt before the workforce; the dead end at the top of the ladder.

'Me?' asked Wolf dubiously.

'Sure. The press love you. You're William Fawkes!'

Wolf sighed: 'Anyone lower on the food chain I can hand this down to?'

'I think I saw the cleaner in the men's loos, but I think it would be better coming from you.'

'Right,' mumbled Wolf.

The phone on the desk started to ring. Wolf went to stand as Simmons answered it, but paused when he held up a hand.

'I've got Fawkes with me. I'll put you on speaker.'

Edmunds' voice was barely audible over the revving engine. Wolf had to sympathise. He knew from experience that Baxter was an appalling driver.

'We're en route to Queen Elizabeth Hospital. Khalid was transferred to their ICU a week ago.'

'Alive?' barked Simmons irritably.

'Was,' replied Edmunds.

'But now?'

'Dead.'

'Head?' Simmons yelled in frustration.

'We'll let you know.'

'Fantastic.' Simmons ended the call and shook his head. He looked up at Wolf. 'They're expecting you outside. Tell them we have six victims. They already know that anyway. Assure them that we are currently in the process of identification and will be contacting the families before making any names public. Don't mention anything about stitching bits together – or your flat.'

Wolf gave a sarcastic salute and left the room. He closed the door behind him and spotted Finlay approaching with two take-away cups.

'Just in time,' Wolf called across the office, which was now filling up with people beginning their day shifts. It was easy to forget that, while the high-profile cases eclipsed the lives of those involved, the rest of the world continued on as normal: people killing people, rapists and thieves running free.

As Finlay passed a desk covered with five huge bouquets, he started to sniff. Wolf could see his eyes watering as he drew nearer. Just as he reached Wolf he sneezed violently, throwing both coffees across the grubby carpeted floor. Wolf looked crushed.

'These effing flowers!' bellowed Finlay. His wife had made him give up swearing when he became a grandad. 'I'll get you another.'

Wolf was about to tell him not to bother when an internal deliveryman emerged from the lift holding yet another impressive armful of flowers. Finlay looked as though he might hit him.

'All right? Got flowers for a Ms Emily Baxter,' announced the scruffy young man.

'Terrific,' grumbled Finlay.

'This has gotta be the fifth or sixth lot for her. Bit of a looker is she?' asked the oafish man, catching Wolf off-guard with the inappropriate question.

'*Ummm* . . . She's – well, very—' Wolf stuttered.

'We don't really think about other detectives in that way,' interrupted Finlay, seeing his friend struggling.

'It depends on . . .' Wolf looked back at Finlay.

'I mean, of course she is,' blurted Finlay, losing his calming hold over the conversation. 'But—'

'I think that everybody's unique and beautiful in their own way,' finished Wolf wisely.

He and Finlay nodded to each other, having flawlessly negotiated a potentially awkward question.

'But he would never . . .' Finlay assured the deliveryman.

'No, never,' agreed Wolf.

The man stared blankly at the two detectives: 'OK.'

'Wolf!' a female officer called across the room, providing him with an excuse to leave Finlay with their visitor. She was holding a phone up at him. 'Your wife's on the line. Says it's important.'

'We're divorced,' Wolf corrected her.

'Either way, she's still on the phone.'

Wolf reached for the receiver when Simmons came out of his office and saw him still standing there.

'Get down there, Fawkes!'

Wolf looked exasperated:

'I'll call her back,' he told the officer before stepping into the idling lift, praying that his ex-wife would not be among the crowd of reporters he was about to face.

CHAPTER 3

Saturday 28 June 2014

6.09 a.m.

Baxter and Edmunds had been made to wait for over ten minutes in the QE's main reception area. Flimsy-looking shutters blocked the entrances to both the café and the WH Smith's and Baxter's stomach rumbled as she glanced again at the piles of Monster Munch sitting just out of reach. At last a morbidly overweight security guard waddled over to the counter and the unfriendly woman on reception pointed in their direction.

'Coo-ee!' she called, waving them over as if summoning a dog. 'Jack will take you down now.'

The security guard clearly had a chip on his shoulder. Begrudgingly, he led them painfully slowly towards the lifts.

'We're kind of in a hurry here,' Baxter snapped, unable to help herself. Unfortunately this only seemed to decelerate the man further.

As they disembarked the lift at basement level, their escort spoke for the first time.

'The "real" police didn't trust us lowly security guards with the intricate task of sitting outside a room, so they took over. Lot of good that did 'em.'

'Was the body guarded at all after it was brought down to the morgue?' asked Edmunds pleasantly, in an attempt to pacify the embittered guard. He had taken out his notebook and was poised to record the response as they walked along the claustrophobic corridor.

'I'm only guessing here,' started the man, with exaggerated deliberation, 'but the police *may* have considered the guy less of a threat after he had died. But as I said, pure guesswork.'

The guard smiled smugly at his own wit. Edmunds glanced at Baxter, expecting her to shake her head or ridicule him for asking stupid questions. Surprisingly, she jumped to his defence instead.

'What my colleague is trying, but failing, to drag out of you is whether the morgue is secure.'

They stopped outside a set of unmarked double doors. The man arrogantly tapped his thick finger against a small 'No Entry' sticker in the window.

'How's that for ya, love?'

Baxter pushed past the obnoxious man and held the door for Edmunds.

'Thank you, you've been most . . .' She slammed the door in the security guard's face. 'Arsehole.'

In contrast to the unhelpful guard, the mortician was welcoming and efficient; a softly spoken man in his early fifties, his greying beard immaculately pruned to match his hair. Within minutes he had located both the hard copy and computer files relating to Naguib Khalid.

'I wasn't actually here when they performed the post-mortem, but according to this the cause of death was identified as Tetrodotoxin. There were traces found in the blood.'

'And this Tetoxin—'

'Tetrodotoxin,' the mortician corrected her without a hint of condescension.

'Yeah, that. What is it? And how is it administered?'

'It is a naturally occurring neurotoxin.'

Baxter and Edmunds stared at him blankly.

'It's poison and he probably ate it. Most TTX fatalities are from ingesting blowfish, a delicacy to some, although, I'm rather partial to a Ferrero Rocher myself.'

Baxter's stomach made another painful growl.

'I've got to go back to my chief inspector and tell him that a *fish* killed the Cremation Killer?' she asked, unimpressed.

'We've all got to go one way or another,' he shrugged apologetically. 'There are of course other sources of TTX out there – some starfish, snails . . . I think I'm right in saying there's a toad . . .'

This did not look as if it reassured Baxter.

'You wanted to see the body?' asked the mortician after a moment.

'Please,' replied Baxter. It was not a word that Edmunds had heard her use before.

'May I enquire why?'

They walked over to the wall of large, brushed-metal freezer drawers.

'To check if he still has a head,' said Edmunds, who was still scribbling notes in his book.

The mortician looked to Baxter. He expected her to smile or perhaps apologise for her colleague's dark sense of humour, but she nodded back sincerely. A little disconcerted, the man located the appropriate drawer, on the bottom row, and gently pulled it out from the wall. All three of them held their breath as the infamous serial killer materialised before them.

The dark-skinned feet and legs were covered in old scars and burns. Next, the arms and groin came into view. Baxter glanced uncomfortably at the two misshapen fingers on the left hand, remembering the night that Wolf had emerged from the holding cell covered in blood. She denied all knowledge of the incident when questioned by her superiors the following day.

As the chest slid into the light, they all stared at the substantial scarring left by the numerous operations to repair the damage sustained during Wolf's attack. Finally the drawer clicked fully open and they gazed down at their own distorted reflections in the metal tray, occupying the space where a head should have rested.

'Shit.'

*

Wolf was loitering outside the main entrance to New Scotland Yard, looking nervously at the huge crowd that had amassed in the shadow of the towering glass building that occupied almost two acres in the heart of Westminster. The finishing touches were being completed to the makeshift podium, erected in the usual media-friendly spot, which incorporated the famous revolving sign as a backdrop.

Someone had once told him that the rotating sign's reflective lettering was intended to symbolise the Met's constant vigilance, the observer's image mirrored back at them, always watching. The same could be said for the rest of the huge building which, on clear days, almost vanished as the mirrored windows adopted the form of the Victorian red-brick hotel opposite and the looming clock tower of 55 Broadway behind.

Wolf's phone started buzzing in his pocket and he cursed himself for not remembering to switch it off. He saw that it was Simmons calling and swiftly answered it.

'Boss?'

'Baxter's just confirmed it: it's Khalid.'

'I knew it. How?'

'Fish.'

'What?'

'Poison. Ingested.'

'It's better than he deserved,' spat Wolf.

'I'm going to pretend I didn't hear that.'

Someone in cargo trousers was gesturing at Wolf.

'It looks like they're ready for me.'

'Good luck.'

'Cheers,' replied Wolf insincerely.

'Try not to mess it up.'

'Right.'

Wolf hung up and checked his reflection, ensuring that his fly was done up and that he did not look any more exhausted and downtrodden than usual. He marched out towards the podium with the intention of getting it over with as quickly as possible;

however, his confidence drained as the noise intensified and he saw the black lenses of the television cameras tracing his every step, like cannons taking aim. For a moment he was back outside the Old Bailey, ineffectively shielding his face as he was bundled into the back of a police van to the unnerving jeers of the unsatisfied press and the violent thudding against the vehicle's metal sides, which would forever infect his sleep.

Apprehensively, he stepped up onto the podium and began his briefly practised statement.

'I'm Detective Sergeant William Fawkes with the—'

'What? Speak up!' he was heckled from the crowd.

One of the men who had assembled the tiny stage ran up and switched on the microphone with a booming static click. Wolf tried not to hear the spiteful laughter emanating from the sea of faces.

'Thank you. As I was saying, I'm Detective Sergeant William Fawkes with the Metropolitan Police and part of the team investigating today's multiple homicides.' *So far so good*, he thought to himself. His audience started shouting questions at him, but Wolf ignored them and continued, 'We can confirm that the remains of six victims were recovered from an address in Kentish Town in the early hours of this—'

Wolf made the mistake of looking up from his notes and instantly recognised Andrea's striking red hair. He thought she looked distraught, which further distracted him. He knocked his cue cards across the floor and stooped down to collect them back up, conscious that he had scribbled a list of details he was not to mention all over one of them. He found the incriminating card and climbed back up to the microphone.

'. . . this a.m. In the morning.' He could feel his throat drying up and knew that he would be blushing bright red like he always did when he was embarrassed, so he speed-read the final card: 'We are in the process of identifying the victims and will be contacting the families concerned prior to releasing any names. Being an ongoing investigation, that is all I can disclose at this time. Thank you.'

He paused for a few seconds, waiting for applause, before realising that it would have been highly inappropriate and that his performance probably would not have warranted it anyway. He climbed back down and retreated from the voices shouting his name.

'Will! Will!'

Wolf turned to see Andrea running over to him. She had managed to dodge the first officer but had been blocked by two others. He was overcome with the same confused anger that had overshadowed their few encounters since the divorce and was almost tempted to let the officers drag her away but decided to intervene when a member of the Diplomatic Protection Group, armed with a Heckler & Koch G36C assault rifle, approached her.

'It's OK. It's OK. Let her through please,' he called grudgingly.

Their last meeting, to discuss further complications regarding the sale of the house, had been an especially frosty affair, so he was taken aback when she rushed over and held him in a firm embrace. He breathed through his mouth, desperate not to smell her hair, knowing that it would be laced with her favourite perfume that he loved so much. When she finally released him, he could see that she was close to tears.

'I can't tell you anything else, Andie—'

'Don't you ever pick up your phone? I've been trying to call you for nearly two hours!'

Wolf could not keep up with her mood swings. Now she seemed genuinely furious with him.

'I'm very sorry. I've actually been a bit busy today,' he said before leaning in to whisper conspiratorially. 'Apparently there was a murder or something.'

'Next to your flat!'

'Yeah,' said Wolf thoughtfully. 'It's a shitty neighbourhood.'

'I've got something to ask you and I need you to tell me the truth, OK?'

'*Hmmm.*'

'There's more, isn't there? The body was stitched together – like a puppet.'

Wolf started babbling uncomfortably:

'How do you . . .? Where did you . . .? Speaking on behalf of the Metropolitan Police, I—'

'It's Khalid, isn't it? The head?'

Wolf grabbed Andrea by the arm and pulled her to one side, as far from the other officers as possible. She produced a thick brown envelope from her bag.

'Believe me, I'm the last person who wants to mention that awful man's name. As far as I'm concerned he destroyed our marriage. But I recognised him from the photos.'

'Photos?' asked Wolf warily.

'Oh my God! I knew they were real,' she said, shell-shocked. 'Someone sent me pictures of the puppet thing. I've already sat on this for hours. I need to get back to work.'

Andrea fell silent as somebody walked past.

'Will, whoever sent me these included a list. That's what I've been trying to call you about because I don't know what it means: six names with a date next to each.'

Wolf snatched the envelope out of her hand and tore it open.

'The first name's Mayor Turnble next to today's date,' said Andrea.

'Mayor Turnble?' asked Wolf. He looked as though the bottom had just dropped out of his world.

Without another word he turned and sprinted back through the main doors. He heard Andrea shout something after him, but the words were indecipherable as they disintegrated against the thick glass.

Simmons was on the phone to the commissioner, who had resorted to unsubtle threats regarding his replaceability as he apologised repeatedly for his team's distinct lack of progress. Simmons was midway through proposing his plan of action when Wolf burst into the office unannounced.

'Fawkes! Get out!' yelled Simmons.

Wolf leant over the desk and held down a button to end the call.

'What the hell do you think you're doing?' asked Simmons, incensed.

Wolf opened his mouth to answer when a distorted voice interrupted from the speakerphone: 'Are you speaking to me, Simmons?'

'Shit.' Wolf jabbed another button.

'You have reached the voicemail of—' started a robotic voice.

Simmons looked horrified and held his head in his hands as Wolf frantically pushed every other button on the phone.

'How do you hang this thing up?' shouted Wolf in frustration.

'It's a big red button with a cro—' the commissioner advised helpfully before a sharp click, followed by silence, confirmed that he had, indeed, been correct.

Wolf scattered the Polaroid photographs of the grotesque body across the desk.

'Our killer's gone to the press with pictures and a hit list.'

Simmons rubbed his face and looked down at the photographs depicting the collective cadaver at various stages of assembly.

'First one's Mayor Turnble – today,' said Wolf.

It took a moment for his words to sink in.

Simmons suddenly snapped into action and took out his mobile phone.

'Terrence!' the mayor answered enthusiastically. It sounded as though he was outside. 'To what do I owe the pleasure?'

'Ray, where are you?' asked Simmons.

'Just walking back up to Ham Gate in Richmond Park – our old stamping ground. After that, I have a fundraiser to get to over in . . .'

Simmons whispered the location to Wolf, who was already on the phone to the control room.

'Ray, we've got a situation: a legitimate threat against your life.'

The mayor took the news surprisingly well:

'Business as usual then,' he laughed.

'Stay where you are. We've got cars on their way to escort you back here until we know more,' Simmons told him.

'Is that really necessary?'

'I'll explain everything when you get here.'

Simmons hung up and turned to Wolf.

'Three vehicles en route. Closest is four minutes out. One's an Armed Response Unit.'

'Good,' said Simmons. 'Get Baxter and what's-his-name back here. Then I want this floor locked down, no one in or out. Make security aware that we'll be bringing the mayor in through the garage entrance. Go!'

Mayor Turnble sat patiently in the back seat of his chauffeur-driven Mercedes-Benz E-Class. He had asked his assistant to excuse him from his busy schedule of commitments on the way back to the car, sensing that it was going to be a long and tedious day.

Only two months earlier he had received a threatening email and been forced to hide inside his Richmond home for an entire afternoon. That was until they discovered that it had been sent by an eleven-year-old boy whose school he had visited earlier in the week. He wondered whether this would prove to be an equally monumental waste of time.

The queuing traffic, already heading into the park to make the most of another glorious weekend, had forced them to move the car. They were now parked outside the recently unoccupied Royal Star and Garter Home. The mayor gazed out at the magnificent building sat atop Richmond Hill and wondered how long it would be before another of London's long, rich histories ended in the anticlimactic dishonour of being converted into apartments for wealthy bankers.

He opened his briefcase, found his brown preventative inhaler and took a deep breath. The endless heatwave had brought with it the soaring pollen counts that played havoc with his breathing and he was determined not to wind up back in hospital for a third time that year. His closest rival was already biting at his heels and he was confident that the day's missed engagements would not go unnoticed.

As he felt the stress build, he lowered his window and lit up a cigarette. The irony of the cigarette box lying alongside his inhalers had long since been lost on him, especially after doing so well to cut down. He could hear the wail of sirens in the distance and was dismayed to discover that they were for his benefit.

A patrol car skidded up beside them and the uniformed officer climbed out to share a short exchange with his chauffeur. Thirty seconds later they were on their way, jumping traffic lights and racing through bus lanes. He prayed that no one was filming this ludicrous overreaction as two more police cars pulled up either side of the all-too-recognisable, Mercedes.

The mayor slid down a little lower in his seat, watching the spacious houses compress into compacted office blocks, jostling for attention in an endless pissing contest that gradually obscured the sky.

CHAPTER 4

Saturday 28 June 2014

7.19 a.m.

Edmunds was almost positive that Baxter had knocked someone off their bike back in Southwark. He closed his eyes as they hurtled along the river on the wrong side of the road, almost obliterating an entire carriage-worth of pedestrians who were attempting to cross the street from where Temple Tube station had spat them out.

Baxter's Audi had blue lights concealed behind the front grille, undetectable when off, and, judging by the number of near misses, not significantly more detectable when on. When she swerved back onto the correct side of the road to weave in and out of the building traffic, Edmunds relinquished his grip on the door handle. During a momentary lull from the deafening engine, to avoid ploughing into the back of a bus, he realised that his phone was ringing. A photo of Tia, an attractive black woman in her mid-twenties, filled the screen.

'Hey, honey, everything OK?' he shouted down the phone.

'Hey, you. You disappeared in the middle of the night, and there's been all this stuff on the news and . . . I just wanted to check in.'

'It's not a great time, T. Can I call you back in a bit?'

Tia sounded put out: 'Sure. Can you pick up some milk on your way home tonight?'

Edmunds pulled out his notebook and made a note beneath the definition of Tetrodotoxin.

'And some beefburgers,' she added.

'You're vegetarian!'

'Burgers!' snapped Tia.

He added it to the shopping list.

'Nutella.'

'What on earth are you making?' he asked.

Baxter glanced over at Edmunds, who made an unmanly screech as his eyes widened in fear. She turned back to the road and spun the wheel violently, only narrowly missing another car.

'Shit!' she laughed in relief.

'OK, fine,' said Edmunds, breathing heavily. 'I've got to go now. I love you.'

They pulled past the security barrier and descended the ramp into the garages below New Scotland Yard, cutting Tia off mid-farewell as the phone lost signal.

'My fiancée,' Edmunds explained. He grinned. 'She's twenty-four weeks.'

Baxter looked at him impassively.

'Pregnant. She's twenty-four weeks pregnant.'

Her expression did not alter.

'Congrats. I was just thinking about how we detectives get way too much sleep, but a crying baby should sort that right out for you.'

Baxter, sort of, parked the car and turned to face Edmunds.

'Look, you're not going to make it. Why don't you stop wasting my time and just go back to Fraud?'

She got out and slammed the car door, leaving Edmunds sitting alone. He had been shaken by her reaction, not because of her bluntness or her unashamed disinterest in his impending fatherhood. Instead, he was disquieted by the suspicion that she had been the first person to actually tell him the truth; he was worried that she was right.

The entire Homicide and Serious Crime department had squeezed into the meeting room, including those not directly involved in the case but who would now be inconvenienced by the emergency lockdown nonetheless. The inadequate air conditioning, wafting through the vents, caught at the edges of the photos on the wall, the enormous reconstructions appearing to sway slightly, just as the real body had while suspended from the high ceiling.

Simmons and Vanita had been talking for over five minutes. Their audience was beginning to grow restless as the temperature in the stuffy room steadily rose.

'. . . through the garage entrance. We will then secure Mayor Turnble in Interview Room One,' said Simmons.

'Better use Two,' someone chipped in. 'One's still got the dripping pipe, and I doubt the mayor wants to add Chinese water torture to his list of troubles today.'

There was sporadic laughter, presumably from people who had unofficially conducted interviews in Room One for that precise reason.

'Room Two then,' said Simmons. 'Finlay, is everything ready?'

'Aye.'

Simmons looked unconvinced by the answer.

Wolf gave his friend a subtle nudge.

'Oh, I've told them to let Emily and . . . and . . .'

'Edmunds,' whispered Wolf.

'What's his first name?' Finlay hissed back.

Wolf shrugged: 'Edmund?'

'. . . Edmund Edmunds through. There's security on all doors, the armed DPG lads in the garage for the meet and the dogs have been through. We closed every blind on this floor and stopped the lifts, which means we're taking the stairs – or Will is, anyway.'

'Excellent,' said Simmons. 'Fawkes, once you've got the mayor, an armed officer will accompany you up here. Keep in mind that it's a big building and we don't know everyone in it. Once you're in the interview room, you're in there for the long haul.'

'How long?' asked Wolf.

'Until we're sure the mayor is safe.'

'I'll get you a bucket,' called out an arrogant detective constable named Saunders, finding his own contribution hilarious.

'I was actually wondering what was for lunch,' replied Wolf.

'Blowfish,' sneered Saunders, testing Simmons' patience.

'Do you think this is a laughing matter, Saunders?' Simmons shouted, perhaps overreacting a little for the sake of the commander. 'Get out!'

The rat-faced detective stuttered like a chided schoolboy:

'I actually physically can't . . . because of the lockdown.'

'Then just sit there and shut up.'

Choosing the worst possible moment to enter the meeting room – Baxter and Edmunds entered the meeting room.

'Nice of you two to join us. I've got a long list of tenuous leads for you to follow up.' Simmons threw Baxter a folder, which she handed straight to Edmunds.

'What did we miss?' Baxter asked the room.

'Will and I are on protection duty,' Finlay answered. 'You and Edmund Edmunds are identifying the bits, and Saunders was being a—'

'Dick?' Baxter suggested, taking a seat.

Finlay nodded, grateful that she had spared him breaking his no-swearing rule.

'OK. Settle down,' ordered Simmons. 'So, while I've got you all here: we've got six dead victims stitched together, a death threat against the mayor, and a hit list of five others.' He pressed on, ignoring the roomful of enquiring looks. 'Does anybody have any—'

'Plus the puppet monster's pointing into Will's window,' interrupted Finlay cheerfully.

'And that. Does anybody have any theories?' A room of blank faces answered Simmons' question. 'Anyone?'

Tentatively, Edmunds raised a hand: 'It's a challenge, sir.'

'Go on.'

'At university I wrote a paper examining the reasons for serial killers to send communiqués to the media or police: The Zodiac Killer, The Happy Face Killer—'

'The Faustian Killer, the baddy from *Seven*,' added Saunders, his impersonation of Edmunds earning him a few spiteful laughs and a glare from Simmons.

'Aren't you the Fraud guy?' someone asked.

Edmunds ignored them.

'Often, but not always, their communication will contain irrefutable proof that they are, in fact, the genuine perpetrator,' he continued. 'Sometimes it's as subtle as details that haven't been made public; other times it's something rather more substantial.'

'Like the photographs sent to Fawkes' wife today,' said Vanita, oblivious of her faux pas.

'*Ex*-wife,' Wolf corrected.

'Exactly. And in very rare cases this is done as a cry for help, literally pleading with the police to stop them killing again. They believe that they are no more than victims of their own uncontrollable urges. Either that or the idea of somebody else claiming credit for their work is unbearable. In both scenarios, consciously or unconsciously, the ultimate intention is invariably the same: to eventually get caught.'

'And you believe that this is one of those rare cases?' asked Vanita. 'Why?'

'The list, for one . . . The definitive time frame . . . The press-baiting . . . I believe the killer will keep their distance as they test the water, but they won't be able to resist getting closer and closer to the investigation. With each subsequent murder, their confidence will grow, fuelling their god complex, goading them into taking greater and greater risks. In the end, *they* will come to *us*.'

The entire room stared at Edmunds in surprise.

'I don't think I've ever heard you speak before,' said Finlay.

Edmunds shrugged bashfully.

'But why me?' asked Wolf. 'Why not point that horrible thing through someone else's window? Why send the pictures to my wife?'

'*Ex*-wife,' Baxter and Finlay chimed in unison.

'Why is my—' Wolf stopped himself. 'Why me?'

'You've just got one of those faces,' smirked Finlay.

The room turned back to Edmunds expectantly.

'It is far less common for a serial killer to single out an individual over the police force as a whole, but it does happen – and when it does, the reasons are always personal. In a way, it's a form of flattery. He must see Wolf, and Wolf alone, as a worthy adversary.'

'That's all right, then. As long as he meant it nicely,' said Wolf dismissively.

'Who else is on this list then?' asked Baxter, eager to change the subject to something on which Edmunds had not written a paper.

'I'll handle this one, Terrence,' said Vanita as she stepped forward. 'At this time we have elected to withhold that information because A, we do not wish to cause a panic; B, we need you all focused on the mayor right now; and C – we don't know for sure that the threat is genuine, and the last thing that this department needs is another lawsuit.'

Wolf sensed several heads turn accusingly in his direction.

The internal line on the meeting room phone rang, and the crowd listened in as Simmons answered.

'Go ahead . . . Thank you.' He nodded to Vanita.

'OK, people, be at your very best today. Meeting adjourned.'

The mayor's Mercedes was already parked by the time Wolf reached the underground car park. Unlike the rest of the building, the subterranean garages lacked the benefit of air conditioning and the heat rising up off the tarmac, laced with the scents of rubber, oil and exhaust fumes, was almost suffocating. The oppressive strip lighting that illuminated all but the darkest corners toyed with Wolf's internal clock. In his exhausted state he wondered whether it was evening again already and checked his watch: 7.36 a.m.

As he approached the car, one of the rear doors swung open and the mayor climbed out, much to the dismay of his now redundant chauffeur.

'Will someone please tell me what the hell is going on?' he snapped as he slammed the door behind him.

'Mr Mayor, I'm Detective Sergeant Fawkes.'

Wolf held out a hand in greeting, and the mayor's anger dissipated instantly. He looked momentarily uneasy before recovering his composure and shaking Wolf's hand heartily.

'Nice to finally meet you in person, Detective,' he beamed, overcompensating, as if posing for a photograph at the charity event he should have been on his way to.

'If you'll follow me, please,' said Wolf, gesturing to the armed officer who would accompany them upstairs.

'One moment, please,' said the mayor.

Wolf removed the hand that he had placed unconsciously against the distinguished man's back in an attempt to hurry him along.

'I would like to be told what's going on, right now.'

Wolf struggled to ignore the conceited tone. He answered through gritted teeth: 'Simmons would prefer to brief you himself.'

The mayor was unaccustomed to being told 'no' and faltered.

'Very well. Although, I must say, I'm surprised that Terrence would send you down here to babysit me. I heard you on the radio this morning. Shouldn't you be working on this serial killer case?'

Wolf was aware that he should not have said anything, but he needed to get the man moving and was already tired of his haughty manner. He turned to the mayor and looked him in the eye.

'I am.'

The mayor was faster than he looked.

If it had not been for the chronic asthma and decades of damage to his lungs, courtesy of the cigarettes, they might not have been able to keep up. The three men slowed to a brisk jog as they entered the main lobby.

The large minimalist space was one of the few areas of the building to have completely shaken off any trace of its 1960s design. The commissioner had point-blank refused Simmons' request to close the lobby and stairwell while they moved the mayor, stating that the armed security, CCTV, metal detectors and building full of police officers already made it the safest place in the city to be.

The lobby was quieter than it would have been during the week, although, there were still several people passing through and loitering around the coffee bar in the centre. Spotting a gap in the pedestrian traffic, Wolf picked up the pace and headed for the door to the stairs.

The mayor, now visibly on edge, was the first to notice the balding man enter the building and start running at them.

'Detective!'

Wolf turned to see the threat and pushed the mayor behind him as the armed officer raised his handgun.

'Down on the floor! Get down!' the officer screamed at the unremarkable man holding a brown paper bag.

He skidded to a stop and raised his hands in dazed shock.

'On the floor!' The officer had to repeat everything twice before the instructions seemed to sink in. 'Drop the bag. Put it down!'

The man tossed the bag away from him, sending it skating across the polished floor in the mayor's direction. Unsure whether this was a deliberate act or simply the misconstrued actions of a nervous man, Wolf pulled the mayor back several steps.

'What's in the bag?' the officer yelled at the man, who glanced up at Wolf and the mayor. 'Eyes down! Look at the floor! What. Is. In. The. Bag?'

'Breakfast!' shouted the terrified man.

'Why were you running?'

'I'm nearly twenty minutes late for work – IT department.'

The DPG officer kept the gun trained on the man and backed towards the bag. He cautiously knelt down beside it and then very, very slowly peered inside.

'We've got some sort of hot wrap,' he told Wolf, as if identifying a suspicious-looking device.

'What flavour?' Wolf called back.

'What flavour?' the officer barked.

'Ham and cheese!' cried the man on the floor.

Wolf grinned: 'Confiscate it.'

They reached the office without further incident. Wolf thanked their escort and then Finlay led them inside. The seven-floor ascent had taken its toll; Wolf could hear a high-pitched whistle every time the red-faced mayor took a breath.

The office felt claustrophobic with all of the blinds closed, the stark artificial light a cheap imitation of the real thing. They walked swiftly through the room of faces watching them from behind computer screens and colourful bouquets. Simmons rushed out of his office when he spotted them coming and shook his old friend's hand.

'It's good to see you, Ray,' he said sincerely before turning to Wolf. 'Trouble downstairs?'

'False alarm,' mumbled Wolf through a mouthful of ham and cheese wrap.

'Terrence, I would appreciate it if you could explain what is happening,' said the mayor.

'Of course, let's speak in private.' Simmons led them into the interview room and closed the door. 'I sent a patrol car over to your house. I thought you would want to know that Melanie and Rosie were safe.'

'I apprec—' The mayor's breathing had worsened, even since walking through the office. He broke into a fit of wheezing coughs and splutters. All too accustomed to the feeling, as though someone were sitting on his chest, he rummaged through his briefcase and found his blue reliever inhaler this time. He took two long, deep breaths which seemed to help a little. 'I appreciate that, thank you.'

The mayor waited expectantly. Taking the hint, Simmons started pacing the room.

'OK, where to start? You heard, of course, that we found six bodies this morning? Well, it's not quite as simple as that . . .'

Over the next fifteen minutes Simmons explained everything that had happened that morning. Wolf remained quiet throughout. He was surprised to hear the boss sharing details that they certainly would not want the press catching wind of, but Simmons obviously trusted his friend implicitly, and Wolf supposed that he had earned the right to know. The only details that Simmons refused to reveal, even when the mayor asked him outright, were the other five names on the list.

'I don't want you to worry. You are more than safe in here,' Simmons assured him.

'And how long exactly do you expect me to hide in here, Terrence?'

'It makes sense to keep you until midnight at least. That way, the killer has failed to follow through on his threat. We'll step up security around you, obviously, but you'll be able to get back to relative normality.'

The mayor nodded in resignation.

'If you'll excuse me, the sooner we catch this bastard, the sooner you can get out of here,' Simmons said confidently, moving towards the door. 'Fawkes will stay with you.'

The mayor got up to speak privately with Simmons. Wolf turned away, as if facing the wall would prevent him overhearing what was being said in the small room.

'Are you sure that is an entirely good idea?' wheezed the mayor.

'Of course. You'll be fine.'

Simmons left the room. From inside they could hear him giving muffled instructions to the officer on the door. The mayor took two more long puffs on his inhaler before turning back to face Wolf. He forced another feigned smile, this one intended to convey his sheer delight at having the infamous detective as company for the day.

'So,' said the mayor, suppressing another violent coughing fit, 'what now?'

Wolf picked up the first wad of paperwork that Simmons had thoughtfully left on the table for him. He put his feet up and leaned back in his chair.

'Now, we wait.'

CHAPTER 5

Saturday 28 June 2014

12.10 p.m.

An atmosphere of exasperation and resentment was manifesting quietly within the hushed office as the wasted hours ticked languorously by. The blatant inequality being exhibited by granting preferential treatment to the 'notable' Mayor Turnble, at the expense of every other second-class victim in the city, had been the heated topic at the core of several whispered conversations. Baxter suspected that this new-found egalitarianism, amongst some of the most chauvinistic and narrow-minded men she had ever known, was rooted more in their own self-importance than in their desire for a fairer world; although, she had to admit, they had a point.

Unconvinced eyes flicked back to the interview room door time and time again, almost hoping for something to happen, if only to justify the inconvenience. There was only so much of the tedious paperwork, which constituted an unglamorous 90 per cent of a detective's job, that people could endure in one sitting. A handful of officers, coming off the back of a thirteen-hour shift, had dragged a whiteboard in front of the grotesque creations that Wolf had plastered across the wall. Unable to go home, they had turned the meeting room lights off in an attempt to get some rest before their next shift began.

Simmons had seriously lost his temper with the seventh person to request special treatment to breach the lockdown and no one had dared ask since. All had had perfectly valid reasons, and he was more than aware that his drastic actions would impact negatively, perhaps irredeemably, upon other equally important cases, but what could he do? He wished that he and Mayor Turnble had not been friends, a detail he was sure would come back to haunt him, because his decisions would have been the same. The world was watching this test of the Metropolitan Police. If they should be proven weak, vulnerable, incapable of preventing a murder that they had prior warning of, the repercussions could be devastating.

Embarrassingly, the commander had made herself at home in his office, so he had temporarily relocated himself to DI Chambers' vacant desk. Simmons wondered if news of the murders had reached him in the Caribbean yet, and whether the experienced detective might have been able to shed any light on the bizarre case had he been there.

Baxter spent the morning tracking down the owner of the flat in which the body had been found. He had believed that a newlywed couple were occupying the old apartment with their newborn baby. Baxter expected that parts of the couple had contributed to the body and did not want to contemplate for too long the fate of the defenceless little baby; however, she discovered with relief that she could find no record of the couple's marriage and that the limited details provided to the trusting landlord had all been fake.

When she called him back an hour later, he admitted that he had been approached privately and accepted cash in hand, posted through his letter box. He told her that he had binned all of the envelopes, never met the tenant in person and then pleaded with her not to report him for undeclared income. Confident that the taxman would catch up eventually, and in no mood to create more work for herself, she moved on, having wasted hours on a dead end.

Edmunds, on the other hand, was feeling elated as he perched on the corner of Baxter's desk. This was, in part, due to the position of his non-desk, situated directly beneath a vent in the ceiling, through which a steady stream of cold air was plunging over his head; more importantly though, he had made significant headway with the pedestrian task that Baxter had assigned him.

Told to find out from whom the prison sourced its food he had quickly learned that the vast majority was prepared on site, but following a food strike in 2006, a company named Complete Foods had been brought in to supply specialist catering for many of its Muslim inmates. A brief call to the prison confirmed that Khalid had been the only inmate to regularly receive the special gluten-free version of the meals. When Complete Foods then admitted that they were investigating a contamination issue after receiving two complaints of people being hospitalised following the consumption of similar meals, Edmunds had to hide his excitement. He wanted to impress Baxter – who was clearly getting nowhere – with his progress.

The floor supervisor at Complete Foods explained that the meals were prepared through the night, ready to be shipped out to prisons, hospitals and schools in the early hours of the morning. Edmunds asked him to compile a list of employees who had been on duty that night and to prepare the surveillance video for their visit the following day. He had just picked up the phone to contact the two companies that had submitted the complaints, confident that he already knew the unfortunate recipient's diagnosis and regrettable outcome, when somebody tapped him on the shoulder.

'Sorry mate, boss's asked you to take over for Hodge on the door. I need him for something,' said the sweating man, who closed his eyes in bliss as he stepped into the blast of cool air.

Edmunds suspected from the man's vague excuse that he was actually just rescuing a friend from the mind-numbing task of standing outside a door for hours on end. He looked to Baxter for help, who just waved him away dismissively. He put the phone back down and unenthusiastically went to relieve the man stood outside the interview room.

*

Edmunds shifted his weight and slouched back against the door that he had been guarding for almost fifty minutes. The lack of sleep had caught up with him now that he was no longer keeping his mind occupied, and the gentle ambience of muted conversation, clicking keyboards and the whirr of the photocopier acted like a lullaby to his exhaustion. His eyelids flickered. He had never longed for anything as much as he wanted to close his eyes at that moment. He rested his heavy head against the door and felt himself drifting off, when a quiet voice spoke unexpectedly from inside the room.

'It's a funny game, politics.'

Wolf jumped at the mayor's sudden, but obviously considered, outburst. The two men had been sitting in silence for five straight hours. Wolf placed the file that he had been reading down on the table and waited for him to elaborate. The mayor sat staring at his own feet. As the pause blossomed into an uncomfortable silence, Wolf wondered whether the mayor even realised that he had spoken out loud. He hesitantly reached for the file again when the mayor finally continued with his thought:

'You want to do good, but you can't unless you're in power. You can't stay in power without votes, and you only get votes by appeasing the public. But then, sometimes appeasing the public requires you to sacrifice the very good that you had set out to achieve. It's a funny game, politics.'

Wolf had absolutely no idea what the appropriate response to this peculiar pearl of wisdom should be, so he waited self-consciously for the mayor to either continue or shut up.

'Let's not pretend that you like me, Fawkes.'

'OK,' replied Wolf, a little too quickly.

'Which makes what you are doing for me today all the more humbling.'

'I'm doing my job.'

'As was I. I want you to know that. Public opinion was not in your favour, therefore, *I* was not in your favour.'

Wolf felt that the phrase 'not in your favour' fell a little short when referencing the relentless tirade of condemnation, the unabashed rallying to whet the appetite of the corruption-fatigued public and the unremitting portrayal of Wolf as a symbol of immorality: a target at which the virtuous could, at last, vent their anger.

Riding a wave of inexhaustible public support against the city's floundering police force, the mayor had unveiled his groundbreaking reports, *Policing and Crime Policy*. He had repeatedly encouraged that Wolf be punished to the full extent of the law during a rousing speech to a roomful of his peers, in which he coined the already well-known slogan 'policing the police'.

Wolf recalled the almost comical turnabout after Naguib Khalid was arrested for the second time. He remembered how this man, still using Wolf as his poster boy, had flaunted his *Health Inequalities Strategy* while damning the inadequate services available to 'our best and bravest' and to the city of London as a whole.

Conducted by a charismatic and unusually popular public figure, the mayor's supporters applauded and rallied obediently in time to his manipulations. The same dedicated voices that had called for Wolf's blood were now campaigning to patch him back up, and one passionate interviewee had even gone on television to demand both.

There was no doubt that without the mayor's influence and his well-publicised crusade to reinstate one of the people's 'broken heroes', Wolf would still be behind bars; however, both men knew that Wolf owed him nothing.

Wolf remained deathly silent, fearful of what he might say should he open his mouth.

'You did the right thing, by the way,' the mayor continued pompously, oblivious to Wolf's drastic change in mood. 'There is a difference between corruption and desperation. I see that now. Personally, I wish you had killed the sick bastard in that courtroom. That last little girl he set alight was my daughter's age.'

The mayor's breathing had calmed during the hours of tense quiet, but this extended period of talking had undone all of his progress.

He shook his blue inhaler and the uninspiring metallic sound, as the dregs of the medicine shuffled against the canister wall, came as no surprise; he had overdosed on over a week's worth of Salbutamol since entering the interview room. Unperturbed, he took another dose and held the precious breath in for as long as he could.

'I've wanted to tell you that for a long time,' said the mayor. 'That it was never personal. I was just doing—'

'Your job, yeah,' Wolf finished bitterly. 'I understand. You were all just doing your jobs: the press, the lawyers, the hero that shattered my wrist and pulled me off Khalid. I get it.'

The mayor nodded. He had not intended to aggravate Wolf, but he felt better for speaking his mind. Despite his current unenviable situation, he felt a small weight lift off his shoulders, something that he had been carrying for far too long. He opened up his briefcase and took out the packet of cigarettes.

'Do you mind?'

Wolf stared at the wheezing man in disbelief: 'You must be joking.'

'We all have our vices,' said the mayor unapologetically. His pomposity had been buoyed by his almost-apology, his authority given free rein now that he no longer felt in any way indebted to Wolf. 'If you expect me to stay locked up in this room for another eleven hours, I expect you not to argue. One now, one at dinner time, that's all.'

Wolf was about to protest when the mayor defiantly placed the cigarette between his lips, sparked his lighter and, with a cupped hand shielding the flame from the air-conditioned breeze, drew the fire towards his face . . .

For a fleeting moment, the two men stared at one another, neither able to comprehend what was happening. Wolf watched as the flame caught where the cigarette wedged the mayor's mouth open and spread instantaneously to consume the entire lower half of his face. The mayor gasped deeply to scream out, but the inferno followed his breath, filling his nose and mouth as it poured into his lungs.

'Help!' yelled Wolf as he reached the man who was silently burning alive. 'I need help in here!'

He grabbed the mayor's flailing arms, uncertain what to do. Edmunds burst through the door and stood open-mouthed as the mayor let out a sickening, guttural cough that showered Wolf's left arm in frothy blood and liquid fire. Wolf momentarily loosened his grip on a thrashing arm and was struck painfully across the face as his own shirtsleeve started to burn. He realised that if he could only get close enough to hold the mayor's nose and mouth closed, the oxygen-starved fire would die out instantly.

Edmunds had rushed back out into the corridor as the fire alarm tripped. The entire office were on their feet, watching as he ripped a fire blanket off the wall. He saw Simmons running between desks towards the room. Edmunds re-entered the interview room. The sprinkler system now raining down over the two men was doing more harm than good; with every mouthful of water that the panicking man sprayed across the room, he spread the flames further, as though he were literally breathing fire. Wolf was still attempting to wrestle him to the ground when Edmunds raised the blanket and charged into them both, dropping all three of them onto the flooded floor.

Simmons splashed into the room and froze in repulsion as Edmunds pulled the blanket off the devastated body that had once been his handsome friend. When it dawned on him that the air he was breathing stank of scorched flesh, he began to gag. Two more officers rushed inside as Simmons backed out. One of them threw another blanket over Wolf's, still burning, arm while Edmunds searched the mayor's neck for a carotid pulse and listened for breathing at the destroyed mouth.

'No pulse!' he yelled, unsure who was even in the room.

The Savile Row shirt disintegrated in his hands as he pulled it open and started counting in time to the chest compressions; however, every time he pushed down on the mayor's sternum, blood and charred tissue flooded the ruined throat. The very first thing that his three-day First Aid at Work course had taught him was the ABCs: without an airway, all the chest compressions in the world could not save him. Edmunds gradually slowed to a stop and slumped onto the soaking floor. He looked up at Simmons, who was standing just outside the door.

'I'm sorry, sir.'

Water streamed out of Edmunds' saturated hair and was running down his face. He closed his eyes as he tried to make sense of the surreal events of the previous two and a half minutes. Somewhere in the distance, he could hear sirens approaching.

Simmons stepped back into the room. His expression was unreadable as he looked down at the charred body of his friend. Forced to look away from the ghastly image that he knew would haunt him for the rest of his life, he turned his attention to Wolf, who was on his knees, holding his blistering arm in pain. Simmons grabbed a handful of his shirt and pulled him to his feet before throwing him back against the wall, shocking everyone in the room.

'You were supposed to protect him!' Simmons screamed with tearful eyes, slamming Wolf into the wall repeatedly. 'You were meant to watch him!'

Edmunds jumped back to his feet before anyone else had reacted and restrained his boss' arms. Following his lead, the two other officers and Baxter, who had just appeared in the doorway, wrestled Simmons away from Wolf and dragged him out of the room. They closed the door on their way out to preserve the crime scene, leaving Wolf alone with the grotesque corpse.

Wolf slid down the wall and sat curled up in the corner. Dazed, he felt the back of his head and stared at the blood on his fingers in confusion. He was surrounded by dozens of tiny oily flames, still burning ferociously across the surface of the rising flood, like Japanese water lanterns guiding lost spirits into the world of the dead. Resting his head against the wall, he watched the flames flicker under the relentless downpour, letting the cold water wash his bloody hands clean.

CHAPTER 6

Saturday 28 June 2014

4.23 p.m.

Andrea climbed out of the taxi and into the shadow of the Heron Tower, London's third-tallest skyscraper. She gazed up at the topmost floors, eclipsing the sun. The unbalanced forms reached incoherently skywards, the lanky metal mast balancing precariously on top, grasping desperately for status at the expense of the aesthetics and, by the looks of it, structural integrity.

The newsroom could not have been housed in a more appropriate building.

She entered the immense reception area and automatically headed for the escalators, intending never to put so much as a foot inside any of the six transparent lifts that propelled impatient businessmen back in the direction of their desks at alarming speed. As she rose gently away from the lobby floor, she admired the colossal aquarium built into the wall behind reception, the immaculate employees apparently unperturbed by the 70,000-litre slice of ocean held at bay by a thin layer of acrylic.

Andrea was thinking about her newest passion in life, scuba diving, as she stared at the colourful blossoms sprouting from the coral and peaceful fish darting in and out of view in the blissfully warm water. She almost tripped over when the travelling staircase jolted her from her thoughts and deposited her unceremoniously onto the stationary floor.

She had received the call to attend the crime scene at 3 a.m. After finally making contact with Wolf, to hand him the disturbing envelope that she had discovered in her post tray, she had remained outside New Scotland Yard with her cameraman for four further hours in order to record half-hourly live updates. This involved repeatedly rehashing the same information to make it appear, although never specifically state, that there had been significant activity and thrilling developments occurring outside on the pavement in front of the police headquarters' closed doors.

After her 11 a.m. bulletin, Andrea had received a phone call from her editor-in-chief, Elijah Reid, instructing her to go home and get a few hours' rest. She had protested obstinately. She had no intention of renouncing her claim over what was sure to become the most sensational story since the Cremation Killings (especially being privy to the troubling contents of the envelope, which she was yet to share with her boss). She was finally persuaded when Elijah swore to phone her immediately at the slightest hint of activity.

It had been a pleasant half-hour stroll in the sunshine, along the palace grounds and past Belgrave Square Garden, back to Knightsbridge and the three-storey Victorian town house that she shared with her fiancé and his nine-year-old daughter. Andrea closed the substantial front door and climbed straight upstairs to the tastefully bland bedroom on the top floor.

She pulled the curtains and lay on top of the covers, fully clothed, in the semi-darkness. She reached into her bag, found her mobile phone and set an alarm. She then removed a file containing photocopies of each and every one of the items that she had surrendered to Wolf and held it tightly against her chest as she closed her eyes, acutely aware of their tremendous significance to the police, to the fated people on the list – and to her.

For over an hour and a half she lay there unable to sleep, staring up at the high ceiling and the ornate detailing surrounding the antique light fitting, weighing up the moral and legal implications of sharing the evidence with Elijah. She had no doubt whatsoever that he would shamelessly parade all twelve of the photographs in front of the world. A tactful promise that 'some viewers may find the following images distressing' would only tantalise the public's insatiable morbid curiosity. She wondered darkly whether the families of the as yet unidentified victims would be watching, finding themselves simultaneously fascinated and repulsed by the vaguely familiar dismemberments.

That morning dozens of journalists had stood side by side in front of the same clichéd backdrop to report the exact same information, each vying for the attention of the spoilt-for-choice viewing public. The fact that Andrea had been contacted directly by the killer would surely give them an edge over the BBC and Sky News, who would undoubtedly reproduce the images within minutes of them being broadcast. However, she knew exactly how to ensure that every television in the country was focused solely on her:

1. The pitch – Andrea would inform the public that she had been contacted by the city's newest serial killer.

2. The tease – They would reveal each of the photographs in turn, describing what was depicted and making wild assumptions to provoke easily influenced imaginations. They may even be able to find an ex-detective, a private investigator – even a crime novelist would do – who would agree to lend their opinion to the unveiling.

3. The promise – Andrea would reveal that included in the package was a handwritten list detailing the identities of the killer's next six victims and the precise dates on which they would die. 'All will be revealed in just five minutes time,' she would promise (long enough for word to spread across the entire planet, yet too little time for the police to disrupt the broadcast).

4. The reveal – With the whole world watching, she would list the names and dates, pausing dramatically between each one like a television talent show judge choosing their finalists. She wondered whether a drum roll would be going too far.

Andrea hated herself for even considering it. There was a strong possibility that the police had not yet contacted the marked people, who undoubtedly deserved to learn of their impending doom at least a little before the rest of the world. Plus, she would be arrested; although, that had never dissuaded Elijah in the past. Even in his short time at the station, Andrea had watched him ruin lives through conjecture, circulate dubiously obtained details of active investigations and attend court twice for withholding evidence and attempting to bribe a police officer.

Having abandoned sleep, she sat up on the bed, no more rested but resolute on a course of action. She would use the photographs; it would land her in trouble, but the benefits to her career far outweighed the inconvenience. She would keep the list secret. It was the right thing to do. She felt proud of herself for still fighting the growing pressure to become as merciless and destructive as her boss.

She reached the corridor that led to the newsroom. Even at this modest height, Andrea instinctively veered towards the wall, ignoring the view out over the rooftops of Camomile Street. When she entered the office, she was struck, as always, by the relentless commotion that persisted twenty-four hours a day. Elijah revelled in the chaos: people shouting at one another, phones ringing discordantly, numerous plasma screens jutting down from the ceiling, subtitles replacing their muted words. She knew that, within minutes, she would acclimatise to it, and the aggressive atmosphere would become no more than background noise.

The newsroom was located on levels ten and eleven. The dividing floor had been removed to create a commodious double-height space. After years of working at regional stations, Andrea found the set-up excessive and wasteful, almost a parody of a newsroom. All she needed was a desk, a computer and a telephone.

The new editor-in-chief had been poached from a hard-hitting US news programme, which had controversially uncovered the rampant corruption festering within a number of well-known brands and companies. He had brought with him a multitude of the patronising Americanisms, team-building exercises and morale-boosting incentives that are increasingly forced upon the chronically reserved English employees.

Andrea took a seat in her neon-yellow (scientific research has discovered a direct correlation between efficiency and bright colours) ergonomic chair opposite the Ben & Jerry's machine and immediately checked her post tray for any further messages from the killer. She removed the file from her bag and was just about to climb the stairs to Elijah's office when people started abandoning their desks to congregate beneath the largest of the television screens.

Andrea noticed that Elijah had also emerged from his office to watch, arms folded, from the balcony. His gaze flickered down to her and then, disinterested, returned to the screen. With no idea what was going on, she got to her feet and stood at the back of the growing crowd.

'Turn it up!' someone shouted.

Suddenly New Scotland Yard's familiar sign appeared and Andrea recognised her cameraman Rory's trademark soft-focus zoom out to reveal a beautiful blonde reporter wearing an inappropriately low-cut summer dress. There was a wolf whistle from somewhere near the front. Isobel Platt had only been working at the station for four months. At the time of her appointment Andrea had considered it an insult to the profession, giving a mindless, cosmetically enhanced, twenty-year-old a position based on no more than her ability to read out loud; she now felt it a personal attack on her and her career.

Isobel was cheerfully informing them that a police spokesperson would be making a statement 'im . . . min . . . ently' while her exposed cleavage dominated the screen to the point where Andrea wondered why Rory was bothering to keep her head in frame at all. She felt tears pricking her eyes and could feel Elijah watching her for a reaction. She focused intently on the screen, refusing to turn around or leave the room, denying him that satisfaction.

It had not been the first time that she had underestimated her editor-in-chief's utter ruthlessness. She understood his reasoning;

in the battle of ratings for the biggest story of the year, why not stick a model in front of the camera as a little extra incentive? She would not have been at all surprised had Isobel reappeared topless for her sign-off.

The startling news of Mayor Turnble's untimely death, while visiting the police HQ for a policies update meeting, barely registered with Andrea as her colleagues gasped and swore accordingly. She was preoccupied with fermenting her self-pity into anger. She would *not* be quietly dismissed from her own story. She turned away from the screen, not lingering to hear what Isobel's breasts had made of the shocking press conference, stormed back over to her desk, collected the file and marched up the stairs towards Elijah. Apparently expecting this, he nonchalantly strolled back into his office and left the door ajar.

Elijah had been screaming and swearing for almost five minutes. He was livid that Andrea had sat on such an explosive story for an entire day. He had told her that she was fired seven times, called her the C-word three times, and physically chased his assistant away when she had come to check that everything was all right.

Andrea waited patiently for him to finish. She found his predictable reaction almost as amusing as the way in which his dubious New York accent became laced with a southern drawl the angrier he got. He was a vain man. He visited the gym both on his way in and back from work and always wore shirts a size too small to emphasise the extent of his obsession. Despite being over forty, his hair showed no sign of grey; instead, a flawless coverage of unnaturally golden hair was slicked back tidily across his scalp. Some of the other women in the office found him heartbreakingly attractive, the very definition of an alpha male. Andrea just found him comically repugnant. She had to wait another minute for his display of dominance to subside.

'These pictures are shitty quality, barely usable,' he spat, masking his excitement as he spread them over his desk.

'Yes, they are. These are just for you,' replied Andrea calmly. 'I have the high-quality versions saved on an SD card.'

'Where?' he asked urgently. When Andrea did not answer, he glanced up at her. 'Good girl, you're learning.'

Although offensively patronising, Andrea could not help but take some pride in the grudging compliment. The playing field had just been levelled; they were two sharks circling a piece of meat.

'The police have the originals?' he asked.

'They do.'

'Wolf?' Elijah had taken a keen interest in Andrea's divorce from the infamous detective. The Cremation Killer scandal had been equally newsworthy across the Atlantic. He grinned. 'Then we can't be accused of withholding evidence, can we? Get the photos to the graphics guys. You can keep your job.'

Andrea was caught off guard. Surely he had understood that her intention was not merely to preserve her employment but to reclaim her ownership of the story. Elijah must have seen the look on her face because his grin turned malicious.

'Don't act like you've been screwed. You've done your job, that's it. Isobel's already there. She'll do the report.'

Andrea could feel the familiar stinging in her eyes, which she desperately tried to conceal as she racked her brain for a countermove: 'Then I'll just—'

'Just what? Quit? Take the photos somewhere else?' he laughed. 'I'm willing to wager that the SD card you used belongs to the company. If I suspect that you are attempting to leave the premises with stolen property, I am well within my rights to have security search you.'

Andrea pictured the small black rectangle wedged between her Starbucks loyalty and PADI registration cards in her purse. They would find it in seconds. But then she realised that she had one last card to play.

'There's a list,' she blurted, talking before her conscience could catch up, 'of the killer's next victims.'

'Bullshit.'

She removed the crumpled photocopy from her pocket and folded it carefully so that only the first line was visible:

Mayor Raymond Edgar Turnble –

Saturday 28 June

Elijah squinted at the greyscale printout that Andrea was keeping well out of reach. He had watched her walk from the television to her desk and then straight up to his office. She'd had no opportunity to fabricate the photocopy.

'I've got five more names and dates below it. And I swear, if you try to take it from me, I'll swallow it whole.'

Sensing that she was deadly serious, he leaned back in his chair and smiled happily, as though they had finally reached the conclusion of a closely fought board game.

'What do you want?'

'It's *my* story.'

'Fine.'

'You can leave Isobel standing out there wasting her time. I'll be presenting my report from the studio.'

'You're a field reporter.'

'You can tell Robert and Marie we won't require them tonight. I'll be needing the entire show.'

A moment's hesitation.

'Consider it done. Anything else?'

'Yes. Lock all the doors until I'm done and don't open them for anyone. We can't let them arrest me until I've finished.'

CHAPTER 7

Saturday 28 June 2014

5.58 p.m.

Wolf sat alone in Simmons' office. He felt as though he was being intrusive for noticing the numerous fresh dents that had been kicked into the ancient filing cabinet and for treading the broken plaster further into the carpet: the first debris of the mourning process. He waited, feeling self-conscious, fiddling absent-mindedly with the damp bandage covering his left arm.

After Simmons had been removed from the interview room, Baxter had gone back to find Wolf slumped beside the mayor's lifeless body as the indoor monsoon raged on. She had never before seen him looking so lost and vulnerable, staring into space, apparently oblivious that she was even there. Gently, she pulled him up onto his feet and led him out into the dry corridor, where a roomful of troubled faces watched their every move with hounding attentiveness.

'For Christ's sake,' huffed Baxter.

She was supporting most of Wolf's weight as they stumbled across the office and through the door into the ladies' toilets. She struggled to get him up onto the countertop between the two sinks. Carefully, she unbuttoned his soiled shirt and slid it slowly off him, taking meticulous care while peeling the melted material out of the weeping and blistered wound that encircled his lower arm. The smell of cheap deodorant, sweat and burnt skin filled the air, and Baxter found herself feeling irrationally on edge, anxious that somebody could walk in at any moment and catch her doing absolutely nothing wrong.

'Sit tight,' she told him, once she had removed as much as she could. She rushed back out into the office and returned a few minutes later with a first aid kit and a towel, which she draped over Wolf's soaked hair. Inexpertly, she ripped open and applied the slimy burns dressing before wrapping sufficient bandage to mummify him around the injured arm.

Moments later, there was a knock at the door. Edmunds came in and unenthusiastically gave up his shirt, having unwittingly admitted to having a t-shirt on underneath. Although tall, Edmunds had the physique of a scrawny schoolboy and the insufficient material barely covered Wolf's bulk, but Baxter supposed that it was better than nothing. With the majority of the buttons done up, she jumped up onto the counter and sat quietly beside him, waiting for as long as it took for him to recover.

Wolf had spent the remainder of the afternoon in a quiet corner writing a detailed report on what had occurred inside the locked room. He had ignored the numerous unsolicited words of advice suggesting that he go home via A & E. At 5.50 p.m. he had been summoned into Simmons' office, where he apprehensively awaited the arrival of his chief inspector, whom he had not seen since his violent eruption hours earlier.

As he waited, Wolf vaguely recalled Baxter and the bathroom, but it all seemed hazy, surreal. He felt a little embarrassed, having neglected his press-ups that morning (and for the preceding four years) and pictured, with a shudder, her seeing his unkempt and slightly tubby body.

He heard Simmons enter the room behind him and close the door. His chief dropped into the chair opposite and removed a bottle of Jameson Irish Whiskey, a bag of ice and a tube of plastic Transformers picnic cups from a Tesco bag. His eyes were still puffy from breaking the news to Mayor Turnble's wife before the press conference. He scooped a handful of ice into two of the cups, topped them up generously and then slid one across to Wolf without a word. They each took a sip in silence.

'Your favourite, I seem to remember,' said Simmons at last.

'Good memory.'

'How's the head?' Simmons asked, as though he were in no way to blame for Wolf's mild concussion.

'Better than the arm,' replied Wolf cheerily, genuinely unsure what the doctors would be able to salvage if Baxter's bandaging was indicative of the treatment underneath.

'Can I be frank?' Simmons did not wait for an answer. 'We both know that you'd be sitting in this chair instead of me if you hadn't screwed up so massively. You were always the better detective.'

Wolf maintained a courteously impassive expression.

'Perhaps,' Simmons continued, 'you would have made better decisions than I did. Perhaps Ray would still be alive if . . .'

Simmons trailed off and took another swig of his drink.

'There was no way of knowing,' said Wolf.

'That the inhaler was laced with an incendiary? That the piles of flowers we've had sat in here for a week were caked in ragweed pollen?'

Wolf had noticed the heap of plastic evidence bags on his way into the office.

'In what?'

'Apparently, it's an asthmatic's kryptonite. And I brought him here.'

Forgetting that he was only holding a picnic cup, Simmons threw his empty glass against the wall, furious with himself. It bounced across the desk anticlimactically and, after a moment, he topped it back up.

'So, let's get this out the way before the commander gets back,' said Simmons. 'What are we going to do about you?'

'What about me?'

'Well, this is the meeting where I tell you you're too close to the case and advise you that it's in everybody's best interests to take you off . . .'

Wolf went to protest but Simmons continued:

'. . . then you tell me to piss off. Then I remind you what happened with Khalid. Then you tell me to piss off again, and I reluctantly agree to let you stay on but warn you that the first flicker of concern from your colleagues, your psychiatrist, or from me, and you'll be reassigned. Good chat.'

Wolf nodded. He was aware that Simmons was putting his neck on the line for him.

'Seven dead bodies and, so far, the only murder weapons are an inhaler, flowers and a fish.' Simmons shook his head incredulously. 'Remember the good old days when people had the decency to just walk up to someone and shoot the bastard?'

'Better days,' said Wolf, raising his Optimus Prime cup.

'Better days!' echoed Simmons as they toasted their glasses.

Wolf felt his mobile phone vibrate in his pocket. He took it out and glanced down at the short message from Andrea:

```
IM SORRY ( )( )
          \ /
           V
```

Wolf was suddenly unsettled. He knew that Andrea was apologising for more than the inappropriate penis drawing that she had, presumably, intended as a heart. He was about to reply when Baxter came storming into the room and switched on the small television on the wall. Simmons was too drained to even react.

'Your bitch of an ex is running with the story,' said Baxter.

Andrea appeared mid-report. She looked incredible. Seeing her objectively like this, Wolf realised that he had taken her beauty for granted – those long red curls pinned up in the style that she usually reserved for weddings and parties, the sparkling green eyes that barely looked real. The reason behind her betrayal was immediately apparent. She was not standing outside by the main road or speaking down a distorted line while an old photograph of her idly loitered on screen like a poor ventriloquist act; she was reporting from the studio, presenting the programme, just as she had always wanted.

'. . . that Mayor Turnble's death this afternoon was, in fact, an act of premeditated murder linked to the six bodies discovered in Kentish Town early this morning,' said Andrea, showing none of the nerves that Wolf knew must have been flitting beneath the surface. 'Some viewers may find the following images—'

'Speak to your wife, Fawkes. Now!' bellowed Simmons.

'Ex,' corrected Baxter as all three of them frantically punched numbers into their phones:

'Yes, I need the number for the newsroom at . . .'

'Two units to 110 Bishopsgate . . .'

'The person you are trying to reach is not available . . .'

Andrea's report continued in the background:

'. . . have confirmed that the head is that of Naguib Khalid, the Cremation Killer. It is unknown at this time how Khalid, who was serving . . .'

'I'm gonna try security at the building,' said Wolf after leaving a curt three-word voicemail for Andrea: '*Call me now!*'

'. . . apparently dismembered before being stitched back together to form one complete body,' said Andrea, on screen, as the horrific photographs appeared one after another, 'which the police are referring to as "The Ragdoll".'

'Bollocks we are,' snapped Simmons, who was still on the phone to the control room.

They each stopped to listen as Andrea continued:

'. . . five further names and the precise dates on which they will die. All will be revealed in exactly five minutes. I'm Andrea Hall. Stay tuned.'

'She wouldn't?' Simmons asked Wolf in disbelief, his hand over the receiver.

When Wolf did not respond, they all resumed their fraught conversations.

*

Five minutes later Wolf, Simmons and Baxter all sat watching the lights fade up on the news studio, which gave the impression that Andrea had been filling the time by sitting alone in the dark. Behind them, their colleagues were crowding round a television that somebody had carried out from the meeting room.

They were too late.

Andrea had, unsurprisingly, failed to reply to Wolf's message. Building security had been barricaded out of the newsroom offices, and the police officers that Simmons had sent were yet to even arrive on scene. Simmons got through to the editor-in-chief whose name he knew all too well. He had informed the insufferable man that he was sabotaging a homicide investigation, for which he could face a prison sentence. When that had no effect, Simmons attempted to appeal to his humanity by admitting that they had not yet even informed the people on the list of the threat against them.

'We're saving you a job then,' Elijah had replied. 'And you say I don't do anything for you.'

He had refused to let them speak to Andrea and promptly hung up. All they could do now was watch with the rest of the world. Simmons poured three fresh glasses of whiskey. Baxter, who was sitting on the desk, sniffed at hers uncertainly but then knocked it back all the same. She was about to ask to see the confidential list, as it would be public knowledge in a matter of minutes anyway, when the programme restarted.

Andrea missed her first cue and Wolf could see that she was anxious, hesitant, having second thoughts. He knew that behind the minimalist desk, her knees would be bobbing up and down as they always did when she was nervous. She looked into the camera, searching the millions of invisible eyes staring back at her, and Wolf sensed that she was looking for him, that she was looking for a way out of the hole that she had dug for herself.

'Andrea, we're on,' a fretted voice hissed in her ear. 'Andrea!'

'Good evening. I'm Andrea Hall. Welcome back . . .'

She spent over five minutes recapping the story so far and recycling the gruesome photographs for the countless viewers who had just switched over. She began to stumble over her words as she explained that a handwritten list had been included with the pictures, and her hands were visibly shaking by the time it came to reading the six death sentences out loud:

'Mayor Raymond Edgar Turnble – Saturday 28 June

'Vijay Rana – Wednesday 2 July

'Jarred Andrew Garland – Saturday 5 July

'Andrew Arthur Ford – Wednesday 9 July

'Ashley Danielle Lochlan – Saturday 12 July

'And on Monday 14 July . . .'

Andrea paused, not for dramatic effect (she had rushed through the list with no sense of showmanship, just desperate for it to be over), but because she had to wipe a mascara-stained tear out of her eye. She cleared her throat and shuffled the papers in front of her, unconvincingly insinuating that a typo or missing sheet had interrupted her flow. Suddenly she put her hands over her face, her shoulders shuddering as the full weight of what she had done dawned on her.

'Andrea? Andrea?' someone whispered from behind the camera.

Andrea looked back up at her record-breaking audience, her big moment, with unbecoming black marks smudged across her face and sleeves.

'I'm OK.'

A pause.

'And on Monday 14 July, Metropolitan Police officer and lead investigator on the Ragdoll murders . . . Detective Sergeant William Oliver Layton-Fawkes.'

CHAPTER 8

Monday 30 June 2014

9.35 a.m.

'Bad.'

'Bad?'

'And sad.'

'Sad.'

Dr Preston-Hall sighed heavily and placed her notebook on the antique coffee table beside her chair.

'You watch the man that you were charged to protect die in front of your eyes and then the person responsible announces their intention to murder you in just a fortnight's time, and all you can muster up for me is that you are feeling "bad" and "sad"?'

'Mad?' tried Wolf, having believed that he was doing well.

This seemed to pique the doctor's interest. She picked up her notebook once more and leaned in closer.

'So, you're feeling angry?'

Wolf considered this for a moment: 'Not really, no.'

The doctor threw her notebook down. It slid off the miniature table and onto the floor.

Apparently, *she* was mad.

Wolf had been visiting the stucco-faced Georgian town house in Queen Anne's Gate every Monday morning since his reinstatement. Dr Preston-Hall was the Metropolitan Police Consultant

Psychiatrist. Her discreet office, advertised only by a brass plaque beside the front door, sat on a quiet road just a three-minute walk from New Scotland Yard.

The doctor's presence only complimented the elegant surroundings. She was in her early sixties now, ageing gracefully, adorned in muted high-end clothing and wearing her silver hair in a meticulously sculptured style. She maintained a stern air of authority: the character of the schoolmistress, ingrained so deeply into children at such a young age so as to never be forgotten in adulthood.

'Tell me, have you been having the dreams again?' she asked. 'The ones about the hospital.'

'You say hospital, I say asylum.'

The doctor sighed.

'Only when I sleep,' said Wolf.

'Which is?'

'Not when I can help it. And I wouldn't really call them dreams. They're nightmares.'

'And I wouldn't call them nightmares,' argued Dr Preston-Hall. 'There is nothing scary about a dream. *You* project the fear onto it.'

'With all due respect, that's a lot easier to say when you haven't already spent thirteen months and a day of your life in that particular hell.'

The doctor dropped the subject, sensing that Wolf would much rather fill their remaining time arguing than telling her anything personal. She ripped open the sealed envelope that he had brought with him and perused the familiar weekly report from Finlay. From her expression, she appeared to think it as big a waste of time, trees and ink as Wolf did.

'Sergeant Shaw seems more than happy with the way you've handled the stress of the past few days. He's awarded you a score of ten out of ten. Lord knows what he's basing his rating system on but . . . good for you,' she said snippily.

Wolf stared out of the open sash window towards the grand houses lining the opposite side of Queen Anne's Gate. Each had been impeccably maintained or else faithfully restored to their former glory. If it had not been for the distant whispers of the chaotic city gearing up for another unrelenting week, he could have bought the illusion that they had travelled back in time. A gentle breeze found its way into the shady room while the morning outside built towards its twenty-eight-degree high.

'I'm going to recommend that we meet twice per week for the duration of this case,' said Dr Preston-Hall, still reading the detailed report that Finlay had scrawled in his clumsy handwriting as Wolf dictated it.

Wolf sat up straight, conscious not to clench his fists in front of the psychiatrist.

'I appreciate your concern . . .'

It did not sound as though he did.

'. . . but I don't have time for this. I've got a killer to catch.'

'And therein lies our problem: "*I*". This is my concern. Is this not what happened before? It is not *your* sole responsibility to capture this person. You have colleagues; you have support—'

'I have more riding on it.'

'And I have a professional obligation,' she said finally.

Wolf had the distinct impression that she might suggest three days per week should he continue to argue.

'So, it's settled then,' she said, flicking through her diary. 'How would Wednesday morning suit you?'

'I'll be doing all in my power to prevent the murder of a man named Vijay Rana on Wednesday.'

'Thursday, then?'

'Fine.'

'Nine o'clock?'

'Fine.'

Dr Preston-Hall signed the paperwork and smiled pleasantly. Wolf got up and headed for the door.

'And William . . .' Wolf turned back to face her, 'take care of yourself.'

*

Simmons had insisted that Wolf take the Sunday off after the ordeals of the previous day. Wolf suspected that he was merely covering his own arse, ensuring that he had been signed off by the psychiatrist before resuming his duties.

He had stopped off at a Tesco Express and bought enough food to hole up for the remainder of the weekend, correctly suspecting that a cluster of reporters would be eagerly awaiting his return outside the entrance to his building. Fortunately he was able to bypass the majority of them by crossing through the police cordon that was still in place while forensics completed their work.

He had used this unwelcome day off to sort through some of the boxes that Andrea had packed up for him months earlier. It looked a rather measly half of the house, and he was reasonably confident that she had not wedged the car into any of the cardboard boxes that lined his walls.

He ignored seventeen calls from her between Saturday night and Sunday, although, he did answer the phone to his mother, who seemed genuinely concerned for all of two minutes before moving on to the more pressing matter of Ethel-next-door's broken fence for the closing forty minutes of the conversation. Wolf promised to come down to Bath to fix it for her one weekend in July; not having to do so would be some consolation, at least, should he be brutally murdered on the fourteenth.

The sound of drilling greeted Wolf as he entered the Homicide and Serious Crime office. A team of stringently vetted workmen had started repairs to the water-damaged interview room. As he made his way across the office, he identified two contrasting reactions from his colleagues. Many gave supportive smiles, someone he did not know offered to make him a coffee, and another (who was not even involved in the case) told him confidently: 'We'll catch 'em'. Others avoided the dead man walking completely, perhaps afraid that whatever poisonous fish, medicine or plant that the killer might choose to dispatch him with would take them down with him.

'Finally,' said Baxter as he approached her and Edmunds' desk. 'Nice day off while we were doing all your work for you?'

Wolf ignored the jibe. He knew better than anybody that hostility was Baxter's go-to move: unhappy – aggression, confused – antagonism, embarrassed – violence. She had been uncharacteristically quiet ever since the news report on Saturday evening and had not attempted to contact him despite being the only person that he might have wanted to speak to. She seemed content to act as though she had never even heard the list and Wolf was happy to indulge her.

'So it turns out that this little bastard,' she gestured to Edmunds, who was sitting right beside her, 'isn't completely useless after all.'

Baxter brought Wolf up to date. They had been forced to abandon the ragweed line of enquiry after an expert had broken the news that it could have been grown in any greenhouse in the country. It was a similar story with the flowers: each bouquet had been purchased from different florists all over London. In every case they had been paid for in cash by post.

Following Edmunds' lead, they had visited the Complete Foods factory and were now in possession of a comprehensive list of employees on duty the night before Naguib Khalid's poisoning. More importantly, they had recovered CCTV footage of an unidentified man entering the premises during the early hours of the morning. Edmunds proudly handed Wolf a USB stick containing the video, looking as though a pat on the head would not have gone amiss.

'There is something that doesn't sit quite right with me,' said Edmunds.

'Not this again,' complained Baxter.

'I found out that the contaminated delivery of specialist meals also went to other places. Three other people consumed the Tetrodotoxin, and two of them are already dead.'

'And the third?' Wolf asked, concerned.

'Not hopeful.'

'It's only blind luck that the goth at St Mary's Academy was on study leave or else we'd have another,' said Baxter.

'Exactly,' continued Edmunds. 'It just doesn't follow that the killer would give us a list of six specific names and then kill three more—'

'Two and a half,' interjected Baxter.

'. . . people at random, and not even claim responsibility for them. Serial killers don't behave like this. This is something else.'

Wolf looked impressed and turned to Baxter.

'I can see why you like him.'

Edmunds looked elated.

'I don't.'

Edmunds' grin deflated.

'I didn't let her share my desk for six months when she was training,' Wolf told Edmunds.

'Moving on!' snapped Baxter.

'Have you got anywhere with the inhaler?' asked Wolf.

'The canister had been custom-welded back together. There was no medicine in it at all, just a chemical I can't pronounce,' said Baxter. 'We're looking into it, but apparently it would be possible to mix from the stores of any school chemistry lab. So don't hold your breath, if you'll excuse the totally inappropriate pun.'

'Speaking of which,' interrupted Edmunds, 'our killer must have been close enough to switch inhalers shortly before the murder, that morning possibly. Why not kill the mayor then? It suggests that his motives are less revenge driven and more about the theatre of it all.'

'Makes sense,' Wolf nodded. He hesitated before bringing up the taboo subject that they had all been skirting around. 'And what's happening with the people on the list?'

Baxter visibly tensed up.

'Nothing to do with us. We're working on identifying the already dead, not the soon to be—' She stopped herself, realising who she was speaking to. 'You'll have to speak to your partner.'

Wolf got up to walk away. He paused.

'Have you heard from Chambers?' he asked casually.

Baxter looked suspicious: 'What the hell do you care?'

Wolf shrugged.

'Just wondered if he knew what was going on. I've got a feeling we're gonna need all the help we can get.'

Wolf had grown tired of the roomful of eyes on his back and had moved into the meeting room where somebody had scribbled 'The Ragdoll' above his two oversized reproductions in an elaborate script. He was growing increasingly frustrated, stubbornly refusing to admit that he had no idea how to play the CCTV footage, trapped inside the stupid little USB stick, through the television.

'There's a hole on the side of the telly,' said Finlay, over fifteen years his senior, as he entered the room. 'No, on the, down – oh, let me do it.'

Finlay removed the USB drive from an air vent on the back of the television and plugged it in. A blue menu screen materialised containing a single file.

'What have I missed?' asked Wolf.

'We sent officers to babysit Garland, Ford and Lochlan. We're only concerned with the ones in London.'

'Because why challenge me to stop him then kill someone on the other side of the country?'

'Aye, something like that. Other forces are sitting on people with the same names, but they're not our concern,' said Finlay. 'Your guess is as good as ours about where Vijay Rana is. He was an accountant living in Woolwich before vanishing off the radar five months ago when the taxman realised he'd been fiddling his numbers. He was on Fraud's to-do list, but it doesn't look like they made much headway. I've asked for the information to be sent over anyway.'

Wolf checked his watch.

'He's got thirty-eight hours till Wednesday. Let's hope, for his sake, we find him first. Who are the others?'

'Garland's a journalist, so no shortage of enemies there. We've got two Ashley Lochlans; one's a waitress and the other's nine years old.'

'But we're keeping officers with both of them, right?' asked Wolf.

'Of course. And Ford's a security guard, I think, or he was until he went off on long-term sick.'

'What's the connection?'

'There isn't one. Not yet. The priority's just been finding them and securing their houses for the time being.'

Wolf was lost in thought for a moment.

'What you thinkin', lad?'

'Just wondering who Vijay Rana screwed over with his dodgy bookkeeping and thinking how it would be a very clever way of finding someone who had disappeared: getting us to find him for them.'

Finlay nodded.

'He might be better off if we leave him under whatever rock he's crawled beneath.'

'He might.'

Wolf was distracted by the stack of paperwork that Finlay had brought in with him. The top page included a photograph of a middle-aged woman in what was presumably supposed to be provocative lingerie.

'What the hell is that?'

Finlay chuckled.

'Your groupies! The Wolf Pack, they call themselves. Now you're a marked man, all the nutters have come out of the woodwork to proposition you.'

Wolf flicked through the first few sheets, shaking his head in disbelief, while Finlay sorted through the other thirty pages, disregarding the rejects onto the meeting room floor.

'Nice touch!' exclaimed Finlay. 'This lass is wearing a genuine vintage "Uncage the Wolf" campaign t-shirt. I've still got mine. Don't look like that in it, though,' he muttered.

Wolf supposed that he should have anticipated this. In the past, he had been disgusted as the vile and dangerous creatures he had hunted were inundated with mail mere days into their lifelong incarcerations. In the same way that he could assume certain traits while profiling a killer, he could almost picture these desperate pen pals: lonely, socially inept women, often previous long-term sufferers of domestic abuse, consumed by the mistaken belief that no one is truly broken, that they alone can fix these misunderstood victims of the law.

Wolf was aware that this bewildering pastime was rife in the US where organisations actively encourage people to communicate with one of the 3,000 inmates on death row. What was the allure? he wondered. Revelling in the tragic, movie-esque finale to a relationship? Those with commitment issues empowered by the enforced timescale? Or simply wanting to be a part of something bigger and more interesting than their own mundane lives?

He knew better than to voice his opinions openly to the public, schooled to react indignantly to any controversial truth or observation for fear of falling victim to the wrath of political correctitude. However, they were shielded from the aftermath of these people's crimes. It was Wolf who had to stare into the unremorseful eyes of these vicious predators. He wondered how many of these ill-informed people would still put pen to paper had they soaked their shoes in the crime scene bloodbath, had they consoled the tattered families left in their pen pals' wake.

'Oooh, look at this one!' shouted Finlay, a little too excitedly, so that several heads in the main office turned round.

He held up a photograph of a beautiful blonde woman in her twenties wearing a fancy-dress policewoman outfit. Wolf paused, lost for words, as he gazed at the picture that would not have looked out of place on the front cover of a men's magazine.

'Bin it,' he finally said, deciding that one narcissistic sociopath vying for his attention was probably enough.

'But . . . Missy . . . from Brighton . . .' Finlay was reading through the rest of the email.

'Bin it!' snapped Wolf. 'How do I play this video?'

Finlay moodily threw the emails into the bin before taking a seat beside Wolf and pressing a button on the remote.

'You're gonna regret that if you're dead in two weeks,' he mumbled.

Wolf ignored the comment and focused on the large television screen. The grainy footage was from a camera high above the Complete Foods factory floor. A pair of double doors were propped open with a box, and in the background was the depressingly monotonous sight of the low-paid staff working robotically towards their next repetitive strain injury.

Suddenly a figure appeared at the doors. It was undoubtedly a man. Edmunds had estimated his height to be fractionally over six feet, having measured the doorway after reviewing the tape. The man was wearing a stained apron, gloves, hairnet and a face mask like the other employees, despite coming in from outside. He walked with confidence, hesitating only for a moment as he decided in which direction to head. Over the next two minutes, he disappeared in and out of shot behind the boxes packaged up for delivery. He then strolled back out through the double doors and into the night without anybody noticing.

'Well, that was a waste of time,' sighed Finlay.

Wolf asked him to rewind and they paused on the best shot of the killer that the pixelated footage would allow. They stared at the covered face. Even after the tech team cleaned it up, there would not be much to go on. He looked to be bald beneath the hairnet, close-shaven at least. The only truly discerning feature was the apron, already covered in what looked like dried blood.

Naguib Khalid should have been impossible to reach, which would suggest that his murder took the most planning. Wolf had assumed, apparently incorrectly, that the killer had murdered him first before pursuing easier targets. He wondered which of the other five victims had already been dismembered at this early stage and, more importantly, why?

CHAPTER 9

Monday 30 June 2014

6.15 p.m.

Edmunds held the two tiny bottles up to the light. One declared itself to be 'Shattered Pink'; the other, 'Sherwood'. Even after three minutes of intense scrutiny, the two nail varnishes looked unequivocally identical to one another.

He was standing in the labyrinthine make-up department that dominated the ground floor of Selfridges. The haphazardly positioned stands acted like an archipelago against an ocean, a first-line defence, taking the full force of the wave of customers flooding in off Oxford Street and filtering them out across the store. He had passed several of the same disorientated faces, people who had become separated from their companions and left to wander aimlessly between the counters of eyeliners, lipsticks and Uplight Face Luminiser Gels that they had no intention whatsoever of purchasing.

'May I help you with anything?' asked an immaculately painted blonde, dressed all in black, whose generous layers of foundation could not cover up the judgemental sneer she wore as she took in Edmunds' flyaway hair and purple nails.

'I'll take these two,' he said happily, smearing purple glitter across her arm as he handed them over.

The woman smiled sycophantically and tottered back round to

the other side of her tiny empire to charge Edmunds an extortionate amount.

'I love Sherwood,' she told him, 'but I adore Shattered Pink.'

Edmunds stared down at the two indistinguishable items sitting pathetically at the bottom of the cavernous paper bag that she had handed him. He made sure to put the receipt straight in the back of his wallet, in the hope that he would be able to claim it back on expenses; if not, he had just blown half of his grocery budget on sparkly nail polish.

'Is there anything else I can help you with today?' the woman asked, reverting back to her former frosty self now that the transaction had been completed.

'Yes. How do I get out of here?'

Edmunds had lost sight of the exit over twenty-five minutes earlier.

'Aim for the escalators and you'll see the doors right in front of you.'

Edmunds wove through to the escalator, only to find himself confronted with the equally daunting fragrance department. He nodded to a man that he had passed on three separate occasions back in make-up and then began his own futile attempt to escape the store.

This unexpectedly lengthy detour on his way home had been due to a development in the case earlier that morning. Once the field team had completed their work at the crime scene, the Ragdoll had been transported back to Forensic Services in the early hours of Sunday morning. This had been a painstaking process due to the importance of preserving the exact posture and weight distribution on each of the various body parts during transport. Ceaseless testing, examination and sample-collecting had taken place throughout the night, but finally, at 11 a.m. Monday morning, Baxter and Edmunds had been permitted access to the body.

Without the surreal haze of the nocturnal crime scene, the incoherent cadaver had been even more repugnant when lit by the unflattering fluorescent light of the crime lab: carelessly cut slabs of flesh rotting slowly in the chilly examination room. The thick stitches connecting them, which had seemed so otherworldly in the heightened atmosphere of the dimly lit apartment, were exposed as no more than violent mutilations.

'How's the case coming?' Joe had asked. He was the forensic medical examiner, who Edmunds thought resembled a Buddhist monk with his all-in-one scrubs and shaved head.

'Fantastic, just finishing up,' replied Baxter sarcastically.

'That well, huh?' grinned the man, who was obviously accustomed to, and appeared to rather enjoy, Baxter's waspish manner. 'Perhaps this'll help.'

He handed her a chunky ring in a clear evidence bag.

'My answer's a resounding no,' she said, making Joe laugh.

'It's from the male left hand. Partial print, not the victim's own.'

'Whose then?' asked Baxter.

'No idea. Might be something, might not.'

Baxter's excitement faded.

'Anything you can tell us to get us started?'

'He,' Baxter's eyebrows arched, 'or she,' then fell, 'definitely had fingers.'

Edmunds let out an involuntary snort which he tried to pass off as a cough when Baxter glared at him.

'Don't worry, there's more,' said Joe.

He pointed to the black male leg, which was decorated with a large operation scar. He held an X-ray up to the light. Two long bright-white bars glowed incongruously against the faded skeleton beneath.

'Plates and screws supporting the tibia, fibula and femur,' Joe explained. 'This was a big operation. "Do we operate? Do we amputate?" kind of big. Someone'll remember doing this.'

'Don't these things have serial numbers or something?' asked Baxter.

'I'll certainly look; although, whether they'll be traceable or not will depend on how long ago the op was done, and this looks like old scarring to me.'

While Baxter studied the X-rays with Joe, Edmunds knelt down to examine the female right arm, which he had noted was pointing creepily towards their reflection in the glass window, more closely. Each of the five perfectly painted nails glittered in a dark purple varnish.

'The index finger's different!' he blurted suddenly.

'Ah, you noticed,' said Joe happily. 'I was just coming to that. It was impossible to tell in the dark apartment, but in here you can clearly see that a different nail polish has been used on that one finger.'

'And that's helpful how?' asked Baxter.

Joe collected an ultraviolet lamp from the trolley, switched it on, and ran it along the length of the graceful arm. Dark bruises appeared and then vanished again as the purple light passed over them, the greatest accumulation occurring on or around the wrist.

'There was a struggle,' he said. 'Now look at these nails: not a single chip. These were painted on afterwards.'

'After the struggle or after death?' asked Baxter.

'I'd say both. I couldn't find any sign of an inflammatory response, which means she died shortly after the bruising was sustained.

'. . . I think the killer is speaking to us.'

Engineering works had closed a small but important section of the Northern line. Finding the prospect of an overcrowded bus less than tantalising, Wolf took the Piccadilly line to Caledonian Road and embarked on the twenty-five minute walk back to Kentish Town. It was not a particularly picturesque route once he had passed through the park and lost sight of the handsome clock tower, its detailing ripened in a charming green rust; however, the temperature had dropped to a tolerable level and the late-evening sunshine had brought a calming air over this part of the city.

The unproductive day had been spent fruitlessly searching for Vijay Rana. Wolf and Finlay had travelled to Woolwich and found the family home in a predictably uninhabited state. The pitiful front garden looked considerably more impressive than it should have, as the long grass and opportunistic weeds encroached across the pathway that led up to the front door. A mountain of unopened post and takeaway leaflets was just visible through a small, lead-lined window.

The information that Fraud had cobbled together had barely been worth the read, and Rana's harassed partner at the accountancy firm had openly admitted that if he had known where his missing partner was hiding, he would have killed him himself. The only promising discovery had been the distinct absence of information on Rana before 1991. For some reason he had changed his name. They hoped if either the Royal Courts of Justice or The National Archives could provide them with a previous name, a multitude of past sins would direct them towards Rana's current whereabouts.

As Wolf approached his block of flats, he spotted a dark blue Bentley with a personalised number plate parked illegally outside the main entrance. Crossing the road in front of the car he registered the silver-haired man sitting in the driver's seat. He reached the front door and was searching for his keys when his mobile went off. Andrea's name flashed up. He promptly put it back in his pocket and then heard the thud of an expensively heavy car door slamming behind him.

'You're ignoring my calls,' said Andrea.

Wolf sighed and turned to face her. She looked immaculate again, having probably spent the majority of the day in front of a television camera. He noticed that she was wearing the necklace that he had given her for their first wedding anniversary but decided against mentioning it.

'I spent most of Saturday night locked up,' she continued.

'That's what happens when you break the law.'

'Give it a rest, Will. You know as well as I do that if I hadn't reported it, someone else would.'

'You know that for certain?'

'You're damn right I do. Do you think if I hadn't broadcast it the killer would just have gone: "Oh, she didn't read it, that's disappointing. I'd better forget this whole chopping people up death list thing"? Of course not. He'd have contacted another news channel and probably made room for me somewhere in his busy schedule.'

'Is that your idea of an apology?'

'I've got nothing to apologise for. I want you to forgive me.'

'You have to apologise first, in order for someone to forgive you. That's how it works!'

'Says who?'

'I don't know – the etiquette police?'

'Because that's a thing.'

'I'm not getting into this with you,' said Wolf, amazed at how effortlessly they could fall into old habits, even now. He looked past Andrea to the elegant car idling at the kerbside. 'When did your dad get a Bentley?'

'Oh, piss off!' she snapped, taking him by surprise.

Slowly it dawned on him why this had offended her.

'Oh my God. That's him, isn't it? Your new squeeze,' he said, wide-eyed as he strained to see through the tinted window.

'That is Geoffrey, yes.'

'Oh, Geoffrey is it? Well he certainly seems very . . . rich. What is he, like sixty?'

'Stop looking at him.'

'I can look at what I want.'

'You are so immature.'

'On second thoughts, you probably shouldn't squeeze him too hard: you might break something.'

Despite herself, the corners of Andrea's mouth curled up.

'Seriously though,' said Wolf quietly, 'is *he* really the reason you left me?'

'*You* were the reason I left you.'

'Oh.'

There was an uncomfortable silence.

'We wanted to invite you out for dinner. We've been sitting out here for almost an hour and I'm starving.'

Wolf made an unconvincing groan of disappointment.

'I'd love to, but I'm actually just heading out.'

'You have literally just got back.'

'Look, I appreciate the gesture, but do you mind if I pass tonight? I've got a hell of a lot of work to do and only one day left to find Rana and—' Wolf realised his slip of the tongue as Andrea's eyes widened in interest.

'You don't have him?' she asked in astonishment.

'Andie, I'm tired. I don't know what I'm saying. I've gotta go.'

Wolf left her on the doorstep and entered his building. Andrea climbed back into the passenger seat of the Bentley and closed the door.

'Waste of time,' said Geoffrey knowingly.

'Far from it,' replied Andrea.

'If you say so. Dinner at the Greenhouse then?'

'You can cope without me tonight, can't you?'

Geoffrey huffed: 'Office, then?'

'Yes, please.'

Wolf unlocked the door to his tatty flat and switched on the television to drown out the sound of the nightly shouting match between the clearly incompatible couple upstairs. The presenter of a property programme was showing some newly-weds around a three-bedroom detached home on the outskirts of an idyllic park in a far more pleasant part of the country. It was simultaneously comical and soul-destroying to listen to them deliberate over the minuscule asking price, which would not have even afforded them the hovel that he was currently occupying in the capital.

Wolf walked to the kitchen window and stared into the blackness of the crime scene opposite. He paused, almost expecting to see the Ragdoll still hanging there, waiting for him. The property show came to an end (the couple decided that they could get more for their money) and a weatherman energetically predicted that the heatwave would come to a spectacular end the following night, with thunderstorms and extremely heavy rain anticipated.

He switched off the television, pulled the blinds and climbed onto the mattress on the bedroom floor with the book that he had been reading for over four months. He made it through another page and a half before drifting off into a disrupted sleep.

Wolf was woken by his mobile phone buzzing on top of his folded clothes from the day before. He was instantly struck by the pain in his left arm and glanced down to find that the wound had wept through his bandages during the night. The room looked strange in the weak morning light, grey rather than the familiar orange that he had grown accustomed to over the previous two weeks. He rolled over and reached for the vibrating phone.

'Boss?'

'What have you done now?' Simmons snapped angrily.

'I don't know. What have I done now?'

'Your wife—'

'*Ex*-wife.'

'. . . has plastered Vijay Rana's face all over the morning news and announced to the world that we are ill-equipped to find him. Are you trying to get me fired?'

'Not on purpose, no.'

'Handle it.'

'Will do.'

Wolf stumbled unsteadily out into the main room. He took two painkillers for his arm and then switched the television back on. Andrea materialised on screen, looking as flawless as ever, but still wearing the same clothes that he recognised from the evening before. With her usual flair for the dramatic, she was reading an undoubtedly fictitious quote from a 'police spokesperson', who implored friends and family of Rana to come forward for his own well-being.

In the top right-hand corner of the screen, a timer counted down the hours and minutes to Wednesday morning. Disconcertingly, with no idea where to even begin the search for Rana, they had only another 19 hours and 23 minutes to wait before the killer could claim his next victim.

CHAPTER 10

Tuesday 1 July 2014

8.28 a.m.

London had returned to its usual monochrome self, the overcast sky propped up by dirty grey buildings that threw dark shadows across an endless expanse of concrete below.

Wolf dialled Andrea's number as he walked the short distance between the Tube station and New Scotland Yard. To his surprise, she picked up almost immediately. She seemed genuinely perplexed by his reaction and insisted doggedly that her sole intention had been to assist the police to atone for the damage that she might have caused. She reasoned that having every pair of eyes in the country looking for Rana could only be a good thing, and Wolf could not really argue with that piece of self-serving logic. He did, however, make her swear to run any further contentious details past him before broadcasting them to the rest of the nation.

Wolf entered the office, where Finlay was already hard at work. He was on the phone to someone at the Royal Courts of Justice, re-emphasising the life and death importance of the simple task that they still had not completed. Wolf took a seat at the desk opposite and flicked through the piles of paperwork left by the night-shift detectives, who had little to show for their efforts. With no better ideas on how to locate Rana, he continued from where his colleagues had left off: the arduous box-ticking exercise of systematically sorting through bank statements, credit card bills and itemised phone records.

At 9.23 a.m. Finlay's phone rang, and he answered it with a yawn: 'Shaw.'

'Good morning, this is Owen Whitacre from The National Archives. I apologise for the length of time it took to—'

Finlay waved at Wolf to catch his attention.

'Have you got a name for us?'

'As a matter of fact, I do. I am faxing over a copy of the certificate to you as we speak, but I thought I should probably contact you directly considering . . . well, considering what we found.'

'What you found?'

'Yes. Vijay Rana was born Vijay Khalid.'

'*Khalid*?'

'So we checked, and he has one sibling listed, a younger brother: Naguib Khalid.'

'Shiatsu.'

'I beg your pardon?'

'Nothing. Thanks,' said Finlay before hanging up.

Within minutes, Simmons had assigned three additional officers to assist Wolf and Finlay delve into Rana's hidden past. They isolated themselves in the meeting room, away from the noise and distractions of the main office, and set to work. They still had fourteen and a half hours to find him.

They still had time.

Edmunds' neck was killing him after a night spent on his inconceivably uncomfortable sofa. He had returned home, to his ex-local authority maisonette, at 8.10 p.m. the evening before to find Tia's mother washing up in the kitchen. He had completely forgotten about the arrangement. She greeted him with her usual warmth and wrapped two bubble-covered hands around him, standing on tiptoes just to reach his chest. Tia, on the other hand, had been far less forgiving. Sensing the tense atmosphere, her mother made her excuses and left as quickly as was polite to do so.

'This has been arranged for more than a fortnight,' said Tia.

'I got held up at work. I'm sorry I missed dinner.'

'You were supposed to pick up dessert, remember? I had to cobble together one of my trifles.'

He was suddenly a little less sorry that he had missed it.

'Oh no,' he said, sounding convincingly disappointed. 'You should have saved me some.'

'I did.'

Damn.

'Is this what life's going to be like from now on? You skipping dinners, turning up at all times with your nails all painted up?'

Edmunds picked self-consciously at the flaking purple varnish.

'It's half eight, T. Not exactly "all times".'

'So it'll be worse then, will it?'

'Perhaps it will. This is my job now,' Edmunds snapped.

'Which is why I never wanted you to move from Fraud,' said Tia, her voice rising.

'But *I* did!'

'You can't be this selfish when you're a father!'

'Selfish?' shouted Edmunds in disbelief. 'I'm out there earning the money for us to survive! What else are we going to live off? Your hairdressing wage?'

He regretted the spiteful retort immediately, but the damage had already been done. Tia stormed up the stairs and slammed the bedroom door behind her. He had hoped to apologise in the morning but left for work before she had even woken up, making a mental note to buy some flowers on the way home.

He met with Baxter first thing, hoping that she would not notice that he was wearing the same shirt from the day before (the others were hanging, freshly ironed, behind the locked bedroom door) or that he could not turn his head to the right. While she was busy contacting orthopaedic surgeons and physiotherapists regarding the reconstructed leg, he had been instructed to find out as much as possible about the plain silver ring.

He searched on his phone for the nearest reputable jewellers and set off, on foot, towards Victoria. When he arrived, the camp salesman was delighted to be of assistance, obviously revelling in the drama of it all. He led Edmunds through to a back room where the relaxed and elegant illusion projected by the front of house was dropped in favour of imposing safes, grubby tools, polishing equipment and feeds from over a dozen hidden cameras, surveying each and every one of the reinforced glass cabinets.

A pasty, scruffy man, hidden out of sight like a leper from the easily intimidated upper-class clientele, took the ring over to his workstation and examined the inner band through a magnifying glass.

'Highest-quality platinum, hallmarked by the Edinburgh Assay Office, made in 2003 by someone going by the initials TSI. You can check with them to find out who that mark belongs to.'

'Wow. Thank you. That's all incredibly helpful,' said Edmunds, making notes, astounded that the man had gained so much from the seemingly meaningless symbols. 'Any idea what a ring like this would sell for?'

The man placed the chunky ring on a set of scales and then produced a dog-eared catalogue from the bottom of one of his drawers.

'It's not a designer brand, which would keep the cost down a little, but we've got similar rings marked up at around the three grand mark.'

'Three thousand pounds?' Edmunds confirmed. He was momentarily reminded of his argument with Tia the evening before. 'That gives us an indication of our victim's social class, at least.'

'It tells you a lot more than that,' said the man confidently. 'This has to be one of the most boring rings that I have ever seen. It has virtually no artistic merit whatsoever. It is the jewellery equivalent of walking about with a fistful of fifty-pound notes: pretentious materialism. All show, no substance.'

'You should come and work for us,' said Edmunds in jest.

'Nah,' replied the man, 'doesn't pay enough.'

By lunchtime Baxter had phoned over forty hospitals. She had excitedly emailed copies of the X-ray and a photograph of the resultant scar when one surgeon confidently claimed responsibility for the limb-saving operation; disappointingly, just five minutes later, he had called back to say he would never have left such horrendous scarring and could be of no further assistance. Without a date or serial number her information was simply too vague.

She watched Wolf in the meeting room. He was also on the phone, working frantically with his team to locate Rana. She still had not even acknowledged the fact that his name had featured on the killer's list, perhaps because she was not sure how he expected her to react. Now, more than ever, she had absolutely no idea what they were to each other.

She was amazed by the way in which he had thrown himself into his work. Weaker men would have gone to pieces, hid, sought sympathy and reassurance from those around them. Not Wolf. If anything, he had grown stronger, more determined, more like the man she had known during the Cremation Killings: the same efficient, ruthless, self-destructive, time bomb. No one else had noticed the subtle shift in him yet, but they would in time.

Edmunds had made impressive progress with the ring. He had already contacted the Edinburgh Assay Office, who had informed him that the hallmark belonged to an independent jewellers in the Old Town. He had sent them a photograph of the ring, crudely annotated with dimensions, and was busying himself comparing nail polishes while he waited for them to return his call. After stopping off at Superdrug and Boots on the way back to the office, he was now the proud owner of another six glittery bottles, none of which matched either of the shades that they were looking for.

'You look like crap,' Baxter informed him after putting the phone down on her forty-third hospital.

'I didn't sleep brilliantly,' replied Edmunds.

'You were wearing that shirt yesterday.'

'Was I?'

'In three months you've never worn the same shirt two days in a row.'

'I didn't realise you were keeping tabs.'

'You had a fight,' she said knowingly, enjoying Edmunds' reluctance to talk about it a little too much. 'A night on the sofa, huh? We've all been there.'

'If it's all the same to you, could we talk about something else please?'

'So, what was it? She doesn't like you being partnered up with a girl?' Baxter swivelled round in her chair and fluttered her eyelashes elaborately at him.

'No.'

'She asked you about your day and you realised you had nothing to say to her that didn't involve dismembered body parts or burning mayors?'

'There's always nail polish,' he smiled, waving his chipped purple nails from the day before at her. He was trying to make a joke to prove that she was not getting to him.

'In which case, you missed something. Birthday? Anniversary?'

When Edmunds did not answer, she knew she was on the right track. She stared at him, waiting patiently for a response.

'Dinner with her mum,' he mumbled.

Baxter burst out laughing.

'Dinner with her mum? Christ, tell her to get a grip. We're trying to catch a serial killer, for God's sake.' She leaned in conspiratorially. 'One bloke I was seeing, I missed his mum's funeral coz I was chasing a boat down the Thames!'

She laughed out loud and so did Edmunds. He felt guilty for not sticking up for Tia, for not explaining that she was still adjusting to the demands of his new role, but he was enjoying sharing some common ground with his partner.

'I didn't hear from him again after that,' she continued.

As her laughter slowly ebbed away, Edmunds thought he could detect genuine sadness beneath the show of insouciance, just a faint flicker as she wondered about all of the things that could have been had she chosen differently.

'You just wait till your sprog pops out on a day we're tied up at a crime scene and you're not there.'

'That's not going to happen,' said Edmunds defensively.

Baxter shrugged and spun back in her chair. Picking up the phone, she dialled the next number on the list.

'Marriage. Detective. Divorce. Ask anyone in this room. Marriage. Detective. Divorce . . . Oh hello, this is Detective Sergeant Baxter with the . . .'

Simmons came out of his office and paused to look over the piles of autopsy photographs that Baxter had littered over Chambers' empty desk.

'When's Chambers back?' he asked her.

'No idea,' she replied, on hold to yet another physiotherapy department.

'I'm sure it was today.'

Baxter shrugged in a way that suggested she neither cared nor wanted to hear any more about it.

'He screwed me for a week when that volcano went off a few years back. He'd better not be "stuck" in the Caribbean. Give him a call for me, will you?'

'Call him yourself,' she snapped, agitated further by the Will Young song blaring down the phone at her.

'I've got a call with the commander. Do it!'

While still waiting to be connected, Baxter took out her mobile and dialled Chambers' home number, which she knew off by heart. It went straight to the answering machine:

'Chambers! It's Baxter. Where are you, you lazy bastard? Shit, I hope the kids don't pick this up. If Arley or Lori are listening, please ignore the word "bastard" and . . . "shit".'

Someone at the hospital finally picked up the other phone, catching Baxter off guard.

'Piss,' she blurted down the mobile before abruptly hanging up.

Wolf felt utterly helpless as the hours ticked by. At 2.30 p.m. he received a call from the officer he had sent to Rana's cousin's house. This, like all of their other possible leads, had turned up nothing. Wolf was positive that friends or relatives were sheltering

Rana and his family. They had vanished without a trace over five months before and had two school-age children in tow, who would have been conspicuous during the week. He rubbed his tired eyes and saw Simmons pacing round his tiny office, dealing with the endless phone calls from his superiors while flicking through the news channels to assess the latest damage.

Another half-hour passed uneventfully before Finlay suddenly shouted out.

'I've got something!'

Wolf and the others dropped what they were working on to listen.

'When Rana's mother died in 1997, she left the house to her two sons, but it was never sold on. A few years later, they signed it over to Rana's newborn daughter. Another tax dodge no doubt.'

'Where?' asked Wolf.

'Lady Margaret Road, Southall.'

'That's got to be it,' said Wolf.

Wolf lost the rock-paper-scissors and sheepishly interrupted Simmons' phone conference. The chief inspector joined them in the meeting room and Finlay explained what he had discovered. The decision was made that Wolf and Finlay would apprehend Rana alone. Discretion would be key to his survival, and it served their purpose to allow the press to tear them apart, flaunting the fact that they had failed to track Rana down, only to reveal him safe and sound on Thursday morning.

Simmons came up with the idea of using his contacts at the UK Protected Persons Service, who were far better equipped to deal with covert transportation and safeguarding, to take joint responsibility for Rana until deemed safe. He had just picked up the phone when there was a gentle knock at the meeting room door.

'Not now!' he bellowed as a junior officer timidly entered the room and closed the door behind her. 'I said not now!'

'I'm very sorry to interrupt, sir, but there's a phone call I really think you need to take.'

'And why do you think that?' Simmons asked patronisingly.

'Because Vijay Rana has just walked into Southall Police Station and given himself up.'

'Oh.'

CHAPTER 11

Tuesday 1 July 2014

4.20 p.m.

Finlay had dozed off at the wheel of the car in the outside lane of the motorway. This had not been as disastrous as it might have been, as they had been sitting in stationary traffic for over forty minutes. The rain was hammering down hard enough to drown out his snores, sounding more like rocks against the thin metal than water. The windscreen wipers had long since stopped having any effect, which was likely to be the reason for the delay up ahead.

In an attempt at anonymity, they had requisitioned a pool car, which they had successfully driven right past the press as they retreated for cover from the sudden rainstorm. Even if they had had sirens, they were trapped in the outside lane of four, and the gridlocked traffic had diffused into every feasible space. They would never have reached the hard shoulder, which stood frustratingly out of reach, less than ten metres away.

Wolf had spoken to Chief Inspector Walker at Southall Police Station. He had immediately struck Wolf as being both competent and intelligent. He had searched Rana on arrival and confined him to a custody cell with one of his men posted at the door. He assured Wolf that only four people, including himself, were aware of Rana's presence in the building. He had sworn his men to secrecy, even from their colleagues out on the road. Walker had closed the station to the public at Wolf's request, claiming a fictional gas leak, and instructed his officers to take their breaks at other stations. Despite the delay, Wolf was satisfied that Rana was in safe hands for the time being.

The five-vehicle pile-up was eventually moved aside to provide entertainment for the dawdling stream of traffic filtering past in the nearside lane. They reached Southall a little over an hour later and the first rumbles of thunder rolled across the dark sky as Wolf and Finlay climbed out of the car. The street lighting was already on, reflecting off the tops of the scurrying umbrellas and the torrent of water flooding the gutters, racing the congested traffic along the high street.

They were both soaked through after their ten-second dash from the car park up to the station's rear entrance. The chief inspector let them inside and then swiftly relocked the door behind them. He was around Finlay's age and proudly sported the familiar uniform. His severely receding hairline suited him so well that it gave the impression he was going bald on purpose. He greeted them warmly and led them through to the break room, where he offered them each a hot drink.

'So gentlemen, is there a plan for Mr Rana?' asked Walker. He directed the question at Finlay, presumably as a courtesy to the older man because he was well aware that Wolf had been making the arrangements.

'It's pretty short notice for Protected Persons to arrange something,' said Finlay, wiping rainwater off his face with a saturated sleeve. 'They won't move until they can guarantee he'll be safe.'

'I shall leave that in your more than capable hands then,' said Walker. 'Please make yourselves at home.'

'I'd like to speak to him,' said Wolf as Walker turned to leave the room.

He took a moment to reply, perhaps searching for the least offensive wording for his response.

'DS Fawkes, you are quite the celebrity at the moment,' he started. Wolf was unsure where he was going with this.

'Although, and I mean no disrespect by this, you were before all this came about anyway, weren't you?'

'Meaning?'

'Meaning that, when Mr Rana came stumbling into reception this afternoon, he was quite distressed. He wanted to distance himself from his wife and children, which is quite understandable under the circumstances. He then broke down and proceeded to weep for his dead brother.'

'I see,' said Wolf, now understanding Walker's reservations: he knew. Wolf was a little irritated; although, he appreciated that the chief inspector was only doing his job. 'I have never met or even heard of Vijay Rana before all this. My only interest in him is in keeping him alive, and I'd say if anybody needs protecting during our meeting, it'll be me.'

'Then you shan't object if I am present at all times during your interview with the prisoner,' said Walker.

'It would certainly make me feel safer,' said Wolf flippantly.

Walker showed them into the custody suite at the back of the building, where the three other officers aware of the situation were waiting tensely. The chief inspector introduced Wolf and Finlay to each of them and then asked the officer standing guard to open the door to Rana's cell.

'We put him at the far end, as far away as we could manage from our other guests,' Walker told them.

The door swung heavily to reveal an open mildewed toilet and the blue mattress and pillow, laid across a wooden bench, that made up the custody cell. Rana was sitting with his head in his hands, still wearing a water-stained anorak. The lock clicked loudly behind them as Walker slowly approached his prisoner.

'Mr Rana, these two officers are in charge of—'

Rana looked up and as his bloodshot eyes settled on Wolf he leapt up from the bench and charged forward. Walker seized one of his arms as he passed and Finlay took hold of the other. They dragged him back over to the bench while he screamed:

'You bastard! You bastard!'

The two experienced officers easily overpowered Rana, who was both short and heavily overweight. A few days' worth of coarse stubble had grown unevenly across his overly large face. He seemed to deflate as he yielded and then started to weep into his pillow. Walker and Finlay cautiously released their grip as the man settled back down. Gradually, the atmosphere calmed.

'My condolences about your brother,' said Wolf with a smirk. Rana's furious eyes fixed back on him. 'He really was a piece of shit.'

'You bastard!' Rana screamed again as Walker and Finlay struggled to wrestle him back onto the bench.

'Dammit, Will,' complained Finlay after a stray knee connected with his groin.

'Do that again, Fawkes,' snapped Walker angrily, 'and I won't even try to stop him.'

Wolf raised an apologetic hand and took a few steps back to lean against the wall. Once Rana had calmed back down, Finlay explained the situation to him: how they had managed to keep news of his surrender contained to a select few, how they were awaiting instructions from Protected Persons, how he would be safe and had made the right decision by giving himself up. As per his training, once he had given Rana enough information to gain some trust, Finlay conversationally switched to his questioning. He asked whether Rana had known any of the other people on the list, names of anyone who may have wished him harm, any recent phone calls or incidents out of the ordinary.

'May I ask you a couple of questions about your brother?' asked Finlay, as politely as Wolf had ever heard him. He was tiptoeing around what they had clearly established to be Rana's pressure point.

Wolf made sure to keep his eyes fixed firmly on the floor, so as not to provoke the situation.

'Why?' asked Rana.

'Because there must be a link between those names on the list and the victims he has already . . . claimed,' explained Finlay softly.

Wolf rolled his eyes.

'OK,' said Rana.

'When did you last have contact with your brother?'

'2004 . . . 2005?' Rana answered uncertainly.

'So that would mean you weren't there for the trial?'

'No. I was not.'

'Why?' asked Wolf, speaking for the first time in over five minutes.

Walker went to grab hold of Rana; however, the man made no attempt to move, nor to answer the question.

'What sort of man doesn't show up for a single day of his own brother's trial?' continued Wolf, ignoring glares from both Walker and Finlay. 'I'll tell you what sort: a man who already knows the truth, who already knows that his brother is guilty.'

Rana did not respond.

'*That's* why you changed your name all those years ago. You knew what he was going to do, and you wanted to distance yourself from it.'

'I never knew he was going to—'

'You knew,' shouted Wolf, 'and you did nothing. How old is your little girl?'

'Fawkes!' yelled Walker.

'How old?' Wolf screamed back.

'Thirteen,' mumbled Rana.

'I genuinely wonder whether your brother would have burned your little girl alive by now if I hadn't stopped him. She knew him, probably trusted him. How long do you think he'd have been able to resist such an easy target?'

'Stop it!' cried Rana, holding his hands over his ears like a child. 'Please, stop it!'

'You, Vijay *Khalid*, owe me!' spat Wolf.

He hammered against the cell door, leaving Finlay and Walker to deal with their whimpering prisoner.

At 7.05 p.m. Wolf received a phone call advising that someone would be with them by 10.30 p.m. at the latest. Protected Persons were still in the process of arranging appropriately trained officers and a suitable safe house considering the immediacy of the threat against Rana's life. Wolf relayed the news to Walker and his officers, who made no effort to disguise that he had already long outstayed his welcome.

Sick of their scathing looks, he decided to fetch some food for Finlay, himself and the prisoner (as a precaution, he had instructed Walker not to feed Rana anything on site). He generously offered to buy chips for everyone, not because he felt he owed them anything but because he could not be sure that they would let him back inside empty-handed.

Wolf pulled on his damp coat and one of the officers held the reinforced door open for him. Apparently the thick metal had dulled the sound of the storm outside. Wolf ran out onto the deserted high street, attempting to time his progress against the mini-tsunamis that flooded the pavement every time a car went through a deep puddle. He found the fish and chip shop and stepped inside onto the slippery, mud-stained floor. As he closed the door on the deafening rain, he realised that his phone was ringing.

'Wolf,' he answered.

'Hello, Will. It's Elizabeth Tate,' said a croaky voice.

'Liz, what can I do for you?'

Elizabeth Tate was a hard-nosed defence lawyer, who also acted as the duty solicitor for a number of central London police stations. She had been in the job for nearly thirty years, a first-line defence for the unprepared imprisoned (from drunks to murderers), a lone voice of support for the isolated and distraught. Although they had had their fair share of disagreements in their time, Wolf liked Elizabeth.

Where other lawyers would lie through their teeth, not for the sake of their undoubtedly guilty client but in defence of their own ego, Elizabeth would defend them as far as the law insisted but no further. On the few occasions that they had fallen out, it had been because she had sincerely believed in her client's innocence, and under those circumstances she was able to fight as ruthlessly and passionately as the best of them.

'I believe that you are, at this moment, guarding a Mr Vijay Rana,' she said.

'Battered sausage and chips twice please, love,' someone ordered in the background.

Wolf covered the speaker as he decided upon a response.

'I don't know what you're—'

'Drop the act. His wife called me,' said Elizabeth. 'I represented him last year.'

'For tax dodging?'

'No comment.'

'For tax dodging.'

'I have already spoken to Simmons, who has agreed to let me meet with my client this evening.'

'Absolutely not.'

'Are you going to make me start quoting the Police and Criminal Evidence Act down the phone at you? I just spent twenty minutes doing just that to your boss. Mr Rana is not only under your protection but under arrest for a crime. We both know that anything he says, to you or anybody else, over the next two days, could further incriminate him to the detriment of his case in court.'

'No.'

'I have agreed to be subjected to a full search of my person and belongings and will, of course, adhere to any other procedures that you have put in place.'

'No.'

Elizabeth sighed.

'Speak to Simmons then phone me back,' she said before hanging up on him.

'What time can you be here?' Wolf mumbled down the phone to Elizabeth as he picked at the last of his soggy chips back at the station.

He and Simmons had argued for ten solid minutes, although it was unrealistic to think that their lawsuit-phobic commissioner would ever back down on such an issue – to deny a prisoner his right to legal advice for a crime that they still fully intended to prosecute him for. Simmons, expecting Wolf to undermine his orders, reminded him of their conversation on Saturday evening. He reiterated that he could have Wolf taken off the case at any given moment. He also made the point that to refuse Rana his lawyer could be grounds to dismiss the case against him; he would have saved a criminal's life only to let him walk free.

Grudgingly, Wolf had called Elizabeth back.

'I need to finish up here at Brentford, then stop off briefly at Ealing on the way over. I should be with you by ten.'

'That's cutting it pretty fine. He's being moved at half past.'

'I'll be there.'

There was a sharp crack of thunder and then all of the lights in the custody suite went out. After a few moments, the eerie glow of the emergency lighting dimmed the darkness a little. A prisoner in one of the nearest holding cells started kicking rhythmically at his door. The dull thudding filled the claustrophobic hallway like a war drum while the muted storm raged beyond the walls. Wolf got to his feet and hung up on Elizabeth.

He realised that his hand was trembling and tried to ignore the reason why: that this was his nightmare, those countless sleepless nights spent on the secure ward, listening to the endless screams flooding the maze of corridors, the futile impacts of desperate bodies breaking against immovable doors. He took a moment to compose himself and then shoved his hand into his pocket.

'I want to check on Rana,' he called to the others beside the processing station.

He and Walker strode down the dark corridor as the steady beat grew towards a crescendo. The officer guarding Rana's room hurriedly unlocked the door. Inside, the cell was pitch black. The weak glow from the corridor barely penetrated the darkness.

'Mr Rana?' asked Walker. 'Mr Rana?'

Finlay appeared behind them wielding a torch. He swung the beam wildly around the room and then steadied it upon the motionless figure lying on the bench.

'Shit,' said Wolf, who rushed into the dark room and rolled Rana onto his back. Pressing two fingers against the man's neck; he searched for a pulse.

Rana's eyes flickered open, and he let out a terrified shriek, having been fast asleep. Wolf sighed in relief as Finlay chuckled out in the corridor. Walker just looked as though 10.30 p.m. could not come quickly enough.

CHAPTER 12

Tuesday 1 July 2014

11.28 p.m.

The last Wolf had heard from the Protected Persons team, they were still stuck on the M25. One of the custody officers had propped his phone up on the counter so that they could all watch the BBC *News* report on the incident causing the delay. Apparently a lorry had jackknifed across the carriageway. Two air ambulances had landed on the motorway and at least one person had been confirmed dead.

The lights had come back on in the custody suite, which was feeling progressively cosier as the storm outside worsened. Finlay was, yet again, asleep in a plastic chair. One officer was guarding Rana's cell, and the other two were exchanging exasperated looks behind Walker's back. Now into the fifteenth hour of a twelve-hour shift, they felt as imprisoned as the people occupying the holding cells.

Wolf was hovering beside the back door, waiting for Elizabeth who had also been severely delayed by the unprecedented weather. The last text he had received from her advised that she was less than five minutes away and instructed him to put the kettle on.

Wolf peered out through the porthole window at the flooded car park, the drowning drains spluttering up filthy water while the building storm gathered strength. Two headlight beams carefully negotiated the corner and a taxi loitered, for over a minute, outside the entrance. A hooded figure holding a briefcase emerged from the back seat, dashed up the steps, and knocked urgently on the metal door.

'Who is it?' called Wolf, unable to make out the face beneath the hood.

'Who do you think?' Elizabeth's raspy voice yelled back.

Wolf pulled the door open and was sprayed with horizontal rain as the gale-force winds, predicted by the Met Office, blew papers and posters across the room. It took all of his strength to force the heavy door closed again.

Elizabeth removed her dripping coat. She was fifty-eight years old and always tied her grey hair back in a tight ponytail. Wolf had only ever seen her wear three outfits. Each looked as though it had been extravagantly expensive when she had purchased it two decades ago, but now appeared worn and outdated. Whenever they met, she had quit smoking again, yet always smelled of fresh smoke, and her garish pink lipstick unfailingly looked to have been applied in the dark. A fond, yellow-toothed smile formed when she looked up at Wolf.

'Liz,' he said in greeting.

'Hello, sweetie,' she said, tossing her coat onto the nearest chair before embracing him and planting two exaggerated kisses on either cheek. She held onto him for a fraction longer than felt normal. Wolf presumed that this was intended to convey her motherly concern over his well-being.

'It is foul out there,' she told the room, in case they had not yet realised.

'Drink?' offered Wolf.

'I would die for a tea,' she told him with enough theatre to warrant a far larger audience.

Wolf left to prepare the tactical drink, leaving Walker and his officers to conduct the security searches. He felt uncomfortable about subjecting a colleague who he had known for so many years, a friend, to a pat-down. At least this way it would appear as though he had no hand in it. He procrastinated for as long as he possibly could before returning to the custody suite to find Elizabeth joking with Finlay, who was sorting through the contents of her briefcase. He had removed an engraved lighter (which she only kept for sentimental reasons) and two expensive ballpoint pens.

'Approved!' smiled Finlay.

He closed up the briefcase and slid it back over to Elizabeth, who drank her tepid tea in a few gulps.

'So, where is my client?'

'I'll take you down to him,' said Wolf.

'We shall need some privacy.'

'There'll be someone on the door.'

'It is a confidential conversation darling.'

'Then you'd better talk quietly,' shrugged Wolf.

That made Elizabeth smile.

'Same old smart-arse, aren't we, Will?'

They had just reached the door to Rana's cell when Wolf's mobile phone went off. The officer on guard let Elizabeth inside and then relocked the door. Wolf was satisfied and walked back down the corridor before answering. It was Simmons calling with two pieces of news. He had just been informed that Protected Persons were mobile, at last, and would be with them within half an hour. He then moved on to the rather more controversial second point: Wolf and Finlay would not be permitted to accompany Rana.

'I'm going with them,' said Wolf firmly.

'They have strict protocols to follow,' argued Simmons.

'I don't give a— We can't just hand him over and let them drive him off to god knows where.'

'We can and we will.'

'You've agreed to this?' Wolf was clearly disappointed in his chief.

'I have.'

'Let me speak to them.'

'Not happening.'

'I'll be polite, I promise. Just let me explain the situation. What's the number?'

Wolf's cheap digital watch beeped midnight while he argued with the man leading the team currently en route to them. He was growing increasingly irate with the pig-headed man, who mindlessly refused to break protocol under any circumstances. Feeling he might have more joy face to face, Wolf called him a 'tosser' and hung up.

'It's a wonder you've got any friends at all,' said Finlay. He was watching a tiny weather forecast with Walker and another officer.

'Winds of up to ninety miles per hour,' a distorted voice warned them.

'They're well trained, those lads,' continued Finlay. 'You need to stop being such a control freak.'

Wolf was about to say something to jeopardise one of his few remaining friendships when he heard the officer unlocking Rana's cell. Elizabeth stepped back out into the corridor. She was still saying her curt farewells to her client as the door was closed and locked behind her. Her bare feet slapped against the beige floor (Walker had confiscated her ludicrously high heels) as she made her way up the corridor. She strode past Wolf without saying a word and collected her possessions from the desk.

'Liz?' he said, confused by her drastic change in mood. 'Everything all right?'

'Fine,' she replied as she wrapped her coat around her. As she fumbled with the buttons, her hands started to tremble. Then, to Wolf's astonishment, she wiped her tearful eyes. 'I'd like to go please.'

She walked over to the door.

'Did he say something to upset you?' Wolf asked. He could feel himself getting angry. He felt protective over this woman who had to deal with the very worst of humanity on a daily basis. He knew that it would have taken an undeservedly vicious jibe to get under Elizabeth's thick skin.

'I'm a big girl, William,' she snapped. 'The door – now, please.'

Wolf walked over and slid the heavy bar across. Another blast of wind and rain accompanied the distant rumble of thunder as Elizabeth stepped outside.

'Your briefcase!' said Wolf, realising that she must have left it in with Rana.

Elizabeth looked terrified.

'I can get it for you. You don't have to see him again,' he said.

'I'll pick it up in the morning.'

'Don't be ridiculous.'

'Jesus, Will, just leave it!' she shouted and then she tottered away down the steps.

'What was all that about?' asked Finlay without taking his eyes off the tiny screen.

Wolf watched Elizabeth turn the corner onto the high street. Slowly, an unsettled feeling began to tighten in his chest. He looked down at his watch: 12.07 a.m.

'Open the door!' he screamed as he sprinted back down the corridor.

The alarmed officer dropped the keys, allowing Walker time to catch up. The lock clunked firmly, and Wolf shoved the weighty door open to reveal Rana sitting upright on the mattress. He heard Walker exhale in relief behind him . . .

. . . and then gasp as he looked again at the seated prisoner.

Rana's head was slumped forward, his face painted the bruised blues and purples of the dead, his bloodshot eyes protruding unnaturally from their sockets. What looked to be piano wire had been coiled several times around his neck, cutting deep lines into the dark skin. More wire sprouted from the inner edge of the open briefcase, obvious now that it was no longer hidden in plain sight.

'Call an ambulance!' Wolf yelled as he tore back along the corridor and out into the night.

He leapt down the slippery steps, splashed through the flooded car park and rounded the corner onto the high street as the torrential rain lashed across his face. Less than thirty seconds had elapsed, yet Elizabeth was nowhere to be seen along the deserted pavement. He ran past dark shop windows, aware that he was disadvantaged by the noise of the storm. Every car that passed sounded more like an aircraft taking off as the spray of surface water built and subsided as they sped by. The millions of raindrops were being amplified as they collided with the metal roofs of parked cars.

'Elizabeth!' he shouted, but the sound was carried away in the wind.

He sprinted past an alleyway between two shops and paused. Retracing his steps, he stood in the dark mouth of the thin passageway, squinting into the blackness. He edged a little further in, listening to the rain strike the glass bottles, discarded packaging and whatever other litter carpeted the invisible alley floor.

'Elizabeth?' he called softly. He edged further in. He could feel the floor cracking beneath his feet. 'Elizabeth?'

He heard a sudden movement and then felt himself being shoved against the cold brick wall. He reached out and almost grabbed a handful of clothing as Elizabeth ran back out onto the street.

Wolf was only a few seconds behind as he emerged into the grainy glow of an orange streetlight. Elizabeth panicked and recklessly darted into the road. An estate car skidded to a stop just inches from her and added the furious blare of its horn to the already deafening night. Elizabeth was now several metres ahead of him. Bizarrely, she took out her mobile phone as her pace began to slow and held it to her ear. Wolf was catching up quickly and could see the blood and dirt covering the soles of her feet from where she had run barefoot through the oily puddles and muddy verges. Finally within earshot, he could hear her panting into the phone:

'It's done! It's done!'

He reached out to grab hold of her, when she suddenly veered back into the road. Instinctively, he followed, unsure whether there was a break in the traffic or not. Elizabeth stumbled across the pedestrian island in the middle of the wide road and tripped onto the tarmac. She climbed back onto her hands and knees to find that Wolf had paused in the centre of the road. She saw the look of horror on his face and turned to follow his gaze just as the double-decker bus bore down on her.

She never screamed.

Wolf moved slowly towards the crumpled shape, which was lying against a kerb over ten metres back down the street. He heard more cars skidding to a halt behind him, throwing headlight beams over the broken body. He could feel tears welling up, too traumatised and exhausted to even attempt to fathom why his friend had done this.

The dazed bus driver staggered over to him while his handful of passengers gawped out at the scene from the comfort of their seats. He wore an expression of hope on his face, hope that the woman might still get up, hope that perhaps she had not even been injured, hope that his life had not just changed forever. Wolf had no inclination to console or even acknowledge the man. He could not be blamed for failing to spot a woman lying in the road in such treacherous conditions, but he had been the one to end Elizabeth's life and Wolf did not trust his temper at that moment.

As another car joined the growing queue of traffic, a fresh section of the dark road was illuminated, and Wolf noticed Elizabeth's cracked phone sitting in the exact spot where the bus had hit her. He slowly crawled over to it and flipped it over to discover that the call was still connected. Holding it tightly to his ear, he could make out rustling and quiet breathing on the other end of the line.

'Who is this?' Wolf's voice cracked as he asked the question.

There was no answer, only the steady breathing of somebody listening in and the sound of industrial machinery operating somewhere in the background.

'This is Detective Sergeant Fawkes with the Metropolitan Police. Who is this?' he asked again; although, he had a feeling that he already knew the answer.

Blue lights were approaching in the distance, but Wolf sat motionless, listening to the killer listening to him. Wolf wanted to threaten him, to scare him, to somehow provoke a reaction out of him but knew that he would never be able to articulate the pure anger and hatred that he was experiencing. Instead, he continued to listen, ignoring the buzz of activity that surrounded him. He did not know why he slowed his breathing to match the killer's, but shortly after there was a loud crackle from the other end of the phone and the line abruptly went dead.

CHAPTER 13

Wednesday 2 July 2014

5.43 a.m.

Karen Holmes waited anxiously for the next traffic report. She never slept particularly well before these early mornings and had been woken several times during the night by the raging storm. She had left her Gloucester bungalow in the dark to find her wheelie bin lying in the middle of the road and one of her fence panels resting against next door's car. She propped the heavy wooden panel back up as quietly as she could and prayed that her unpleasant neighbour would fail to notice the additional scratches to his bonnet.

Karen dreaded her monthly visit to the firm's main offices in the capital. Her colleagues all claimed hotels and dinners on expenses; but she had nobody that she could reasonably ask to look after her dogs on such a regular basis, and their well-being was her priority.

The traffic on the motorway was already beginning to build, and a seemingly endless average speed check had slowed her progress in order to protect mile upon mile of plastic cones, teasing that somebody might possibly commence some work, somewhere, at some point in the near future.

Karen looked down to fiddle with her radio, paranoid that she had missed a report. As she glimpsed back up at the road, she noticed a large black bag lying between the steel barriers of the central reservation. Something about the size and shape of it struck her as unusual. Just as she drew level with it, at forty-nine miles per hour, she could have sworn that she saw it move. When she glanced in the rear-view mirror, all she could see was the Audi saloon that had inexplicably decided to accelerate right up to her bumper before overtaking at ninety miles per hour, either too rich or too stupid to be concerned with speed cameras.

She continued along the motorway, noting that there was a junction in another two miles. She did not have time to stop, even if she had been sure that she had seen something, which she was not. The bag had probably been blown there in the high winds and her car had disturbed it as she passed, yet Karen was unable to shake the feeling that there was something inside, something about the way that it had moved.

Both of her Staffordshire bull terriers had been rescue dogs, found together and left for dead in a skip. The thought always made her feel physically sick. As she came out of the roadworks, a BMW flew past at over a hundred miles per hour, and Karen was confident that anything alive inside would not be for much longer.

She turned the wheel suddenly and her ancient Fiesta vibrated violently as she drove across the rumble strips and pulled onto the slip road. She would only delay her journey by fifteen minutes by going back to check. She looped around the roundabout and rejoined the motorway in the opposite direction.

It was difficult to remember exactly how far down the monotonous road the bag had been, so Karen slowed down when she thought she was getting close. She spotted it ahead, switched on her hazard lights and pulled onto the hard shoulder, stopping level with it. She watched the black bag for over a minute, feeling foolish and angry with herself, as it sat perfectly still until being blown about by the next speeding vehicle. She indicated right and was about to pull back into the inside lane when the bag suddenly lurched forward.

Karen's heart was racing as she waited for a gap in the traffic, got out of the car and ran across three lanes to climb over the central reservation. She could feel the force of the cars passing only a few metres away, spraying her with dirt and oily water. She knelt down and hesitated.

'Don't be snakes. Please don't be snakes,' she whispered to herself.

As she spoke, something in the bag made another deliberate movement towards her, and she thought that she could hear whimpering. Cautiously, she took hold of the papery material and tore a small hole in one end. Slowly, Karen ripped the gap wider and wider, worried that whatever was inside might run straight out into the oncoming traffic. In her heightened state, she accidentally tore halfway down the material and fell back in horror as a head of dirty blonde hair spilled out over the tarmac and the bound and gagged woman feverishly took in her surroundings. She looked up at Karen with huge pleading eyes and lost consciousness.

Edmunds had a spring in his step as he passed through security at New Scotland Yard. He had made it home in time to take Tia out for dinner as an apology for the previous night. They had both made an effort to get dressed up and, for a couple of hours, were happy to pretend that such extravagances came naturally to them. They enjoyed three courses and Edmunds had even ordered a steak. The illusion had only been ruined by the irascible waitress, who had yelled to her supervisor across the restaurant that she had no idea how to put Tesco Clubcard vouchers through the till.

Edmunds' mood had also been lifted by finally finding a match to the nail polish. He was not yet sure how this information would be of help, only that it was an important step towards identifying the Ragdoll's female right arm. He entered the office and saw that Baxter was already at her desk. Even from the opposite side of the room, he could tell that she was in a foul mood.

'Morning,' tried Edmunds cheerfully.

'What the hell are you grinning at?' she snapped.

'Nice night,' said Edmunds with a shrug.

'Not for Vijay Rana it wasn't.'

Edmunds sat down to listen. 'Is he . . .?'

'Not for a woman I've known for years called Elizabeth Tate. And not for Wolf.'

'Is Wolf all right? What happened?'

Baxter briefed Edmunds on the events of the previous night and the discovery of the young woman earlier that morning.

'The bag's with forensics, but when the ambulance crew got there they found this hanging off her foot.'

Baxter handed Edmunds a small plastic evidence bag containing a morgue toe-tag.

'"Care of: Detective Sergeant William Fawkes",' read Edmunds. 'Does he know yet?'

'No,' she said. 'Wolf and Finlay were up all night. They've been stood down for the rest of the day.'

An hour later, a female officer escorted the petrified woman through the busy office. She had been brought in directly from the hospital and was still caked in grime. Her face and arms were decorated in cuts and bruises and her matted hair covered every shade between bleached blonde and black. She reacted in alarm to every sudden noise and new voice.

News had already reached the department that she had been identified as Georgina Tate, Elizabeth's daughter. She had apparently been absent from work for two days and her mother had phoned in on her behalf citing personal issues. No missing persons report had been filed. Even from these snippets of information, it was not difficult to piece together what had transpired, and Baxter felt unsettled by how easy it had been to coerce a woman that she knew to be strong, resourceful and unwaveringly moral into murder.

'She doesn't know yet,' said Baxter solemnly as Georgina Tate was shown into the renovated interview room.

'About her mother?' asked Edmunds.

'Doesn't look in any fit state to hear it, does she?'

Baxter started packing up her things.

'Are we going somewhere?'

'We're not,' said Baxter. 'I am. With no Wolf or Finlay, guess which mug's been left to sort all their shit out on top of my own. Who's number four on the list?'

'Andrew Ford, the security guard,' said Edmunds, a little surprised that Baxter needed to ask.

'Complete arsehole. Big drinker. Managed to knock out a female officer's tooth last night when she tried to stop him trashing the place.'

'I'll come with you.'

'I can handle it. Then I've got a meeting with Jarred Garland, the journalist, who's due to die in . . .' Baxter counted it out on her fingers, 'three days. He's decided to spend his final week reporting how useless he thinks we all are and how it feels to be on a serial killer's hit list. I've been asked to "pacify" and "reassure" him.'

'*You*?' asked Edmunds incredulously. Fortunately Baxter took his disbelief as a compliment. 'What do you want me to do?'

'Find out if Georgina Tate remembers anything useful. Chase up about the ring; we need to know who it was made for. See if the medical examiners have anything new for us, and get hold of Elizabeth Tate's mobile phone the second it's released by forensics.'

Baxter left the office, and Edmunds realised that he had not even told her about the nail varnish. He placed the small bottle on the desk, feeling foolish for getting so excited about his trivial investigation while Wolf was out there chasing reluctant killers around Southall, having kidnapped women delivered to the office and holding phone conversations with criminal royalty. It was all horrible, of course, but he had to admit he was a little jealous.

'This is beautiful,' laughed Elijah excitedly as the photograph he had just purchased for two thousand pounds was projected onto the conference room wall. 'And I mean *beautiful*.'

Andrea was holding her hand over her mouth and was grateful that no one else in the darkened room could see the tears rolling down her cheeks. The picture was anything but beautiful; in fact, it was probably the saddest thing that she had ever seen: a black-and-white photograph of Wolf on his knees, lit beneath a solitary streetlight, the sparkling rain and car headlights reflecting off the puddles and shop windows like stage lights. She had seen Wolf cry perhaps two or three times during their marriage and each time it had broken her heart.

This was so much worse.

He was sat in the flooded road beside the mangled body of an older woman, still gently holding her bloodied hand as he stared into space with a look of utter defeat painted across his face.

He was broken.

Andrea glanced around at the faces of her colleagues: smiling, applauding, laughing. She could feel herself shaking in anger and disgust. At that moment she despised each and every one of them and wondered whether she would have worn the same delighted look had she not once loved the man in the photograph. She was disturbed to admit that she might.

'Who's the roadkill?' Elijah asked the room to a series of shrugs and shaking heads. 'Andrea?'

Andrea focused on the image, attempting to hide her eyes from the others.

'How would I know who that poor lady is?'

'Your ex-husband seems keen on her,' said Elijah.

'A little too keen,' the balding producer in the corner of the room shouted out to the amusement of the others.

'Thought you might recognise her,' finished Elijah.

'Well, I don't,' said Andrea as pleasantly as she could, although, several people shared surprised looks.

'No matter. It's TV gold either way,' said Elijah, unfazed by her tone. 'We'll open with the photograph and the counter ticking down the hours that Rana, or whatever his name is, has to live. We'll do a bit about the ongoing search for him and then back to the photograph for speculation and fabrication.'

Everyone in the room apart from Andrea chuckled.

'Who is this woman? Why's the lead detective on the Ragdoll case at a traffic accident rather than searching for the next victim?

Or was this somehow connected to the murders? The usual.' Elijah waited expectantly. 'Anything else?'

'"Hashtag: notonthelist" is trending right now,' said an irritating young man, who Andrea had never seen without a phone in his hand, 'and our Death Clock app's been downloaded over fifty thousand times already.'

'Shit. Should've charged for it,' cursed Elijah. 'How's the Ragdoll emoji coming?'

Another man tentatively slid a piece of paper across the table to him. Elijah picked it up and stared at it in confusion.

'It's hard to capture the full extent of the horror in a cartoon,' the nervy man explained defensively.

'It'll do,' Elijah told him, tossing the picture back in his direction. 'But lose the boobs. Bit inappropriate for the kids, don't you think?'

Apparently satisfied that he had done his good deed for the decade, Elijah adjourned the meeting. Andrea was the first to get up and leave the conference room. She was not sure herself whether she was going to head down to make-up or carry straight on out through the exit. She only knew that she desperately wanted to see Wolf.

Simmons stood staring at the enormous Ragdoll collages on the meeting room wall. He looked immaculate, wearing full dress uniform, apart from the deep scuff to his right shoe that he had not been able to polish out. He had damaged the leather while furiously kicking the metal filing cabinet in his office just minutes after seeing his friend lying charred and still on the flooded interview room floor. It seemed fitting, somehow, to wear them that afternoon, a private symbol of loss and friendship in what was sure to be an impersonally regimented and formal affair.

The service for Mayor Turnble was due to take place at St Margaret's, in the grounds of Westminster Abbey, at 1 p.m., his family having requested a private funeral at a later date once the body was released. Before that, Simmons was scheduled to hold a press conference to confirm the deaths of Vijay Rana and Elizabeth Tate. He was struggling to keep his temper in check as the PR team bickered amongst themselves regarding the best way to put a 'positive spin' on the situation.

Simmons watched as Georgina Tate was led out of the interview room that he had not yet worked up the courage to return to and was not at all sure he ever would. He would never forget the sight of his friend's blistered and peeling face, and he could still smell burning flesh whenever he revisited the unwelcome memory.

'OK, how about this: focusing on the fact that we managed to stop this Tate woman,' suggested a lanky young man, who looked about fifteen years old to Simmons, 'one less killer out on our streets, isn't it?'

Simmons slowly turned round to face the three-person team, armed with their charts and graphs, highlighted sections of the morning's newspapers glowing like the toxic waste that it was. He went to say something, shook his head in blatant disgust, and left the room.

CHAPTER 14

Wednesday 2 July 2014

11.35 a.m.

Baxter took a District line train to Tower Hill and unenthusiastically followed Jarred Garland's vague directions away from the station. Keeping the Tower of London on her left, she set off down the congested main road. Why they couldn't have met either at his home (where he should have been, sheltering under police protection), or at the newspaper offices, was beyond her.

In an unexpected turn of events, the amoral, self-publicising, rabble-rousing journalist had requested that she meet him at a church. She wondered whether Garland had turned to religion in his final days, as so many do. If she had believed in anything, she was sure that she would have found the brazen cheek of these curtain-call epiphanies mildly insulting.

The dark clouds overhead were beginning to break, allowing the sun to warm the city for a few intermittent minutes at a time. After ten minutes of walking she caught sight of a tall church tower and turned down the next side street. As she came round the corner, with bright sunshine flickering down on her, her mouth dropped open.

The pristine church tower of St Dunstan's in the East loomed high above its own ruined walls. Thick, vibrant trees sprouted up through an imaginary roof and out through the tall arched windows, while climbing plants had tangled themselves up the stone walls only to spill back over the other side in dense formations that cast strange shadows across the intimate gardens. It looked like something plucked from a children's story: the secret wood in the city, hidden in plain sight, invisible from the dull office buildings that stood with their backs to it.

Baxter entered through the metal gates, stepped into the ruined church and followed the gentle trickle of water beneath an enormous archway, strangled in thick vines, to a cobbled courtyard built around a small fountain. A couple were attempting to take a photograph of themselves and an overweight woman was feeding the pigeons. She walked over to the solitary figure sitting quietly in the far corner.

'Jarred Garland?' she asked.

The man looked up in surprise. He was a similar age to Baxter, dressed in a fitted shirt with the sleeves folded up and was moderately attractive with a clean-shaven face and overly styled hair. He looked her up and down with an arrogant smile.

'Well, today just got a whole lot better,' he said with a strong East End accent. 'Have a seat.'

When he patted the space to his right, Baxter sat down to his left. Garland smiled broadly at this.

'Why don't you wipe that stupid grin off your face and tell me why we couldn't meet at your office?' Baxter snapped.

'Newspapers don't really like having detectives snooping around their offices if they can help it. Why couldn't we meet at yours?'

'Because detectives don't really like having smug, shit-stirring, opportunistic journalists . . .' She pulled a face as she sniffed the air, 'wearing awful aftershave snooping around their offices, full stop.'

'You've read my column, then?'

'Not by choice.'

'I'm flattered.'

'Don't be.'

'So what did you think?'

'What's that saying about not biting . . .?' Baxter trailed off.

'Don't bite the hand that feeds you?'

'No, that's not it. Oh yeah: don't bite the hand of the only protection you've got standing between you and a prolific, ruthless, genius, serial killer.'

This time, a smirk formed over Garland's boyish features.

'You know, I've already started on today's article. I begin by congratulating the Met on yet another successful execution.'

Baxter wondered how much trouble she would land herself in were she to punch the man that she was supposed to be protecting.

'But that's not entirely true, is it? You outdid yourselves. Detective Fawkes scored you a two-for-one!'

Baxter did not respond and glanced around the gardens. Garland must have thought he had hit a nerve; in fact, she was actually checking for witnesses should she lose her temper.

The sun had disappeared behind a cloud while they were talking, and the secret garden had taken on a more sinister appearance in the shade. Suddenly the image of a house of God being ripped apart from the inside out felt a little discomforting, its strong walls crumbling in the hold of the snakelike vines, dragging it piece by piece down into the earth, irrefutable proof that there was nobody left in this godless city that cared enough to save it.

Having thoroughly ruined her newest picnic spot for herself, Baxter turned back to Garland and spotted the top of a thin black box poking out of his shirt.

'Oh, you arsehole!' said Baxter as she snatched the mini-recorder from his pocket. A red recording light was flashing.

'Hey, you can't—'

Baxter smashed it onto the cobbled floor and ground it beneath her heel for good measure.

'S'pose I deserved that,' admitted Garland with surprising good grace.

'Look, this is how this works: you've got two police officers posted outside your house. Use them. Wolf will be in touch tomorrow—'

'I don't want him. I want you.'

'Not an option.'

'Look, Detective, this is how this works: I am not a prisoner. I have not been arrested. The Metropolitan Police have no hold over me, and I am under no obligation to accept their help. And, in the nicest way possible, you don't have the best track record so far. I will be willing to work with you on this, but on my own terms. First: I want you.'

Baxter stood up, in no mood to negotiate.

'Second: I want to fake my own death.'

Baxter rubbed her temple and winced, as though Garland's stupidity was causing her physical pain.

'Think about it. If I'm already dead, the killer can't kill me. We'd have to do it realistically, though, like in front of an audience.'

'You could be on to something,' said Baxter.

Garland's face lit up as she sat back down beside him.

'We could swap your face with John Travolta's . . . Oh no, wait, that was a movie. How about we teleport . . . no. Got it: we hire a jet fighter, I think Wolf's got that category on his licence, and we blow a helicopter out of the—'

'Hardy-har-har,' said Garland, a little embarrassed. 'I feel you're not taking me seriously.'

'That's because I'm not.'

'My life's at stake,' said Garland, and, for the first time, Baxter thought she could hear fear and self-pity in his voice.

'Then go home,' she said.

She got back up and walked away.

'Thank you so much, I really appreciate it. You too. Bye.'

Edmunds put down the receiver just as Baxter returned to the office following her meeting with Garland. He pinched his leg painfully beneath the desk to ensure that he was not smiling when she came over.

She hated it when he smiled.

She sat down at her computer, huffed loudly, and began sweeping crumbs off her keyboard and into her hand.

'Did you actually eat any of whatever this was?' she snapped.

He decided not to mention that he had been far too busy to take lunch and that she was holding the remnants of her own breakfast granola bar. Baxter glanced up to find him watching her patiently with a strained look on his face. He looked as though he might explode with excitement.

'OK, let's hear it,' she sighed.

'Collins and Hunter. It's a family-run law firm based in Surrey with several specialist branches and partnerships scattered across the country. They have a long-standing tradition of presenting their employees with a ring . . .' Edmunds held up the evidence bag containing the thick platinum ring. 'This precise ring, in fact, after five years of service.'

'You're sure?' asked Baxter.

'Yes.'

'That can't leave us a big list to choose from.'

'Twenty to thirty at the most, according to the lady I spoke to. She's sending me the complete list, including contact details, this afternoon.'

'It's about time we caught a break,' Baxter smiled.

Edmunds was amazed how different she looked when she was happy.

'How did it go with Garland?'

'He wants us to kill him. Drink?'

Baxter's shocking response was only eclipsed by her offer to make him a drink. It had never happened before and Edmunds panicked.

'Tea,' he blurted out.

He hated tea.

Five minutes later Baxter returned to their shared desk and set a milky tea down in front of him. She had evidently forgotten (or never listened in the first place) that Edmunds was lactose intolerant. He pretended to sip it with exaggerated delight.

'What time's Simmons due back?' she asked. 'I need to talk to him about this Garland situation.'

'Three, I think.'

'Did they get anything out of Georgina Tate?' Baxter asked him.

'Not much,' replied Edmunds, consulting his notebook. 'Caucasian. But we knew that already. Scars covering his right forearm.' It took him a moment to decipher his own scribble at the bottom of the page. 'Oh yeah. You had a call while you were out: Eve Chambers. She said you had the number.'

'Eve phoned?' asked Baxter, puzzled that Chambers' wife had returned her call.

'She sounded quite distressed.'

Baxter immediately took out her mobile phone. Unable to speak in private with Edmunds sitting two feet away, she got up and moved on to Chambers' vacant desk. The phone was answered on the second ring.

'Emily,' said a relieved voice.

'Eve? Is everything all right?'

'Oh yes, I'm sure it is, my love. Just me fretting like the silly old bugger I am. It's just . . . I got your answerphone message yesterday.'

'Yeah, sorry about that,' said Baxter awkwardly.

'Oh, not to worry. I presumed it was just a mix-up at your end, but then Ben never came home last night.'

Baxter was confused: 'Never came home from where, Eve?'

'Well, from work, dear.'

Baxter sat up a little straighter, suddenly alert, and carefully considered her reply so not to unduly worry the kind-hearted woman on the other end of the phone.

'When did you get back from holiday?' Baxter asked conversationally.

'Yesterday morning, and Ben had already left for work by the time I got home. No food in the fridge, no note to say welcome home . . . That man!'

Eve let out a strained laugh. Baxter rubbed her head. She was getting more confused every time Eve opened her mouth and was trying not to get stroppy with her.

'OK, why did you get back home later than Chamb— . . . than Ben?'

'I'm sorry, my love. I don't understand.'

'When did Ben get back from holiday?' Baxter almost yelled.

There was a long pause on the other end of the line before Eve's angst-ridden voice replied in a hoarse whisper:

'He didn't come on holiday.'

During the stunned silence, in which Baxter struggled to form any useful thoughts, Eve started to weep down the phone. Chambers had already been missing for over two weeks without a single person realising. Baxter could feel her heart racing, her throat drying up.

'Do you think something's happened to him?'

'I'm sure he's fine,' said Baxter unconvincingly. 'Eve?'

Only distant crying answered her.

'Eve, I need to know why Ben didn't come on holiday with you . . . Eve?'

She was losing her.

'Because he wouldn't shut up about it to me,' continued Baxter in the most light-hearted tone she could muster. 'He was showing me pictures of your sister's house on the beach and the restaurant on stilts. He was really looking forward to it, wasn't he?'

'Yes dear, he was. But he rang me at the house on the morning we were due to fly out. I was all packed up and waiting for him. He'd been in to see Dr Sami first thing to collect his medication and ended up getting himself admitted to hospital for "observations". He sent me a message the following day to say he'd been given the all-clear and was heading back into work.'

'What else did he say?'

'He said he loved me and that he'd been having some problems with his leg of late. Hadn't wanted to worry me. I said I'd stay, of course, but he was absolutely adamant that I go rather than waste the money. We had an argument about it.'

Eve began to cry again.

'His leg, Eve?'

Baxter recalled Chambers walking with a slight limp at times, but she had never seen it severe enough to cause a problem or heard him complain about it.

'Yes, you know dear, from that accident he had years ago. Comes home aching and sore most nights. Doesn't like to talk about it. Plates and rods and . . . he almost lost it . . . Hello?'

Baxter had dropped the phone and was already frantically searching through Chambers' desk drawers. She was shaking violently and beginning to hyperventilate as she pulled the entire top drawer out and showered the contents over the desk. People were watching her in embarrassed bewilderment.

Edmunds approached as she poured a second drawer of paperwork, stationery, painkillers and junk food over the floor. She had already dropped to her knees and started sorting through the mess when he knelt down opposite her.

'What are we looking for?' he asked softly. He spread the pile across the carpet, unsure what Baxter needed to find so desperately. 'Let me help.'

'DNA,' whispered Baxter, her breathing rate steadily increasing.

She wiped her tearful eyes and yanked the bottom drawer out of the cabinet. She was about to upturn it over the floor when Edmunds reached in and picked out a cheap plastic comb.

'Like this?' he asked, holding it out to her.

She crawled over to take it from him, burst into hysterical tears and started sobbing uncontrollably against his chest. Edmunds put a hesitant arm around her and angrily waved off the assembling spectators.

'What's all this about, Baxter?' he whispered.

It took her a minute to compose herself enough to answer him. Even then, she could barely talk between her harried breaths:

'The Ragdoll . . . The leg . . . It's Chambers!'

CHAPTER 15

Wednesday 2 July 2014

7.05 p.m.

Wolf was still wearing his shoes when he finally crawled onto his uninviting mattress at 8.57 a.m. He and Finlay had worked through the night at the two crime scenes, a quarter of a mile apart – preserving evidence, containing media coverage, conducting witness interviews, and compiling statements. When Finlay eventually dropped him off outside his building, just as the rest of the city was heading out to work, they were both too drained to speak. Wolf had simply patted his friend on the shoulder and climbed out of the car.

He watched Andrea's first broadcast of the day, sitting on his hard floor with a mouthful of toast, but had switched it off when the photograph of him beside Elizabeth's crumpled body appeared. He dragged himself into the bedroom and fell asleep within moments of closing his eyes.

He had hoped to get his arm looked at by an actual doctor but slept straight through until 6 p.m., when he received a phone call from Simmons. After a few words about Mayor Turnble's service, Simmons had briefed him on the day's progress and the media fallout from the night before. Following a hesitant pause, he went on to tell Wolf about Baxter's discovery. Forensics had confirmed that hair lifted from the comb in Chambers' desk had been an exact match to the right leg of the Ragdoll. Lastly, he reminded Wolf that he could still walk away from the case whenever he wanted.

Wolf had cooked himself a microwaveable meatball pasta, but after his conversation with Simmons, he was unable to get the image of the killer's stained apron out of his head. He had wondered, while watching the fuzzy CCTV footage, whose blood had already dried into the dirty apron, who had died even before the killer had claimed his fêted trophy in the form of Naguib Khalid. Now it all made sense. The killer had been forced to murder Chambers before he could leave the country.

He sat down in front of the television only to discover that the nightmarish photograph had been shared around the news channels, all of whom seemed to be filling airtime by debating whether Wolf was a suitable choice to hold such a prominent role in the case. He managed just two mouthfuls of his fleshy-looking meal before giving up on it. He was about to get up to scrape it into the bin when the intercom buzzed. Frustratingly, he was still unable to open any of the windows; otherwise, he might have been able to rid himself of both an intrusive reporter and his revolting dinner in one fell swoop. Reluctantly, he pushed a button on the receiver.

'William Fawkes: media scapegoat, male model and dead man walking,' he answered cheerfully.

'Emily Baxter: emotional wreck and moderately drunk. Can I come up?'

Wolf smiled, pushed another button, quickly tossed the worst of the mess through the bedroom door and closed it. He opened the front door to Baxter, who was dressed in tight jeans, black ankle boots and a lacy white top. She was wearing smoky blue make-up around her eyes and a sweet floral perfume that drifted over the threshold. She handed him a bottle of red wine as she stepped into the depressingly tatty room.

Wolf could never get used to the sight of Baxter in such casual clothing, despite knowing her for so many years. She looked younger, dainty and delicate; someone more suited to dances and dinner parties than dead bodies and serial killers.

'Chair?' he said.

Baxter looked around the unfurnished room.

'Do you have one?'

'That's what I was asking you,' said Wolf dryly.

He dragged the box labelled 'Trousers & Shirts' into the centre of the room for her and found some wine glasses in the one that he was about to sit on. He poured them each a conservative glass.

'Well, the place is certainly looking . . .' Baxter trailed off with an expression that suggested she did not want to touch anything. She then looked at Wolf, with his crumpled shirt and messy hair, in much the same way.

'I only just got up,' he lied. 'I stink, and I need a shower.'

They both sipped their wine.

'You heard?' she asked.

'I heard.'

'I know you weren't his biggest fan, but he meant a lot to me, you know?'

Wolf nodded with his eyes glued to the floor. They never talked like this.

'So, I cried into my trainee's arms today,' said Baxter, utterly mortified with herself. 'I'll never live it down.'

'Simmons said you were the one who figured it out.'

'Still . . . my trainee! It would've been OK if it was you.'

There was a heavy pause, stretched further by the knowledge that they were both picturing him with his arms wrapped around her.

'I wish you'd been there,' mumbled Baxter, accentuating the unpropitious image, her huge smoky eyes flicking up to gauge Wolf's reaction.

He shifted uncomfortably on his box, smashing something inside, as Baxter generously topped up their glasses and leaned in closer.

'I really don't want you to die.'

She slurred slightly, and Wolf wondered how much she had already had to drink before arriving at his. She reached across and took his hand.

'Can you believe she thought there was something going on between us?'

Wolf took a moment to catch up with the non sequitur: 'Andrea?'

'I know! Crazy, right? I mean, if you think about it, we basically suffered all the negatives of having an affair but got to enjoy none of the . . . positives.'

Her wide eyes were watching him again. Wolf let go of her hand and got to his feet. Baxter sat back and sipped her wine.

'Let's go out and find something to eat,' he suggested enthusiastically.

'I'm not really—'

'Sure you are! There's a noodle place just down the road. Let me jump in the shower. Five minutes and we'll go.'

Wolf almost ran into the bathroom. He had to wedge a towel beneath the ill-fitting door to keep it closed and got undressed as quickly as possible.

Baxter felt light-headed as she got to her feet. She wobbled over to the kitchenette, downed the rest of her glass, then filled it up with tap water. She refilled it and drank three more while staring into the empty apartment opposite, where the mastermind behind all of this misery and death had proudly displayed his monster.

She thought of Chambers making that phone call to Eve, presumably under duress, in a desperate attempt to protect her.

The muffled sound of running water permeated the paper-thin bathroom wall.

She pictured Elizabeth Tate lying broken in the rain, that black-and-white photograph of Wolf holding her hand.

Wolf was humming tunelessly in the echoic shower.

She thought about Wolf and how she knew she could not save him.

Baxter placed her glass in the sink, checked her reflection in the microwave, and walked over to the bathroom door. For the second time that day, her heart was racing in her chest. A crack of light between the door and the frame told her that either Wolf could not, or purposely had not, locked it. She put her hand on the rusty handle, took a deep breath . . .

There was a knock at the front door.

Baxter froze, still clutching the wobbly piece of metal. Wolf was still humming in the shower, unaware. There was another, more urgent, knock. She swore under her breath, stormed over to the front door and swung it open.

'Emily!'

'Andrea!'

The two women stood in uncomfortable silence, neither sure what to say next. Wolf emerged from the bathroom with a towel wrapped around his waist. He was halfway to the bedroom before he noticed them both watching him accusingly. He stopped, stared at the unenviable situation developing in the doorway, shook his head and shut himself in the bedroom.

'This all looks very cosy,' said Andrea with equal measures of relish at being right all along, and indignation.

'I suppose you'd better come in,' said Baxter, stepping aside and folding her arms defensively. 'Box?'

'I'll stand.'

Baxter watched Andrea as she inspected Wolf's shabby flat. She looked as boringly perfect as usual and her designer heels made an irritating clicking sound as she tottered about.

'This place is . . .' Andrea started.

'Isn't it, though?' said Baxter, keen to make clear to the wealthy woman that *her* middle-class apartment bore no resemblance to this hovel.

'Why does he live here?' whispered Andrea.

'Well, I'm guessing because you royally screwed him in the divorce,' said Baxter angrily.

'Not that it's any of your business,' whispered Andrea, 'but we are going to split the house fifty-fifty.'

They both glanced around the small room in awkward silence.

'And for your information,' Andrea continued, 'Geoffrey and I helped Will financially when he first came out of hospital.'

Baxter picked up the half-empty bottle of red wine.

'Wine?' she offered pleasantly.

'Depends, what kind is it?'

'Red.'

'I can see that. I meant: where is it from?'

'Morrisons.'

'No, I mean . . . I'll pass.'

Baxter shrugged and returned to her box.

Wolf had been dressed for well over five minutes but was still standing in his dreary bedroom waiting for the shouting in the next room to subside. Baxter had accused Andrea of profiting from the misery of others, which Andrea had taken offence to, even though, without question, she had. Andrea had then accused Baxter of being drunk, which she had taken offence to, even though, without question, she was.

When the argument turned to Wolf's relationship with Baxter, he finally came out of hiding.

'So how long has this been going on?' Andrea snapped at them both.

'Me and Baxter?' Wolf asked innocently. 'Don't be ridiculous.'

'Ridiculous?' shouted Baxter, affronted, not helping the situation. 'Just what is so ridiculous about maybe, perhaps, sort of liking me?'

Wolf winced, fully aware that whatever he said next would be wrong.

'Nothing, I didn't mean it like that. You know I think you're beautiful and smart and amazing.'

Baxter smiled smugly at Andrea.

'Amazing?' Andrea shouted. 'And you're still seriously trying to deny it?' She turned on Baxter. 'Do you live here with him then?'

'I wouldn't live in this shithole if my life depended on it,' retorted drunk Baxter.

'Hey!' yelled Wolf. 'Granted, it's a doer-upper.'

'Doer-upper? It's a knock-downer!' laughed Andrea, who had just trodden in something sticky. 'All I'm asking is for you to be honest. What does it matter now?'

She walked over to speak to Wolf face to face.

'Will . . .'

'Andie . . .'

'Were you having an affair?' she asked calmly.

'No!' he bellowed in frustration. 'You threw away our marriage over nothing!'

'You two practically lived together for months on end. Do you really expect me to believe that you weren't having sex?'

'Well *we* managed it just fine!' he shouted in her face.

Wolf grabbed his coat and left the flat, slamming the door, leaving Andrea alone with Baxter. There was a long silence before either of them spoke.

'Andrea,' said Baxter softly, 'you know that nothing in the world would give me more pleasure than to give you bad news, but nothing ever happened.'

The argument was over, years of suspicion and accusation obliterated with a single sincere sentence. Andrea sat down on a box, stunned that something she had believed so entirely had never actually happened.

'Wolf and I are friends, nothing more,' murmured Baxter, more for her own sake than Andrea's.

She had made a complete fool of herself in her confusion over their undeniably complicated relationship, her own need for comfort and reassurance in light of Chambers' death, and in her panic at the prospect of losing her best friend.

She shrugged. She would just have to blame it on the booze.

'Who was the woman in the photograph with Will?' asked Andrea.

Baxter rolled her eyes at her.

'I don't want her name,' she said defensively. 'Just . . . did he know her well?'

'Well enough. She didn't deserve . . .' Baxter had to tread carefully, so as not to disclose any of the details surrounding Vijay Rana's murder. 'She didn't deserve any of it.'

'How's he holding up?'

'Truthfully? It reminds me of before.'

Andrea nodded in understanding, remembering all too well the closing act of their marriage.

'It's all too personal, too much pressure. It's consuming him again,' said Baxter, struggling to articulate the change in Wolf that only she had noticed.

'You have to wonder if that's the intention,' said Andrea. 'Pushing his buttons, ensuring Will is so fixated on catching them that he can't even contemplate saving himself.'

'Aren't catching the killer and saving himself the same thing?'

'Not necessarily. He could run – but he won't.'

Baxter smiled weakly: 'No, he won't.'

'You know, we've had almost this exact conversation before,' said Andrea.

Baxter looked wary.

'Don't worry, I've never told a soul, and I never will. My point is that we've already made the decision what to do.'

'One word to Simmons and he'd be taken off the case, but I can't do it to him,' said Baxter. 'I'd rather he was out there self-destructing than just sitting in here waiting to die.'

'Decision made then. Keep quiet. Just help him as much as you can.'

'If we could just save one of them, prove the killer isn't infallible, it wouldn't all seem so hopeless.'

'What can I do to help?' asked Andrea, genuinely.

Baxter was suddenly struck with an idea; however, it was a huge risk discussing something of such importance with a woman who had already been arrested for distributing sensitive material across worldwide media. She had absolutely no intention of even contemplating Garland's idiotic suggestion of faking his own death, but if she had an opportunity to use the press as an ally rather than a hindrance, for once, there might be another way to stack the odds in their favour.

Andrea appeared sincere and was clearly deeply concerned about Wolf. She was also Baxter's best hope of successfully accomplishing her plan.

'I need you to help me save Jarred Garland.'

'You want *me* involved?' Andrea asked.

'And your cameraman.'

'I see.'

Andrea read between the lines of Baxter's outlandish request. She could picture Elijah's triumphant face at exposing the Metropolitan Police's troubling level of desperation. He would probably suggest that she play along for a while before breaking the story the evening before the murder.

It would be career suicide for a news reporter to deliberately mislead the public, no matter how honourable the intentions; how could they ever trust her again?

She remembered the smiling faces of her delighted colleagues in the conference room, grateful to Elizabeth Tate for dying so violently, as if she had stepped out in front of that bus for their benefit. She clenched her fists as she imagined them rejoicing over Wolf's lifeless body, expecting her to 'add some drama' to what would already be the worst day of her life.

She could not be there for that. They all repulsed her.

'I'll do it.'

CHAPTER 16

Thursday 3 July 2014

8.25 a.m.

Wolf called in at the office en route to his 9 a.m. session with Dr Preston-Hall. He sat down at his desk and swore when he kicked over his overflowing wastepaper bin. A sly look around the room for an empty and unguarded replacement suggested that the cleaners' workload had not increased proportionally with that of the department.

Following a token effort to tidy up after himself, Wolf was touched to discover that Finlay had gone to the trouble of completing the laborious monitoring form on his day off. A Post-it note attached to the front read:

What a load of faecal matter! See you at meeting. Fin.

He removed the note, assuming that the doctor would not appreciate Finlay's candour, and stared at Chambers' empty desk for a moment, picturing Baxter's uncharacteristic breakdown of the previous day. He hated to think of her so upset. He had only ever witnessed her that distraught once in all of the time that they had known each other, and it had affected him more than anything else on that traumatic and surreal day.

There had not been room inside the Old Bailey courtroom for Baxter, but she had stubbornly insisted on accompanying Wolf to hear the verdict of the Khalid trial. By that stage he had been suspended from work and everybody on the team was facing a formal investigation into the handling of the case. He had not wanted her to come. The rift between him and Andrea had come to a spectacular head during the week, which had ended in the police being called to their terraced cottage in Stoke Newington, adding fuel to the fabricated domestic abuse stories. Regardless, Baxter had pulled some strings and been permitted to wait outside in the palatial Great Hall for hours on end.

Wolf could still picture the foreman clearly (he looked just like Gandalf) and remembered the clerk asking for the verdict. Everything after that was a blur: shouts of panic, the smell of floor polish, a bloody hand pressed against a white dress.

The only thing that he vividly remembered was the intense pain as the dock security officer shattered his left wrist with a single vicious blow, metal displacing bone. That, and seeing Baxter standing amidst the chaos, tears streaming down her face, asking him repeatedly, 'What have you *done*?'

As he stopped struggling and allowed the horde of police officers to restrain him, he watched her take the arm of the blood-spattered juror and lead her out to safety. When Baxter disappeared through the heavy double doors, he had believed that he would never see her again.

Wolf's reverie was interrupted by an annoying beeping and the familiar assortment of whirrs and bangs that always emanated from the malfunctioning fax machine. He could see Baxter, deep in conversation with Simmons in his office. They had not had any contact since he walked out of the flat, and both women were gone by the time he had traipsed back home. He felt a little guilty, but had far too much on his mind to get stuck in the middle of their enduring feud. With no time to do anything useful, he picked up the monitoring form and left the office.

Wolf's session with Dr Preston-Hall had not gone at all well and he was relieved to leave the fusty office behind and step back out into the reliable drizzle of a British summer. Although it was warm, he pulled his coat on over his white shirt. He still had the small trophy sitting on the corner of his desk that Finlay had presented to him after getting caught in a hailstorm wearing the same cheap garment: Miss Wet T-shirt 2013. He had been self-conscious about it ever since.

He thought about the meeting as he ambled back towards New Scotland Yard. Dr Preston-Hall had voiced her concerns regarding the amount of pressure that he was under and the effect of seeing another two people die in front of him just since their meeting on Monday. Fortunately no one had gotten around to informing her about Chambers' death.

Although the sessions should have been based solely upon the information provided in Finlay's reports and the doctor's own confidential conversations with Wolf, it had been impossible to avoid the photograph that had dominated the news reports the previous day.

The doctor said that the photo was the most honest thing that he had ever given her to work with, albeit unintentionally, and that anyone could see that the man clutching the dead woman's hand was breaking apart. She told him that she would be phoning Simmons to advise that Wolf 'take a less prominent role in the investigation going forward', whatever that meant, and then promptly dismissed him again until Monday morning.

The office was half empty when Wolf returned. Two teenagers had been killed in a gang-related stabbing in Edmonton overnight, and a third was critically ill in hospital. It was another reminder that London was carrying on as usual and that the Ragdoll murders, the lives of those marked to die, and Wolf's own fight for survival, were nothing more than interesting topics of conversation for the millions of people not involved.

There was a message waiting for him when he got back to his desk. Andrew Ford, the security guard and number four on the list, had been demanding to speak to Wolf in person since the previous morning. He was becoming increasingly aggressive towards the officers assigned to him as time wore on. Apparently Baxter had attended in his stead, only to have been swiftly rebuffed by the boorish man.

When they were called into the meeting room, Wolf took the empty seat beside Baxter, who had reverted to her usual unapproachable self, complete with dark make-up and bored expression.

'Morning,' he said casually.

'Morning,' she replied brusquely, not meeting his eye.

He gave up and turned to speak to Finlay instead.

1. (HEAD) Naguib Khalid 'The Cremation Killer'
2. (TORSO) – ?
3. (LEFT ARM) *platinum ring, law firm?*
4. (RIGHT ARM) *nail varnish?*
5. (LEFT LEG) – ?
6. (RIGHT LEG) Detective Benjamin Chambers

A – ~~Raymond Turnble~~ (Mayor)
B – ~~Vijay Rana/Khalid~~ (Brother/accountant)
C – Jarred Garland (Journalist)
D – Andrew Ford (Security guard/alcoholic/pain in arse)
E – Ashley Lochlan (Waitress) or (nine-year-old girl)
F – Wolf

They all stared at the list in silence, hoping that inspiration might strike and an obvious link would suddenly present itself. They had spent the first twenty minutes of the meeting arguing themselves in circles, which had prompted Simmons to scrawl their current progress up on the flipchart in his almost illegible handwriting. Seeing it written down like this, they had achieved a decidedly underwhelming amount.

'The Cremation Killings must be the key,' said Finlay. 'Khalid, his brother, Will . . .'

'His brother had nothing to do with the trial,' said Simmons, adding an annotation to the list. 'He wasn't even there.'

'Maybe when Alex gets back with a name for us it'll make more sense,' said Finlay with a shrug.

'It won't,' interjected Baxter. 'Edmunds has got twenty-two people who owned those rings. Not one of them was involved in Khalid's trial.'

'Ben was, though, wasn't he?' asked Finlay.

There was an uncomfortable pause on mention of the name. Finlay looked guilty for bringing up his deceased colleague, as though he were just another part of the puzzle.

'Chambers was involved, but no more than anyone else in this room,' Baxter replied unemotionally. 'And even if he was, how would it link to the rest of the list?'

'How thoroughly have we delved into these other people's backgrounds?' asked Simmons.

'We're doing the best we can, but could really use some more help,' said Baxter.

'Well, there isn't any,' snapped Simmons irately. 'I've already got a third of the department helping out on this. I can't spare anyone else.'

Baxter backed off, appreciating the amount of pressure that her chief was under.

'Fawkes, you've been unusually quiet, any thoughts?' asked Simmons.

'If Khalid's trial was the key, why would I be on the same list as him? It makes no sense. They want the Cremation Killer dead but also the person who tried to stop him?'

There was a puzzled silence.

'Could be because it was famous,' suggested Finlay. 'Maybe Ben had a big case that caught his attention too.'

'It's a thought,' said Simmons. 'Look into it.'

At that moment Edmunds burst into the room looking sweaty and dishevelled.

'The ring belonged to Michael Gable-Collins,' he said triumphantly. 'Senior partner at Collins and Hunter.'

'Collins and Hunter? Why does that ring a bell?' asked Finlay.

Wolf shrugged.

'Forty-seven years old, divorced, no children. Interestingly, he attended a partners' meeting last Friday lunchtime,' continued Edmunds.

'So we have an approximate twelve-hour window between that meeting and the discovery of the Ragdoll,' said Simmons, adding the blue-blooded name to the list.

'And he definitely wasn't at the trial?' asked Finlay, ignoring Baxter's exasperated sigh.

'I'm still looking into it, but not directly. No,' said Edmunds.

'So we're no closer to finding a link then?' said Finlay.

'Oh, the trial's the link,' said Edmunds simply.

'But you just said this bloke had nothing to do with it.'

'He did though. They all did. We just haven't worked it out yet. Khalid is the key.'

'But—' Finlay started.

'Moving on,' Simmons interrupted, glancing down at his watch. 'Jarred Garland has requested that Detective Baxter take the lead on his protection. I have discussed this at length with her and expect you all to assist her with anything that she needs.'

'Wait, wait, wait!' exclaimed Wolf.

'She will be out of the office for the remainder of today and tomorrow in relation to this. Fawkes will, of course, be happy to continue work on her enquiries in her absence,' said Simmons firmly.

'I need to be with Garland,' said Wolf.

'You need to consider yourself lucky to still be here at all after the phone call I received from *you-know-who-hyphen-what* this morning.'

'Sir, I have to agree with Wolf on this,' said Edmunds, surprising everyone with his commanding tone. Baxter looked like she might throw something at him. 'The killer has made the challenge to Wolf. If we alter that dynamic there's no telling how he might respond. He will consider it an insult.'

'Good. I certainly hope he does. I've made my decision.'

Edmunds shook his head: 'In my opinion, it's a mistake.'

'I may not have a fancy PhD in Cops and Robbers like you, Edmunds, but, believe it or not, I have dealt with a few murderers in my time,' snapped Simmons.

'Not like this one,' said Edmunds.

Finlay and Baxter shifted uncomfortably in their seats as Edmunds obstinately refused to back down.

'Enough!' shouted Simmons. 'You are still on a probationary period here. You would do well to remember that. The killer will attempt to murder Jarred Garland on Saturday whoever is babysitting him. Garland, on the other hand, will not consent to our involvement *unless* Baxter is the one doing the babysitting.

'Baxter, bring Fawkes up to speed on your work. Thank you all for the headache. Now go away.'

As the meeting adjourned, Edmunds walked over to speak to Baxter.

'You little prick,' she hissed at him. 'What's gotten into you?'

'I—'

'This is a huge deal for me, and it's hard enough without you doubting my abilities and embarrassing me in front of my boss.'

Baxter noticed Wolf loitering in the doorway, waiting for a chance to speak with her in private.

'Know what you're doing the rest of the day?' she asked Edmunds.

'Yes.'

'Then you can explain it to him.'

She got to her feet and stormed out of the room without acknowledging Wolf. Edmunds smiled weakly at him.

'How are you on your nail varnishes?' he asked.

Wolf had phoned the medical examiner to enquire whether they had found anything new in relation to the three unidentified body parts. He was told that they were still running tests and had nothing of investigative value to offer him. He needed to get across to Peckham at some point to meet with Andrew Ford, but was waiting around to speak to Baxter before she left the office.

For some reason Edmunds had suddenly appeared at the end of his desk and had not left, even though Baxter had been in Simmons' office for thirty-five minutes and her station was sitting empty. Edmunds had been attempting to make conversation, but Wolf was too distracted, watching them, to really engage with him.

'I had a thought,' said Edmunds. 'Our killer is methodical, resourceful and clever. He hasn't slipped up once yet. Which got me thinking: he's done this before. Think about it. This person has perfected their art—'

'Art?' asked Wolf dubiously.

'That's how he'll see it, and there's no denying that as awful as the murders are, they are nonetheless, objectively speaking, impressive.'

'Impressive?' Wolf snorted. 'Edmunds, are you the killer?' he asked, straight-faced.

'I want to look into old case files,' this caught Wolf's attention, 'for examples of unusual MOs, murders of supposedly inaccessible victims, amputations and mutilations. Somewhere out there he's left a trail.'

Edmunds had hoped that Wolf would support his idea, perhaps even be impressed by his thinking. Instead, he became angry.

'We have four of us working this case full-time: four! That's it. Do you actually think we can spare you to go swanning about looking for a needle in a haystack while people are dying out there?'

'I was – I was just trying to help,' stammered Edmunds.

'Just do your job,' snapped Wolf as he got to his feet and rushed across the office to intercept Baxter, who had just finished with Simmons.

'Hey,' he said.

'Not happening.'

Baxter had a file in her hands as she strolled past him towards her desk.

'If this is about last night . . .'

'It's not.'

As they passed the meeting room, Wolf grabbed Baxter's wrist and pulled her inside, attracting strange looks from the people sitting nearby.

'Hey!' she shouted.

Wolf closed the meeting room door.

'I'm sorry I walked out last night. We still had things to talk about. She just made me so mad . . . I shouldn't have left you with her. I apologise.'

Baxter looked impatient.

'Do you remember the bit when I said you were beautiful and smart and . . .'

'Amazing,' she reminded him with a smirk.

'Amazing,' nodded Wolf. 'She didn't like that, did she?'

Baxter smiled broadly: 'No. No she didn't.'

'So let me help you with this Garland situation. I can't sit with Edmunds any longer. He tried to paint my nails a few minutes ago!'

Baxter laughed: 'No, but thank you.'

'Come on, you're the boss. I'll do whatever you say.'

'No. You need to be less controlling. You heard Simmons; he's on the verge of taking you off the case altogether. Just drop it.'

Wolf looked desperate.

'Excuse me,' said Baxter, trying to leave the room.

Wolf did not move from the doorway: 'You don't understand. I *need* to help.'

'Excuse me,' she said more forcefully.

Wolf attempted to snatch the file out of her hand. The plastic folder twisted and cracked under the strain as it bridged the space between them. She had seen him like this before, during the Cremation Killer investigation, when she had lost him so entirely to his obsession, when he had no longer been able to tell friend from foe.

'Let . . . go . . . Will.'

She never used his Christian name. She tried again to pull the Garland file free of his grip but couldn't. All she had to do was shout for help. A dozen officers would burst through the door and

Wolf would be taken off the case. She wondered whether she had done the wrong thing by letting it go on this long, by ignoring the signs. She had only wanted to help him, but enough was enough.

'I'm sorry,' she whispered.

She raised her free hand to bang against the frosted glass but, at that moment, Edmunds came blundering into the room, accidentally opening the door into Wolf's back.

Wolf released his grip.

'Sorry,' said Edmunds. 'I've got a Constable Castagna on the phone for you about Andrew Ford.'

'I'll call them back,' said Wolf.

'Apparently he's threatening to jump out of the window.'

'Constable Castagna or Ford?'

'Ford.'

'To escape or kill himself?'

'Fourth floor, so fifty-fifty.'

Wolf smiled at this, and Baxter watched his transformation back into his normal, irreverent self.

'Fine, tell them I'm on my way.'

He smiled warmly at Baxter and followed Edmunds out. Baxter waited out of sight behind the frosted glass. She exhaled deeply and then crouched down before she could fall over. She felt light-headed and emotionally drained from making such a significant decision, only to be left feeling as indecisive as ever. She got back up before anyone entered the room, took a steadying breath, and stepped back out into the office.

CHAPTER 17

Thursday 3 July 2014

3.20 p.m.

Wolf had to catch an overground train to Peckham Rye Station, which felt like an irrationally enormous undertaking to him. To reward himself, he bought an extra-hot, double-shot skinny macchiato with sugar-free syrup but then felt rather emasculated when the man behind simply ordered 'Coffee. Black'.

He ambled along the main road towards a set of three council tower blocks standing proudly over everything else in the vicinity, blissfully unaware or merely undeterred that the rest of the population regarded them as unwelcome eyesores and would tear them down given half a chance. At least the designers of these particular monstrosities had chosen to paint them a perfect 'miserable, drizzly, smoggy, London-sky grey', which rendered them almost invisible for 90 per cent of the year.

Wolf approached the one labelled 'Shakespeare Tower', unconvinced how much of an honour the great man would have considered it, and sighed as he took in the familiar sights and sounds. Perhaps a dozen flags depicting the St George Cross had been draped out of windows, pledging allegiance to this great country or at least to eleven dependably disappointing footballers. A dog, Wolf guessed a Staffordshire bull terrier or German Shepherd, was barking incessantly from the five-foot balcony that it had been shut out on, and an exhibition of rancid undergarments had been displayed, drying in the rain like grotesque modern art.

Some would accuse him of being bigoted or classist, but they had not spent half of their working lives in identical buildings to this all over the city. He felt that he had earned the right to hate them.

As he approached the main entrance, he could hear shouting from round the back of the building. He walked along the side of the tower block and was surprised to find a grubby-looking man, wearing only a vest and underpants, hanging off a balcony above him. Two police officers were trying in vain to pull him back over, and several neighbours had ventured out onto their own balconies, camera phones at the ready in case they were fortunate enough to capture him fall. Wolf watched the bizarre scene in amusement until one pyjama-clad neighbour eventually recognised him.

'Ain't you that detective off of the telly?' she shouted down at him in a husky voice.

Wolf ignored the nosy woman. The man hanging off the balcony suddenly stopped yelling and peered down at him casually sipping his coffee.

'Andrew Ford, I presume?' said Wolf.

'Detective Fawkes?' asked Ford with an Irish twang.

'Yep.'

'I need to talk to you.'

'All right.'

'Not here. Come up.'

'All right.'

Wolf shrugged indifferently and headed for the main entrance while Ford inelegantly clambered back over the railings. When he got upstairs, he met an attractive Asian police officer at the door.

'Are we glad to see you,' she told him.

When she spoke, Wolf noticed the large gap in her smile and could feel himself getting angry.

'Did *he* do that to you?' he asked, gesturing to his own mouth.

'Not intentionally. He was thrashing about and I should have left him to it. My own stupid fault.'

'Bit unstable to be a security guard, isn't he?'

'He's been signed off work for the past year. He basically just drinks and rants now.'

'Where did he work?'

'Debenhams, I think.'

'What does he want with me?'

'He says he knows you.'

Wolf looked surprised: 'Probably arrested him.'

'Probably.'

The officer showed Wolf into the cluttered flat. DVDs and magazines littered the hallway, while the bedroom appeared to be no more than a dumping ground. They entered the poky lounge, where bottles of cheap vodka and boxes of extra-strength lager covered every surface. The only sofa was hidden beneath a cigarette-burned duvet, and the whole place had a faint odour of sweat, vomit, ash and overflowing rubbish.

Andrew Ford was almost ten years his junior, yet looked far older than Wolf. His unkempt hair grew in sporadic patches around his balding head. He was ill-proportioned – gaunt, with a small but defined beer belly, and he had a yellow tinge of jaundice to his skin. Wolf waved in greeting. He had no intention of touching the filthy man.

'Metropolitan police officer and lead investigator on the Ragdoll murders . . . Detective Sergeant William Oliver Layton-Fawkes,' Ford recited excitedly, giving him a short applause. 'But it's Wolf, right? Cool name. Just a wolf amongst sheep, aren't you?'

'Or pigs,' Wolf said indelicately as he looked around the revolting room.

Ford looked as though he was about to attack him but then burst into laughter instead.

'Coz you're a cop. I get your meaning,' he said, in no way getting Wolf's meaning.

'You wanted to talk?' asked Wolf, hoping that Baxter might want to take the lead on this one as well.

'Not with all these . . .' he screamed the next words, 'pigs around!'

Wolf nodded to the two officers and they left the room.

'We're sort of brothers in arms, aren't we?' said Ford. 'Just two upstanding gentlemen of the law.'

Wolf felt it a bit of a leap, the man from Debenhams describing himself as a 'gentleman of the law', but he let it slide. He was, however, getting impatient.

'What did you want to talk about?' he asked.

'I want to help you Wolf.' Ford tilted his head back and howled loudly.

'Well, you're not.'

'You've missed something,' said Ford smugly. 'Something important.'

Wolf waited for him to continue.

'I know something you don't know,' Ford sang childishly, enjoying this unfamiliar position of power.

'That pretty officer whose tooth you knocked out . . .'

'The Indian?' Ford made a dismissive gesture.

'. . . She said you knew me.'

'Oh, I know you Wolf, but you don't remember me at all, do you?'

'So give me a clue.'

'We spent forty-six days in the same room, but we never spoke.'

'OK,' said Wolf uncertainly, hoping that the two officers had not wandered too far.

'I didn't always work at a department store. I used to be somebody.'

Wolf looked blank.

'And I can see that you're still wearing something that I gave you.'

Wolf looked down at his shirt and trousers in confusion. He patted his pockets and glanced at his watch.

'Warmer!'

Wolf rolled up his sleeve, exposing the substantial burns to his left arm and his digital wristwatch. It was only a cheap model that his mother had bought him last Christmas.

'Hot, hot, hot!'

Wolf removed the watch to reveal the rest of the thin white scar that ran across his wrist.

'The dock security officer?' asked Wolf through gritted teeth.

Ford did not answer straight away. He rubbed his face agitatedly and walked over to the kitchen to collect a bottle of vodka.

'You're selling me short,' he finally replied in mock offence. 'I am Andrew Ford: the man who saved the Cremation Killer's life!'

He took an angry swig from the bottle, which dribbled down his chin.

'If I hadn't been so heroic dragging you off him, he wouldn't have survived to murder that last little girl. Saint Andrew! That's what I want on my gravestone. Saint Andrew: assistant child killer.'

Ford began to cry. He slumped down onto the sofa and pulled his disgusting duvet over him, knocking a precariously balanced ashtray over the floor.

'There, that's all. Send those pigs away. I don't want saving. I just wanted to tell you . . . to help you.'

Wolf stared at the wretched creature as it took another swig from the bottle and switched on the television. The theme tune to a children's programme blared at full volume as Wolf showed himself out.

Andrea watched in stunned silence as her cameraman, Rory, dressed as a spaceship captain, beheaded an alien being (that looked suspiciously like his friend Sam) with a Pulse-Bō (foil-covered stick). Green slime exploded liberally from the resultant stump as the rest of the overacting body eventually ceased to move.

Rory hit the pause button.

'So, what d'ya think?'

Rory was in his mid-thirties but was dressed like a scruffy teenager. He was a little overweight, had a thick ginger beard and a friendly face.

'The blood was green,' said Andrea, still a little dazed by the gory video. It had been low-budget but effective.

'He was a *Kruutar* . . . an alien.'

'Right. I appreciate that, but Emily will need to see red blood if we're going to stand any chance of convincing her to do this.'

Andrea had arranged to meet Baxter and Garland at Rory's film studio: StarElf Pictures, which had turned out to be a garage round the back of Brockley Station. Although in no way related to the plan discussed the previous evening, she, Garland, Rory and his co-producer/actor/best friend Sam were debating the best way to fake a person's death while they waited for Baxter to arrive.

After watching over a dozen death scenes from StarElf's back catalogue, they had concluded that eviscerations were problematic, beheadings were realistic but perhaps a little excessive and that explosions occasionally went wrong (Sam's big toe still sat pride of place in a pickling jar above the workstation). The decision was made that a straightforward bullet to the chest was the way to go.

A flustered Baxter had finally arrived forty minutes late and been less than impressed to find Rory and Sam wasting time indulging Garland by setting up a live test of the gunshot. After fifteen solid minutes of arguing and Garland threatening several times to take his chances alone, Baxter begrudgingly agreed to stop shouting long enough to hear them out. She inspected her surroundings dubiously and Garland could tell that she was understandably sceptical regarding the competence of the StarElf team. Fortunately, she was yet to notice the toe-jar above her head.

'I know you have reservations, but we can do this,' Rory enthused as he prepared his presentation. They had met in passing five days earlier, when Baxter had accidentally introduced his beloved camera to the Kentish Town pavement. Luckily Rory was not one to hold a grudge and seemed genuinely excited by the prospect of their clandestine assignment.

He and Sam explained animatedly how the incredibly realistic effect, used in motion pictures and theatre productions all over the world, was achieved by concealing a thin bag (usually a condom) filled with fake blood underneath a person's clothing. A small explosive called a squib, which looked troublingly like a tiny stick of dynamite, was attached to the rear of the bag to propel the blood outwards. They would be using a watch battery to supply the current to spark the contained explosion, powered by a transmitter of Rory's own design. Finally, a thick rubber-lined belt had to be worn between the skin and the explosive to protect from burns and projectiles.

As Andrea stepped outside to make a phone call, Rory bumbled over wielding the Glock 22 that he intended to shoot Garland with and casually offered him the weighty weapon as though it were a bag of crisps. Garland looked uncomfortable as he inexpertly inspected the gun, and Baxter winced as he trustingly peered down the end of the barrel.

'Looks real,' said Garland with a shrug.

'It is,' said Rory cheerfully. 'It's the bullets that aren't.'

He poured a pile of blanks into Garland's hand.

'Cartridges filled with gunpowder to create the muzzle flash and the bang but with no bullet on top.'

'But they remove the firing pins from prop guns, right?' asked Baxter, instinctively ducking as Garland waved it in her general direction.

'Usually they do, yeah,' said Rory, avoiding the obvious question.

'And on this one?' Baxter pushed him.

'Not so much, no.'

Baxter put her head in her hands.

'It's totally legal,' said Rory defensively. 'I've got a licence. We know what we're doing. It's completely safe. Look . . .'

He turned to Sam, who was adjusting one of the video cameras.

'You filming?' he asked.

'Yeah?' said Sam, looking worried.

Without warning, he disengaged the safety and pulled the trigger. There was a deafening bang as a spray of dark red blood exploded out from Sam's chest. Andrea came rushing back inside. Baxter and Garland stared in horror at the rapidly growing puddle of blood. Sam threw his screwdriver down and frowned at Rory.

'I was going to change my t-shirt first, you penis,' he said before returning to the camera.

'That looked incredible!' exclaimed Garland.

They all looked at Baxter expectantly, whose expression remained decidedly unimpressed.

She turned to Garland: 'Could I speak to you outside a minute?'

Baxter unlocked the car so that they could talk in private. She cleared the mess on the passenger seat into the footwell.

'Just to make myself perfectly clear,' she started. 'We are not going to fake your death. It is possibly the stupidest thing I've ever heard.'

'But—'

'I told you I had a plan.'

'But didn't you—'

'We're already placing far too much trust in these people as it is. Can you imagine what would happen if word got out that the Metropolitan Police had been reduced to faking deaths to keep people alive?'

'"To keep people alive", being the important part of that sentence,' said Garland, who was becoming increasingly agitated. 'You're thinking like a police officer!'

'I *am* a police officer.'

'It's my life; it's my decision.'

'I won't do it,' said Baxter. 'Final answer. If you don't want my help, fine. But I've got a plan, and I'm asking you to trust me.'

She pulled a face, appalled by the words that had just come out of her mouth. Garland looked equally surprised. Not one to miss out on an opportunity to use his impending murder as a dating tool, he reached for Baxter's hand.

'OK . . . I trust you,' he said before whimpering pathetically as Baxter twisted his wrist in on itself.

'OK, OK, OK!' he gasped until she finally let go.

'Dinner?' he asked, unperturbed.

'I told you, you're not my type.'

'Successful? Determined? Handsome?'

'Doomed,' said Baxter with a smirk as she watched his self-satisfied expression crumble.

She would never normally have tolerated his sleazy advances, but after her disastrous failed seduction of Wolf the night before, she was quite enjoying the attention.

'Good safety net though, if you didn't fancy a second date,' said Garland, quickly recapturing his self-assurance.

'I suppose it is,' smiled Baxter.

'Is that a *yes* then?' asked Garland hopefully.

'No,' she said, smiling.

'But it's not a *no* either, is it?'

Baxter thought about it for a moment: 'No.'

A towering floodlight cast counterfeit moonlight over the seemingly endless underground archives, spilling long shadows across row after row of metal shelving units and reaching down the narrow aisles like fingers extending out of the dark. Edmunds had lost all track of time as he sat reading, cross-legged, on the hard warehouse floor. Scattered around him lay the contents of the seventeenth cardboard evidence box on his list: photographs, DNA samples, witness statements.

With both Baxter and Wolf otherwise engaged, he had seized this opportunity to visit the Central Storage Warehouse, located in a secure facility on the outskirts of Watford. Over a gruelling five-year period, the inconceivable feat of scanning, logging and photographing every record held by the Metropolitan Police had been completed; however, the physical evidence still had to be retained.

While items relating to lesser crimes could be returned to the families or destroyed after a period of time set by the court, all evidence concerning homicide or serious crimes was kept indefinitely. This would be stored locally at the relevant police station for a time, dependent on space and resources, and then transferred to the secure temperature-controlled archives. Cases were so often reopened when fresh evidence came to light, appeals were made or when advancements in technology revealed something new, that these assorted souvenirs of death would be preserved to long outlive those involved.

Edmunds stretched his arms out and yawned. He had heard another person wheeling a trolley a couple of hours earlier but was now alone in the colossal warehouse. He packed the evidence carefully back into the box, finding nothing to suggest a connection between this headless victim and the Ragdoll Killer. Sliding the box back onto the shelf, he crossed it off his list. It was only then that he realised the time: 7.47 p.m. Cursing loudly, he jogged towards the distant exit.

His phone was returned to him once he had passed through security and he climbed up the stairs to ground level to discover that he had five missed calls from Tia. He had to return the pool car to New Scotland Yard and drop into the office before he could even think about heading home. He dialled Tia's number and braced himself for her reaction.

Wolf was approaching the end of his second pint of Estrella as he sat outside the Dog & Fox on Wimbledon high street. He was the only person braving the chilly outdoor tables, especially now that an ominous rain cloud had settled overhead, but he did not want to miss Baxter returning home to her trendy apartment across the street.

At 8.10 p.m. he saw her black Audi almost take out a pedestrian on the corner before parking up the side road. He abandoned the rest of his now lukewarm beer and started making his way over. He was ten metres away when Baxter climbed out of the car laughing. Then the passenger door swung open and a man he did not recognise stepped out.

'One of these places must sell snails, and I'm doing it,' said the man.

'I don't think the idea's to bring your last meal back up,' said Baxter with a smirk.

'I refuse to go without first putting a disgusting, slimy, dirty mollusc into my mouth.'

Baxter opened the boot, removed her bags and then locked the car. Wolf, sensing an awkward situation developing, panicked and crouched behind a postbox as they started to approach. Baxter and her acquaintance had actually walked past him before noticing the imposing man crawling on the pavement.

'Wolf?' asked Baxter in disbelief.

Wolf casually got back to his feet and smiled, as if this was how they normally greeted one another.

'Hi,' he said, before offering his hand to the sharply dressed man. 'Wolf – or Will.'

'Jarred,' said Garland, shaking his hand.

Wolf looked surprised: 'Oh you're . . .'

He let the question disintegrate when he noticed Baxter's impatient expression.

'What the hell are you doing here? Why were you hiding?'

'I was worried it might be awkward,' mumbled Wolf, gesturing towards Garland.

'And it's not now?' she asked, going red. 'Could you give us a moment?' she said to Garland, who wandered up towards the high street.

'I was coming to see you to apologise for last night and this morning and, well, everything really,' said Wolf. 'I thought we might grab a bite to eat, but it looks like you've already got . . . plans.'

'It's not what it looks like.'

'It doesn't look like anything.'

'Good, because it's not.'

'I'm glad.'

'You are?'

The conversation was becoming excruciating with all that was not being said.

'I'm gonna go,' said Wolf.

'You do that,' replied Baxter.

He turned around and walked away in the opposite direction to the station, just to escape. Baxter swore under her breath, angry with herself, and then went to join Garland at the end of the road.

CHAPTER 18

Friday 4 July 2014

5.40 a.m.

Baxter had barely slept. She and Garland had had dinner at the Café Rouge down the road, which, as luck would have it, had run out of escargots. In feigned disappointment, Garland had promptly ordered a steak instead before the dubiously French waiter could suggest some other inedible delicacy. She had been too distracted by Wolf's impromptu visit to be much company and, despite his best efforts, had arranged for Garland's protection detail to collect him from the restaurant by 10 p.m.

She struggled to carry her bags up the narrow stairs to her apartment alone but knew that Garland would have read imaginary subtext into her acceptance of his offer of help. She unlocked the door and stumbled into her pristine one-bed flat. Her cat, Echo, came skidding across the wooden floor to greet her in the hallway. The temperature was refreshingly cool thanks to a gentle breeze pouring in from the open skylight. After kicking her shoes off on the mat, she carried her things through to the bedroom and set them down on the thick white carpet. After feeding Echo, she treated herself to a large glass of red wine, collected her laptop from the living room and climbed onto the bed.

She had spent over fifty minutes clicking around aimlessly on the Internet, checking her emails, catching up on over a month's worth of news on Facebook. Another one of her friends was pregnant, and she had received an invite to a hen do in Edinburgh. She adored Scotland but wrote an unnaturally girly message apologising for not being able to make it without even checking her diary.

Her mind kept returning to Wolf. He had made it quite clear how he felt, or rather did not feel, the previous night. She now had bruises on her arm from where he had grabbed her earlier in the day and then he had shown up wanting to take her out for dinner. Had this just been out of guilt? Had he regretted rejecting her? Was she sure that he *had* even rejected her? Bored thinking about it, she poured herself another glass and switched on the television.

With Garland not due to die until Saturday, the Ragdoll murders had taken a backseat on the late-night news programmes, which were more concerned with the capsized oil tanker off the coast of Argentina that was leaking over three hundred gallons of oil per hour towards the Falkland Islands. Garland had grown on her a little over dinner, but she had to admit that, even on Saturday, he would have been upstaged by the poor little penguins retreating from the encroaching sludge.

Only when they had exhausted every conceivable topic of conversation relating to the oil spill, share prices, the assorted wildlife of the Falklands, the unsubstantiated possibility of terrorist involvement, the likelihood of the oil travelling across the Atlantic Ocean to pollute British shores (none whatsoever), did they return to the murders to debate the rationale behind Garland's very public approach to the threat against him. Doing nothing to calm her nerves, Baxter switched the television off and read a book into the early hours.

Just after 6 a.m. she opened up her laptop and went to the newspaper's website. Due to the unprecedented demand for Garland's *Dead Man Talking* column, the paper had been uploading the latest edition every morning at the same time, turning the web page into a prime piece of cyber real estate. An irritating video either selling perfume, make-up or a Charlize Theron movie refused to close down in the centre of the screen. When it eventually disappeared of its own accord, the short statement that she and Andrea had prepared together materialised. It had already had over a hundred thousand hits:

One hour exclusive interview to the highest bidder (by 09:30 BST), to take place Saturday morning at an undisclosed London hotel. 0845 954600.

Despite Garland's openness in his articles throughout the week, Andrea had been confident that the lure of a worldwide exclusive with the man fated to die would prove too enticing to resist. Baxter's plan was no more than a simple diversion. With Andrea's assistance they would pre-record a half-hour interview with Garland, which would then be broadcast 'live' on Saturday morning. When the worldwide media inevitably descended upon their chosen hotel in the capital, erroneously advertising Garland's whereabouts to the killer, he would already be safe in the hands of Protected Persons on the other side of the country.

The effectiveness of the plan was routed in its banal plausibility: the greed and self-exploitation of the opportunistic journalist, the ensuing dogfight between the infinitely powerful news companies and the assumed anonymity of a 'secret' rendezvous. They had set up a recorded message requesting that bidders state their offer and leave contact details. This was futile, of course, but would justify Andrea's presence, television camera on hand, at the hotel. Garland had chosen the lobby of the ME London in Covent Garden as the setting for the deception. When Baxter had asked why, he simply answered that it was going to look 'mind-blowing' on camera.

She checked the time, shut down her laptop and got changed into her workout clothes. The sun had just risen high enough over the city to blaze through the living room windows as she stepped onto the treadmill. Closing her eyes against the blinding sun, she put in her earphones and turned up the volume until she could no longer hear the rhythmic thudding of her steps.

*

Sam was already getting Garland set up when Andrea arrived at the freshly graffiti-tagged door to StarElf Pictures. She had received a call from Garland late the previous night, in which he had begged her to help him.

'You know we can pull this off,' he had said.

'I'm sure Emily has her reasons for saying no,' reasoned Andrea.

'Her hands are tied by the police, yours aren't . . . *Please.*'

'I could speak to Emily again.'

'She'll stop us.' Garland sounded desperate. 'Once it's done, she's got no choice but to play along. She knows as well as we do it's my best shot.'

There was a long pause before Andrea replied.

'Be at StarElf by eight,' she sighed, praying that she was doing the right thing.

'Thank you.'

Andrea stepped inside. Garland was unbuttoning his shirt while Sam fiddled with the transmitter.

'Morning. That's some exquisite new artwork on the door,' she complimented Sam.

'Those bloody skater kids trying to get in again,' he muttered, heading back across the room to Garland. 'I've told Rory to stop letting them in here.'

'Pass us the padding, will you?' said Sam, gesturing to the thick protective belt on the desk behind her, which would absorb the force of the modest explosion.

She picked it up, feeling the hard rubber lining beneath the thin material, and handed it to him. Without his shirt on, Garland was surprisingly skinny, and the entire left side of his body was peppered in unattractive moles. He had replicated David Beckham's famous guardian angel tattoo across his upper back, which looked absurd mounted on such an unsubstantial canvas.

'Breathe in,' said Sam, who wrapped the material around Garland's ribcage and fastened it up at the back.

He then attached the condom filled with fake blood, one of the squibs from the box and the watch battery receiver. While Garland got dressed again, Andrea made Sam check and double-check the gun and blanks. It felt wrong to be going behind Baxter's back like this, so she figured the least she could do was ensure that no detail was overlooked.

Sam had bestowed some last-minute acting advice upon Garland regarding how to die convincingly. She hoped he was not listening, having already endured his disembowelled ogre making a rambling ten-minute speech and his rookie police officer sneezing at his own funeral.

Sam left twenty minutes before Baxter arrived, a balaclava, the transmitter and the blank-loaded gun concealed on his person.

'Nervous?' asked Andrea, hearing Baxter's car crunching over the gravel outside.

'About tomorrow, yeah,' replied Garland.

'Well, if this morning goes to plan . . .'

'That's what I'm nervous about. We've got no way of knowing, do we? We'll only know whether he bought it or not when he either tries to kill me – or not.'

'Which is why Emily's getting you as far away from London as possible tonight – unless she's killed us both herself before then, of course,' joked Andrea anxiously.

Baxter walked in through the door and checked her watch: 'Time to go.'

Baxter had not known what she was expecting, but it definitely was not this. On arrival at the hotel, she and Garland had been ushered into a black lift, which took them up to the lobby. The doors slid apart and she had only taken a few steps across the glossy black floor before pausing to gawp in wonder at the surreal reception area.

They were standing in the mood-lit base of a huge marble pyramid. A curiously oversized book lay open on a stand in front of them, while white sofas reflected in the dark floor, as though they stood in water. The scattered side tables and substantial reception desk, like flawless blocks of obsidian, looked to have grown naturally up out of the floor. Animated jellyfish were projected onto the polished marble walls, swimming against gravity as they climbed the inside of the pyramid and fading into oblivion where the sun burned through a triangle of natural light over a hundred feet above.

'Come on,' said Garland, pleased to have finally impressed the determinedly unimpressed Baxter.

A member of staff handed them each a glass of Prosecco and then led them over to one of the leather sofas when Garland told her that they were meeting somebody. If she recognised either of them, she had shown no sign of it.

'I really enjoyed dinner last night,' said Garland as he watched the mesmerising jellyfish struggling to escape the pyramid.

'Yeah, food's always good,' said Baxter evasively.

'I meant the company.'

'Café Rouge?'

Garland smiled and took the hint to leave the subject for the time being.

'Where are we going afterwards? You know, after the interview?' he whispered.

Baxter shook her head and ignored the question.

'No one can hear us,' he hissed.

'Protected Persons already have a house set up from . . .'

'The last person you couldn't save,' Garland finished bitterly.

Baxter failed to notice Sam walking through the reception area and into the toilets but did register the abrupt change in Garland.

'They're here,' he said nervously.

Andrea was still on the phone to Elijah when she and Rory entered ME London. As the lift doors closed, she lost reception, cutting Elijah off as he listed the questions that she was to ask Garland. He wanted her to gear the interview so that Garland came across as challenging the killer, defiant until the end.

'No one likes a massacre,' he had said moments earlier. 'People want a fight.'

She had not bothered to phone him back after stepping into the magnificent lobby. Rory had gone off to get some filler shots of the giant book and the pyramid, although, they were all confident that the footage was more likely to feature in his next movie. The member of staff who had not recognised Baxter or Garland certainly recognised Andrea and looked excitedly at the group making a show of the introductions. The news of Garland auctioning off his final interview had been widely reported all morning. Andrea caught the woman before she could scuttle off.

'This is a distinguished hotel,' said Andrea. 'We may be having a dry run now but we are under no obligation to return tomorrow for the real thing. As such, I expect nothing less than the utmost discretion from you and your colleagues. Make sure that they are also aware of my expectations.'

'Of course,' smiled the woman, as though it had never crossed her mind to take a discreet selfie with the Ragdoll Killer's next victim. She walked over to reception to reprimand the staff who were watching them avidly.

'Do you think she bought it?' asked Andrea.

'Maybe,' replied Baxter, looking concerned. 'Let's just do the interview and get out of here.'

Edmunds had spent another night on the sofa. By the time he had returned home, just after 10 p.m., Tia was already asleep and had locked him out of their bedroom. He stayed up into the early hours, Googling further murder cases to look into.

He had spent the morning researching background information on Michael Gable-Collins. By leaving the platinum ring on the Ragdoll's hand, the killer evidently had wanted them to identify him, although it was not clear why. Positive that Khalid was the key to everything, Edmunds had worked tirelessly and eventually found the link between them.

The law firm, Collins and Hunter, had represented Khalid in court; however, Michael Gable-Collins had no other attachment to the case. He had never attended a single day of the trial and, as a partner and a specialist in family law, had no involvement in the preparation work, which appeared to have been supervised by Charlotte Hunter.

Although the law firm took on hundreds of cases each year, he was confident that it was more than just coincidence and arrived at work early to continue his search for a link between them all. He had compiled a full list of names attached to the Khalid trial, from lawyers to witnesses, the staff, to the people who had signed into the public gallery. He would go through each of them one by one if he had to.

Andrea performed her introduction into the camera and was a little unsettled by the thought of the colossal audience soon to critique their scarcely rehearsed theatre piece.

'. . . joined this morning by journalist Jarred Garland, the third victim named by the Ragdoll Killer. Good morning, Jarred.'

Rory adjusted position to frame both Andrea and Garland in the shot. They were sitting opposite each other on the white leather sofas.

'Thank you for speaking to us during what must be an unimaginably difficult time for you. Let's begin with the most obvious question: why? Why has this person, this serial killer, chosen you?'

Baxter was engrossed in the interview. She could tell that Garland was on edge. He was scared; something was wrong. The door to the men's toilets creaked open, and Sam stepped out into the lobby unnoticed, dressed all in black with the balaclava covering his face. He was already holding the gun in his right hand.

'I wish I knew,' said Garland. 'As I'm sure you have experienced yourself, Ms Hall, working in journalism doesn't always make you friends.'

They both forced a nervous laugh.

There was a shriek from one of the women on reception, and Rory spun with the camera to film the approaching gunman. Baxter instinctively rushed at the masked man and did not slow even when she recognised his vaguely familiar voice and it dawned on her what was happening.

'Goddamn you, Jarred Garland, you son of a bitch!' he improvised.

Rory ran out of the gunman's way and turned the camera back on Garland, who looked terrified as he got to his feet. The gunshot was deafening, resonating off the polished surfaces, and Andrea screamed on cue as blood exploded out from the centre of Garland's chest. Baxter landed heavily on top of Sam as Garland fell back onto the sofa as planned – and then a blinding white light appeared from the wound, spitting sparks across the black floor. He started screaming over the hissing sound, like a firework burning, thrashing about and clawing at the belt around his chest.

Dropping the camera, Rory raced over to help him. He could hear glass shattering and felt the intense heat radiating from the spark as it orbited Garland's body. In his panic, he reached desperately for the fastening and then realised, in revulsion, that his fingers had disappeared deep within Garland's chest cavity.

He then tried pulling forcefully on the belt, but most of the rubber lining had already melted into the skin. There was another sound, like glass shattering, and Rory fell back onto the floor as some sort of liquid burned away the skin on his hands.

Baxter ran over in a daze.

'Don't!' shouted Rory in agony. 'It's acid!'

'Call an ambulance!' Baxter ordered the reception staff.

All of a sudden, having completed its circle, the white spark died out. Only the sound of Garland's laboured breathing remained. Baxter ran to the sofa and took Garland's hand.

'You're gonna be all right,' she promised him. 'Andrea . . . Andrea!'

Andrea was sitting staring at him in paralysed shock. Slowly, she turned to look at Baxter.

'Reception must have a first aid kit with burns dressings. Go get it,' Baxter instructed her, unsure whether he had been burned by acid or heat or something else entirely.

Several sets of sirens were already approaching as Andrea returned to the sofa with the basic first aid box. Every gasp was clearly agony for Garland. He had rested his head back on the sofa, watching the jellyfish climbing the walls, heading towards the light at the end of the tunnel.

Baxter met Andrea's eye as she took hold of the box.

'What have you done?' she asked in horror, before turning back to Garland. 'You're gonna be all right,' she said again soothingly, even though she knew she was lying. Part of his melted shirt had fallen away, and she could see a section of his charred lung fighting to inflate between two ribs. She did not even want to imagine the damage that was obscured from her view. 'You're gonna be all right.'

Armed police flooded the lobby and surrounded Sam, who had at least had the sense to drop the gun before they arrived. Once it was deemed safe, paramedics followed them inside and carefully lifted Garland onto a stretcher. Baxter saw them share a telling look before rushing him towards the lifts. Another crew were wrapping burns dressings around Rory's disfigured hands.

Where Garland had been sitting, splinters of glass sparkled in the ambient lighting. The largest piece looked like a thin rod that had broken at the top. She could see several spots on the sofa where the leather had burned away entirely. She got up and followed the paramedics to the lifts, determined to stay by Garland's side for as long as he was still with them.

Edmunds looked around the office in confusion. He had been so immersed in his work that he had not noticed the rest of his colleagues abandoning their desks to gather round the large television. A stunned silence had fallen over the department, bar the ever-ringing phones and Simmons' muffled voice coming from inside his office, undoubtedly speaking with the commissioner.

Edmunds got up. As he approached the back of the crowd, he caught a fleeting glimpse of Andrea on screen. Although no stranger to televised appearances, she clearly was not featuring in the context that he and the rest of the country had grown accustomed to. Instead of sitting behind a desk, she was running alongside paramedics as the shaky camera phone footage struggled to keep her in frame. He spotted Baxter in the background, leaning over someone on a stretcher. It could only have been Jarred Garland.

At last, they cut back to the newsroom. Edmunds' colleagues began returning to their desks and, gradually, conversations started up again. It had been common knowledge that Baxter had taken the lead on Garland's protection and many had criticised her decision to allow the man, who had been so publicly damning of their work, to appear on live television.

Several new questions were now being asked: why had Baxter been parading Garland around in public anyway? Was the person who shot him the Ragdoll Killer? What had actually happened to him? Conflicting reports said that he had either been shot or burned up.

Only one question interested Edmunds however: why had the killer acted a day early?

CHAPTER 19

Friday 4 July 2014

2.45 p.m.

Due to the severity and unknown etiology of Garland's injuries, he had been blue-lighted directly to A & E at the Chelsea and Westminster Hospital, where a consultant from their specialist burns unit had been standing by. Baxter had held his hand the entire journey and only let go when a domineering staff nurse had demanded that she leave the room.

Andrea and Rory had arrived in a second ambulance minutes later. From what Baxter could see beneath the glutinous burns dressing, his left hand looked as weepy and sore as it had back at the hotel, but a large chunk of flesh was now missing from his right palm, the injury more closely resembling a bite wound than a burn. The paramedic returned from speaking with the staff nurse and led Rory away to see the consultant.

Baxter and Andrea sat, not talking to one another, outside a Starbucks down the road. Garland had been rushed up to surgery over two hours earlier, and they were yet to hear anything from Rory. Baxter spent the majority of that time trying to find out where Sam had been taken, in order to corroborate the outrageous story that was, undoubtedly, falling on deaf ears.

'I just don't understand what happened,' mumbled Andrea as she fiddled with a broken coffee stirrer.

Baxter ignored her. She had already made it quite clear that asking for Andrea's help had been one of the biggest mistakes she had ever made and that she genuinely wondered whether there was something fundamentally wrong with her.

'You literally can't be trusted with anything,' Baxter had told her. 'Does that not sink in when everything you seem to touch turns to shit?'

She was tempted to relight their argument but decided that no good could come from it, and Andrea clearly already felt as guilty and upset as Baxter did.

'I thought I was helping him,' said Andrea, talking to herself. 'It's like you said: if we could just save one of them, it all wouldn't seem quite so hopeless for Will.'

Baxter hesitated, electing whether or not to tell Andrea about him blockading her inside the meeting room the previous morning. She decided to keep it to herself.

'I think we're going to lose him,' whispered Andrea.

'Garland?'

'Will.'

Baxter shook her head: 'We're not.'

'You two should . . . If you want to . . . You seem . . . He should be happy.'

Baxter somehow deciphered Andrea's garbled meaning but ignored the implied question.

'We're not,' she said again firmly.

*

I.M SORRY. ILL COOK 4US 2NT. LOVE U X

Edmunds was sitting at his half of Baxter's desk, trying to text Tia without Simmons seeing. She had ignored his first three apologies.

'Edmunds!' barked Simmons, directly behind him. 'If you've got time to text, you've got time to go to forensics and find out what the hell happened today.'

'Me?'

'Yes, you,' spat Simmons, who stared in abhorrence towards his office when the phone started ringing again. 'Fawkes and Finlay are on the other side of the country and Baxter's still at the hospital. So that leaves me, you, and only you.'

'Yes, sir.'

Edmunds packed away what he was working on, quickly tidied the desk so Baxter would not shout at him, and left the office.

'How's she doing?' asked Joe, looking as monk-like as ever as he washed his hands in the forensics lab. 'I saw the news.'

'I think the entire country did,' said Edmunds. 'I haven't heard from her, but Simmons has. She's still at the hospital with Garland.'

'That's thoughtful of her, but unnecessary, I'm afraid.'

'They're operating on him, so they must think there's a chance.'

'There isn't. I've spoken to the burns specialist there to make him aware of what they're up against.'

'Which is?'

Joe waved Edmunds over to a workstation, where pieces of shattered glass, collected from the hotel sofa, waited under a microscope. A few drops of residual liquid sat pathetically at the bottom of a test tube. A metal rod, attached by wires to a piece of equipment, had been dipped into it. What remained of the protective belt had been laid out on a tray, pieces of Garland's skin still clinging sickeningly to the rubber.

'I take it you're aware they were trying to simulate a gunshot to fake Garland's death?' asked Joe.

Edmunds nodded: 'Simmons told us.'

'Good plan. Brave,' said Joe genuinely. 'So, how does one murder someone with a fake gunshot? Modify the gun? Swap out the blank bullets? Replace the tame explosive behind the blood bag, right?'

'I guess.'

'Wrong! All these things would be checked and double-checked. So our killer decided to refashion the protective belt that would be strapped across Garland's chest. It's just a strip of rubber inside some material, no threat to anyone.'

Edmunds moved over to the remnants of the belt, covering his nose against the stench of scorched flesh. Several strands of charred metal protruded haphazardly out from the rubber.

'Strips of magnesium coiled around the rubber lining,' said Joe, apparently indifferent to the smell, 'wrapped around his chest and burning through the poor bastard at a few thousand degrees Celsius.'

'So, when they triggered the blood bag . . .'

'They ignited the magnesium coil. I found some accelerant coating the sections at the front to ensure that it caught.'

'Where does the glass fit into all of this?' asked Edmunds.

'Overkill, if you'll excuse the term. The killer wanted to ensure that Garland wouldn't survive. So, he strapped several vials of acid to the inside of the belt for good measure, which then exploded into his exposed flesh under the intense heat . . . Oh, and not forgetting the fatal spasms and oedema on inhalation of the toxic vapour.'

'Jesus.' Edmunds was scribbling frantically in his notebook. 'What sort of acid?'

'I'm not really doing it justice by calling it an acid. This stuff is worse, far worse. It's what they call a superacid, probably triflic, approximately a thousand times stronger than your run-of-the-mill sulphuric acid.'

Edmunds took a step back from the innocent-looking test tube.

'And Garland's got this stuff eating away at his insides?' said Edmunds.

'You see my point? It's hopeless.'

'This stuff must be hard to get hold of?'

'Yes and no,' answered Joe unhelpfully. 'It's widely used industrially as a catalyst, and there's a concerning demand for it on the black market for its weaponisable qualities.'

Edmunds sighed heavily.

'Not to fear, you've got far more promising leads to look into,' said Joe cheerfully. 'I found something on the Ragdoll.'

Baxter stepped away from the table to take a call from the hospital. In her absence, Andrea unenthusiastically removed her work phone from her bag and switched it on. Eleven missed calls: nine from Elijah and two from Geoffrey, received before she remembered to tell him she was safe. There was one new voicemail. She braced herself and held the phone to her ear.

'Where are you? Hospital? Been trying to get hold of you for hours,' started Elijah, inconvenienced. 'Spoke to one of the staff at the hotel. She said you were filming something when it happened. I need that footage here, now. I've sent techie Paul over to the hotel with a spare key to the van. He'll upload it from there. Call me when you get this.'

Baxter returned to the table to find Andrea looking shaken.

'What?' she asked.

Andrea put her head in her hands: 'Oh God.'

'What?'

Andrea looked up at Baxter in resignation.

'They've got the footage,' she said. 'I'm sorry.'

Everything she touched really did turn to shit.

They had been called back to the hospital and were forced to barge their way through the wall of television cameras and reporters that had besieged the main entrance. Andrea noticed that Elijah had sent Isobel and her cameraman to report on this latest horrifying incident that she now found herself at the centre of.

'Taste of your own medicine,' Baxter pointed out after a police officer allowed them through and they had reached the safety of the lifts.

A nurse showed them into a private room, and Baxter could tell instantly from her demeanour what she was about to say: despite their best efforts, the extent of the damage was too great and Garland's heart had stopped on the operating table.

Even though she had been expecting this and had only known Garland for three days, she broke down into tears. It was impossible to imagine ever ridding herself of such an immense burden of guilt. She could almost physically feel it pulling in her chest. He had been her responsibility. Perhaps had he not felt that he had to plan it all behind her back . . . Perhaps if she . . .

The nurse told them that Garland's sister had been informed and was alone in a room down the hall if they wanted to sit with her, but Baxter could not face it. She asked Andrea to wish Rory a speedy recovery and left the hospital as quickly as she could.

Joe removed the now infamous Ragdoll corpse from the freezer and wheeled it into the centre of the lab. Edmunds had hoped to never see the horrible thing again. As a final insult to the poor woman whose torso had already been so gruesomely connected to five separate body parts, a fresh set of stitches now ran along the centre of her chest, forking off between her small breasts and ending at either shoulder. Though they had established at the crime scene that the amputations and mutilations had taken place after death, he could not help but feel that this nameless pale-skinned woman had been punished the most.

'You found something in the post-mortem?' asked Edmunds, feeling unfairly angry at Joe for the one misaligned stitch he had spotted.

'Huh? No, nothing.'

'So?'

'Take a moment and then tell me what's not right about this body.'

Edmunds gave him a despairing look.

'Apart from the obvious, of course,' Joe added.

Edmunds looked over the grotesque cadaver, not that he really needed to. He doubted that he would ever be able to shake the image from his memory. He hated being in the same room as it. Although it was completely irrational, there was still something macabre about it. He looked back at Joe blankly.

'No? Look at the legs. Taking into account that they're different skin colours and sizes, they have been cut and attached almost symmetrically. But the arms are a different story altogether: one complete female arm on one side . . .'

'Not that we needed the entire arm to identify the nail polish,' Edmunds chimed in.

'. . . and then just a hand and a ring on the other.'

'So the arm belonging to the torso must be significant in some way,' said Edmunds, catching up.

'And it is.'

Joe took several images from a folder and handed them to Edmunds, who flicked through them in confusion.

'It's a tattoo.'

'It's a tattoo that she had removed. Very effectively, I might add. Metallic content from the ink is still visible through radiography, but the infrared image is even clearer.'

'What is it?' asked Edmunds as he flipped the image upside down.

'Your job,' smiled Joe.

Simmons had been sitting in his stifling office with the commander for over an hour, listening to her make her usual threats that she was only ever 'passing on' from above. She had then reiterated several times that she was on his side before criticising his detectives, his department as a whole, and his own ability to manage them. He could barely breathe in the windowless room and could feel his temper fraying as the temperature continued to soar.

'I want DS Baxter suspended, Terrence.'

'For what, precisely?'

'Need I spell it out? She basically killed Jarred Garland herself with this, frankly ridiculous, plan.'

He was so tired of listening to the torrent of self-righteous poison that seemed to flow perpetually from this woman. He could feel sweat running down the side of his head and fanned himself with an incredibly important piece of paperwork.

'She swears she knew nothing about it,' said Simmons. 'And I believe her.'

'In which case she is incompetent at best,' retorted Vanita.

'Baxter's one of my best detectives and is more dedicated to, and familiar with, this case than anybody – apart from Fawkes.'

'Another of your impending catastrophes. Do you think I don't know the consultant psychiatrist has advised that he take a step back from the case?'

'Well, I've got a serial killer out there who, through the medium of terrifying corpse pointing through window, has expressed his expectation of Fawkes' involvement,' snapped Simmons, a little more harshly than he had intended.

'Terrence, do yourself a favour. You need to show that you condemn Baxter's reckless actions.'

'She didn't know! So what would you have suggested she do differently?'

He was losing his temper now. He just wanted to get out of the cramped little sweatbox.

'For starters, I—'

'Wait a minute, I don't give a damn,' he snarled, 'because you have *no idea* what my team are dealing with out there, and how could you? You're not a police officer.'

Vanita smirked at his uncharacteristic outburst.

'And are you, Terrence? Really? Sat here in your little cupboard. You made a conscious decision to become a manager. You had best start acting like it.'

Simmons was momentarily derailed by her scathing remark. He had never thought of himself as being isolated from the rest of his team.

'I will not suspend, reassign or even reprimand Baxter for doing her job and putting her life on the line today.'

Vanita got to her feet, revealing the full extent of her garish outfit.

'We'll see what the commissioner has to say about that. I've scheduled a press conference for five o'clock. We need to make a formal statement about what happened this morning.'

'Do it your damn self,' snapped Simmons, also getting to his feet.

'I beg your pardon?'

'I will not be doing any more press conferences, listening to any more of your arse-covering politics or sitting in here on the phone while my colleagues are out there in harm's way.'

'Think very carefully before you continue.'

'Oh, I'm not resigning. I've just got more useful things to be doing right now. You can see yourself out.'

Simmons slammed the door as he left. He cleared a space at Chambers' empty desk and booted up the computer.

Baxter was at her desk by the time Edmunds returned to the office. He did a double-take as he passed Simmons, who was on the Internet researching Garland's most controversial stories. Hurrying over to her, he gave her a hug and, astonishingly, she did not shy away.

'I've been worried about you,' he said as he took a seat.

'I had to stick around until . . . for Garland.'

'He really didn't stand a chance,' said Edmunds. He filled her in on his conversation with Joe and the discovery of the tattoo.

'We need to start by—'

'*You* need to start by,' corrected Baxter. 'I'm off the case.'

'What?'

'Simmons told me the commander's pushing for my suspension. At the very least, I should expect to be reassigned by Monday. Simmons will take my place and Finlay's agreed to babysit you.'

Edmunds had never seen Baxter so downtrodden. He was about to suggest that they get out of the office, take the infrared images around some tattoo parlours, when the scruffy internal mailman approached them.

'DS Emily Baxter?' he asked, holding a thin, handwritten envelope decorated with courier stickers.

'That's me.'

She took the envelope off him and was about to tear it open when she realised he was still staring at her.

'Yes?'

'Normally flowers I'm luggin' up 'ere for you, ain't it? Where are they all anyways?'

'Bagged up as evidence, tested by forensics, and burned after they killed a man,' she said matter-of-factly. 'Thanks for bringing them up here though.'

Edmunds smirked as the dumbfounded man turned and swaggered away without another word. Baxter ripped the envelope open. A thin coil of magnesium dropped out onto the desk. She and Edmunds shared a concerned look, and he passed her a pair of disposable gloves. She pulled out a photograph of her climbing into the back of the ambulance alongside Garland's stretcher. It had been taken from the perspective of the large crowd that had gathered to watch the ensuing chaos outside the hotel. A message had been scrawled on the back of the picture:

If you won't play by the rules, neither shall I.

'He's getting closer, just like you said he would,' said Baxter.

'He can't help himself,' said Edmunds as he closely examined the photograph.

'It's properly punctuated.'

'Not too big a surprise. He's obviously well educated,' said Edmunds.

'"If you won't play by the rules, neither shall I",' Baxter read aloud.

'I don't buy it.'

'You don't think it's him?'

'Oh, I think it's him. I just don't buy it. I wasn't going to bring this up today with all you've been through but—'

'I'm fine,' insisted Baxter.

'Something isn't right. Why would he murder Garland a day earlier than he said?'

'To punish us. To punish Wolf for not being there.'

'That's what he wants us to think. But he's gone back on his word at the expense of a perfect score sheet. He would see this as a failure on his part.'

'What's your point?'

'Something spooked him into murdering Garland early. He panicked. Either we got too close or he genuinely believed that he wouldn't be able to get to Garland tomorrow.'

'He was going into witness protection.'

'So was Rana before Elizabeth Tate got to him first. Besides, no one but you knew that's where he was going. So, what was different?'

'Me? I was in charge. Neither the team or Wolf were involved.'

'Exactly.'

'What are you saying?'

'I'm saying that either we accept the possibility that the killer has all of us under surveillance and believed this morning to be his last chance before Garland disappeared . . .'

'Seems unlikely.'

'. . . or that somebody with in-depth knowledge of the case is leaking him information.'

Baxter laughed and shook her head.

'Wow, you really know how to make friends, don't you?'

'I hope I'm wrong,' said Edmunds.

'You are. Who here would want Wolf dead?'

'No idea.'

Baxter thought about it for a moment.

'So what do we do?' she asked.

'We keep this between the two of us.'

'Naturally.'

'And then we set a trap.'

CHAPTER 20

Friday 4 July 2014

6.10 p.m.

Wolf awoke to discover that he was back in London. He and Finlay had driven the entire breadth of the country and back in order to surrender Andrew Ford to the Protected Persons team. Neither of them knew Ford's final destination, although, they could be reasonably confident that it was a remote location in South Wales, having rendezvoused with the officers in the car park of the Pontsticill Reservoir, somewhere in the Brecon Beacons.

Ford had been tiresome company during the four-hour drive, especially after news of Garland's premature demise had reached the mainstream radio stations. When they pulled into a service station, Wolf had attempted to phone Baxter but only got her voicemail. Finlay resigned himself to buying their passenger a bottle of vodka for the remainder of the journey, in the hope that it might shut him up for a little while.

'Here you go, Andrew,' said Finlay when he returned to the car. Ford ignored him and Finlay sighed heavily. 'Fine. Here you go, Saint Andrew, assistant child killer.'

Ford had regaled Finlay with his story about the time he saved the Cremation Killer's life from a ferocious but honourable wolf, and had since refused to respond to anything but his full title. He had already severely disrupted their day by declining to leave his squalid Peckham flat that morning, which meant that they were late to the handover and were now returning to the capital at rush hour.

At least the reservoir itself had been an unexpected surprise. They had climbed out of the car to the roar of rushing water. The scene would have been impressive enough, with the sun blazing over the miles of forest-framed blue water, but a thin steel walkway reached out from the shore towards what appeared to be the uppermost chamber of a sunken tower. Arched windows dissected the light stone walls, and an iron weathervane stood atop the blue copper spire, as if retreating from the rising water that had already claimed the rest of the imagined castle.

Beneath the precarious walkway, a huge void had opened up in the water, sucking the reservoir endlessly into the blackness below, as if an enormous plug had been ripped from the Earth, threatening to drag the final piece of the tower into the abyss. They had watched it for a while before beginning the return journey.

Wolf yawned loudly and sat up straight to ascertain where they were.

'Late night?' asked Finlay, who was struggling not to break his no swearing rule as an Audi arrogantly pushed ahead of him at a set of traffic lights.

'I don't sleep that well any night, to be honest.'

Finlay looked over at his friend.

'What are you still doing here, lad?' he asked. 'Just go. Get on a plane and go.'

'Where? My stupid face is plastered across every newspaper on the planet.'

'I dunno – the Amazon rainforest, the Australian outback? You could wait it out.'

'I can't live like that, looking over my shoulder for the rest of my life.'

'Which might be a damn sight longer.'

'If we catch him, it's over.'

'And if we don't?'

Wolf shrugged. He did not have an answer for him. The lights changed to green and Finlay pulled away.

Andrea was met with a standing ovation when she returned to the newsroom. People were patting her on the back and muttering congratulations as she wove through them towards her desk. She was conscious that she still had the dead man's fake blood splattered across her blouse, despite scrubbing at it in the hospital toilets.

She was worried sick about Rory, who had to stay in hospital for periodic irrigation of his wounds to counteract the acid, which was still eating away at his flesh almost eight hours after the incident. The consultant had warned her that he would most likely lose the thumb on his right hand and, should any further nerves be lost, the use of his index finger.

As the spontaneous applause dissipated in an uncoordinatedly awkward fashion, Andrea sat down. The footage of Garland burning alive was playing in slow motion on the ceiling screens as the channel broadcast it for the hundredth time that day. Rory's discarded television camera had captured everything, the crack in the lens framing the shot beautifully. She looked away in revulsion and found the note that Elijah had left her:

Apologies. Had to go. Actual footage of the murder: genius! Meeting Monday AM to discuss future – you've earned it. Elijah.

The vague message could only mean that he was planning to offer her a permanent anchor position, the job of her dreams and yet, far from feeling elated, she felt empty. She absent-mindedly picked up the brown envelope in her post tray and ripped it open. Something dropped out of it and onto the desk. Andrea inspected the small coil of metal before removing a photograph of her and Rory exiting the ME London.

She took out her phone and texted Baxter. Although this second communiqué from the killer was huge news and only further confirmed her claim over the story, she placed the contents back inside the envelope and locked it away in her drawer.

She was not playing this game any more.

The unstable cluster of candles in the centre of the wooden Ikea table looked equal parts romantic and fire hazard. Tia had been left to close up the salon, meaning that Edmunds had arrived home before her and immediately set to work on dinner. She had been delighted to come home to find him making such an effort and put the meal for one that she had picked up in the freezer. They enjoyed an evening together, fuelled by white wine and Waitrose dessert, the way they used to before Edmunds' transfer.

Before leaving work, Edmunds had printed out a stack of old case files, which he planned to sort through once Tia had gone to bed. He had stashed them on top of the high kitchen cupboards, where five-foot Tia would never find them, but completely forgot that they were even there as the hours ticked by until the conversation turned to the baiting subject of his job.

'Were you there?' Tia asked, unconsciously rubbing the bump in her belly. 'When that poor man . . .'

'No.'

'But your boss was? I heard the Indian commander lady mention her name.'

'Baxter? She's not really my boss. She's . . . I suppose she might as well be.'

'So what were you working on while all that was happening?'

Tia was obviously trying to show an interest in his work. Although it was confidential, he did not feel as though he could shoot her down. He decided to share the least important aspect of the investigation with her, which would serve the dual purpose of putting her mind at ease regarding the mundane nature of his role within the team.

'You saw the pictures of the Ragdoll on the news? Well, the right arm belonged to a woman.'

'Who?'

'That's what I'm trying to find out. She was wearing two kinds of nail varnish, which we believe is a clue to her identity.'

'Two types on one hand?'

'The thumb and three of the fingers were painted in Crushed Candy, but the last one is something slightly different.'

'You really think a nail varnish can tell you who this lady is?'

'It's all we've got to go on,' shrugged Edmunds.

'It'd have to be a pretty special one, wouldn't it?' said Tia. 'To be of any help, I mean.'

'Special?'

'Yeah, like there's this one stuck-up old bag who comes into the salon once a week to get her nails done, and Sheri has to order the stuff in specially because it's got real gold flakes in it or some rubbish.'

Edmunds was listening to Tia attentively.

'They don't sell it in most shops because it's way too easy to nick and costs about a hundred pounds a bottle.'

Edmunds grabbed Tia's hand excitedly.

'T, you're a genius!'

After just half an hour of searching for limited-run and ludicrously expensive nail polishes on the Internet, Edmunds thought he had found his elusive missing shade: Chanel Limited Edition Feu De Russie 347.

'This stuff was being sold at the 2007 Moscow Fashion Week for ten thousand dollars a bottle!' read Tia as Edmunds topped up their glasses.

'For nail polish?'

'It was probably a charity thing,' she shrugged. 'Even so, I bet there aren't too many people out there walking around with a bottle of this in their bag.'

The next morning, Baxter received a text from Edmunds asking her to meet him at the Chanel Boutique on Sloane Street at 10 a.m. When she reminded him that she was being taken off the case come Monday, he had simply reminded her that it was still only Saturday.

She was running late after sleeping through her alarm and had been stuck behind a wheelchair for almost two minutes. Following Garland's horrific death, she had wanted nothing more than to vegetate and feel safe, so had curled up on the sofa watching Friday-night television. She had also managed to finish off two whole bottles of wine by herself.

When the wheelchair got stuck on a drain cover, she seized the opportunity to overtake and found Edmunds waiting for her a little further down the road. She had been thinking a lot about his theory that one of the team was leaking information. The more she thought about it, the more preposterous it seemed. Wolf, obviously, was not involved and she trusted Finlay implicitly. Simmons was facing disciplinary action for fighting her corner, and, although she would never tell him to his face, she trusted Edmunds as much as any of them.

Edmunds handed her a lukewarm takeaway coffee and told her all about Tia's discovery. She appreciated that he had reverted to addressing her like his bad-tempered superior. There was no trace of the pity or reassurance that she had so desperately needed the day before, and his faith in her gave her confidence in herself again.

A manager had come across to meet them from the Oxford Street store. The woman, who was refreshingly efficient, spent over an hour making phone calls and checking accounts on their behalf. Eventually she produced a list of eighteen transactions, seven of which had names and delivery details attached.

'There were others,' the well-spoken woman told them, 'that were sent out for auctions, prizes, charity events. The people that we hold contact details for are naturally our best clients . . .'

The woman trailed off as she read through the printout.

'Problem?' asked Baxter.

'Mr Markusson. He is one of our regulars at Oxford Street.'

Baxter took the list off the woman and read the contact details.

'Says here he lives in Stockholm,' said Baxter.

'He divides his time between Stockholm and London. He and his family own property in Mayfair. I'm absolutely positive I have a delivery address. If you'll excuse me a moment . . .'

The woman dialled the number for their main branch again.

'What are the odds Mr Markusson is nuding it up in some sauna in Sweden right now?' Baxter mumbled to Edmunds.

'Oh, he's not dear,' said the woman, holding the phone theatrically far away from her. 'He came in yesterday.'

Simmons had made a point of sitting at Chambers' desk again. Several people had approached him with trivial problems, shift swaps and holiday requests but he had refused to deal with all but the most pressing issues in order to concentrate on the task at hand.

His wife had not taken the news of his potential demotion well, and he had spent the majority of the night reassuring her that they would still be able to afford the mortgage and could still go on their summer holiday. They would get by. They always did.

He was in the middle of the mind-numbing task of checking Edmunds' list of names from the Khalid trial against the Missing Persons database one at a time. He was not as convinced as Edmunds that the murders were all centred around Khalid; however, he had nothing more promising to be working on.

His concentration was beginning to waver when, on the fifty-seventh name, he finally got a match. He double-clicked the report to bring up the complete details. It was dated Sunday 29 June, the day after the Ragdoll's discovery, and had been generated by the Metropolitan Police. It had to be one of their three unidentified victims.

'Son of a bitch,' murmured Simmons.

Baxter and Edmunds climbed the steep steps up to the front door of the four-storey town house, located on a leafy but busy side street in Mayfair. They had to knock twice before they heard the sound of footsteps clicking down the hallway towards them. A sinewy man answered the door, a coffee in one hand, his phone clamped between his ear and his shoulder. He had bright blond hair, which he wore in a long but tidy style, was clearly very muscular and was wearing an expensive shirt over blue jeans. A strong aroma of aftershave wafted over them as he looked at them impatiently.

'Yes?'

'Mr Stefan Markusson?'

'That's right.'

'Police. We need to ask you a few questions.'

In contrast to the first impression that he had given, Markusson had been amiable and welcoming. He led them through his incredible home, which could only be described as Georgian sci-fi, and into the living room where an entire glass wall had been folded back to open it up on to the decked garden. Baxter was sure that Rory would have loved it and was determined to take some pictures for him if their host left them alone at any point.

Markusson sent his adorable daughter back upstairs when she came down to see who had come to visit, and Edmunds wondered whether they were wasting their time when his beautiful two-armed wife went off to prepare them some iced tea. Baxter's experience, however, had taught her that men seldom bought such extravagant gifts for their wives and that they were far more likely to get honest answers with her out of the room.

'So, how can I help you?' asked Markusson, his accent more noticeable now.

'We believe you were in Moscow in April 2007,' said Baxter.

'April 2007?' Markusson stared into space. 'Yes, fashion week. My wife, she drags us to all of these shows.'

'We need to ask you about something you bought while you were out there . . .' Baxter paused, expecting the man to remember his ten-thousand-dollar purchase. Apparently, he did not. 'A bottle of Chanel nail polish?'

At that moment Mrs Markusson returned with their drinks, and Baxter noticed the uncomfortable look on her husband's face.

'Why don't you go keep Livia company?' Markusson told his wife, squeezing her affectionately from his chair. 'We'll head out soon.'

Baxter rolled her eyes as the beautiful blonde scuttled obediently from the room and Edmunds noticed a dramatic shift in her mood.

'The ten grand polish then?' she asked, just as the door clicked shut.

'It was for a woman who I met when I was here in London. I was travelling a lot back then, and it gets very lonely when—'

'I honestly don't give a toss,' interrupted Baxter. 'What is this woman's name?'

'Michelle.'

'Surname?'

'Gailey, I think. We'd have dinner when I was in town. She loved all of this fashion stuff, so I bought her a gift.'

'And you met how, exactly?' asked Baxter.

Markusson cleared his throat. 'Dating website.'

'Rich-shits.com?'

Markusson took the insult on the chin, apparently considering it deserved.

'Michelle wasn't from money; my reason for getting her the present,' explained Markusson. 'To avoid complications, it seemed wise to date someone of a *different* social standing.'

'I bet it did.'

'When was the last time you saw her?' asked Edmunds, scribbling, as usual, in his notebook. Distractedly, he took a sip of his iced tea and started spluttering. Baxter ignored him.

'I called it off when my daughter was born back in 2010.'

'That's mighty fine of you.'

'I haven't seen her since. It's funny . . .'

'What is?' asked Baxter.

'I've been thinking about her a lot in the last week, probably because of all these things in the news.'

Baxter and Edmunds shared a glance.

'Which things?' they asked in unison.

'The Cremation Killer turning up dead. Naguib Khalid, is that his name? It's just that Michelle and I spoke a great deal about him the last time I saw her. It was a big step for her.'

'What was?' they both chimed together again.

'Her being assigned to him,' said Markusson thoughtfully. 'She was his probation officer.'

CHAPTER 21

Monday 7 July 2014

9.03 a.m.

Wolf ignored the call from Dr Preston-Hall's assistant as he entered the Homicide and Serious Crime department. He had, unofficially, discharged himself from her care. Seeing as she had already effectively declared him unfit for work, he could see no reason to waste another moment of his precious time in the old battleaxe's company.

Simmons only had grounds to overrule the psychiatrist's advice because of the premature and very public death of Jarred Garland. With so little time, and the odds already stacked against them, he could not risk provoking the killer further, and the communiqué sent to Baxter following the murder had made it quite clear that Wolf's involvement was to continue.

By Simmons' reckoning, the risk of having one unstable detective out on the streets was far outweighed by the insinuated threats of a serial killer: additional victims? Disregarding the stipulated dates again? Leaking more sensitive information to the press?

They weren't coping as it was.

Oddly, Wolf could not help but feel a little appreciative towards the ruthless monster, who planned to murder him in a week's time, for keeping him in a job. He had no intention of buying him a card, but every cloud . . .

On the spur of the moment, Wolf had decided to head down to Bath for the weekend. Although he had barely entertained the notion of his own demise, something inside him had yearned for the furnace-like front room of the house he'd grown up in, his mother's overcooked beef Wellington, and a pint at the local with his oldest friend, who was apparently destined to live, work and die within a two-mile radius of their senior school.

He had taken the time to listen to the same stories that his dad had been telling for his entire life and had, after all this time, understood why they were worth revisiting so regularly. Only once, during a lull in the conversation, had his parents briefly touched upon the subject of the murders and their son's impending doom; his father had never been the touchy-feely type. They had apparently discussed it at 'great length' while Wolf had been in the shower (a subtle dig at him for using too much hot water) and arrived at their usual solution to most of life's problems: he could move back into his old room upstairs.

'Doubt this fella will want to trek all the way down here,' his father told him confidently.

In the past, Wolf might have found their naivety and trivialisation infuriating, but on this occasion he found it endearingly humorous. His dad then got cross with him for laughing at his opinion.

'I might not be one of your big city know-it-alls but that doesn't mean I'm thick either,' he snapped. For some reason, he had always had an issue with the capital and had treated his son differently ever since he abandoned their 'dull little town' for better things. 'Bloody M4's a menace. Roadworks and average speed checks the entire way!'

Unfortunately this only set Wolf off again, irritating his father further.

'William-Oliver!' his mother had chided him when William Senior stormed out to 'make a cuppa'.

He hated the way that she always double-barrelled his first names. As if their pretentious surname wasn't bad enough. She appeared to consider hyphens camouflage for their modest means, just as the immaculate garden and financed car parked in front of the house in no way matched the tired rooms inside.

Wolf did a few jobs around the house; however, this did not extend to Ethel next door's bloody fence, and he almost crippled himself diving behind the garden wall when she had suddenly emerged from her porchway to accost him.

He felt well rested and invigorated for the week ahead, but then, with a single glance up at the busy office, he realised that everything had changed.

The commander looked to have taken up residence in Simmons' office again. Simmons, meanwhile, appeared to have relocated onto Chambers' old desk and inherited Edmunds in the process, who was sitting alongside him and sporting two very black eyes. Baxter was deep in conversation with a detective named Blake, who everyone knew she could not abide and who had no attachment whatsoever to the Ragdoll case.

On the flipchart in the meeting room, two additional names had been added to the list of dead victims, and Wolf found a note from Finlay waiting on his desk asking him to meet him at the Irish embassy in Belgravia once he had 'finished at the shrink's'. They were to take charge of Andrew Ford's protection there, which was mildly vexing because Wolf distinctly remembered leaving Ford in South Wales and driving away.

Bewildered, he made his way over to Simmons and Edmunds, whose nose was clearly broken up close.

'Morning,' he said casually. 'So, what did I miss?'

Madeline Ayers had worked for Collins and Hunter for a four-year period and had acted as Naguib Khalid's defence lawyer for the duration of the high-profile trial. Simmons had recognised the name on the Missing Persons report immediately. Ayers had spearheaded the pejorative, and often propagandising, assault on Wolf and the Metropolitan Police Service as a whole. She had become a household name with her flippant remarks and controversial quotes from inside the courtroom, including famously suggesting that Wolf take her client's seat in the dock.

Seeing Ayers' name had been confirmation that Edmunds had been right in his convictions all along: this was, and always had been, about Khalid. The process of dispatching officers to her home in Chelsea had merely been a formality in order to officially confirm that the pale, fragile torso holding the mismatched Ragdoll together was hers. Despite this tragic, but promising, step forward in the investigation, the team were no closer to understanding Michael Gable-Collins' connection to the case.

Barely three hours later, Baxter and Edmunds had returned to the office with confirmation that Khalid's probation officer, Michelle Gailey, was their fifth unidentified victim, courtesy of a ten-thousand-dollar nail varnish and an extravagantly duplicitous Swede. Somewhat overshadowed by more pressing matters at the time, it turned out that Khalid had been found guilty of driving while disqualified and had been under Michelle Gailey's supervision when he claimed his final victim.

Out of the six body parts that made up the Ragdoll, only one remained unidentified. Although none of the other people involved in the trial had been reported missing, Simmons was now positive that their final victim's name was staring up at him from the page. He began working back from the top of the list and would only cross off a name once he had made direct contact or was satisfied that they had been sighted since the Ragdoll's discovery.

By dawn on Sunday morning, Rachel Cox had been nearing the end of her night shift in a quaint cottage close to the picturesque Welsh village of Tintern. She had only been working for Protected Persons for a little over a year, but this had been by far the most pleasant location that they had sent her to in that time. Unfortunately, it had also been the most trying.

Andrew Ford spent the majority of his time either screaming obscenities at Rachel and her colleague or throwing things around the delicate little house. On Friday night he had almost burned the thatched cottage down after an unsuccessful attempt to build a fire, and on Saturday afternoon it had taken both of them to physically stop him from leaving the grounds.

Finlay had given her a piece of advice back at the reservoir, which she had dismissed at the time, but she was now seriously considering going into town after a couple of hours of sleep and smuggling a few bottles of alcohol into the house. She would have to keep it from her supervisor, but she had no doubt that it would make the remaining nights with their Irish house guest more bearable.

Thankfully, Ford had finally run out of steam at around 3 a.m. and fallen asleep. Rachel sat at the gnarled wooden table in the warm kitchen under the cosy glow spilling in from the hallway light. She was listening to the snores and holding her breath every time there was a pause in the guttural sounds, praying that he had not woken up. When she could feel herself getting drowsy again, she followed her supervisor's advice and got up to patrol the grounds.

She tiptoed across the creaky floorboards, unlocked the heavy back door as quietly as she could and stepped out into the chilly morning. Slipping her boots on, she walked along the wet grass in the predawn light and could feel herself waking up. The cold air stung her eyes and she wished that she had thought to bring her jacket out with her.

As she rounded the wall to the front garden, she was startled by a ghostly figure standing fifty metres away by the front gate.

Rachel was directly beneath the bedroom where her armed colleague was sleeping. She would be down there in under twenty seconds if Rachel called out, but she did not want to wake her unnecessarily, nor draw attention to the fact that she had left her radio on the kitchen table, so decided to investigate herself.

She cautiously took out her pepper spray and approached the featureless figure, silhouetted against the glowing hills behind. The temperature seemed to be dropping with every step she took away from the safety of the house and her forced, slow breaths were now adding an eerie mist to the already intimidating scene.

A few minutes later and the sun would have climbed above the undulating horizon. As it was, Rachel had silently moved to within ten metres of the figure and was still unable to make out a single discernible feature, only that it was tall and fixing something to the front gate. They showed no sign of being aware of her presence until she was forced to step out onto the gravel path. The cold stones crunched loudly beneath her boots and the dark figure abruptly stopped what it was doing to stare in her direction.

'Can I help you?' asked Rachel as confidently as she could. She had been trained to only reveal herself as a police officer as a last resort. She took another step closer. 'I said, can I help you?'

Rachel was furious with herself for leaving the radio behind. She was now almost fifty metres from the cottage and would have to shout loudly to have any hope of waking her colleague. She wished she had done it sooner. The figure stood motionless. It did not respond, but she was close enough to hear its raspy breathing and see the rhythmic clouds of mist filling the space between them, like smoke warning of the fire to come.

Rachel's nerve finally gave out. She took a huge cold breath to cry for help, and the figure bolted.

'Coombes!' she yelled as she burst through the gate and pursued the shadow downhill along the muddy track that ran alongside the woods.

Rachel was twenty-five years old and had been the star runner at her university. She was rapidly closing the gap between them as they stumbled down the steepening slope, which was growing increasingly uneven underfoot. It was surreally silent; the only sound in the tranquil hills was that of their laboured breathing and heavy footsteps as the chase continued.

'Police! Stop!' she panted.

The sun was rising with every passing moment, and the tips

of the dark trees were now painted in golden sunlight. Rachel could now make out that she was chasing an imposing man with a closely shaven head and a deep scar running diagonally across his scalp. He was wearing heavy boots and a black or dark blue coat that billowed out behind him as he ran.

Suddenly he veered off the track and leapt awkwardly over the barbed wire fence surrounding the woods.

Rachel heard him cry out in pain before scrambling back to his feet and disappearing through the treeline. She reached the spot where he had hurdled the fence and abandoned her pursuit. Sometimes it was difficult to remember the training once the adrenaline had kicked in, but she was only armed with pepper spray. She had already ascertained the man's imposing size and therefore, suspected that the dense woodland would be of greater advantage to him than to her. Besides, she had what she needed.

She knelt down to look at the dark blood pooling around a coil in the metal spike. Without anything to cut the wire with, and unable to leave the evidence unattended, she took a clean tissue from her pocket and soaked up what she could. With one eye on the treeline, she began the long, steep, ascent back up the hill.

Baxter had been the first member of the team to arrive at the office on Sunday morning and had picked up the urgent message to contact Protected Persons. She had to go through an arduous twenty-minute process of identity checks and security numbers before finally being connected to Rachel, who informed Baxter of the incident and the brown envelope that she had found tied to the gate of the cottage on her return. It had contained a single photograph, taken the previous afternoon, of Rachel and her colleague struggling with Ford in the front garden.

Rachel and her supervisor had been reassuringly competent and thorough. They had local police combing the woods, had cordoned off the muddy footpath to preserve footprints, and had bagged the bloodstained tissue that Rachel had collected and the section of fence that the trespasser had injured himself on, both of which were already in transit to the Met's forensic lab.

If it had been their killer's first mistake, they fully intended to capitalise on it.

It was clear that Andrew Ford was no longer secure at the safe house. With Simmons unable to get hold of Wolf, he had sent Baxter and Edmunds to collect Ford while he worked on alternative arrangements. After a few personal calls to contacts that he had met through Mayor Turnble, he was connected to the ambassador of the Embassy of Ireland.

The embassy had seemed a logical choice as it was already overseen by the armed diplomatic protection officers and had security measures engineered into the building as standard. Simmons had been as open with the ambassador as he could, and was upfront about Ford's drinking problem and volatile behaviour.

'No need to check his passport then,' the ambassador had joked.

He had invited Ford and the Metropolitan Police to utilise the top floor of the embassy until the situation had been resolved, and Finlay had drawn the short straw of spending Sunday night there.

Edmunds had returned home on Sunday evening, exhausted from his day of travelling. They had left Ford in Finlay's care and then Baxter had kindly dropped him home.

'Don't let the cat out!' Tia screamed at him as soon as he stepped over the threshold.

'The what?'

He almost tripped over the tiny tabby kitten as it sped past him and collided with the front door.

'T? What is this?' he asked.

'He's called Bernard, and he's going to keep me company while you're out at work,' said Tia challengingly.

'A bit like the baby will?'

'The baby's not here yet though, is it?'

Edmunds stumbled through to the kitchen as the affectionate kitten rubbed up against his legs. Tia was clearly delighted, though, and had not even complained that he was home late, so he decided not to object or remind her that he was severely allergic to cats.

On Monday morning, Vanita had assumed Simmons' role and taken charge of the case. Simmons, back at Chambers' desk, was rather looking forward to being a more intimate part of the unit – less so to the disciplinary action awaiting him when things calmed down. Baxter, meanwhile, had been reassigned to normal duties.

Her first case had been a woman who stabbed her cheating husband to death. Boringly, she had admitted to it. Baxter, therefore, faced several hours of tedious form-filling to complement her five seconds of investigative work. She also had to work alongside Blake, one of the obnoxious Saunders' crowd, who had always had a thing for her. It was fortunate she was such a gifted actress that nobody had picked up on the fact that she could not abide the man.

Simmons had scribbled the weekend's updates onto the scruffy board in the meeting room:

1. (HEAD) Naguib Khalid 'The Cremation Killer'
2. (TORSO) – ? – Madeline Ayers – (Khalid's defence lawyer)
3. (LEFT ARM) *platinum ring, law firm?* – Michael Gable-Collins – *why?*
4. (RIGHT ARM) *nail varnish?* – Michelle Gailey – (Khalid's probation officer)
5. (LEFT LEG) – ?
6. (RIGHT LEG) Detective Benjamin Chambers – *why?*

A – ~~Raymond Turnble~~ (Mayor)
B – ~~Vijay Rana/Khalid~~ (Brother/accountant) *not at trial*
C – ~~Jarred Garland~~ (Journalist)
D – Andrew Ford (Security guard/alcoholic/pain in arse) – *Dock security officer*
E – Ashley Lochlan (Waitress) or (nine-year-old girl)
F – Wolf

*

Edmunds had all but forgotten about the newest addition to their family as he got ready for work that morning but received a stark reminder when he accidentally trod on the sleeping fluff-ball in the hallway and stumbled face first into his front door.

Tia had, of course, sided with Bernard, and told Edmunds to stop scaring him by bleeding so profusely.

CHAPTER 22

Monday 7 July 2014

11.29 a.m.

The moment the 'On Air' light went out, Andrea pulled off her microphone, hurried out of the studio, and back into the newsroom. Elijah had scheduled their meeting for 11.35 a.m., and as she climbed the stairs up to his office, she still had no idea what she would say should he offer her what she had always wanted.

When she had agreed to help Baxter she had had every intention of leaving the cut-throat profession behind; however, her misguided attempt at redemption had backfired horribly, while catapulting her fame and journalistic influence to dizzying new heights. Somehow, in her fight to free herself from the dirt, she had only succeeded in digging herself further in.

Elijah spotted her coming and, for the first time ever, opened the door for her before she even had time to knock, robbing her of a few additional seconds that she so desperately needed in order to make up her mind. He smelled faintly of sweat, and dark patches were beginning to form under his arms. He was wearing a fitted sky-blue shirt that looked as though it would split should he tense anything, and tight black trousers that emphasised his absurdly disproportioned profile.

He offered her one of his revolting espressos, which she declined, and then droned on about how he was seldom surprised but had to admit that she had shown a killer instinct he had not believed her capable of. He clicked a button to bring a graph up on the projector behind him and began reeling off numbers without even glancing at it. Andrea had to stifle a laugh because half of the lopsided chart he was referring to had disappeared out of the office window, which he would have realised had he not been too conceited to even turn his head.

She zoned out as he congratulated her for her sterling work on Garland's murder, as though it had been a live television event that she had meticulously choreographed, which, in a nauseating way, it had been. While flashbacks of Garland thrashing around occupied her thoughts, Elijah finally reached his point.

'. . . our newest prime-time newsreader!'

He deflated when Andrea failed to respond.

'Did you hear what I said?' he asked.

'Yes. I heard,' said Andrea quietly.

Elijah relaxed back in his chair, popped a piece of chewing gum into his mouth and nodded knowingly. As he continued, he unconsciously pointed a condescending finger at her.

Andrea was tempted to rip it off.

'I get what this is,' he said, chewing with his mouth open. 'This is about Wolf. You're thinking: he can't seriously expect me to sit there in front of a camera and report my own ex-husband's death to the world, can he?'

She hated it when he put words in her mouth; although, on this occasion he was spot on. She nodded.

'Well, tough shit, precious,' he snapped. 'That's what's gonna make it so compelling. Who'll be watching the dreary BBC when they could be watching the love of Wolf's life only learning of his passing as she reads it out on air. Un . . . missable!'

Andrea laughed bitterly and got up to leave.

'You're unbelievable.'

'I'm a realist. You're gonna go through it anyway. Why not do it on camera and make yourself a star in the process? Oh! You could convince him to do an interview the night before. How heartbreaking would that be? We could actually broadcast you saying your goodbyes.'

Andrea stormed out of the office and slammed the door behind her.

'Think about it!' he yelled after her. 'I'll expect your answer, one way or another, by the weekend!'

Andrea was due back in front of the camera in twenty minutes. She calmly walked into the women's toilets, checked that no one was in any of the cubicles, locked the door and burst into tears.

Edmunds yawned loudly as he waited for Joe in the empty forensics lab. He had elected to stand in a cramped corner between a clinical waste bin and a fridge. Coincidentally, it just so happened to also be the furthest point away from the large cadaver freezer, which he glanced up at every few seconds between scribbling in his notebook.

He had stayed up well past 3 a.m., sifting through the case files that he had stashed on top of his kitchen units. Although Tia had no hope of finding them up there, her new pet, using the curtains as a climbing aid, did. And had subsequently thrown up all over a very important witness statement. He felt worryingly tired considering that it was not even lunchtime. At least his exhaustion was worthwhile; he had come across one case that certainly warranted further investigation.

'Wow! What the hell happened to you?' asked Joe as he entered the lab.

'It's nothing,' replied Edmunds, stepping out from his corner and touching his broken nose self-consciously.

'Well, it's definitely him,' announced Joe. 'All three photographs were taken by the same camera.'

'Please say you found something from the blood.'

'I could, but I'd be lying. He's not in our database.'

'Which means we've never arrested him,' said Edmunds, more for his own benefit. He could now confidently rule out a large percentage of the archived case files.

'Blood type: O-positive.'

'The rare one?' asked Edmunds hopefully.

'Common as muck,' said Joe. 'No sign of mutation or illness, no alcohol or drugs. Eye colour: grey or blue. You know, for the most twisted serial killer in recent memory, his blood is deplorably dull.'

'So you've got nothing?'

'I didn't say that. The boot prints are size eleven, and the cast of the tread pattern is a combat boot, so maybe military?'

Edmunds got his notebook back out.

'The crime scene forensics guys found traces of asbestos, tar and a lacquer in the imprints along with considerably higher levels of copper, nickel and lead than the surrounding soil. A warehouse maybe?'

'I'll look into it. Thank you,' said Edmunds, closing his book.

'Hey, I heard they identified our torso. Did you ever work out what that tattoo was?' asked Joe.

'It was a canary escaping a cage.'

Joe looked puzzled: 'Funny thing to get removed.'

Edmunds shrugged.

'I suppose she realised that some canaries belong in cages after all.'

The Embassy of Ireland was an imposing five-storey building that overlooked the grounds of Buckingham Palace from its large corner plot position in Belgravia. On this breezeless and sunny day, Wolf entered the grand portico under the shadow of the wilted flags that protruded out over the busy pavement. The grand entranceway doubled as a bridge over the litter-hoarding service area that provided a fire escape to the basement level below.

Wolf had been in a number of embassies in his time, none by choice, and had always been left with the same impression: the high ceilings, old paintings, ornate mirrors and comfortable-looking sofas that appeared as though no one had worked up the courage to sit on them yet; it was like visiting a well-off relative who simultaneously wanted to appear welcoming and for you to leave before you could break anything. This one was no exception.

Once Wolf had passed through security in the public areas, he was confronted with a grand staircase framed by intricately embellished duck-egg-blue walls. He was stopped on three separate occasions on his way up, which was encouraging, and reached the top floor to be greeted by the familiar sound of Andrew Ford's raised voice filling the civilised hallway.

Wolf looked out at the palace in the distance for a tranquil moment before going to face the pugnacious man again. He smiled at the armed officer on the door, who did not return the gesture, and entered the opulent room to find Finlay calmly watching television while Ford writhed about on the floor like a badly behaved toddler.

The room clearly functioned as an office under normal circumstances. The computers, desks and filing cabinets had either been removed entirely or stacked against the far wall to accommodate their ungracious guest. Someone had even gone to the trouble of equipping the room with a camp bed, kettle, sofas and the television at very short notice.

A creature of habit, Ford had evidently slept in front of the TV on the pristine leather sofa, because the same smelly, stained duvet from his bedsit now lay draped across it. It was a peculiar sight, this dirty train wreck of a man living in such decadent surroundings, and Wolf could not believe that, of all his possessions, he had chosen this rancid piece of bedding to drag across the country and back again.

'Wolf!' shouted Ford, as though they were old friends. He howled excitedly.

Finlay waved cheerfully from the other, duvet-free, sofa.

'What noise does he make when he sees you?' Wolf asked Finlay.

'Afraid I cannae repeat it. Wasn't very friendly though.'

Ford got up off the floor and Wolf saw that his hands were trembling constantly. The Irishman then rushed over to the window to peer out over the street below.

'He's coming Wolf. He's coming to kill me!' said Ford.

'The killer? Well . . . yeah,' said Wolf in confusion. 'But he's not going to.'

'He is. He is. He is. He knows things, doesn't he? He knew where I was before. He'll know where I am now.'

'He will if you don't move away from that window. Sit down.'

Finlay watched in resentment as the childlike man, who had made the last seventeen hours of his life a living hell, obeyed without argument. Wolf took a seat next to his friend.

'Good night?' he asked cheerily.

'I'm gonna kill him myself if he carries on like he has been,' Finlay muttered.

'When was his last drink?'

'Early hours,' said Finlay.

Wolf knew from experience the toll that the withdrawal symptoms could take on a long-term alcoholic. Ford's heightened anxiety and the onset of delirium tremens was not a promising sign.

'He needs a drink,' said Wolf.

'Believe me, I asked. The ambassador said no.'

'Why don't you take a break?' Wolf told Finlay. 'You must be dying for a cigarette.'

'I'm the one who's going to die here!' yelled Ford in the background.

They both ignored him.

'And while you're out, pick us up a couple of bottles of . . . *lemonade*,' suggested Wolf with a significant look.

Simmons walked past Vanita's door carrying a coffee.

'*Chaachaa chod*,' she murmured, using her favourite Hindi insult.

Because of him, she had spent the entire morning wading through the backlog of paperwork and post that he had left unactioned. She opened up the next email: another update, sent out to everyone involved in the Ragdoll investigation. She noticed Chambers' name included in the list of recipients and sighed. Simmons had cancelled his pass card to the building immediately after learning of his death, as per the protocols, but the endless task of removing the veteran officer from their databases and collecting in his equipment sat somewhere near the bottom of her to-do list.

Supposing that it was bad form to circulate a dead colleague's name on each and every one of the incessant updates, she quickly typed out a request to have him deleted and moved on to the next job on her list.

Simmons and Edmunds had been working silently for over an hour, despite sitting only eighteen inches apart. Edmunds felt surprisingly relaxed around his irritable senior officer. Perhaps three months of Baxter had toughened him up, but the quietness felt comfortable, just two professionals absorbed in their work, efficient, intellectual souls, sharing a mutual respe—

Simmons turned to Edmunds, interrupting his train of thought.

'Remind me to order you a desk later, will you?'

'Of course, sir.'

The silence felt considerably less comfortable after that.

Simmons was still working on the labour-intensive task of contacting each and every one of the remaining eighty-seven names on the list. On his first pass, he had only managed to cross off twenty-four. He had turned the page back over and started again from the top, positive that once they had identified this final victim, the entire puzzle would make sense.

Edmunds, whose idea it had been to compile the list in the first place, was not sure how or when Simmons had claimed ownership over his part of the investigation but was not about to question it. He had his hands full anyway, searching for all possible links between the Ragdoll victims and Naguib Khalid.

Although he had not found a connection between Chambers or Jarred Garland, he figured that police officers and journalists both tended to accrue long lists of enemies over the years. He had, instead, decided to focus his attention on Michael Gable-Collins, Mayor Turnble and the waitress, Ashley Lochlan.

He felt frustrated. Something connected this assorted group of people but even knowing that Khalid was the key, they were somehow failing to see the entire picture.

Baxter was at the scene of a serious sexual assault in an alleyway just two streets down from Wolf's apartment. It really was a shitty area. She had annoyed Blake by refusing to climb into a skip to help him search for evidence and was supposed to be asking for witnesses instead but had distracted herself by thinking about Wolf and Finlay in the Irish embassy, with just a day and a half to go until the attempt on Andrew Ford's life. She missed Edmunds too. She had got so used to him following her around like a puppy that she had actually barked an order into thin air earlier that morning.

She was bored. It was a terrible thing to admit while in the midst of investigating the most horrific ordeal of a young woman's life, but she was. She thought back to the feeling of hopelessness she had experienced as Garland thrashed around just metres away from her. She remembered holding his hand, willing him to survive and the nurse coming in to break the news of his death.

She missed the adrenaline. It had been one of the worst days of her entire life and yet, given the opportunity to do it all over again, she would. Was there something wrong with her? Were haunting memories better than none at all? Feeling fear and peril preferable to feeling nothing? And were these the sort of questions that the killer asked himself to justify his own atrocities?

Scaring herself, she decided to go and do some work.

Wolf and Finlay were watching a rerun of *Top Gear* at almost inaudible volume while Ford snored loudly from beneath the duvet on the other sofa. He had passed out after approximately one and a half bottles of 'lemonade' and given the two detectives a blissful hour of quiet.

'Thomas Page,' rasped Finlay as quietly as he could.

'What?' asked Wolf.

'Thomas Page.'

'Bastard. He knocked out t—'

'Two of your teeth at a crime scene when you were in training. I know.'

'He always had a temper.'

'And you were always a smart-arse,' replied Finlay with a shrug.

'Why are you bringing him up any—'

'Hugh Cotrill,' interrupted Finlay.

'Tosser,' spat Wolf, almost waking Ford. 'My first arrest for theft and he was the system-playing prick that got him off.'

'He was doing his job,' said Finlay with a smile. He was clearly antagonising Wolf intentionally.

'He got his watch nicked by his own client, the prick. What's your point?'

'My point is: you are a lot of things Will but forgiving is not one of them. You hold grudges. You probably hate me for something I said or did to you once upon a time.'

'Said,' clarified Wolf with a smirk.

'That mess over there isn't particularly likeable on a good day, but you must *really* hate him. He broke your wrist in three . . .?'

Wolf nodded.

'. . . places and probably saved Khalid's life.'

'Again,' said Wolf, 'what's your point?'

'Nothing in particular. It's just funny how things work out, isn't it? You in charge of protecting a man that I don't believe for a second you give a damn about saving.'

'You're right about one thing,' whispered Wolf after they were both distracted by the television for a moment. 'It is funny how things work out. Somehow I've ended up in a position where I want to save this piece of shi—'

Wolf stopped himself from swearing, and Finlay nodded in approval of his self-restraint.

'. . . this man's life more than anything else I have ever done, because if we can save *him* then maybe, just maybe, we can save *me*.'

Finlay nodded in understanding and gave Wolf a painfully sincere slap on the back before returning to his show.

CHAPTER 23

Tuesday 8 July 2014

6.54 a.m.

'Let me go!' screamed Ford as Wolf, Finlay and the diplomatic protection officer struggled to drag the frenetic man back into the room. 'You're killing me! You're killing me!'

The gaunt and jaundiced man had been surprisingly strong, and the three of them had barely managed to heave him back over the threshold during the three-minute panic. He still had a firm grip on the thick door frame, and his legs were kicking out at them violently. In the background, Andrea addressed the world through the television, the Death Clock hovering above her head counting down Ford's final hours. She cut back to a reporter out in the field, and Wolf was horrified when he and his colleagues suddenly appeared on screen battling with Ford.

He almost lost his grip on the crazed man when he turned to locate the camera, wielded by a lunatic hanging precariously out of a window in the building opposite. Thankfully, the DPG officer had called for backup, and at that moment two more armed men came rushing to their aid.

'Get the blinds!' Wolf shouted desperately.

Both officers glanced at the television and understood the situation immediately. One of them ran to the windows while the other took hold of Ford's thrashing legs. Hopelessly outnumbered,

Ford went limp and started to weep.

'You're killing me,' he sobbed repeatedly.

'We need to get those reporters out of that building,' Wolf told the newcomers, who nodded and hurried back out of the room.

'You're killing me!'

'Shut up!' snapped Wolf.

He needed to speak to Simmons. He had no idea where they stood legally in detaining Ford against his will, and thanks to one, admittedly, resourceful cameraman they could all technically be charged with assault. He was aware that he should approach Vanita with issues such as this, but knew that her answer would be biased by the PR team and in ensuring that she was covering her own arse. Simmons, on the other hand, knew how the real world worked.

Half an hour later, Wolf had discussed the situation with Simmons, who had fortunately arrived admirably early for work. They were agreed that, unlike Garland's threat to decline their input, Ford could not confidently be classed as 'of sound mind'. It was, therefore, in his best interests for the police to temporarily revoke his right to freedom.

It was a grey area at the best of times and they were, frankly, grasping at straws. Protocol would dictate that a qualified medical practitioner thoroughly assess the patient and sign off on it; however, after the Elizabeth Tate incident, there was no way on earth that Wolf was permitting anybody access to Ford.

The ambassador had returned to the embassy after seeing the news report. Wolf felt a little guilty about how insolently he had acted towards the influential man, who had bent over backwards to accommodate them. Wolf had accused his staff of selling information to the press and demanded (not that he had any right) that he conduct a full inquiry into the source of the leak. He would have to apologise later.

He was overly tired and irritable after a difficult night with Ford and had vented his anger at the wrong person. Yet again his frustrations should have been directed at Andrea, who had heedlessly jeopardised another life in her selfish pursuit of ratings. This time he was not going to let her simply shrug off the impact of her continued interference. He would ensure that she was held accountable should anything happen to this man.

Simmons had suggested that they find somewhere else for Ford to go, but Wolf disagreed. Half of the city's press had gathered on the street below. He could hear the frenzied buzz of activity seeping through the draughty windows even as they spoke on the phone. They would never have been able to move Ford without exposing him to the ever-growing crowds or being followed. They were in a secure building and would be able to protect him best from there.

When Wolf returned to the room, Ford was speaking calmly to Finlay. He seemed resigned and surprisingly dignified considering the scene thirty minutes earlier.

'You were doing your job,' said Finlay. 'What possible reason would you have had to let someone, who had just been declared innocent, be beaten to death in front of you?'

'You can't seriously be trying to tell me you think I did the right thing?' laughed Ford bitterly.

'No. I'm telling you that you did the *only* thing you could do.'

Wolf closed the door quietly, so as not to disturb the intriguing conversation.

'If you hadn't stepped in and Khalid had died, there's a very good chance he'd never have been exposed as the Cremation Killer and Will here,' Finlay gestured towards him standing in the doorway, 'would've spent the next twenty-five years of his life in prison.'

'A little girl died,' said Ford with tears in his eyes.

'Aye. And a good man was spared,' said Finlay. 'I'm not saying it was a good thing that Khalid survived. I'm just saying . . . things happen.'

Finlay took out the ancient pack of cards that he always carried around with him and dealt out three piles. His talk with Ford seemed to have calmed the unpredictable man down, but it had also affected Wolf as he took a seat on the sofa. He had always dwelled on the negative repercussions of that traumatic day; he had never even considered the positive.

He picked up his disappointing hand and watched Finlay closely. After years of playing with him, he knew that he was a dirty cheat. Ford burst into tears after looking through his cards, which was not much of a poker face.

'Got any threes?' asked Finlay.

'Go fish.'

Blake had a weak bladder and an appreciation for Earl Grey tea. Edmunds had deduced this after watching his comings and goings for the past day. Edmunds waited for him to pass his and Simmons' desk before getting to his feet and rushing over to see Baxter at the back of the room. He had two minutes.

'Edmunds! What the hell are you doing?' asked Baxter as he crouched down to avoid attracting attention.

'Someone told the press and therefore the killer about the embassy,' he whispered.

'I'm not allowed to talk about the case with you.'

'You are the only person I trust.'

Baxter warmed a little. Everyone had been treating her like a leper since the Garland fiasco. It was reassuring to know that one person, at least, still valued her opinion.

'You can trust all of them. Anyone could have blabbed about the embassy: you've got DPG, the staff, whoever's in that building opposite. You *really* need to drop this. Now get out of here before you get me in trouble.'

Edmunds hurried back to his desk. A few moments later, Blake walked by with a mug in his hand.

By early afternoon Simmons had eliminated forty-seven of the eighty-eight names on the list while Edmunds continued looking for connections between the victims. When the standard checks and protocols had turned up nothing, he had reverted to his fraud training and borrowed a colleague's passwords to access his old department's specialist software.

Within fifteen minutes he had found something and scared Simmons half to death by leaping out of his seat. They moved into the meeting room to talk in private.

'Ashley Lochlan,' said Edmunds triumphantly.

'The next victim?' said Simmons. 'What about her?'

'Back in 2010, she was married and going by the name of Ashley Hudson.'

'We must have known that?'

'We did, but the computers weren't looking for a second bank account in a different name that was only open for ten months. On the fifth of April 2010, she paid two and a half thousand pounds cash into her Hudson account,' said Edmunds, handing Simmons a printout.

'That was around the start of Khalid's trial.'

'I looked into it. She was working in a pub for minimum wage at the time. She then paid in a second two thousand five hundred a fortnight later.'

'Interesting.'

'Suspicious,' Edmunds corrected him. 'So I looked through our other victim's accounts for that period and found two matching withdrawals made by one Mr Vijay Rana.'

'Why would Khalid's brother be transferring five grand to a barmaid?'

'That's what I'm about to ask her.'

'Do it. Excellent work Edmunds.'

At 4 p.m., Wolf heard the muffled sounds of the officers changing over through the door. They had switched the television off after that morning's incident, although it was only a token gesture, seeing as they could quite clearly hear that the sea of spectators, police cars and reporters flooding the road beneath them were yet to get bored and move on.

With the exception of a couple of fleeting episodes, Ford had maintained his new-found calm and given Wolf and Finlay a rare insight into the man that he had once been. If anything, he seemed defiant, determined, spurred on by the bloodthirsty mob waiting expectantly outside.

'I've already let one serial killer ruin my life. I'm not about to let another decide when to end it.'

'That's the spirit,' said Finlay encouragingly.

'I'm taking back control,' said Ford. 'And today seems as good a time as any.'

As a security precaution, they had closed all of the windows and dropped the blinds. Despite borrowing a fan from down the hall, the room was stifling. Wolf unbuttoned his cuffs and rolled up his sleeves, exposing the healing burn that covered his left arm.

'I never asked,' said Ford, gesturing to Wolf's injury. 'What happened?'

'It's nothing,' replied Wolf.

'He was injured when Mayor Turnble . . .' Finlay trailed off.

'So, both of you are taking a huge risk just by being near me, aren't you? For all you know, he could just fire a rocket launcher up here.'

The thought had clearly not crossed Finlay's mind and he looked to Wolf in concern.

'I've not got long anyway,' said Wolf cheerfully as he peered through a gap in the blind.

'I don't want anyone getting hurt for me,' said Ford.

Wolf had been watching a group of three people out on the street for over five minutes. They had caught his attention because they had settled away from the rest of their fellow spectators and looked to be waiting for something. Two of them had carried a large canvas bag to the spot and set it down in the middle of the closed road. Wolf watched as each of them pulled a different animal mask over their face. Soon, they were joined by six others.

'Finlay!' Wolf called from the window. 'Can you get hold of the officers down on the street?'

'Aye. What is it?'

'Trouble.'

Two of the masked group, a cartoon monkey and an eagle, crouched down and pulled the bag open. They removed what they needed, barged their way through the crowd and ducked beneath the police tape.

'Child killer!' one of the slightly muffled voices called up to them.

'The saviour of the Cremation Killer!' yelled his female counterpart.

The police officers on crowd control were swift to remove the two people who had crossed the cordon, but the remaining seven, who had lingered behind, had now caught the attention of the media as they produced banners, boards and a megaphone from the large bag. A woman wearing a shark mask began ranting over the already raucous street.

'Andrew Ford deserves what is coming to him!' she thundered. 'If he had not saved the Cremation Killer's life, Annabelle Adams would still be alive today!'

Wolf looked back into the room to gauge Ford's reaction, expecting it to set him off again. Surprisingly he had not moved. He just sat listening to the distorted assault upon him. Unsure what to say, Finlay switched the television back on, found a children's programme and turned the volume right up in an attempt to drown out the commotion outside. Wolf thought that the gloomy, grand room resembled Ford's impoverished bedsit all of a sudden.

'Spare the Devil and God will strike thee down!'

The protesters had started chanting the same faux-religious slogan repeatedly. One of them was talking animatedly to a reporter while the ringleader suggested that Ford had been involved with Khalid since the beginning.

'Has this ever happened before?' Wolf asked Ford, without taking his eyes off the threat below.

'Not like this,' replied Ford distractedly. In an almost inaudible whisper, he joined the chant: 'Spare the Devil and God will strike *me* down.'

Some of the police at street level had gathered around the protesters; although, while they remained peaceful, they had no grounds to disperse them. Wolf gestured for Finlay to join him at the window.

'You think this is his doing?' mumbled Finlay, reading his mind.

'I don't know. But it doesn't feel right.'

'Want me to go down there and ask some questions?' Finlay offered.

'No. You're better with him than I am. I'll go.'

Wolf took one last look at the group of masked people before heading for the door.

'Wolf,' said Ford, as he was leaving. 'Take back control.'

Wolf smiled politely at the bizarre comment, shrugged at Finlay and left the room. As he reached the ground floor, he received a phone call from Edmunds, who told him about his discovery involving Ashley Lochlan.

'She's refusing to talk to anybody but you,' said Edmunds.

'I'm busy,' said Wolf.

He had barely taken a step out of the embassy before a wave of reporters swelled forward towards him. He wondered if perhaps he should have sent Finlay. Ignoring the shouts of his own name, he ducked beneath the tape and pushed through the crush, following the sound of the chanting.

'It's important,' said Edmunds. 'She might be able to finally tell us what the connection is between you all. From there, we'll stand a real shot of working out who is doing this to you.'

'Fine. Text me the number. I'll call her when I can.'

Wolf hung up. A large space had formed around the seven disruptive protesters. Up close, the cartoonish masks felt far more sinister: venomous voices spat from unmoving smiles and furious eyes burned through the dark holes in the plastic. The most intimidating of them, both in stature and behaviour, was wearing a slack-jawed wolf mask. He carried two mounted boards high above his head as he stamped around the others, chanting aggressively. Wolf noticed that he was limping slightly, presumably an old injury from where the last rubber bullet had bounced off his rear end.

Making sure to avoid the bellicose man, Wolf approached the woman in the shark mask who still had the megaphone held up to her mouth. He snatched it off her mid-sentence and threw it against the wall of the building behind, where it split apart with an electrical squeal. The incriminating television cameras were following his every move greedily.

'Hey! You can't . . . Wait, aren't you that detective?' asked the woman, now adopting a far more feminine and middle-class tone.

'What are you doing here?' Wolf demanded.

'Protesting,' she shrugged.

Wolf could sense her smug smile obscured from his view and looked unamused.

'Jesus Christ. Lighten up.' She lifted up her mask. 'The truth is, I don't know. None of us do. There's this website where people advertise for, like, flash mobs or girls to stand around outside hotels to make boy bands look more popular. Today it was for people to stage a protest.'

'What site?'

She handed him a leaflet with the details printed on it.

'They were handing them out at my college.'

'Do you get paid for it?' asked Wolf.

'Of course. Why else would we do it?'

'You sounded pretty passionate about it before.'

'It's called *acting*. I was reading from a card.'

Wolf was very conscious of the number of people listening in. In an ideal world, he would not have been questioning her on live television.

'How are you getting paid?'

'Cash, inside the bag. Fifty quid a piece.' She sounded bored by his questions. 'And, before you ask, we all met at a grave in Brompton Cemetery. The bag was already there waiting for us.'

'Whose?'

'Bag?'

'Whose grave?'

'That name I read out before – Annabelle Adams?'

Wolf tried to conceal his surprise at the answer.

'That bag and everything in it is evidence in a murder investigation,' he said, kicking the empty holdall back in front of the group.

They whined and swore but obeyed the physical instruction and threw the boards, banners and cue cards into an untidy pile.

'And the masks,' Wolf barked impatiently.

One by one they reluctantly surrendered six of the colourful masks. Two of the protesters immediately pulled their hoods up over their heads to conceal their identities, even though, technically, they had done nothing wrong.

Wolf turned round to address the final protester in the wolf mask, who had so far ignored the instructions. The imposing man was still chanting breathlessly while he trampled the perimeter he had carved out of the crowd, as if marking his area. Wolf stepped out in front of the man. The ironically friendly-looking wolf had been depicted licking its lips and salivating. He barged heavily into Wolf and then continued on another lap.

'I'll be needing those,' shouted Wolf, gesturing to the two boards that he was carrying over his head, inscribed with the now familiar chant.

Wolf stepped back out into the man's path and braced himself for the worst. He was precisely the sort of person that Wolf would have expected to respond to such an advert, hiding behind a mask, empowered by his anonymity, opportunistically seeking out large crowds and overwhelmed security as occasions to commit blatant acts of violence, vandalism and theft.

Wolf had no qualms about arresting the thug, who came to a stop mere inches from his face. He was unaccustomed to having to stand up straight to match someone's height and recoiled slightly at the underlying smell, medicinal, rotting, that seemed to emanate from behind the plastic. Eerily, the wild, light blue eyes staring out at him looked as though they could have actually belonged to the creature.

'Boards. Now,' said Wolf, in a tone that would have cowed anyone aware of his controversial past.

Wolf refused to break eye contact. The man turned his head to the side, much like a real animal: inquisitive, measuring up a new challenger. Wolf could sense the cameras at his back, drinking in the tense stand-off and praying that it might escalate. Suddenly, the man threw both of the boards he had been holding across the concrete.

'And the mask,' said Wolf.

The man showed no intention of complying.

'The mask,' he repeated.

This time, it was Wolf who leaned in aggressively. He could feel the tip of the plastic nose brushing against his own, the smell nauseating, as they shared one another's hot breath. They stood like this for ten excruciating seconds until, to Wolf's surprise, the man's pale eyes darted up towards the upper windows of the embassy behind him. All around him, people started gasping and shouting as they too spotted what the wolf had seen.

Wolf turned to see Ford balancing precariously on the pitched roof as Finlay hung out from a small window, calling him back. The crowd took a sharp intake of breath as Ford stepped out of reach of Finlay's grasping hands and staggered across the open rooftop to a chimney, like a tightrope walker losing balance.

'No, no, no!' hissed Wolf.

He shoved the confrontational protester aside and started pushing his way through the crowd. Diplomatic protection officers appeared at sporadic windows alongside Ford and on the floor below.

'Don't do this, Andrew!' shouted Finlay, who was now out on the window ledge with half of his body lying across the unstable roof.

Part of a tile broke away and seemed to fall forever before cracking the windscreen of a police car below.

'Don't move, Finlay!' Wolf screamed up at him as he emerged from the sea of people. 'Don't you move!'

'Wolf!' shouted Ford.

Wolf skidded to a stop and stared up at the man whose scruffy hair was blowing about in a breeze that he could not even feel at street level. He could hear a fire engine blasting its bullhorn as it rushed across the city towards them.

'You've gotta take back control!' Ford said again, but this time Wolf understood his meaning.

'If you do this . . . If you die, he wins!' yelled Finlay. Crouched on the sloping roof, he clung desperately to the windowsill as more debris showered down over the street.

'No. If *I* do this, *I* win.'

Ford released his grip on the chimneystack and tentatively raised his trembling arms to balance himself. The traffic on the main road had come to a standstill as people abandoned their vehicles to watch this worldwide news unfold first-hand. The crowd below was quiet, except for the whispered bulletins from distracted reporters. The fire engine could only have been a few streets away.

Finlay had shuffled halfway between the safety of the window and the chimney stack. There were shouts of horror from the spectators when Ford almost lost his balance. He closed his eyes with his arms outstretched and swayed unsteadily above the edge.

'Things happen,' he said, so quietly that only Finlay could hear.

Then he let himself fall forward.

Finlay scrambled across the space between them, but Ford had already dropped out of reach. Wolf could only watch helplessly, with the other two hundred people out on the road, as he plummeted silently past the windows and then dropped out of sight into the basement service area with a dull thud.

For a moment, all was still – and then the army of reporters surged forward, overpowering the handful of police officers in their desperation to broadcast the first gruesome images of the aftermath. Wolf ran to the black metal fire escape and jumped the last six steps in his haste to reach Ford. As he approached the body, which had twisted unnaturally on impact, he realised he was standing in the copious amounts of blood that had leaked freely from the back of the man's skull.

Before he had even checked for a pulse, the sun had been chased off the fresh corpse by the shadows of the people above. Too traumatised to care that he was undoubtedly posing for yet another iconic photograph, Wolf sat back against the wall, surrounded by the growing puddle of blood, and waited for help.

Three minutes later the service area was heaving with police officers and paramedics. Wolf got to his feet to climb back above ground, where he would be able to watch the fire service rescue Finlay from the rooftop, who was now clinging to the chimney stack for dear life. A trail of red footprints followed Wolf over to the metal stairs where he had to wait for an obese coroner to finish his protracted descent.

Wolf put his hands in his pockets and frowned in confusion. He removed an unfamiliar piece of paper and cautiously unfolded it to reveal a single bloody fingerprint soiling the centre of the crumpled page. A hint of dark lettering was showing through from the other side. He turned it over to find a short message scrawled in the killer's distinctive handwriting:

Welcome back.

He stared at it in utter bewilderment, wondering how long he had been carrying it around with him and how the killer had ever managed to—

The wolf mask!

'Get out the way!' yelled Wolf as he shoved past the hefty man on the stairs.

He surfaced out onto the chaotic road, searching frantically through the crowds for any of the protesters. Weaving between the people packing up equipment or leaving the scene now that the show was over, he reached the spot where the confiscated boards and banners had been thrown into a pile.

'Move!' he shouted at the dawdling pedestrians as he climbed on top of a bench for a better viewpoint.

He spotted something on the floor in the centre of the road and pushed his way through to find the plastic wolf mask cracked and dirty from where it had been trampled into the concrete.

Wolf stooped down to pick it up, knowing that the killer would still be there, watching him, laughing at him, revelling in the undeniable power that he had held over Ford, that he continued to hold over the media and, as much as Wolf hated to admit it, that he held over him . . .

ST ANN'S HOSPITAL

Wednesday 6 October 2010

10.08 a.m.

Wolf stared out at the sun-dappled gardens that surrounded the grand old building. The few patches of light that had managed to fight their way through the dying foliage above danced across the neat lawn to the choreography of a gentle breeze.

Even the concentration required to enjoy the tranquil scene was taking its toll upon his fatigued mind. The medication that he was force-fed twice a day had left him in a perpetual half-waking state, not the warm uncoordination of an alcohol-provoked daze – more distant, apathetic, defeated.

He understood the need for it. The common areas were populated with people suffering the entire spectrum of mental health disorders: those who had attempted suicide sharing tables with those who had killed, those spiralling into depression through feelings of worthlessness talking to others with delusions of grandeur. It was a recipe for disaster diluted through medication, although, Wolf could not help but feel, born out of a need to control rather than actually cure.

He was losing track of the days and weeks, existing as he did in the surreal routined confines of the hospital, where he and his fellow detainees would roam the halls aimlessly in their pyjama-style scrubs, were told when to eat, when to wash, when to sleep.

Wolf could not be positive how much of his current condition was attributed to the drugs and how much to the insomnia-induced exhaustion. Even in this semi-catatonic state he feared nightfall, the hush before the storm as the bruise-eyed night-shift workers escorted the patients back to their rooms and the confinement that brought out the true psychosis contained within the walls of the handsome old hospital. Every night he would wonder why these people struggled on, petrified of being left alone with themselves, their pathetic crying in the dark.

'Open up,' instructed the impatient nurse standing over him.

Wolf opened his mouth and stuck out his tongue to prove that he had swallowed the handful of brightly coloured pills.

'You understand why we had to transfer you onto the secure ward, don't you?' she asked him, as if speaking to a child.

Wolf did not answer.

'If I can tell Dr Sym you've been better about taking your meds, I'm sure she'll move you back.'

When Wolf turned his attention back to the window she huffed and went off to annoy someone else.

He was sitting in a quiet corner of the Rec Room, an almost perfect recreation of his sixth-form common room, complete with stackable bright orange school chairs. Table Tennis Man was growing increasingly irate, as he did every day at this time, somehow managing to lose his one-player match. The Two Pink Ladies, as Wolf knew them, due to the colour of their scrubs, were making simple models out of plasticine, and a group were occupying the tatty sofas surrounding the large television; he was vaguely aware of his name being mentioned, before a member of staff rushed over to replace the Mayor of London with SpongeBob SquarePants.

Wolf shook his head in disbelief as he regarded the nursery-school scene before him, after what had been a particularly disruptive and violent night in the residential wing. One of the Pink Ladies cheerfully kneaded blood into her plasticine flower. Wolf winced as she continued, oblivious to the pain in her destroyed fingernails, presumably sustained while clawing frantically at an immovable door.

He wondered whether he shared this trait with these people: the capacity for such extremes. He knew, deep down, that he would have killed Khalid in front of all those people, no matter what the consequences, any sense of self-preservation lost.

He would have ripped him apart.

Perhaps 'normal' people had more control over their emotions. Perhaps what he considered normal, in fact, wasn't.

His thoughts were interrupted when a tall black man in his mid-twenties got up from in front of the television and approached his table beside the window. Bar the few occasions when it had been absolutely inescapable, Wolf had avoided all contact with anybody since his incarceration. This had even extended to Andrea, who had given up on her attempts to call the hospital and had wasted a journey down there, only for him to refuse to leave his room.

Wolf had seen the man around. He always wore bright red scrubs with bare feet. He had struck Wolf as being, in the main, reserved and thoughtful, which was why it came as such a surprise when he gestured to one of the plastic chairs and waited patiently for a reply.

Wolf nodded.

The man carefully lifted the chair back from the table and sat down. A faint smell of infection surrounded him as he held both hands out to Wolf, linked by the metal handcuffs that the staff equipped him with whenever he entered the communal areas.

'Joel,' the man said through a thick south London accent.

Wolf used his strapped-up wrist as an excuse not to take his hand. Despite the man's calm demeanour, he appeared unable to sit still, and Wolf could hear a foot tapping nervously against the floor beneath the table.

'I thought I knew you,' grinned Joel, pointing at Wolf with both hands. 'Moment you stepped through that door, I said: "I know him".'

Wolf waited patiently.

'When I saw what you did, I thought to myself: "This guy, he don't just *think* that the Cremation Killer; he *know*." Right? That be the freak who killed them girls. Right? And they just let him go.'

Wolf nodded.

Joel swore and shook his head.

'You tried. You did the right thing going for him like you did.'

'You know,' started Wolf, speaking for the first time in weeks. His voice sounded different to how he remembered. 'I appreciate the sentiment, but it would probably mean more had I not watched you whispering into a bowl of cereal all morning.'

Joel looked mildly insulted.

'A man with a god would know the difference between whispering and praying,' said Joel accusingly.

'And a man with his sanity would know the difference between a bowl of Coco Pops and his deity,' quipped Wolf with an unconscious smirk. He suddenly realised how much he missed trading insults with his colleagues.

'OK, OK. Be that way,' said Joel as he got back up. 'I'll see you around, *Detective*.'

Joel went to leave but paused and turned back to Wolf.

'My grandpa used to say: "A man without enemies is a man without principals."'

'Wise words,' nodded Wolf. He felt exhausted by their fleeting exchange. 'But I'm guessing advice like that is also the reason you're in here.'

'*Nah*. I choose to be in here, don't I?'

'Is that right?'

'As long as I'm in here, I'm alive.'

'"A man without enemies . . ."' Wolf recited thoughtfully.

'Ain't got no enemies left, *Detective* . . .' said Joel, turning his back to Wolf and walking away, '. . . that's the problem.'

CHAPTER 24

Wednesday 9 July 2014

2.59 a.m.

Edmunds' watch beeped 3 a.m. He was sitting in the centre of a puddle of light spilling from a buzzing lamp that dangled down from the high ceiling of the Central Storage Warehouse. This was his fourth visit to the archives and he realised that he had started looking forward to these solitary nights.

He found the perpetual darkness peaceful and the temperature-controlled climate pleasant: warm enough to remove his jacket yet cool enough to keep him awake and alert. As he took in another dusty breath, watching the particles spinning in the air around him, he felt overwhelmed by the sheer volume of history buried there.

It was like a game without an end. Inside each of the tens of thousands of identical cardboard boxes lay a puzzle waiting to be verified, or perhaps even solved for the very first time. It was easier to focus upon the challenge that they posed to him rather than the distressing realisation that each and every one of the uniform boxes represented a life lost, lives ruined, all lined up in a tidy row and enjoying the respectful silence like graves in a catacomb.

The day's events had confirmed his suspicions beyond any doubt. Yet again, the killer had known where to find his supposedly hidden target.

Baxter was being naive.

It was true that somebody at the embassy could have leaked Andrew Ford's location; only, this had not been an isolated incident. This was now the fourth occasion on which they had been betrayed and, worse still, nobody but him could see it.

He had lied to Tia again, telling her that he had drawn the short straw and been roped into a stakeout, thus buying himself another precious night with which to hunt the killer into the past. He was in there, somewhere in that enormous warehouse, Edmunds was sure of it, the first tentative steps of the monster that was now running towards them at full pelt.

On Monday night he had stumbled upon an unresolved case from 2008 in which a home-grown Islamic fundamentalist had died inside a secure cell. No one had signed in or out of the building during the estimated time of death and the CCTV footage had corroborated this. The body of the otherwise healthy twenty-three-year-old had displayed signs of suffocation; however, there had been no other evidence to support this, and the death had eventually been accredited to natural causes.

His Internet searches had also turned up the suspicious death of a marine on a military base. After Joe's promising identification of the boot print, Edmunds had made a formal written request to the military police, asking them to disclose the entire case file, but was yet to hear anything back.

He had spent the last hour sorting through the evidence of a murder that had happened back in 2009. The heir to a multinational electronics corporation had mysteriously vanished from a hotel suite despite two bodyguards sitting less than twenty feet away in the next room. Enough blood had been present at the scene to declare the young man dead, yet no body was ever discovered. There had been no useful fingerprints, DNA, or security footage for the police to even begin looking for a killer, which meant that there was nothing of use to Edmunds to link the case to the Ragdoll murders. He made a note of the date and packed the contents back inside the box.

The cool air was keeping him going. He did not feel even remotely tired, but he had promised himself that he would leave by 3 a.m. at the very latest and get home for a couple of hours of sleep before work. He flicked back to his list of the five other cases that he had hoped to get through and sighed. He got to his feet, stacked the box back on the shelf and began the long walk down the shadowy aisle.

As he neared the end of the high shelving units, he realised that the dates on the labels had reached December 2009, the month of the next murder on his list. He glanced down at his watch: 3.07 a.m.

'One more,' he told himself as he located the appropriate box and dragged it off the shelf.

At 8.27 a.m. Wolf entered an uninviting block of flats on a run-down side road off Plumstead high street. He had given up on sleep again, mainly because he now had the unsettling image of the wolf mask to add to his list of reasons not to close his eyes for any length of time. The killer's overconfidence had shaken him. It had been a risk to visit the embassy at all, reckless to join the protest that he had organised, and narcissistically self-destructive to have confronted Wolf as he had.

Wolf recalled Edmunds promising them that the killer would not be able to resist coming in closer and closer as time went on, drawn by a burning desire to eventually get caught. He wondered whether the incident outside the embassy had been the killer's plea for help, whether desperation, rather than arrogance, had driven his actions.

He climbed the muddy stairs, trying to remember whether it had rained since the storms a week earlier. On the third floor, he pulled a peeling fire door open to access the yellowed corridor. There was no sign of the two police officers that should have been stationed outside Ashley Lochlan's door.

He approached Flat 16, which looked to have the only freshly painted front door in the building, and was about to knock when the two officers bumbled out into the corridor holding toasted sandwiches and cups of coffee. They were both startled to find the imposing detective standing there.

'Morning,' said the female officer through a mouthful of bacon and toast.

Wolf's stomach grumbled.

She offered him the other half of her breakfast, which he politely declined.

'Know when you'll be moving her?' asked her youthful-looking colleague.

'Not yet,' said Wolf a little curtly.

'Oh, I didn't mean it like that,' said the man quickly. 'Quite the opposite actually – she's an absolute delight. We're going to miss her.'

The female officer nodded in agreement. Wolf was surprised. The trusty set of stereotypes that had always served him so well had had him expecting a pyjamas-only, smoke-hazed, cat rescue on the other side of the door, yet the two officers were clearly in no hurry to leave.

'She's just jumped in the shower. I'll show you in.'

The female officer unlocked the front door and led him into the immaculate flat that smelled of fresh coffee and bacon. A warm breeze was blowing the net curtains across the colourful flowers on the living room table. The airy space had been tastefully decorated in pastel paints and real wood floors with matching work surfaces. Photographs covered an entire wall and baking apparatus had been left to dry beside the kitchen sink. He could hear water running in the next room.

'Ashley!' shouted the officer.

The water stopped.

'Detective Sergeant Fawkes is here to see you.'

'Is he as handsome as he looks on the television?' a soft Edinburgh accent called back.

The officer looked awkward and then, to her horror, Ashley continued: 'I agree he looks like he needs a good scrub before you could take him anywhere, but—'

'He actually looks like he might fall asleep at any moment,' the officer shouted over her.

'Let him know there's coffee in the kitchen when you show him in.'

'Ashley . . .'

'Yeah?'

'He's already in.'

'Oh! Did he hear?'

'Yes.'

'Arse.'

The police officer could not leave the uncomfortable situation quickly enough and rushed outside to join her colleague. Wolf could hear things scraping, spraying, and shutting behind the thin partition wall and sniffed himself self-consciously as he stood in front of the wall of photos. They were simple, genuine: a recurring beautiful woman at the beach with friends, sitting in a park with an elderly man, at Legoland with what looked to be her young son. His heart sank as he stared at the two delighted faces on what had obviously been a perfect day.

'That's Jordan. He's six now,' said a voice behind him in the attractive accent that sounded a million miles away from Finlay's rasping tones.

Wolf turned to find the same stunning woman from the photographs towel-drying her dark blonde hair in the bathroom doorway. She had clearly just thrown on a pair of tiny denim shorts and a light grey vest top. Wolf's gaze lingered over her glistening long legs before returning to the photograph in embarrassment.

'Don't be creepy,' he whispered to himself.

'Sorry?'

'I said: where is he?'

'I'm pretty sure you said: "don't be creepy".'

'Nope.' Wolf shook his head innocently.

Ashley gave him a funny look.

'I sent him off to my mum's after . . . Well, after the deranged serial killer threatened to murder us all, to be quite frank.'

Wolf was making a valiant effort not to stare at her legs.

'Ashley,' she said, holding her hand out to him.

He was forced to walk over to her, to smell the strawberry shampoo that she had just washed out of her hair, to notice her bright hazel eyes and spot the dark patches on her top where her damp skin had soaked through the thin material.

'Fawkes,' he said, after almost crushing her delicate hand in his. He stepped back as quickly as he could.

'Not William?'

'Not William.'

'Then you can call me Lochlan,' she said with a smirk, before looking him up and down.

'What?'

'Nothing. It's just . . . you look different in person.'

'Well, the press only photograph me if I'm standing next to a dead body, so . . . sad face.'

'You're not trying to tell me that this is your take on a happy face?' Ashley asked, laughing.

'This?' said Wolf. 'No. This is my been up for a week, misunderstood hero, possibly the only person brave and smart enough to catch a genius serial killer, face.'

Ashley laughed: 'Is that right?'

Wolf shrugged as she stared at him, intrigued.

'Breakfast?' she suggested.

'What have you got?'

'The best café in the world just down the road.'

'One: the best café in the world is Sid's, round the corner from mine. And two: you're under home protection. You can't leave.'

'You'll protect me,' she said dismissively as she started pulling windows closed.

Wolf was torn. He knew that he should not indulge her, but he was enjoying their conversation and did not want to do anything to ruin it.

'I'll just put some shoes on,' she said as she headed towards the bedroom.

'You could consider some trousers too,' he suggested.

Ashley stopped and looked at him in mock offence. She caught him glancing back down at her legs again before looking away.

'Why? Am I making you nervous?'

'Far from it,' said Wolf indifferently. 'You just look horrible. *Bleh*! I can't take you out with me looking like that.'

Ashley laughed again at his unconvincing insult. She walked over to the clothes horse, untucked her vest top so that it dropped to the top of her thighs, and then slid out of the denim shorts. Wolf was too stunned to even try to look away. She then wriggled into a pair of skintight ripped stonewash jeans before effortlessly scooping her hair up into a messy ponytail that only made her look more attractive.

'Better?' she asked him.

'Not in any way,' he answered honestly.

She smirked. She never behaved like this, but, with possibly only three days to live, she was enjoying flirting with the man who only had five days left himself. Sliding her feet into a pair of well-worn Converse All Stars, she grabbed her keys off the kitchen table.

'How do you feel about heights?' she asked him quietly.

'Don't want to fall off them,' he replied, confused.

Ashley grinned. She tiptoed past the front door, walked out onto the balcony and then turned back to Wolf:

'Shall we?'

Wolf felt that Ashley had overhyped the dismal little café. The contents of his fry-up seemed to have a life of its own as the various items glided across the plate over a film of grease. Ashley had not even managed to finish her toast. He suspected that she had merely wanted an excuse to get out of the flat and had never actually been inside before, doubting that anybody would make the same mistake twice.

'No offence, Lochlan, but this café is—'

'I work here.'

'. . . good. It's good.'

They had attracted a number of looks on their short journey down the high street, although Wolf could not be sure whether this was people recognising them or simply staring at Ashley. They had chosen a spot beside the window, as far away from the other steel-gutted patrons as possible, and talked easily about nothing in particular for over twenty minutes.

'I've been worried about you,' blurted Ashley when Wolf had believed they were still on the subject of favourite Bon Jovi albums.

'I'm sorry?'

'How are you . . . dealing with everything?'

'Let me get this straight. You're due to die in three days' time and *you're* worrying about *me*?' asked Wolf, seizing the opportunity to put his cutlery down.

'You're due to die in five days' time,' she shrugged.

This caught him off guard. He had been so caught up with the investigation that he had not realised how quickly his own big day was approaching.

'I've been watching the news a lot,' said Ashley. 'There's not much else to do when you're locked up in four rooms. It's like watching a cat playing with a mouse, and the more destroyed you look, the more whoever's doing this seems to tease you.'

'I didn't know I had a destroyed look,' joked Wolf.

'You do,' Ashley said simply. 'What happened to those people, whatever happens to me, it's not your fault.'

Wolf let out an involuntary snort. She was wasting her time trying to make him feel better.

'You seem weirdly *OK* about the whole thing,' he said.

'I'm a strong advocate for fate.'

'Not to burst your bubble, but from what I've seen, if there is a god we have a serious problem because he is not on our side.'

'It's good I'm not talking about God then. Just – things have a funny way of working out.'

'Such as?'

'Such as life bringing you here to me this morning: two people who should never have met, so that I finally have the chance to atone for something I did years ago.'

Wolf was intrigued. Instinctively, he looked around to ensure that no one was listening in. He had been so captivated by Ashley that he had almost forgotten where they were. The flawless woman looked preposterously out of place in such dour surroundings. It was the polar opposite to watching Andrew Ford squatting in the lavish embassy.

'Promise you'll let me finish before you . . . just promise.'

Wolf folded his arms defensively and leaned back in his chair. They both knew that Edmunds had found the five thousand pounds from Vijay Rana's account.

'Four years ago I was working in a pub in Woolwich. It was a rough period for us. Jordan was only one and I was trying to separate from his father, who was not a nice man at all. I could only work part-time while my mum looked after Jordan.

'Vijay was a regular there. He'd come in most lunchtimes and we were quite friendly. On more than one occasion he'd seen me in tears about money or the divorce. He was a kind man. He used to leave me ten-pound tips, which I'd try to give back to him, but he wanted to help. It meant a lot.'

'Maybe he wanted something more than just to help,' said Wolf bitterly. He had no love for Khalid's brother.

'He wasn't like that. He had a family. So, one day he came to me with a proposition. He told me that a friend of his was in trouble with the police but that he knew they were innocent. He offered me five thousand pounds just to say that I had seen someone on my walk home at a specific time. That's it.'

'*You* gave the false statement?' Wolf asked darkly.

'I was desperate – and I'm ashamed to say that I agreed to do it. I didn't think it could really make that much of a difference, and at the time me and Jordan had about fifteen pounds to our name.'

'It made *all* the difference.'

Wolf had lost any trace of affection for Ashley and watched her with furious eyes.

'That's the thing. As soon as I realised it was the Cremation Killer case that I had lied about, I panicked.' Ashley was becoming tearful. 'I wouldn't help someone accused of the things that man was walk free for all the money in the world. I went straight round to Vijay's house, you've got to believe me, and I told him I couldn't do it. I wouldn't mention his involvement or the money. I'd just say that I was mistaken.'

'And what did he say?'

'He tried to talk me out of it, but I think he understood. On the way home, I called the law firm that had been present for my witness statement.'

'Collins and Hunter.'

'And I got put through to one of the senior lawyers.'

'Michael Gable-Collins?'

'Yes!' said Ashley, surprised.

It had not yet been made public that he was dead.

'I told him that I needed to retract my statement and he started threatening me. He began reeling off the charges that I was guilty of: contempt of court, impeding a police investigation, perhaps even an accomplice to the murders! He asked me if I wanted to go to prison, and when I told him about Jordan he said social services would be involved and that they might even take him away from me.'

Ashley was visibly shaken just from the memory of this terrifying conversation. Despite himself, Wolf handed her a napkin.

'It was too high-profile a case for his firm to lose, no matter what the cost,' said Wolf.

'He told me to keep my "stupid mouth shut" and said he'd do all in his power to keep me out of the courtroom. That was the last I ever heard about it directly. Then I watched the events unfold and what you did to try to stop the man that I had helped free, and I – I am so, so sorry.'

Wolf silently got up from the table, took out his wallet and dropped a ten-pound note next to his half-full plate.

'It's not me you need to apologise to,' he said.

Ashley burst into tears.

Wolf walked out of the café, leaving the endangered woman, whose safety he was responsible for, sitting in the corner alone.

CHAPTER 25

Wednesday 9 July 2014

10.20 a.m.

Edmunds felt drunk on exhaustion. He had eventually left the archives at 6 a.m. and had been sitting at his shared desk in the office less than an hour later. His hopes for a doze before the department filled up with those fortunate enough to be working the more sociable shifts had been scuppered when Simmons heaved himself into the chair beside him at 7.05 a.m. Showing a work ethic and obsessive streak only surpassed by Edmunds' own, he had given himself a head start on the day to complete his enquiries regarding the remaining seven names on the list.

Edmunds sent Tia a text to say that he missed her and was going to do his best to get back on time that evening. He had even suggested that they go out for something to eat. He had hesitated before pressing send. The idea of committing himself to additional hours of exhaustion was unappealing, but he thought he should make the effort and was feeling guilty about his innocent, but no less reprehensible, stakeout lie.

After revealing his expertise in criminal communiqués during the initial team meeting, he had unofficially become the department's criminal behaviourist, a role for which he was neither qualified nor being financially rewarded. The commander had requested he prepare a report on the latest note that the killer had so daringly placed on Wolf's person.

It had not taken Joe long to ascertain that the bloody fingerprint from the note was a match to the sample taken from the barbed wire fencing. Edmunds could, therefore, confidently conclude that the message was no more than another taunt. The killer was demonstrating the insignificance of his misstep in Wales and had literally handed them a sample of his own DNA to prove just how incapable they were of stopping him. The fact that he had chosen to deliver the message in person indicated the heightened degree of his growing god complex and suggested to Edmunds that he intended it all to end spectacularly in just five days' time.

He woke with a start. His half-typed report waited on the screen in front of him, the cursor flashing impatiently at the end of his last word. The screensaver had not even activated. He must have only closed his eyes for a moment but somehow felt even worse for it. Offering to make Simmons a drink, he went into the kitchen. While he waited for the kettle to boil, he splashed cold water on his face over the mug-filled sink.

'You didn't get hit again?'

Edmunds finished drying his face to catch Baxter stealing his hot water. The heavy bags beneath his eyes emphasised the bruises left by his broken nose.

'Is Tia knocking you around?' she asked in mock concern.

'I told you, I tripped over the cat.'

'OK. Did you "trip over the cat" again?'

'No. I've just not slept.'

'Because?'

He had managed to keep his visits to the archives secret until this point. He considered finally confiding in Baxter but then decided against it.

'Sofa,' he said, knowing that she would readily accept his relationship troubles as sufficient explanation. 'What are you working on today?'

'Some bloke jumped off Waterloo Bridge and drowned. Left a note and everything. Quite possibly the most straightforward suicide in history, except that some CSI-watching constable has, for no good reason, declared that it looks suspicious. After that, we've got to head over to Bloomsbury for a puddle of blood. The guy's probably taken himself down to A & E: mystery solved.'

She sighed heavily, however Edmunds thought it sounded far more interesting than his day was shaping up to be.

'Have you seen Wolf?' she asked.

'He's not been in.'

Blake appeared in the kitchen doorway. He had started wearing a suit and combing his hair since being partnered with Baxter.

'Ready?' he asked.

'Gotta go,' said Baxter, pouring away her coffee and adding the mug to the already precariously stacked pile in the sink.

Andrea had just got off the phone with Wolf when she stepped out of the taxi. It had been a decidedly unsuccessful conversation, courtesy of the car noise at her end and the background chatter of whichever busy high street he had been walking down at the time.

She had wanted to check in with him. The production team at the newsroom were already making preparations for the rapidly approaching concluding day of the Ragdoll saga. Unfortunately Wolf had been in no mood to speak to her.

He criticised her and her team for broadcasting Andrew Ford's precise location in the embassy and, perhaps unfairly, accused her of facilitating the killer's manipulation of an already paranoid and unhinged mind by televising the protest. She listened to his lecture without argument, even though it had been completely irrational, as every news channel in the world had done the same.

When she had suggested that she buy him dinner, he told her to leave him alone and abruptly hung up. Although she would never vocalise it, she was angry with him for being so petty and judgemental during what might well have been one of their last-ever interactions. It was obvious from the way he had been talking that the idea of not surviving to see next Tuesday had scarcely crossed his mind, making her wonder whether he had finally stepped across the blurred line between optimism and denial.

Elijah was pressuring her for an answer regarding the promotion and it had occupied the majority of her thoughts ever since their meeting. She felt frustrated with herself for the disparity of her indecision. At any given moment she could either be determined to hand in her notice and walk away with what little remained of her moral integrity, or resolute on accepting the position that would be filled with or without her.

She and Geoffrey had discussed it the night before, sitting in the late-evening sun on the patio of their small but beautifully landscaped, garden. As with all things in their relationship, he had made no attempt to influence her decision. It was what made them work so well together. He respected Andrea's independence, that she had grown so accustomed to during her marriage to Wolf. She and Geoffrey chose to spend time together, but they never *needed* to.

Geoffrey had been watching the Ragdoll story unfold with the rest of the world and had never so much as raised an eyebrow at Andrea's sensationalist reporting style, her groundless conjecture, or even the Death Clock, which even she considered a grotesquely shameful gimmick. He had only ever asked that she be careful. His shelves full of war books had taught him that, throughout history, messengers were chosen for their ability to communicate, the speed with which they could reach the intended ear and, more troublingly, their expendability.

Geoffrey listened patiently as the temperature dropped and the strategically positioned garden lights were activated one by one in the falling darkness. He had made the argument that, if she were to take the promotion, her decision would be purely driven by ambition. They did not need the money and she had already established herself as a credible and talented reporter. As perceptive as ever, he had suggested that she speak to Wolf, realising that his opinion was the only one that truly mattered to her on the subject.

Their brusque conversation that morning had made Wolf's position quite clear.

Finlay was keeping one eye on the commander's office as he walked across the room to Simmons and Edmunds' desk. He could see that the tiny but terrifying woman was agitated as she gesticulated wildly while speaking to somebody on the phone. He perched on the corner of the desk, sitting firmly on top of Edmunds' work.

'She's not a happy bunny,' Finlay told them.

'Why's that?' asked Simmons.

It was strange for him, begging for scraps of information from the office gossip when he was so accustomed to being the first to know.

'Will,' said Finlay. 'What else? Apparently he took Ashley Lochlan away from her protected flat.'

'What for?'

'Breakfast. And then stormed off and left her in a café. Her protection team put in a formal complaint. She wants him suspended.'

'On her head be it,' said Simmons. 'What's he playing at?'

Finlay shrugged.

'It's Will, so who knows? He's staying well clear of the office today. I'm off out to meet him now.'

Simmons was rather enjoying the school-like clandestinity taking place right under the boss' nose.

'If she asks, I'm making arrangements for Ashley Lochlan's safe house, which is actually true,' said Finlay.

'We're heading out too,' said Simmons.

'We are?' asked Edmunds. 'Where?'

'I've still got four people on this list unaccounted for,' said Simmons. 'One of them is dead. We're going to find out which one.'

Simmons and Edmunds had treated themselves to Greggs' sausage rolls, as evidenced by the trail of pastry running along the pavement behind them as they neared the third address on the list.

They had already visited the home of the court stenographer and discovered that she had died of cancer back in 2012. They had then learned that His Honour Judge Timothy Harrogate and his wife had emigrated to New Zealand. Fortunately, a neighbour had had contact details for their son, who woke them up in the middle of the night to confirm that they were both alive and well.

The sun emerged from behind a cloud as they strolled past Brunswick Square Gardens and approached the identical brick town houses on Lansdowne Terrace. They located the correct black door and found it ajar. Edmunds knocked loudly, and they stepped into an intricately tiled communal hallway. An engraved plaque directed them upstairs to 'The Penthouse', which struck them both as being rather pretentious in a four-storey building.

They climbed the echoic staircase and reached the corridor that serviced the top-floor apartment. Faded photographs adorned the wall, most depicting an aged gentleman in the company of far younger, and considerably more attractive, women in exotic places. The blonde that the man had his arm around on a yacht appeared not to have made it to shore, where the next picture showed a bikini-clad redhead relaxing beside him on the beach.

There was a loud smash from inside the apartment and, as they drew closer, they could see that this door had also been left unlocked. Sharing a concerned look, they quietly pushed it open. The gloomy hallway boasted the same original tiles as the entrance hall below. They crept past closed doors towards the light at the end of the corridor and the sound of footsteps against a hard floor.

'You tit! I told you not to touch it.'

Edmunds paused. He and Simmons recognised the snide, condescending tone instantly.

'Baxter?' Edmunds called out.

Straightening up, he walked out into the main room, where Blake was on his hands and knees collecting up pieces of the, presumably expensive, vase he had just dropped.

They both looked bewildered as Edmunds and Simmons joined them.

'What the hell are you two doing here?' she asked.

'Ronald Everett, missing juror from the Khalid trial,' said Edmunds.

'Oh.'

'You?'

'I told you earlier: puddle of blood, no body.'

'Where?' asked Simmons.

'Everywhere.'

She gestured to the floor behind the large sofa. There, a halo of dark, dried blood covered the white tiles that surrounded the saturated rug.

'Jesus,' said Edmunds.

'I think we can safely assume that your Mr Everett is no more,' said Baxter callously.

On seeing the bloodbath at his feet, Edmunds was reminded of one of the archived case files he had been reviewing overnight: puddle of blood, no body ever discovered. There was no way that it was simply a coincidence.

'What's wrong?' Baxter asked him.

He could not tell anyone about his private investigation until he was certain that he had found something concrete.

'Nothing.'

He glanced at his watch. He had promised to take Tia out for dinner but could still get to the archives, spend an hour there, and get back again in time if he left straight away.

'This mess doesn't really fit with our killer's meticulous, exacting standards,' said Simmons. 'Not a drop was found at any of the other victims' homes.'

'Perhaps he's not quite as infallible as we've built him up to be,' suggested Edmunds, crouching down to look at the flecks of blood running up the side of the sofa. 'Maybe this was just the only victim he murdered and carved up in their own home and there are other puddles of evidence still scattered elsewhere around the city.'

At that moment the forensics team arrived and Edmunds seized his chance to escape. He made his excuses to Simmons, telling him that he needed to finish up some paperwork back at the office, and then ran downstairs and jogged back towards the Tube station.

*

Wolf's phone beeped. He glanced at the short text message:

I DESERVED THAT EARLIER. DINNER? L X

'What are you grinning about?' Finlay asked him as they walked back to New Scotland Yard.

Wolf ignored him and dialled the number on the text.

'Hello, Detective Fawkes.'

'Hello, Ms Lochlan.'

Finlay looked at him in surprise.

'How did you get this number?'

'Remember Jodie, who you met earlier?'

'Who put in a complaint about me?'

'That's the one. She phoned a friend, who phoned a friend who knows you.'

'I'm surprised you want to have dinner,' said Wolf.

Finlay shot him another strange look.

'Well, lord knows neither of us ate much at breakfast,' she laughed.

'I mean, I think I owe you an apology.'

'I won't hold it against you; you haven't got long left. Seven?'

'At yours, I presume?'

'I'm afraid so. It would appear that you got me grounded.'

'I'll have a "good scrub" beforehand.'

Finlay did not even bother to react this time.

'You do that. Later, Fawkes.'

She hung up before he could respond. Wolf stopped walking.

'I take it I'm to cover for you, as per?' said Finlay.

'I have somewhere to be.'

'Wear that nice aftershave we got you for your birthday, but don't wear that awful blue shirt you always put on.'

'I love that shirt.'

'It makes you look pregnant. Maggie's words, not mine.'

'Anything else?'

'Have fun,' said Finlay with a sly grin.

'I can always tell when you're lying, old man,' said Baxter.

She had bumped into Finlay in the kitchen and casually asked about Wolf. After he had fumbled through his first answer, she had subjected him to five solid minutes of questioning. He was beginning to break and she knew it.

'He wasn't feeling well.'

'Because of the headache?'

'Aye.'

'But you said stomach ache before.'

'That's what I meant, stomach ache.'

'Wait, no. You *did* say headache.'

She was quite enjoying torturing her friend.

'OK. You win. He went back to Ashley Lochlan's.'

'Simmons said they'd argued.'

'They made up.'

'So, why aren't you going?'

Finlay clearly did not want to answer the question, but he knew that Baxter was not going to let it go.

'I wasn't invited.'

'Invited?'

'To dinner.'

'Dinner?'

Baxter's jovial mood suddenly soured and she went very quiet. Finlay was not sure what to say next, so busied himself by making a coffee. When he turned back round to offer Baxter one, she was gone.

CHAPTER 26

Wednesday 9 July 2014

7.05 p.m.

Wolf hoped that his walk in the rain down Plumstead high street had watered down the potency of his new aftershave. After befouling himself with the well-intentioned gift, he had sprayed some along the walls of his flat in the hope that it might keep whatever was scratching behind the plasterboard at bay. He had spent a rare half-hour selecting the perfect outfit and combing his hair in nervous preparation for his first date in a decade, only to come out the other end looking exactly the same as he did every other day.

He stopped at an off-licence on the way and picked out the only two bottles of red and white that he recognised (Baxter's favourites) before purchasing the last remaining bouquet from the garage next door. The limp flowers looked so pathetic that he was seriously questioning whether he had just paid good money for something that had grown naturally out of the old bucket from which he had plucked them.

He made his way up the spine of the run-down tower block and greeted the two police officers standing guard. Neither looked particularly happy to see him.

'We've put in a complaint about you,' the female officer challenged him.

'You'll feel bad about that if I'm dead in a week,' said Wolf.

He smiled; she did not. He squeezed between them and knocked on Ashley's door.

'Try not to leave her crying this time – *mate*,' said the male officer, who was obviously jealous of their dinner date.

Wolf ignored the comment but started to wish that he had responded with something just to fill the awkward silence when Ashley still had not answered the door twenty seconds later. When she did finally unbolt the new security features that had been added to her front door, she looked stunning. Wolf thought he heard the other man audibly gasp behind him. She was wearing a lacy pale pink dress and had pinned her hair up in loose curls. She looked ridiculously overdressed for a quiet meal at home.

'You're late,' she said abruptly before striding back into the flat.

Wolf uncertainly followed her inside and slammed the door on the miserable gargoyles standing watch.

'You look amazing,' he said, wishing that he had worn/owned a tie.

He handed her the wine and the bouquet, which she politely placed in a vase of water in a token attempt to resuscitate them.

'I know it's a bit much, but I might not have another chance to get dressed up so I sort of went all out.'

Ashley opened the red for herself and the white for Wolf. They talked in the kitchen while she occasionally stirred the food. They covered all of the cliché first date topics: family, hobbies, aspirations, using the most tenuous of links to bridge the gap between the subject of the conversation and one of their funniest tried and tested stories. Wolf was suddenly reminded of his dad. And for the first time since this had all begun, they both felt normal, as if there was an indefinite future ahead of them, as if this first evening together could still blossom into something special.

The dinner that Ashley had cooked for them was delicious. She repeatedly apologised for the 'burnt bits' nonetheless, not that Wolf could find any. She poured the dregs of each bottle into their glasses as she served dessert, and the conversation became more melancholy but no less enthralling.

Ashley had warned him that the flat became unbearably hot after cooking. When he self-consciously rolled up his shirtsleeves, she had been intrigued rather than repulsed by the burn covering his left arm. She dragged her chair over to look at it more closely, gently running her fingers over the sensitive, scarred skin in fascination.

Wolf could smell the strawberry in her hair again and the sweet scent of wine on her breath as she turned to look up at him, inches from his face, sharing the air between them . . .

. . . The wolf mask.

Wolf flinched and Ashley pulled away. The image disintegrated instantly, but it was too late. He had completely ruined the moment and could see the rejection painted on her face. He desperately wanted to save what had already been one of the most enjoyable nights he could remember.

'Sorry,' he said.

'No, I'm sorry.'

'Can we try that again? You know, your hand on my arm, you looking up at me, etcetera.'

'Why did you pull away from me?'

'I pulled away, but not from you. The last person who got that close to me was the man who's trying to kill us . . . Yesterday.'

'You saw him?' Ashley's eyes were wide.

'He was wearing a mask.'

Wolf explained what had happened outside the embassy. Something about him facing down the masked man, the wolf, meeting its eye and refusing to look away, sparked something in Ashley, and she gradually came in closer once more. Her hand was back on his arm. He could smell the subtle hint of wine on her breath. She breathed in heavily and parted her lips . . .

Wolf's phone went off.

'Bollocks!' He looked at the screen and almost hung up but then smiled apologetically and stood up to take the call. 'Baxter? . . . Who? . . . No, don't do that . . . Where? . . . I'll be an hour.'

Ashley looked annoyed and started clearing the table.

'You're going then?'

Wolf was in love with that accent and very nearly changed his mind on hearing the disappointment in it.

'A friend's in trouble.'

'Shouldn't they call the police?'

'Not that kind of trouble. Believe me, if it was anybody else I'd tell them where to go.'

'They must be very special to you.'

'Irritatingly . . . yes.'

Edmunds opened his eyes and had no idea where he was for a few seconds. He had drooled all over his own arm and was lying on a mattress of paperwork, staring up at the canyon of shelving units running in either direction. He had been so exhausted, and the combination of the darkness and quiet had been too much for him. Bracing himself, he looked down at his wrist: 9.20 p.m.

'Bugger!'

He threw everything littered across the floor back into the evidence box, slid it onto a shelf and started running towards the exit.

Wolf barely had enough money on him to pay the extortionate taxi fare before climbing out in front of Hemmingway's on Wimbledon high street. He fought his way through the alfresco drinkers and flashed his identification at the bar.

'She's passed out in the toilets,' the girl pulling pints told him. 'Someone's with her. We were gonna call an ambulance, but she insisted we try you first. Wait, you're that detective . . . Wolf. *The* Wolf!'

Wolf was already well on his way to the toilets by the time she reached for the camera phone in her pocket. He thanked and dismissed the waitress who had been good enough to sit with Baxter until he arrived. He knelt down beside her. She was still conscious but only responded if he pinched her or shouted her name.

'Just like old times,' he said.

He draped her jacket over her head to hide her face, predicting that the girl behind the bar would have told every one of the amateur photographers out there that the man from the news was in the ladies' toilets then he scooped Baxter up in his arms and carried her out.

The doorman had cleared a path through the crowd for him. Wolf suspected it was more to get the intoxicated woman outside before she vomited again than out of concern for her welfare, but the assistance was appreciated all the same. He carried her along the street and almost dropped her down the narrow staircase up to her apartment. He somehow managed to unlock the front door and was met by the sound of the radio blaring. Stumbling through to the bedroom, he dropped her onto the bed.

He pulled her boots off and tied her hair back like he had countless times before, albeit not for a long time. Then, he went into the kitchen to fetch the washing-up bowl and switched off the music before feeding Echo. There were two empty wine bottles in the sink and he cursed himself for not asking the bar staff how much extra they had served her.

He filled two glasses with water, gulped his down, and went back through to the bedroom where he placed the bowl beside the bed and the glass of water on the bedside table, then he kicked off his shoes and climbed up next to her. Baxter was already snoring.

He turned off the lamp and stared up at the dark ceiling, listening to the first patters of rain against the window. He hoped that Baxter's recent relapses had been solely due to the stress that they were all under, and that she still had some control over the vice that had never fully relinquished its grip on her. He had helped her hide it from everybody for so long, too long. As he settled in for another sleepless night, periodically checking that she was still breathing and cleaning up after her, he wondered whether he was really helping at all.

Edmunds was soaked through by the time he arrived home to find all of the lights out. He stumbled through the dark hallway as quietly as he could, presuming that Tia was already asleep; however, when he reached the open bedroom door, he saw that the bed was still made.

'T?' he called.

He went from room to room, switching on lights and noticing the things that were missing: Tia's work bag, her favourite jeans, the walking trip-hazard of a cat. She had not left a note; there was no need. She was at her mother's. He had let her down one time too many, not just during the Ragdoll case but ever since the transfer.

He slumped onto the sofa, which he had expected to be sleeping on that evening, and rubbed his tired eyes. He felt terrible for upsetting her so much, but they only had to struggle through another five days before it would all be over one way or another. Surely Tia could see that the end was in sight.

He considered calling her but knew that she would have turned her phone off. He looked at the time: 10.27 p.m. His soon-to-be mother-in-law must have come to collect her because she had left the car out on the road. Grabbing the keys off the hook he switched off the lights and, despite his exhaustion, stepped back out into the night.

He hit hardly any traffic and made excellent time across the city. He reversed into a parking space directly outside the building and hurried over to the security guard. The man recognised him immediately and they made small talk while Edmunds provided his identification and surrendered his personal possessions in order to sign back into the archives.

The wine had helped Wolf drop off to sleep, but less than an hour later he had been woken by the sound of Baxter retching into the en suite toilet. He lay in the darkness, the glow of the bathroom light seeping between the door frame, listening to the chain flush, cupboards opening and closing and then her gargling and spitting mouthwash into the sink.

He was about to get up to head home, satisfied that she was functioning effectively enough to make it through the night unaided, when Baxter wobbled back into the bedroom, rolled onto the bed and slapped a drunken arm across his chest.

'How was your date?' she asked him.

'Short,' replied Wolf, both annoyed with Finlay, who could not keep a secret to save his life, and suspecting that Baxter's poorly timed indiscretion had, in fact, been timed very intentionally.

'Shame. Thank you for coming to get me,' she said, almost asleep again already.

'I nearly didn't.'

'But you did,' she whispered as she drifted off to sleep. 'I knew you would.'

Edmunds' hunch had paid off. He managed to locate the box that he had been working on earlier and had abandoned on completely the wrong shelf in his haste to get home. He had returned to the case from 2009: the heir to a powerful corporation that had vanished from a secure hotel suite, a puddle of blood, no body. He studied each of the crime scene photographs individually and had finally found one that confirmed his suspicions.

On the wall beside the pool of blood, a set of eight tiny spatter stains had been evidenced and dismissed, understandably, as 'further blood'; however, the scene looked uncannily similar to the room that he had visited earlier that day. Armed with the knowledge that they now possessed, it was obvious that this apparently insignificant spatter pattern had actually been caused while the murderer was dismembering the deceased victim in order to remove the body from an otherwise inescapable situation.

It was their killer. Edmunds was sure.

He started packing the evidence back into the box excitedly. At last, he felt as though he had found something promising enough to share with the team. As he got up, a piece of paper dropped out of the lid and onto the floor. It was the standard form that accompanied every box in the warehouse: a list of names, dates signed in and out, and a brief description of the reason for removing it from the archives. Edmunds crouched down to tuck it back inside the lid but then spotted a familiar name at the bottom of the page, the last person to have reviewed the evidence:

Detective Sergeant William Fawkes – 05/02/2013: Blood spatter analysis
Detective Sergeant William Fawkes – 10/02/2013: Returned to store

Edmunds was confused. There had been no paperwork from Wolf and no forensics report since the original back in 2009. The most likely scenario was that Wolf had been led to this case while investigating another. Perhaps he had unintentionally stumbled across this previous victim of the Ragdoll Killer, unwittingly drawing his attention. That would explain the personal nature of the challenge and also the clear level of admiration: the one police officer that the killer deemed worthy.

It was all falling into place.

Edmunds was elated. He would ask Wolf about it in the morning, who might be able to point him towards other examples of their killer's early work. Encouraged by his discovery, he switched aisles and started searching for the next case on his list.

At long last, they were hunting the hunter.

CHAPTER 27

Thursday 10 July 2014

7.07 a.m.

The sun was blazing in through the open doorway, casting hazy shadows across the bed. Wolf opened his eyes. He was alone in Baxter's room, lying fully clothed on top of the covers. The rhythmic thud from the other room of footfalls springing off the treadmill had woken him.

With great effort he got up and collected his shoes from where he had kicked them off at the bottom of the bed. He walked into the sunny living room and waved listlessly at Baxter, who was dressed in her workout clothing and was still sporting the lopsided ponytail that he had given her the night before. Had he not known better, he would have said that she looked rested and revitalised. She had always been able to recover quickly. It was part of the reason she had been able to hide her debilitating problem from so many for so long.

She did not acknowledge him as he went into the open-plan kitchen and set about making a coffee.

'Do you still keep a . . .' he started.

Baxter's skin was glistening with sweat as she maintained the demanding pace. She looked annoyed at having to remove her earphones to hear him.

'Do you still keep a spare toothbrush around?' asked Wolf.

They had always had an unspoken agreement by which Baxter would keep a stock of emergency toiletries in case Wolf ended up staying over at short notice. At one stage it had become a regular occurrence. As innocent as it had been, it was no wonder that Andrea had become so suspicious of their relationship.

'Bottom drawer, bathroom,' she said curtly before replacing her earphones.

Wolf sensed that she was looking for a fight but he was determined not to rise to the bait. This was typical of Baxter. She was embarrassed by her behaviour and would express it by being thoroughly unpleasant.

The kettle boiled and Wolf held up a mug to silently ask her whether she would like a drink. She huffed loudly and ripped the earphones back out.

'What?!'

'I was just asking if you wanted a coffee.'

'Oh, I don't drink coffee. You know that better than anyone. I only drink wine and ridiculous-looking cocktails.'

'Is that a *no* then?'

'That's what you think of me, isn't it? Poor drunken mess who can't even look after herself. Admit it.'

Wolf's resolve was weakening.

'I don't think that,' he said. 'Just going back to the coffee . . .'

'I didn't need you coming round like this, you know? But now you can go off on your merry way feeling all noble and superior. Do me a favour: don't bother next time.'

She was getting out of breath the longer she ranted.

'I wish I hadn't bothered this time!' he shouted. 'I should have left you crawling around on that toilet floor instead of ruining my dinner.'

'Oh yeah, your dinner with Ashley Lochlan. How sweet. I've got a really good feeling about that relationship. I reckon it's going places, just so long as neither of you are brutally murdered in the next four days!'

'I'm going to work,' said Wolf, heading for the door. 'You're welcome, by the way.'

'I don't know why you're doing it to yourself,' Baxter yelled after him. 'It's a bit like naming a cow at an abattoir!'

The front door slammed, knocking a canvas print of the New York skyline off the living room wall. Buzzing with adrenaline, Baxter increased the speed of the treadmill, put her earphones back in and turned up the volume.

Wolf was in a foul mood by the time he reached the office and stormed over to Finlay's desk, where his friend was eager to hear all about his date with Ashley.

'What the hell did you go and do that for?' Wolf snapped.

'Come again?'

'Telling Baxter about my dinner with Lochlan.'

'Tried not to, but she knew I was hiding something.'

'Then you should have made something up!'

'Should I now?'

Wolf watched as Finlay, ever the source of joviality and positivity in the department, transformed back into the brawling Glaswegian bobby he had once been. Wolf took his hands out of his pockets in case he needed to react quickly – Finlay's left hook was legendary.

'It's what a friend would do,' said Wolf.

'I'm Emily's friend as well.'

'All the more reason. Now you've hurt her feelings.'

'Oh, *I've* hurt her feelings? *I* have?' Finlay was talking very quietly, which was never a good sign. 'I've watched you lead that poor lass on for years. Whatever's going on between you two already cost you your marriage and yet you're still at it now, which either means you actually *do* want her but are too gutless to take the plunge or you *don't* and are too gutless to cut her loose. Either way, you've got four days left to man up.'

Wolf was speechless. Finlay had always fought his side over everything.

'I've got a lead to follow up on. I'm heading out,' said Finlay, getting up.

'I'll come with.'

'No, you won't.'

'We've got a progress meeting at ten,' said Wolf.

'Cover for me,' smiled Finlay bitterly.

He slapped Wolf sharply on the back and walked away.

At 9.05 a.m. Wolf ignored another call from Dr Preston-Hall and expected to hear the commander's phone ring at any moment. Finlay had left in a temper and he had already heard Baxter yelling at someone from across the office.

Edmunds was oblivious to all of this. He had spent the last ten minutes preparing the documents that he wanted to discuss with Wolf and was excited to see his reaction. He gathered up the papers and ran through the opening lines that he had been practising in his head as he made his way over to Wolf's desk.

'Gabriel Poole Junior, 2009,' announced Edmunds.

He thought he saw a fleeting look of recognition, but Wolf just sighed heavily and looked up at him impatiently.

'Is that supposed to mean something to me?'

Wolf's lack of reaction had been disappointing, but Edmunds continued on enthusiastically.

'I was hoping that it might,' he said. 'Heir to an electronics empire, vanished from a hotel suite, body never recovered. Any of this ringing any bells?'

'Look, I don't want to be rude, but isn't there anyone else you could talk to about this? I'm not much company.'

Edmunds' confidence had been shaken by Wolf's disinterest. He realised that he had not explained himself very well.

'Sorry, let me start again. I've been looking into archived cases—'

'I thought I told you not to.'

'You did, but I assure you, I did it all in my own time. Anyway, I found someth—'

'No. Not "anyway". If a superior officer instructs you not to do something, you don't do it!' Wolf yelled, attracting the entire office's attention to Edmunds' dressing down. Wolf got to his feet.

'If you'll just g-give me a chance to explain,' Edmunds

stammered. He could not understand how the innocent conversation had deteriorated so drastically, but he was not prepared to walk away either. He had important questions that needed answering. 'I found something really promising.'

Wolf came round to the front of the desk. Edmunds took this as a sign that he was willing to listen and held the first document out to him. Wolf slapped the entire pile out of his hands and onto the floor. There were schoolyard jeers and laughter at the insult. Baxter was on her way over to them and Simmons, reverting back into chief mode, was on his feet.

'I need to know why you booked out the Poole evidence,' said Edmunds. His voice was raised, but the tremble betrayed his nerves.

'I don't think I like your tone,' said Wolf, squaring up to the gangly young man.

'I don't think I like your answer!' replied Edmunds, surprising everybody, including himself. 'Why were you looking into it?'

Wolf grabbed Edmunds by the throat and slammed him back against the meeting room wall. Black cracks forked outwards through the tinted glass.

'Hey!' yelled Simmons.

'Wolf!' shouted Baxter, running over to them.

Wolf released Edmunds, who had a trickle of dark blood running down his neck. Baxter stepped between them.

'What the hell, Wolf?' she shouted in his face.

'You tell your little lapdog to stay away from me!' he bellowed.

She barely recognised the wild-eyed man in front of her.

'He's not mine any more. You're losing it, Wolf,' she told him.

'*I'm* losing it?' he screamed, red-faced and intense.

Baxter understood the unspoken threat. He was a hair's breadth away from exposing the secret that she had concealed for years. She braced herself, actually feeling relieved that she could finally stop pretending.

But he hesitated:

'Tell him he'd better have something concrete if he's going to start throwing accusations around,' said Wolf.

'Accusations about what?' asked Baxter.

'I wasn't accusing you of anything,' snapped Edmunds. 'I just wanted your help.'

Vanita, having missed the beginning of the disagreement, emerged from her office.

'With what?' Baxter barked at both of them.

'He's been wasting time on my old case files rather than doing his job!'

'Oh, piss off,' spat Edmunds uncharacteristically. Blood was running between his fingers where he held his head.

Wolf lunged forward, but Simmons blocked him. Baxter leaned in to whisper to Edmunds.

'Is that true?' she asked him.

'I've found something.'

'I told you to leave this alone,' she snapped.

'I *found* something,' he repeated.

'I can't believe you're taking his side,' said Wolf.

'I'm not! I think you're both dicks!' shouted Baxter.

'Enough!'

The office went deathly silent. Vanita was livid as she marched up to the squabbling group.

'Edmunds, get that head seen to. Baxter, go back to your own team. Fawkes, you're suspended as of this moment.'

'You can't suspend me,' he said dismissively.

'Try me. Get out!'

'Commander, I have to agree with Wolf,' said Edmunds, leaping to his attacker's defence. 'You can't suspend him. We need him.'

'I will not have you tearing my department apart from the inside,' she told Wolf. 'Get out. You're done.'

There was a tense moment in which everybody waited with bated breath for Wolf's reaction. Anticlimactically, he simply laughed bitterly, pulled his arm out of Simmons' grip and shoulder-barged Edmunds on his way out.

*

Only Simmons and Vanita were in attendance for the scheduled progress meeting at 10 a.m. The twelve names were listed on the flipchart, which stood proudly in the centre of the room like a completed jigsaw puzzle. Unfortunately, identifying the final victim, Ronald Everett, had not been the revelation that Simmons had hoped. They were still missing something.

'Just us then,' smiled Simmons.

'Where is DS Shaw?' she asked.

'No idea. Finlay's not picking up his phone. Edmunds has been taken down to A & E for stitches, and you just suspended Fawkes.'

'Just come out and say it if you think I made a bad call, Terrence.'

'Not bad,' said Simmons, 'just brave.'

'He's a liability. You can't blame him, all things considered, but we've finally reached the stage where he's doing more harm than good.'

'I wholeheartedly agree, but I can't coordinate this thing by myself,' he said. 'Let me have Baxter back.'

'I can't. Not after the Garland fiasco. I'll assign you someone.'

'We don't have time for that. Ashley Lochlan dies in two days, Fawkes two days after that. Baxter knows the case. Keeping her away *would* be a bad call.'

Vanita shook her head and muttered something.

'OK, but I'm documenting my objections to this. She's your responsibility now.'

'The Beautiful Blood-spattered Juror,' said Samantha Boyd as she stared at the infamous photograph of her standing outside the Old Bailey. 'Their name for me. It's not like I've got that printed on my business cards or anything.'

Finlay could barely recognise the person sitting across the table from him as the same woman from the picture. There was no doubt that she was still attractive, but her long platinum-blonde hair was now dark brown and styled in a boyish fashion. She was wearing heavy make-up that distracted from her sky-blue eyes that pierced through even the black-and-white versions of the photograph, and her clearly expensive clothing was flattering but in no way attention-grabbing.

The third most famous person from the most famous court case in living memory had agreed to meet him in a fashionable Kensington coffee shop. He had thought it closed for refurbishment when he first arrived, but none of the shopping-bag-toting clientele or tattooed staff appeared the least bit concerned about the exposed piping, dangling bulbs or un-plastered walls.

Finlay's expedition out of the office had not been prompted by his argument with Wolf. He had made the arrangement the evening before. As good as money-tracking, footprint-testing and blood-spatter analysis were, he firmly believed that the most effective way of gathering evidence was simply to ask the right people the right questions. He knew his colleagues thought him old-fashioned, a dinosaur. He would happily admit that he was stuck in his ways and had no intention of changing now, less than two years from retirement.

'I've tried very hard to get away from this,' Samantha told him.

'Can't have been all bad. Good for business, I'd expect.'

He took a sip of his coffee and almost choked on it. It tasted like something Wolf would have asked for.

'Absolutely. We couldn't keep up with the orders, especially for that white dress. We ended up turning people away.'

'And yet?' asked Finlay.

She considered her answer carefully before continuing.

'I wasn't posing for a photo that day. I was looking for help. I never wanted to be famous, especially not because of something so . . . horrible. But suddenly I was "The Beautiful Blood-spattered Juror" and that's all I was to people after that.'

'I can understand that.'

'With respect, I don't think you can. The truth is that I am ashamed of the part I played that day. By then we were so influenced by the indiscretions of Detective Fawkes and the accusations being made against the police that I think we let it overshadow our decision. Most of us did anyway. Ten out of twelve of us made an irreparable mistake, and I think about the repercussions of that every single day.'

There was no trace of self-pity in her voice, merely an acceptance of responsibility. Finlay took out a recent photograph of Ronald Everett and placed it down on the table between them.

'You recognise this man?'

'How could I not? I had to sit next to the horrible old pervert for forty-six days. I wouldn't call myself a fan.'

'Can you think of any reason someone would want to harm Mr Everett?'

'You obviously haven't met the man. My first guess: he probably pawed over the wrong man's wife. Why? Has something happened to him?'

'That's confidential.'

'I won't tell.'

'Neither will I,' said Finlay, putting an end to the topic. He thought hard before asking his next question. 'When you think back to Mr Everett, was there anything that makes him stand out from you and the rest of the jurors?'

'Stand out?' she asked. She looked blank and Finlay wondered whether it had been a wasted journey. 'Oh, only . . . we never proved it.'

'Never proved what?'

'Me and a few other jurors were approached by journalists offering to buy information off us for silly sums of money. They wanted to know what we were discussing behind closed doors, who was going to vote which way.'

'And you think Everett took them up on the offer?'

'No. I'm positive he did. Some of the stuff they were printing had come directly out of our jury bundle and then poor Stanley, who had fought for a guilty verdict right from the very beginning, woke up one morning to find his face plastered across the papers, who claimed to have exposed his strong anti-Muslim views and family ties to Nazi scientists or something similarly absurd.'

'Aren't you supposed to avoid the news during these things?'

'You remember that trial? It would have been easier to avoid air.'

Finlay suddenly had a thought. He dug around in his file for something and then placed another photograph on the table.

'By any chance, was this one of the journalists who approached you?'

She stared down at the photograph intently.

'Yes!' she gasped. Finlay sat up attentively. 'This is the man that died on the news, isn't it? Jarred Garland. My God. I didn't recognise him before. He had long greasy hair and a beard when I met him.'

'You're positive it's the same man?' asked Finlay. 'Look again.'

'Without question. I'd know that sly smile anywhere. You should be able to check it easily enough though if you don't believe me. I had to call the police to come and escort him off my property when he followed me home one night and refused to leave.'

Edmunds could not stop poking at the lump on his head where the nurse had glued the skin back together. He had spent the hours in the waiting room replaying the conversation with Wolf in his head and had transcribed it almost word for word in his notebook. He could not understand how Wolf had misinterpreted his meaning so entirely.

He was tired. Perhaps he had unintentionally come across as disrespectful or accusing. Accusing him of what, though? Edmunds wondered whether Wolf had lied about recognising the case and knew full well that he had forgotten to include the updated forensics report. His overreaction might have been in self-defence.

The one positive thing to have come out of his trip to A & E was that Tia had been forced to reply to his texts. She had even offered to come out of work to sit with him, but he assured her that he was fine. They had agreed that she would stay with her mother for the rest of the week as he would barely be at home and he promised that he would start making up for everything after that.

Conscience-free, he trained it back across town to Watford and then caught a taxi out to the archives. Robotically, he went through the usual routine to gain access to the warehouse but paused outside the little office at the bottom of the stairs. He normally strode right past the door labelled 'Administrator', but on this occasion, he knocked politely against the glass and stepped inside.

The small middle-aged woman behind the obsolete computer looked exactly as he had predicted: deathly white skin, oversized glasses and unkempt. She greeted him enthusiastically, like a conversation-starved elderly relative, and he wondered whether he was her first visitor in quite some time. He agreed to sit but declined the offer of a drink, suspecting that it would cost him at least an hour of his precious time.

After she had told him all about her deceased husband, Jim, and the friendly ghost that she swore haunted the subterranean mausoleum, Edmunds gently guided the conversation back on track.

'So everything has to go through this office?' he asked.

'Everything. We scan the barcodes in and out. If you take one step through that door without a validated code, every alarm in the place goes off!'

'Which means that you can tell me who has been looking at what,' said Edmunds.

'Of course.'

'Then I'm going to need to see any box that DS William Fawkes has ever booked out.'

'All of them?' she asked in surprise. 'Are you sure? Will used to come here a lot.'

'Every single one.'

ST ANN'S HOSPITAL

Sunday 17 October 2010

9.49 p.m.

Wolf shuffled languidly back towards his room in preparation for the night staff's rounds at 10 p.m. The tired corridor was filled with artificial light and the smell from the hot chocolate trolley, a misleading name, as the tepid drink reduced in temperature every time a patient threw a cup of it in a member of staff's face.

He rolled a small ball of plasticine around in his fingers, stolen off the Pink Ladies a week earlier, which he fashioned each night into makeshift earplugs. Although nothing could silence the perpetual screaming, these at least made it only a distant horror.

He passed several open doors leading to vacant rooms as their occupiers squeezed every last second of television out of the evening before their enforced curfew came into effect. As he turned the corner into another deserted corridor, he heard whispering from one of the darkened rooms. He gave the doorway a wide berth as he passed, overhearing the muted prayers recited at speed under the speaker's breath.

'Detective,' called the whispered voice before continuing with the remaining lines.

Wolf paused, wondering whether he had imagined it, the medication playing tricks on him again. He peered into the blackness. The door was slightly ajar. The shard of light penetrating the darkness revealed only the hard floor and part of a black torso bent over a bare leg in prayer. Wolf went to move away when the whispering stopped once more.

'Detective,' it repeated before beginning a new verse.

Wolf cautiously approached the heavy door and pushed. It swung stiffly on its old hinges with a weary creak. From the relative safety of the doorway, he reached blindly for the light switch that he knew was situated somewhere to the right of the door. The recessed fluorescent strip buzzed to life but had been smeared with either food or dried blood, its brightness reduced to an imitation candlelight that threw dark shadows across the walls. The small space reeked of infection and whatever it was that had burnt onto the plastic casing.

Joel faltered in his prayer to shield his eyes from the polluted light. He was only wearing frayed underwear, leaving the substantial scarring to the rest of his body exposed; however, these were not souvenirs from a past accident or violent attack but self-inflicted mutilations. Crosses of various sizes littered the dark canvas, many scars aged white with time, others still red-raw and inflamed.

The rest of the small room matched its guest: a Bible lay haemorrhaging pages on the yellow-stained bed, individual verses torn crudely from their gospels and glued with saliva to every available surface, overlapping where God's message overwhelmed the room's insufficient size.

As if emerging from a trance, Joel slowly looked up at Wolf and smiled.

'Detective,' he said softly before gesturing around the room. 'I wanted to show you this.'

'I wish you hadn't,' replied Wolf, his own voice barely louder than a whisper, as he tried to cover his nose in the politest way possible.

'I been thinking a lot about you . . . about your situation. I can help you,' said Joel. He ran his hand across his disfigured chest. 'And this – this is what's gonna save you.'

'Self-harm?'

'God.'

Wolf suspected that the self-harm route might have produced more tangible results.

'Save me from what, Joel?' he asked wearily.

Joel burst out laughing. Wolf had had enough and turned to leave.

'Three years back, my little sister was killed – murdered. Drugs debt,' said Joel. 'Owed some pretty bad people a hundred and fifty quid – so they cut her face off.'

Wolf turned back to look at Joel.

'I-I mean, I ain't gotta tell you. You know. You know what I wanted to do to them. Woulda made it real slow. Woulda made them feel it.' Joel stared into space as he pictured enacting his revenge with a cruel smirk. 'I tooled up. Went looking. But these ain't the kinda people you get close to. I felt helpless. Know what I'm saying?'

Wolf nodded.

'Desperate times, right? So, I took the only option I had left, the only way to make things right. I made a trade.'

'A trade?' asked Wolf, transfixed by the story.

'My soul for theirs.'

'Your soul?'

Wolf glanced around at the Bible that surrounded them and sighed. He felt foolish for indulging his fanatical host for as long as he had. He could hear a member of staff struggling to escort someone back to their room out in the corridor.

'Goodnight Joel,' he said.

'Week later, I find a bin bag waitin' on my doorstep, just a regular black bin bag. There was so much blood. I mean, it was on my hands, my clothes . . .'

'What was in the bag?'

Joel did not hear the question. He could see it staining his hands once more, could smell the metallic blood. He started muttering under his breath and crawled across the room towards his few worldly possessions. He ripped another page from his decimated Bible and scrawled across it in crayon.

Wolf realised that, this time, he was not reciting a prayer but a number. He cautiously took the page from Joel's outstretched arm.

'It's a phone number,' said Wolf.

'He's coming for me, Detective.'

'Whose number is this?'

'"This is the second death, the lake of fire,"' quoted Joel, reading the relevant verse off the back wall.

'Joel, whose number—'

'Eternal damnation. Who wouldn't be afraid?' A tear rolled down his cheek. He took a moment to compose himself and then met Wolf's eye. 'But you know what?' He looked up at the creased page that Wolf held in his hands and smiled sadly:

'It was worth it.'

CHAPTER 28

Friday 11 July 2014

7.20 a.m.

Baxter thought she might have damaged her Audi, which was frustrating because she was always so careful with it and knew she was an excellent driver. She had had no choice but to park just off the high street in an open space that had been miraculously transformed from a rubble-strewn building site into a functional car park simply by installing a ticket machine in the far corner.

She was on her way to prep Ashley for the move later that day. On Vanita's orders they were to keep their involvement simple. She and Edmunds would collect her from her flat in an unmarked car and rendezvous with Simmons on the outskirts of the city. Ashley would then change vehicle and be driven to the south coast, where Protected Persons would be waiting with a boat. As before, the final destination had not been shared with them.

Baxter stepped into the third-floor corridor. The two sleep-deprived officers sitting outside Ashley's door got to their feet when they heard her coming. Baxter took out her identification and introduced herself.

'You might want to give it a few more minutes,' smirked the female officer.

The male officer looked annoyed. Baxter ignored the advice and banged loudly against the blue door.

'I'm on a tight schedule,' she said.

She could see the two officers exchanging irritated looks out of the corner of her eye.

'I told you, I don't think they're up yet.'

'They?' asked Baxter.

At that moment, the lock clicked loudly and the door swung open. Wolf was halfway through buttoning up his shirt and froze when he saw Baxter standing in the doorway.

'Hey,' he said dumbly.

Baxter's expression shifted from confused to hurt to angry. Without a word, she clenched her fist, turned her shoulder and swung at Wolf with all her weight behind it. He had taught her well. The satisfying blow made contact with his left eye, and he stumbled backwards. The two police officers watched in surprise, but neither made any attempt to intervene.

Baxter suspected that she had broken a finger and tried to shake off the pain. Then she turned on her heel and stormed off back down the corridor.

'Baxter! Will you please just stop for a second?' Wolf had followed her out of the building, down the street, and into the potholed car park. 'I hate to use the dead man walking card, but I could be dead in three days' time. Please.'

Reluctantly, Baxter stopped. She turned to face him and folded her arms impatiently.

'We are not a couple,' said Wolf, 'and never have been.'

Baxter rolled her eyes and turned back towards the car.

'We are something else,' he said sincerely, 'something confusing, infuriating, special and messy. But we are not a couple. You can't be angry with me about this.'

'You just carry on waltzing about doing whatever you want like usual.'

'I will, and that's my point. I'm not couple material. Andrea will tell you that.'

Baxter made to walk away again and Wolf gently took her arm.

'Don't touch me!' she shouted, and he let her go.

'Look, I just need you to know that . . .' Wolf was struggling to find the words, 'that nothing I've done . . . that I never intended to hurt you.'

Baxter unfolded her arms and looked at him for a long moment.

'Go screw yourself, Wolf,' she said before marching back in the direction of Ashley's building.

Wolf looked hurt but did not try to pursue her.

'Baxter!' he yelled after her. 'Protect the little girl!'

She continued walking away.

'If he can't get to Ashley, I think he'll come for her!'

Baxter turned onto the high street and disappeared out of sight without acknowledging him.

After the non-meeting the day before, Vanita had rescheduled the case review for 9.30 a.m. Baxter came rushing into the office with just two minutes to spare. Thanks to Wolf, her frosty encounter with Ashley had overrun considerably and then she had hit heavy traffic trying to get back into the city.

Edmunds came bounding over before she had even put her bag down in the greasy stain on her desk, a souvenir from the night shift's nocturnal supper. He looked tired and unusually untidy.

'Christ's sake,' huffed Baxter, moving her bag to the floor. 'This place is going to shit.'

'I need to speak to you,' Edmunds said urgently.

'Not now. It's been a shitty morning already.'

'I think I've found something, but I don't fully understand it.'

Baxter could see Vanita watching them from inside the meeting room.

'Then share it with everyone. Come on.'

She tried to step around him.

'That's the thing. I really do need to discuss it with you first.'

'Jesus, Edmunds! Afterwards,' she snapped.

She jogged into the meeting room and apologised for being late. Anxiously, Edmunds followed her inside, where the flipchart of information now looked impressively complete.

1. (HEAD) Naguib Khalid 'The Cremation Killer'
2. (TORSO) – ? – Madeline Ayers – (Khalid's defence lawyer)
3. (LEFT ARM) *platinum ring, law firm?* – Michael Gable-Collins – ~~*why?*~~ *spoke to AL*
4. (RIGHT ARM) *nail varnish?* – Michelle Gailey – (Khalid's probation officer)
5. (LEFT LEG) – ? – Ronald Everett – *juror – leaking information to JG*
6. (RIGHT LEG) Detective Benjamin Chambers – *why?*

A – ~~Raymond Turnble~~ (Mayor)
B – ~~Vijay Rana/Khalid~~ (Brother/accountant) *not at trial, paid off AL*
C – ~~Jarred Garland~~ (Journalist) *bought information off RE*
D – ~~Andrew Ford~~ (Security guard/alcoholic/~~pain in arse~~) *– Dock security officer*
E – Ashley Lochlan (Waitress) or (nine-year-old girl) *faked witness statement*
F – Wolf

The meeting began with Vanita recapping the plan to deliver Ashley Lochlan to Protected Persons later that afternoon. When Baxter noticed the additional annotations that had been scrawled on to the board, Finlay told them about his conversation with Samantha Boyd and how Ronald Everett had been selling information to Jarred Garland. He handed out a selection of articles written by Garland around the time, all unremittingly criticical of either Wolf, the Metropolitan Police or the neo-Nazi, Muslim-hating juror.

Edmunds had barely been listening. Bar the few hours of involuntary sleep that his body had forced upon him in the dark archives, he had basically been up for four days straight. He was starting to suffer with the side effects of his obsession. He could barely concentrate on anything for more than a few moments and was regularly losing periods of time, five minutes here, ten there, staring blankly into space. He had developed a slight twitch in his left eye and was suffering with several painful mouth ulcers, a sign that he was feeling run-down.

He had completed his task of sorting through every evidence box that Wolf had signed out over the years and had found something deeply troubling amongst the other routine investigations. For a period between 2012–13, Wolf had looked into seven archived files that clearly resembled their killer's distinctive methods. One of the autopsies had even cited triflic acid as the cause of the 'horrific internal injuries'.

It was clear that Wolf had been hunting a serial killer, and yet there was no open case file linking the murders together and not one document relating to his investigations included in any of the boxes. He had been trailing this unnamed killer in secret, but why?

It had occurred to Edmunds that the period in question would have been shortly after Wolf's reinstatement. Disregarding all protocols and procedures, perhaps he had wanted to catch this killer alone to prove himself after all of the controversy and allegations that had ripped his reputation to shreds. Perhaps he had even wanted to prove it to himself.

That still did not explain why he had not shared this invaluable information with them once the Ragdoll murders began. There was no way that he had not recognised his killer's telltale signs.

Edmunds desperately needed to speak to Baxter about it all.

'We're still no closer to identifying who would want all of these people dead,' said Vanita in frustration. Her way of stating the facts sounded more like an accusation of incompetence. 'None of the relatives of Khalid's victims are flagging up as the vigilante type.'

Simmons handed Edmunds the pile of articles written by Garland and he began flicking through them.

'Chambers still doesn't link to Khalid in any way,' Baxter pointed out. She was now able to bring up her friend's name without getting overly angry or upset.

One of the articles caught Edmunds' attention. Garland had interviewed Mayor Turnble and the piece was about as damning and slanderous as the newspaper could confidently print without winding up in court. The mayor had been busy promoting his new strategies and had openly invited the 'victimised' Naguib Khalid to assist him in finalising his new *Policing and Crime Policy* report. Garland had purposely asked leading questions with which to encourage the mayor's increasingly vehement attack on the Met's most disgraced detective.

'Almost looks like Will's hit list,' quipped Finlay. 'If he wasn't on it, of course.'

'Faustian, you could say,' smiled Simmons.

Finlay chuckled.

Edmunds slowly lowered the article he had been reading and turned to Finlay. An incoherent thought began to form somewhere within his fatigued mind. He glanced back down at the article in his lap and then up at the flipchart in the centre of the room.

All of a sudden, something clicked.

It all finally made sense.

'It's Wolf!' he gasped, dropping the articles on the floor and pressing his hands firmly against his temple, forcing his disjointed thoughts into order.

'I was joking,' said Finlay uncomfortably.

The others shared concerned looks as Edmunds started mumbling names to himself. He leapt up out of his seat and laughed.

'We've been so blind,' he said. He started pacing up and down. 'I've been wrong this entire time. Khalid was never the key; it's Wolf. It was Wolf all along!'

'What the hell are you talking about, Edmunds?' asked Baxter. 'Wolf's one of us.'

Finlay pulled a face and shook his head at her reassuringly.

Edmunds ripped the completed list of victims off the flipchart and let it drop to the floor.

'Hey!' shouted Simmons, but Vanita gestured to let Edmunds continue.

He started scribbling excitedly.

1. The Cremation Killer – Wolf obsessed – already tried to kill once
2. The defence lawyer – discredited Wolf's evidence – got Khalid cleared
3. The law firm boss – knew the witness statement was fake
4. The probation officer – inexperienced – allowed Khalid to kill again
5. The juror – leaking sensitive information to Garland
6. Chambers –
7. Mayor – shamelessly used Wolf before and after Khalid killed final girl
8. Khalid's brother – paid Lochlan for fake witness statement
9. Journalist – printed lies about Wolf, used information to influence public/jury
10. Security officer – saved Khalid's life, broke Wolf's wrist
11. The witness – lied for money, contradicted Wolf's evidence
12. Wolf – the deception

'This is ridiculous, right?' said Baxter. She looked to her colleagues for support. 'I mean, none of you is actually buying any of this crap?'

'Chambers?' Edmunds asked her. 'What's the missing link?'

'It seems awfully convenient that Wolf roughs you up a bit yesterday and now, all of a sudden, you start accusing him of – I don't even know what,' she replied.

'Chambers?' Edmunds repeated.

'There's no connection,' she said defiantly.

'What's the link?' Edmunds shouted at her, dominating the room.

'I told you, nothing!'

Finlay cleared his throat and turned to her. Baxter scowled at him.

'I don't believe a word of it either, lass, but we need to go along with it to get it sorted out,' he said.

Baxter refused to talk.

'Will always believed Ben sent the letter,' said Finlay.

'Which letter?'

'The one to Professional Standards,' Finlay continued, 'saying he was obsessed and unstable and advising his reassignment.'

Finlay glanced back at Baxter, but she would not even look at him.

'It was the final nail in the coffin when it got read out in court,' recalled Simmons, who was looking increasingly troubled. 'That letter saved Khalid.'

'These are substantial allegations, DC Edmunds,' said Vanita, stating the obvious. 'Substantial allegations require substantial proof.'

Edmunds remembered something. He was already flicking through the pages of his notebook. He started paraphrasing:

'28 June – guard duty outside interview room. Overheard discussion between Mayor Turnble and DS Fawkes: "I understand. You were all just doing your jobs: the press, the lawyers, the hero that shattered my wrist and pulled me off Khalid."'

'Fawkes said that?' asked Simmons in concern.

'Word for word,' said Edmunds. 'He named three of our victims before we had even started looking into them.'

'It's not enough,' said Vanita. 'Not to invite the shit storm that's going to hit us if we go down this path.'

Edmunds walked out of the meeting room and returned with the first of the archived evidence boxes. He handed each of his colleagues the relevant documents attributed to the case, along with the incriminating sign-out sheet.

'You all remember Wolf's reaction to me discovering this yesterday?' asked Edmunds. 'Well, I've got six more beneath my desk – our desk.'

'This explains everything,' said Baxter. 'Wolf clearly spooked this freak and now the killer's acting in self-defence.'

'I considered that, but did Wolf tell anybody here about any of this?' Edmunds asked the room. 'Boxes of invaluable evidence that could have saved these people's lives? That could save his life?'

No one responded.

Edmunds squatted down and held his hands over his eyes, rocking back and forth gently on his heels. He grimaced as though he were in pain and started whispering nonsensical snippets of information to himself:

'Wolf IDs him . . . He approaches him . . . Leaks details of the case . . . No. No, but he doesn't just do that because these are Wolf's enemies – *this* is Wolf enlisting him.'

'I've heard enough of this shit,' said Baxter, getting up to leave.

Edmunds turned back to his uncomfortable audience:

'Wolf wanted revenge, justice, call it what you will, for Annabelle Adams, for her family, for himself,' he started, still piecing it all together even as he spoke. 'None of these people's corruption, inaction or opportunism had been answered for, while he was serving time in a psychiatric hospital and another young girl was lying dead.

'So, he gets reinstated and starts actively looking into unsolved murders. After all, an unsolved murder means an uncaptured killer. He conducts his investigation in secret, finds these seven old cases and somehow discovers the identity of the killer. Ah, but instead of arresting him, he uses him to bring retribution down upon everyone that he holds accountable.

'The ingenious twist was to add his own name to the list, making the entire thing about him. Wolf knew that no one would suspect him if his life was under threat. I mean, think about it: if Wolf's name wasn't on there, he would have flagged up as a suspect from the get-go.'

There was a knock at the glass door.

'Not now!' all five of them bellowed in unison at the mousy woman, who scurried away back to her desk.

'If, and that's a big *if*, Fawkes did discover the identity of the killer,' said Simmons, ignoring Baxter's glare, 'that would mean the answer is somewhere inside these seven boxes.'

'It would,' nodded Edmunds.

'This is ridiculous,' hissed Baxter.

'If you're right, we should assume that Fawkes was passing information to the killer the entire time,' said Vanita.

'That would certainly explain a lot,' said Edmunds. 'I've been concerned about the possibility that we might have a leak for a good few days now.'

Edmunds looked to Baxter for confirmation, but she purposely ignored him. Vanita sighed.

'Then we have a real shot at saving Ashley Lochlan,' she said, 'as Fawkes won't be involved.'

Finlay and Baxter glanced at one another.

'Am I missing something?' asked Vanita.

'Wolf was with her this morning,' said Baxter impassively. 'It looked like he'd stayed the night.'

'Is there a rule left that man hasn't broken?!' exclaimed Vanita, glaring accusingly at Simmons. 'We'll need to make Ms Lochlan aware of the situation. DC Edmunds, assuming you are right about this, do you believe the killer is aware that Fawkes is behind it all?'

'That's tricky to answer.'

'Try.'

'I can only speculate.'

'Then speculate.'

'No. Wolf clearly considers himself far cleverer than all of us, including the killer. I can't see that he would want to leave any loose ends. I also don't believe for a moment that this killer would willingly allow one of his victims to survive after promising the world his murder. It's a point of pride for him. To fail would be an embarrassment.'

'Which can only mean that Fawkes intends to get to him first,' said Vanita.

Baxter threw a handful of paperwork against the cracked glass wall and stood up again.

'This is complete bullshit! This is *Wolf* we're talking about here!' She turned to Finlay. 'Your *friend*, remember?'

'Aye, but look at the facts, Emily,' he replied, looking ill.

Baxter turned on Edmunds.

'You've had a thing about a mole on the team for days and this convenient little story just so happens to fit in perfectly for you, doesn't it? If anyone thinks they're cleverer than everyone else, it's you!' She looked pleadingly at her colleagues. 'What if Wolf's being set up? Has anyone thought about that, huh?'

'Maybe he is,' said Simmons soothingly, 'but we need to bring him in either way.'

'I agree,' said Vanita, picking up the meeting room phone. 'This is Commander Vanita. I need an Armed Response Unit to attend William Fawkes' home address immediately.'

Baxter was shaking her head in disbelief. She slid her mobile phone out of her pocket.

Finlay was watching her closely. 'Emily,' he said firmly.

She grudgingly put it away.

'Be aware, suspect may be dangerous,' Vanita continued on the phone. '. . . That's correct: suspect . . . that's affirmative. I am ordering you to arrest DS Fawkes.'

CHAPTER 29

Friday 11 July 2014

12.52 p.m.

Baxter glanced in the rear-view mirror. Ashley sat nervously in the back seat, staring out at the heaving streets they were crawling through at an agonisingly slow pace.

Baxter had asked Finlay to drive, which appeared to have shocked him more than anything else he had heard on what had already been, by anyone's standards, an unusually shocking day. He had taken them on the most absurd route across the city and it was taking all of her self-restraint not to comment on it as the set of temporary traffic lights up ahead allowed another two cars to pass by the crater that had been dug out of the city centre.

Baxter had point-blank refused to even speak to Edmunds, let alone sit in a car with him for a two-hour round trip. She pictured him back at the office, barely able to conceal the stupid grin on his face as he trespassed into Wolf's affairs, collating his evidence to use against him.

Apparently, Wolf had not been at home when the Armed Response Unit arrived at his building and kicked down the door to his unimpressive apartment. As they sat there in the queue that Finlay had found for them, a team of their colleagues were ransacking the tiny flat, finally unpacking the piles of boxes that Wolf had left collecting dust since moving in.

The bare bones of the situation had been explained to Ashley. She said she had no idea about Wolf's current whereabouts and had not known anything about the suspension. As the last person to have seen Wolf, Baxter had had no choice but to elaborate on their parting conversation; however, she decided to omit the punch in the face, knowing that the irrelevant detail would only provoke further questions that she was in no mood to answer.

They had collected Ashley at 12.15 p.m. and were due to rendezvous with Simmons at 1.30 p.m. in the car park of Wembley Stadium. She had already called to warn him that they were running late. Neither of the women had spoken a single word to one another and even Finlay had struggled to maintain his trademark buoyancy and prevent the car from sinking into a lasting silence.

Baxter felt very exposed. They had been sitting on the same road for almost ten minutes, while pedestrians weaved in and out of the stationary traffic, some passing mere inches away from their endangered passenger. When three cars (two legally and one BMW) made it through the lights, Baxter realised exactly where they were.

'What the hell are we doing in Soho?' she asked.

'You asked me to drive.'

'Yes, but I thought "in the right direction" was implied.'

'Which way would you have gone then?'

'Shoreditch, Pentonville, Regent's Park.'

'There are roadworks all around King's Cross.'

'Good thing we didn't get stuck in any of those.'

There was the ping of an incoming text message and Ashley slyly looked at her phone.

'What the hell?' said Baxter. 'They were supposed to take that off you.'

She held out her hand impatiently while Ashley typed a hurried reply.

'Now!' snapped Baxter.

Ashley switched the phone off and handed it over. Baxter pulled out the battery and the sim card before dropping it into the glove compartment.

'Tell me, why are we all risking our arses trying to keep you hidden when you're sat there pissing around on your phone?'

'She gets the message,' said Finlay.

'Perhaps you could Facebook a nice selfie outside the safe house when you get there.'

'She gets it, Emily!' snapped Finlay.

The car behind honked its horn and Finlay looked back up to find that the two cars in front were gone. He pulled up to the red light, where the imposing Palace Theatre dominated the crossroads.

'Is that Shaftesbury Avenue?' asked Baxter, appalled. 'On what planet was this ever going to be the quickest—'

The car door slammed.

Baxter and Finlay both whipped round to stare at the empty back seat. Baxter threw the passenger door open and climbed out. She spotted Ashley pushing her way through a group of tourists in matching backpacks before disappearing around the corner onto Shaftesbury Avenue. Baxter took off after her on foot. Finlay jumped the red light, only to narrowly avoid a head-on collision with a car coming from the other direction. He swore for the first time in years and was forced to reverse back.

Ashley took the first road on the left. By the time Baxter reached the corner, she had swung right and passed beneath the ornate Paifang archway that marked the entrance to Chinatown. Baxter arrived at the gateway. Red and dirty-gold pillars held a decorative green roof high above the street below. She had lost sight of Ashley, who had slowed her pace to a brisk walk, knowing that she would blend seamlessly into the endless crowds filtering through the narrow corridor of shops and restaurants.

'Police!' Baxter shouted, holding her ID out in front of her.

She started fighting through the continual flow of distracted tourists passing beneath the strings of red lanterns that criss-crossed into the distance. Shop owners laughed and shouted to one another incomprehensibly, music clashed discordantly as it escaped the open windows of the street-side eateries, and unfamiliar smells infused the polluted London air as she snaked between the street vendors. If she did not get a visual on Ashley in the next few seconds, she knew she would lose her altogether.

She spotted a bright red bin beside a matching lamp post, painted to complement the colourful archways. She pulled herself up onto it, gaining strange looks from the more attentive of the crowd, and looked out over the sea of heads. Ashley was over twenty metres ahead of her, sticking close to the shopfronts as she approached another Paifang archway and the O'Neill's pub that denoted a stark return to reality.

Baxter jumped down and started running for the exit, shoving people aside as Ashley came back into view. She was only five metres behind when Ashley passed beneath the archway and an unfamiliar car came skidding to a halt in front of her. Ashley ran into the road and climbed into the passenger seat. The driver saw Baxter coming and wheelspun as he accelerated fiercely. Baxter had one hand against the driver's window as the car swerved violently away from her and then sped out onto Shaftesbury Avenue.

'Wolf!' she called desperately after him.

He had looked right at her.

She repeated the number plate again and again to ensure that she had it memorised. She was breathing heavily as she took out her phone and dialled Finlay's number.

Edmunds heard Vanita's undignified reaction to Ashley Lochlan's voluntary kidnapping from his seat out in the main office before she dragged him and Simmons back into the meeting room to inform them of this latest development. Edmunds had been busy working through the archived boxes one at a time and Simmons was in the middle of sifting through Wolf's phone records for the previous two years.

'She is positive that it was Wolf?' Edmunds asked in confusion.

'Positive,' said Vanita. 'We've flagged up the number plate as a top priority.'

'We need to keep this to ourselves,' said Simmons.

'Agreed,' said Vanita.

'But the public could help us find them. We have absolutely no idea where he's taking her,' said Edmunds. 'She's in danger.'

'We don't know that for certain,' said Vanita.

'No,' corrected Edmunds. 'We haven't built an airtight case against him yet, but we know he's behind it.'

'You need to wake up, Edmunds,' snapped Simmons. 'Can you imagine the fallout from announcing to the world that our lead detective masterminded the entire thing? And then we let him drive away with his next target to boot!'

Vanita nodded along thoughtfully.

'But—' started Edmunds.

'A touch of diplomacy goes a long way in situations such as this, and I for one have no intention of losing my job over it until we know, beyond any conceivable doubt, that Fawkes is guilty,' Simmons told him. 'Even then, there will be a time and a place to trickle out the details of what transpired.'

Edmunds was disgusted. He stormed out of the meeting room and slammed the door behind him, extending the large crack in the glass wall created by his own head the previous morning.

'Very nicely handled. It's good to see that there's still a manager in there somewhere,' said Vanita. 'Maybe when you get this cops and robbers phase out of your system, there will still be some hope for you.'

Edmunds swung the door to the men's toilets open and kicked the metal bin across the tiled floor in frustration. He felt like laughing and crying simultaneously; the irony of Wolf being protected by the very self-serving, red-taped, arse-covering bureaucracy that had landed them all in this situation had not been lost on him. If he stood any hope of making his superiors act, he needed to find irrefutable proof of Wolf's guilt.

He needed to get into Wolf's head before he started covering his tracks, before he was thinking clearly. He needed him at his most vulnerable.

*

Baxter and Finlay pulled into the South Mimms services on the outskirts of the city. Ashley's reassembled phone revealed that she had been texting Wolf with their location at every step of the journey. The one incoming message from Wolf had simply read:

WARDOUR ST. RUN.

They had returned to Ashley's flat to search for any clue as to where they were heading but had left empty-handed, then on their way back to New Scotland Yard, they received a phone call. The parking enforcement company that operated at the services had contacted the police when their automatic number plate recognition camera had issued a fine to the flagged-up car.

The dilapidated Ford Escort had been left unlocked and virtually out of fuel, suggesting that Wolf had no intention of returning for it. The useless CCTV footage showed them abandoning the car before disappearing out of sight, presumably to change vehicle. Wolf now had a four-hour head start on them.

'How does any of this fit Edmunds' brilliant theory?' asked Baxter as they walked back through the car park.

'I don't know,' said Finlay.

'It doesn't. She chose to run off with him of her own accord. She willingly changed cars with him here. He's trying to save her, not kill her!'

'I guess we'll find out when we find him.'

Baxter laughed as though Finlay was being naive.

'Problem is, we're not going to find him.'

Edmunds reread the selection of NHS posters pinned haphazardly across the notice board as he waited opposite the small reception window in the entrance of St Ann's Hospital. He looked up hopefully every time one of the casually dressed employees buzzed in or out through the secure main doors. He was beginning to doubt his own idea, unsure what he realistically expected to learn in exchange for the five-hour round trip.

'Detective Edmunds?' a careworn woman finally asked.

She buzzed them in and led him through the maze of bleak corridors, only pausing to swipe her card whenever a door blocked their path.

'I'm Dr Sym, one of the primary AMHPs here,' she said, too quickly for Edmunds to even scribble down the meaningless jumble of letters. She flicked through the handful of paperwork in her hands and posted something into a colleague's pigeonhole. 'You had some questions about one of our—'

The woman spotted someone she urgently needed to speak to: 'Sorry.'

Jogging off down the corridor, she left Edmunds standing outside the entrance to the Rec Room. Ever the gentleman, he opened the door for an elderly woman, who dawdled out without acknowledging him as he peered inside. The majority of the room's occupants were sitting around the television, which was blaring at an uncomfortable volume. A man tossed a table tennis bat across the room in a temper and another was reading beside the windows.

'Detective!' the harried woman called from along the corridor.

Edmunds let the door swing shut and caught up with the doctor.

'Let's stop by the residential wing on the way to my office,' she said, 'then I'll dig Joel's file out for you.'

Edmunds stopped walking: 'Joel?'

'Joel Shepard,' she said impatiently before realising that Edmunds had never actually stated which patient he had wanted to discuss with her.

'Joel Shepard?' Edmunds repeated for his own benefit. He recognised the name from one of the archived case files, one from Wolf's list. He had dismissed it as unrelated to the investigation.

'I'm sorry,' said the flustered woman, rubbing her tired eyes. 'I just presumed you were here about his death.'

'No, no,' said Edmunds quickly. 'I'm not being very clear, am I? Tell me about Joel Shepard.'

The doctor was too drained to register Edmunds' abrupt change of mind.

'Joel was a very disturbed young man – sweet though, in the main.'

Edmunds took his notebook back out.

'He suffered with crippling paranoia, schizophrenic behaviours and vivid delusions,' she explained as she unlocked the door to Joel's old room. 'But given his past history, none of that should come as too much of a surprise.'

'Remind me, if you would,' said Edmunds.

The doctor sighed.

'Joel's sister died – was killed, brutally. He, in turn, butchered the men responsible. Evil breeds evil.'

The room was unoccupied. The walls had been whitewashed, yet the eerie shadows of dark crosses bled through to stain the pristine canvas. Scripture scarred the floor beneath their feet and the inside of the door was decorated in deep scratches.

'Sometimes you can't just scrub away the things our more troubled patients leave behind,' the doctor said sadly. 'We're at capacity, but have to leave this room empty because we obviously can't put anybody else in here.'

The room felt cold, the air stale and soiled. Edmunds did not want to spend a moment longer than he needed to on the wrong side of its door.

'How did he die?' asked Edmunds.

'Suicide. Overdose. It shouldn't have happened. As you can imagine, we monitor every single pill dispensed in here. We still don't know how he managed to hoard enough to—' She stopped herself, realising that she was thinking out loud.

'How did he justify the murders?' asked Edmunds, running his hand over the largest and most prominent cross.

'He didn't. Not directly. Joel was under the impression that a demon, perhaps even the Devil himself, had "claimed their souls" on his behalf.'

'A demon?'

'You asked,' shrugged the doctor. 'His delusion was all-consuming. He irrefutably believed that he had made a deal with the Devil and that it was only a matter of time before it came to collect what Joel had promised.'

'Which was?'

'His soul, Detective,' she said, checking her watch. 'Faustian or what?'

'Faustian?' asked Edmunds, trying to remember where else he had heard the term used.

'As in the stories: Robert Johnson goes down to a dusty crossroads with nothing but the clothes on his back and a battered old guitar . . .'

Edmunds nodded, now understanding the reference. He knew his mind was playing tricks on him, but several of the faded crosses now looked darker than when he had entered.

'Would it be possible to see William Fawkes' old room while I'm here?' he asked casually, already heading for the door in his haste to leave.

The doctor was clearly surprised by the request: 'I don't see how—'

'It will only take a minute,' Edmunds insisted.

'Very well,' she huffed irately, before leading him along the corridor and opening the door to another whitewashed room. Clothing and personal possessions were littered over the basic furniture. 'As I said, we're at capacity.'

Edmunds paced across the room, his eyes scanning the featureless floor, before lying on his front to peer under the metal bed. He then walked over to the bare wall and began systematically running his hands over the fresh white paint.

The doctor looked uneasy: 'May I ask what you're looking for?'

'The things you can't just scrub away,' mumbled Edmunds. He climbed up onto the bed to inspect the back wall.

'We conduct an extensive damage report whenever a room is vacated. If anything had been left behind, we would have known.'

Edmunds dragged the bed noisily across the floor and crouched down to search the blank space behind for some invisible trace of Wolf. His fingers paused over a series of indents that had been obscured by the bed frame.

'Pen?' he called, refusing to look away for fear of losing them.

The doctor hurried over and handed him the stubby pencil from her shirt pocket. Edmunds snatched it off her and started scribbling frantically over the area.

'Excuse me Detective!'

Dark shapes slowly appeared from nowhere: letters, words. Finally, he dropped the pencil, sat down on the edge of the bed and took out his phone.

'What is it?' asked the concerned woman.

'You're going to need to find somewhere else for this patient to go.'

'As I already explained—'

Edmunds spoke over her:

'I'll then need you to lock this door behind you and ensure that it isn't opened for anyone, or anything, until the forensic team arrive. Is that clear?'

Wolf and Ashley were into the final mile of their four-hundred-mile journey. They had only stopped once since swapping the Ford Escort for the inconspicuous van that Wolf had left there overnight. It had been a noisy and uncomfortable way to ascend the country, but for just three hundred pounds it had gotten them to where they needed to be with twenty minutes to spare. They pulled up in a 'drop-off only' bay outside the terminal and rushed in through the main entrance to Glasgow Airport.

The radio had prattled incessantly in the background for seven hours straight. There had been a lot of discussion about Ashley's imminent murder, and a high street betting shop had been forced to apologise after it had been revealed that they were distastefully taking bets on which hour her heart would stop.

'Bastards,' Ashley had laughed, surprising Wolf again with her plucky attitude.

The same sound bite had been played repeatedly and Wolf winced every time he was forced to relive the moment that Andrew Ford made contact with the earth below. An exclusive interview with one of Ashley's 'closest friends' had come as a surprise to her, mainly because she had no idea who the woman being interviewed was. Wolf was glad to hear the news programmes struggling to fill airtime. It meant that the police had not yet publicised the fact that he had absconded with their next victim.

Gambling that his colleagues had not yet put out an All Ports Warning on them, he had spoken to the airport's head of security just ten minutes earlier and, as requested, the man was awaiting their arrival when they entered the terminal at 8.20 p.m.

He was a handsome black man in his mid-forties and was wearing a flattering suit with a security badge swinging from the pocket like a carefully chosen accessory. Wolf noted that he had sensibly posted two armed police officers close by following the unusual phone call.

'Ah, Detective Fawkes, it actually is you. I wasn't sure,' said the man, shaking Wolf's hand firmly. 'Karlus DeCosta, head of security.'

DeCosta turned to Ashley and held out his hand.

'And Ms Lochlan, of course.' He pulled a face intended to convey sympathy for her current predicament. 'How may I be of service to you both?'

'There's a plane leaving for Dubai in seventeen minutes,' said Wolf bluntly. 'I need her to be on it.'

If DeCosta was surprised by the request, he did not show it.

'You have a passport?' he asked Ashley.

She took it out of her bag and handed it to him. Professionally, he carefully inspected it despite the time constraints.

'Come with me,' he said.

They passed through security and commandeered one of the electric shuttle carts to expedite their journey to the gate. A robotic female voice announced the final call for the flight over the public address system.

DeCosta, who was apparently accustomed to such harried requests, swung suddenly to the right and drove the cart down an empty travelator. This struck Wolf as unnecessary because he had already radioed the gate and instructed them not to close it until he got there. He appeared to be enjoying himself though.

'There's a plane leaving for Melbourne two hours after you land in Dubai,' Wolf told Ashley quietly.

'Melbourne?' she asked in shock. 'That's your plan? Go on holiday? No. I can't. What about Jordan? And my mum? You wouldn't let me phone them and they'll be hearing all this stuff on the news and . . .'

'You've got to keep moving.'

Ashley looked distraught, but after a moment she nodded:

'Shouldn't we tell Karlus?' she asked, gesturing to their escort, who was now leaning out of the vehicle like an action hero as they trundled along the carpeted floor.

'No. I'll make the call myself just before you land. I don't want anyone but us knowing where you're going,' said Wolf. 'By the time you step off the plane in Melbourne it'll be 5.25 a.m. Sunday morning. You'll be safe.'

'Thank you.'

'When you get there, head straight to the Consulate-General and tell them who you are.' Wolf took her delicate hand in his and scrawled a mobile phone number across the back of it. 'Just let me know you made it.'

They arrived at the gate a few minutes before take-off. DeCosta went to speak to the staff while Wolf and Ashley climbed off the back of the cart and looked at one another.

'Come with me,' she said.

Wolf shook his head: 'I can't.'

Ashley had anticipated the answer. She took a step closer, pushing herself up against him, and closed her eyes.

'Ms Lochlan,' called DeCosta from the ticket desk. 'We need to get you boarded, right now.'

Ashley smiled coyly at Wolf and turned away.

'Later, Fawkes,' she called back casually.

'Later, Lochlan.'

DeCosta closed the gate once she was on board and requested that the control tower give the plane priority take-off. Wolf thanked him for his help and asked to remain behind. He would be able to negotiate customs himself. His own passport was sitting stiffly in his inside jacket pocket. He was not even sure why he had picked it up. It had only made it harder to refuse Ashley when she had inevitably asked him to run away with her, to escape the mess that awaited him back in London while he still could.

He watched longingly as Ashley's plane took its position on the runway, roared down the asphalt and then ascended into the colourful evening sky, away from danger, away from him.

CHAPTER 30

Saturday 12 July 2014

2.40 a.m.

Police Constable Dean Harris was sitting in his usual uncomfortable armchair beside the window in the grand but unwelcoming living room. He was reading by the light of an expensive-looking table lamp that he had balanced precariously on the windowsill and was ignoring the muted television altogether. He had only put it on to provide himself with a bit of company to help him through another lonely night in the unfamiliar house.

The other constables in his unit had all been incredibly jealous to learn of his involvement in the Ragdoll case. They were still at a stage in their careers where they kept count of the number of dead bodies that they had seen, and 'Welshie' was their hero, being the only member of the group to have actually tasered someone.

Dean acted aloof about his posting but had been secretly proud. He told his family, of course, knowing that the news would spread like a virus, embellishing the importance of his role and inventing a job title for himself that he could no longer remember. What he had not anticipated was spending two lonely weeks guarding a little girl who just so happened to share a name with the killer's actual target.

The Lochlan family had all but ignored him as they carried on with their inconvenienced lives. They had tolerated his presence in their home and were naturally on edge, refusing to let little Ashley even go to the bathroom alone, though they knew, just as he did, that their nine-year-old daughter had no attachment whatsoever to this serial killer or anybody else involved. But at least he was not the only one. There were probably dozens of Ashley Danielle Lochlans all over the country reluctantly sharing their homes with equally reluctant police officers.

Dean was distracted from his book when there was a loud creak from upstairs followed by a whirring sound. He returned to his page but had lost his place. Over the past fortnight he had come to recognise all of the large old house's idiosyncrasies. That particular sound had been the heating kicking in automatically as the temperature dropped in the dead of night.

He yawned loudly and checked his watch. The graveyard shifts were always the hardest. Although he had adjusted to the pattern and managed seven hours of sleep during the day, he could feel himself getting tired. Six o'clock in the morning felt a long way away.

He removed his glasses and rubbed his sore eyes. When he opened them again, the room looked much brighter, throwing ominous shadows across the walls that flickered and changed position in time with the erratic television programme. It took him a moment to realise that something had triggered the powerful security light in the front garden.

Dean got up and peered out through the tall window. The timed sprinkler system had clearly tripped the motion sensor as the spinning jets performed their synchronised routine for their one-person audience. The beautifully landscaped garden was otherwise empty, so he sat back down to stare at the silent screen, watching the nonsensical pictures cut back and forth enthusiastically, as if anybody cared at that time in the morning.

Twenty seconds after the sprinklers shut off, the bright light went out and the room seemed darker than ever. Dean relaxed into the hard chair and rested his eyes, which stung when he closed them. Suddenly his eyelids were glowing fleshy orange, and he opened his eyes to be blinded by a white light that was flooding the room from outside. He stumbled across to the next window and looked out to discover that the security light was now pointed back at the house, casting the rest of the garden into darkness.

There was a violent bang at the back door. With his heart racing, Dean grabbed his tactical vest off the back of the chair. Slowly, he stepped out into the hallway, which was filled with the eerie light, and shuffled towards the door, distracted by the spots flashing before his dazzled eyes. He remembered too late that he'd removed his own pristine taser hours earlier to get comfortable and had left it against the chair leg in the other room. He pulled on his vest as he passed between the rows of despondent-looking portraits, gripping his extendable baton above his head, ready to strike.

The security light went out behind him.

Dean was plunged into darkness. He held his breath. He could hear something approaching along the corridor and swung wildly in panic, hitting nothing but air and the wood-panelled wall. Before he could strike again, something solid connected with his forehead, and he fell in the blackness.

He had no idea whether he had been unconscious or not when he reached for his Airwaves radio and pushed the panic button, which would transmit everything he said over an open channel. The green glow emitting from the tiny screen reflected off the shiny walls, guiding Dean as he staggered back to his feet and towards the light switch.

'Met control, send more units,' he slurred before losing balance and dropping the radio onto the floor.

He slumped against the light switch. Above his head, the mini-chandelier came to life, revealing a set of muddy footprints leading down the hallway and ascending the stairs towards Ashley's bedroom. Dean snatched the baton off the floor and stumbled up the staircase to the landing, where the rapidly fading boot prints turned sharply towards the girl's elaborately decorated door.

Dean burst inside, wielding the weapon over his head, only to find the cluttered room empty. The final traces of mud on the cream carpet led to the open balcony doors. He looked out over the deserted garden and then sat down against the metal railings, having lost the adrenaline that had been distracting him from the giddiness. He took out his phone and while he waited for backup to arrive, texted the number that had been given to him earlier that evening.

Edmunds had fallen asleep underneath his jacket. He had now spent more nights on his sofa over the past couple of weeks than he had in his bed. Baxter, however, was wide awake at the kitchen table, reading the text that she had just received. Quietly, she climbed the uncarpeted stairs to check on the entire Lochlan family who were holed up and sound asleep in Edmunds and Tia's bedroom.

Wolf had been right. He had warned her that the killer would come for the girl if he could not reach Ashley. He had already demonstrated his willingness to murder at random. The three dead, fussy eaters, collateral damage of Khalid's poisoning, were testament to that. It should have come as no surprise at all that he was prepared to murder an innocent child in preservation of his ego.

Vanita had hesitantly agreed to let Baxter move the family, believing it to be a complete waste of time for everyone involved. Baxter had offered to put them up at her apartment. At least, that was what she told the team.

She still had not ruled out the possibility that Wolf was being set up. After all, this was the second Ashley Lochlan that he had tried to save in a day. She had decided to phone the only person that she utterly trusted, despite still being furious with him.

With Tia staying at her mother's, Edmunds had graciously agreed to accommodate Baxter and her aristocratic refugees. After showing them in, and despite his exhaustion, he had rushed out to the convenience store to buy some essentials that he could ill afford. Baxter was thankful that he had – it meant he was not there to see the wealthy family's appalled faces as they explored the measly confines of their temporary home.

'He should fire his maid,' Baxter heard Mrs Lochlan murmur to her haughty husband when she stepped in a pile of cat biscuits on the kitchen floor.

Edmunds had crashed out on the sofa during dinner, meaning that he had neither eaten his beans on toast nor had the chance to speak to Baxter in private. It was probably for the best, she thought. Nothing had changed. He believed that Wolf was guilty, and there was nothing she could say to change his mind. He did not know him like she did.

As Baxter constructed her argument in defence of Wolf to use against Edmunds in the morning, she picked her phone back up and wrote out a short text:

GIRL SAFE. NEED TO TALK. CALL ME. X

She knew that Wolf would have disposed of his phone to prevent them from tracking him but she pressed the send button anyway, needing to feel in some way still connected to the most important person in her life, unable to even contemplate the very real possibility that she might never see him again.

Andrea silently climbed out of bed so as not to wake Geoffrey. She wrapped her dressing gown around her and then crept downstairs to the kitchen. She could see the sun beginning to rise into the ink-blue sky through the glass roof that was to blame for the room's wildly fluctuating temperature. Even in winter, the showroom-perfect space would become unbearable while the sun passed overhead on a clear day and yet, before daybreak on a summer's morning, her toes had gone numb just from walking across the freezing tiles.

She had closed the door behind her, needing privacy, and sat at the breakfast bar with a glass of orange juice as she held her phone to her ear. It was strange that, even after years apart, she felt completely comfortable phoning Wolf at 5 a.m. She could not say the same for anybody else in her life, not even Geoffrey.

She had grown so accustomed to her ex-husband's irregular working patterns over the years that she knew he was just as likely to be awake in the middle of the night as he was in the middle of the day. But truthfully, it went deeper than that. She knew that he was there for her, never more than a phone call away, prepared to listen whenever she needed to talk, whether he had been asleep or not. It was something that she had always taken for granted, until now.

For the sixth time in twelve hours she was diverted to his voicemail and chose to end the call rather than leave another garbled message. She would try again on her way to work. Elijah was expecting her answer regarding the promotion by the end of the day and she had reached the stage where she had given up even thinking about it, hoping to miraculously channel the correct response when required.

Geoffrey got up at 6 a.m. as usual and Andrea made a conscious effort not to bring up the well-worn subject over breakfast. He must have been as sick of the topic as she was and there was nothing that he could say to help her anyway. He had wished her luck before heading up for his shower, just to let her know he had not forgotten, and then he disappeared upstairs.

Andrea left the house at 6.20 a.m. to get a head start on what was sure to be another exhausting 'Death Clock' day of news. Once she arrived at the newsroom, the reason for Wolf's lack of response became apparent. She found her inbox full of emails and photographs from people expecting some form of financial recompense for their sightings of Wolf and Ashley Lochlan. The unreliable list of widely spread locations reminded her of a story that she had covered years ago about an escaped snow leopard: there were sightings at two different service stations, Glasgow Airport, riding on the back of a cart – and a blurred photograph sent only minutes earlier from Dubai.

Unsure what to make of any of it, Andrea sent Baxter a text to check that everything was all right then she went down to make-up early to ensure that she avoided Elijah when he walked in. She did not need reminding of the enormous decision that lay before her or need him pressuring her for an answer.

She still had ten hours in which to decide.

*

Baxter was still sat at the kitchen table when she heard Edmunds beginning to stir. She quickly shoved the Glock 22 that she had borrowed from evidence back into her bag. She had had no intention of leaving herself or the Lochlan family unprotected and had no difficulty in accessing the evidence from her own investigation. It had then only taken a quarter of an hour of rummaging through drawers and other evidence boxes to gather a handful of the .40 S&W bullets that fitted the magazine.

Edmunds staggered, bleary-eyed, into the kitchen and groaned when he saw the pile of mess waiting for him in the sink. Apparently the Lochlans had never been faced with the prospect of washing up after themselves and had made it through another night without having to learn.

'Morning,' he yawned.

He shuffled over to the kettle.

'Thank you for putting us up,' said Baxter.

Edmunds was still half-asleep and could not tell whether she was being sincere or not.

'The killer came for her, just like Wolf said,' Baxter told him.

Edmunds abandoned his coffee and sat down at the table.

'He got away,' she told him when he looked hopeful. 'The kid watching the house is being treated for a concussion, but he'll be fine.'

Baxter paused as she prepared to deliver her well-rehearsed argument.

'Look, I don't blame you for yesterday or for looking into the possibility of Wolf's involvement. Considering the evidence you found, you wouldn't be doing your job if you didn't.'

'The tech guys said he'd been Googling Madeline Ayers the day after we found the Ragdoll,' started Edmunds, but Baxter talked over him:

'You don't know him like I do. Wolf has a code. He is probably the most moral person I have ever known, even if that sometimes leads him to do illegal and horrible things.'

'Isn't that a bit of a contradiction?' asked Edmunds as carefully as he could.

'We all know there are times when the law and the right thing don't line up like we'd like them to. Wolf would never do any of these things you—'

Baxter paused mid-sentence as Edmunds got up and pulled a file out of his workbag. He dropped it onto the table in front of her.

'What's this?' she asked warily.

She showed no intention of picking it up.

'I took a trip down to the coast this afternoon, to St Ann's Hospital.'

Baxter's expression darkened. It was obvious that she thought he had crossed a line.

'What makes you think you've got the right—'

'I found something,' said Edmunds, raising his voice over hers. 'In Wolf's room.'

Baxter looked furious. She snatched the folder off the kitchen table and opened it up. The first photograph depicted a small white-washed room with most of the furniture displaced. She looked up at Edmunds impatiently.

'Go on,' he prompted.

The second photograph showed what looked to be a dirty mark on the back wall.

'Riveting,' said Baxter, shuffling the photograph to the back of the pile before glancing down at the third and final picture. She stared at it in silence for over a minute before her face scrunched up and she had to hide her tearful eyes from Edmunds.

The photograph in her lap had captured the familiar names etched deep into the rough surface, those that Wolf considered responsible, the dark lettering like shapes obscured by smoke, black and burnt forever into the fabric of the old building.

'I'm sorry,' Edmunds said softly.

Baxter shook her head and tossed the file back across the table.

'You're wrong. He was sick back then! He couldn't have . . . He . . .'

She knew that she was lying to herself. She felt as though everything she had ever known was wrong; after all, if she had been naive enough to believe in Wolf, what other delusions had she been living her life by? The man that she had tried to live up to, had attempted to emulate, had wanted to be with, *was* the monster that Edmunds had warned her he was.

She could hear Garland's death screams. She could smell the stench of the mayor's charred remains, could remember embracing Chambers when nobody was watching, wishing him a happy holiday.

'It's him, Baxter. There's no doubt. I'm sorry.'

Slowly, she met Edmunds' eye and nodded.

There was no doubt.

CHAPTER 31

Saturday 12 July 2014

8.36 a.m.

'Was it you?' Vanita hissed at Finlay as she stormed into the meeting room. She turned to Simmons. 'You?'

Neither of them had any idea what she was talking about. Enraged further by their blank expressions, she snatched the remote control off the stand and flicked through the channels until she found Andrea sitting behind her news desk with the Death Clock superimposed above her head. Vanita turned up the volume as an out-of-focus image filled the screen.

'. . . depicts Ashley Lochlan being escorted through Dubai International by Head of Security Fahad Al Murr,' read Andrea.

A short camera phone video played in slow motion.

'And here, we can clearly see Detective Sergeant Fawkes and Ashley Lochlan speeding through Glasgow Airport's Terminal One.'

'We knew all this,' said Finlay.

'Wait for it,' snapped Vanita.

Andrea reappeared on screen.

'A source close to the investigation has exclusively revealed to us that Ms Lochlan served as a witness on the Cremation Killer trial and has links to other victims of the Ragdoll murders. The source went on to confirm Detective Fawkes' involvement in the operation to chaperone Ms Lochlan out of the country.'

'Clever girl,' smiled Finlay.

'I beg your pardon?' spat Vanita.

'Emily. She's leaked nothing of importance but enough to prove that *this* Ashley Lochlan is the killer's target. There's no point in him making another attempt on the little girl now or any other Ashley Lochlans out there. She just told the world that he's going to fail.'

'She just told the world that the Metropolitan Police are so incompetent that this woman is better off taking her chances on her own than letting us protect her!' said Vanita.

'She's saving lives.'

'But at what cost?'

The phone in Vanita's office started to ring. She cursed under her breath and then marched out, calling Simmons after her like a dog. Simmons hesitated and met Finlay's eye.

'Terrence!' she called again, and Finlay watched in disgust as he hurried after her.

'The subservience of leadership,' he muttered to himself.

Edmunds stepped aside for Simmons and entered the meeting room. Quietly, he unpacked his workbag, showing no interest in the news report, having already thoroughly discussed the matter with Baxter.

'So, it's Will then?' asked Finlay.

Edmunds nodded solemnly and offered him the file that he had just removed from his bag, but Finlay refused it.

'I believe you,' he said, before turning his attention back to the television.

'If you don't mind me saying, you don't seem all that surprised,' said Edmunds.

'When you've been in as long as I have, nothing surprises you any more. It just makes you sad. If I've learned anything, it's that if you push anyone far enough, eventually they're going to push back.'

'You're not trying to justify Wolf's actions?'

'Of course not. But over the years I've seen so many otherwise "good" people doing horrible things to each other – husbands strangling cheating wives, brothers protecting sisters from abusive partners. In the end you realise . . .'

'Realise what?'

'That there are no "good" people. There are just those who haven't been pushed far enough yet, and those that have.'

'You don't sound like you want Wolf caught.'

'We have to catch him. Some of those people didn't deserve what happened to them.'

'And you think some did?'

'Aye, some did. Don't worry, lad. I want to catch him more than any of you because, more than any of you, I don't want him getting hurt.'

Vanita and Simmons returned to the meeting room looking sheepish and took their seats. Edmunds handed them each a copy of the profile that he had created for their killer.

'We are running out of time,' he told them, 'so I have gathered together everything we know about our killer, along with some educated assumptions to narrow down the search: Caucasian male, six foot to six-four, bald or closely shaven hair, scarring to right forearm and back of head, size eleven boots, standard army issue pre-2012, either is or was a soldier. Very high intelligence, which he tests on a regular basis to fuel his ego. Emotional detachment, trivialisation of the value of human life, relishes the challenge and wants to be tested. He's bored, so it's likely that he's not a soldier any more. The theatre of it all tells us that he enjoys it. He'll be a loner, an outsider, unmarried, basic accommodation. Considering London prices, my money's on a studio flat in a bad area.

'People who join the army solely because they like killing tend to make themselves known and wind up dishonourably discharged after either doing or being suspected of doing something appalling. As we don't have his prints in the system, he must have only been suspected of something; although, we can't rule out injury either, considering the scars.'

'That's a lot of guesswork,' said Simmons.

'Educated guesswork, and it's somewhere to start,' said Edmunds unapologetically. 'We need to compile a list of names that fit the description and were discharged from the military in the years leading up to the first archived case in 2008.'

'Excellent work yet again, Edmunds,' said Vanita.

'With your permission, I would like to continue working through the evidence with Finlay. It would be helpful if DCI Simmons could start compiling the list of names for me.'

Simmons did not appreciate their newest recruit delegating him work and was about to say so when Vanita answered:

'Whatever you need,' she told him. 'I presume that Baxter is out looking for Fawkes, then?'

'Baxter won't leave that girl's side before midnight, and all the orders, threats and pleading in the world aren't going to change her mind. I wouldn't waste your time,' said Edmunds.

Finlay and Simmons shared a stunned look. Was he giving the *commander* orders now?

'The killer has systematically been drawn in closer and closer with each murder. He plans to finish this face to face. If we find him, we find Wolf.'

The meeting was adjourned. Vanita and Simmons headed back towards her office while Edmunds lingered behind to speak to Finlay in private. He closed the meeting room door and then hesitated, unsure how best to approach the unusual subject.

'Finlay . . . weird question.'

'OK?' said Finlay, glancing at the closed door.

'You and Simmons were talking about something yesterday.'

'You're going to have to be a wee bit more specific,' laughed Finlay.

'Faustian,' said Edmunds. 'I was wondering what you meant by that.'

'Honestly, I barely remember what *this* meeting was about.'

The notebook came out.

'We were discussing the victims and then you said: "almost looks like Will's hit list, if he wasn't on it" and then Simmons said: "it's almost Faustian" or something to that effect.'

Finlay nodded as the memory returned to him.

'It was nothing. A stupid joke,' he said.

'Could you explain it please?'

Finlay shrugged and took a seat.

'A few years back we had a run of people swearing blindly to their innocence despite the piles of bodies accumulating around them.'

'Blaming demons or the Devil?' asked Edmunds, fascinated.

'Aye, the Faustian alibi, as it became known,' smirked Finlay.

'And how would one go about arranging something like that?'

'Come again?'

'In practical terms, I mean.'

'Practical terms?' asked Finlay in confusion. 'It's an urban legend, lad.'

'Humour me.'

'What's all this about?'

'It might be important – please.'

Finlay looked at his watch, conscious that they had precious little time.

'All right. Story time: there are these numbers floating about out there, just regular mobile phone numbers. No one knows who they belong to, and no one's ever been able to trace them. They're only ever live for one call before being disconnected. If a person comes into possession of one of these numbers, and are so inclined, they can offer up a trade.'

'A deal with the Devil,' said Edmunds, captivated by the story.

'Aye, a deal with "the Devil",' sighed Finlay. 'But like any story involving the Devil, there's a catch: once he's done doing your bidding, he will expect something in return . . .'

Finlay paused and gestured for Edmunds to lean in closer.

'Your soul!' he bellowed, making Edmunds jump.

Finlay coughed and spluttered as he laughed at his nervy colleague.

'Do you think there could be any truth to it at all?' asked Edmunds.

'The Devil on Pay As You Go? No. No, I don't,' said Finlay, now looking serious. 'You need to concentrate on more important things today, all right?'

Edmunds nodded.

'All right then,' said Finlay.

Mr and Mrs Lochlan were watching television in Edmunds' tatty lounge. Baxter could hear Ashley playing upstairs in the bedroom from her seat at the kitchen table. She was about to get up to make something to eat when Ashley suddenly went quiet.

Baxter got to her feet, straining to listen over the blaring television in the other room, but relaxed when she heard Ashley's thunderous footsteps running along the landing and then bounding down the stairs. She came rushing into the kitchen with an assortment of hair clips and flowers clasped haphazardly over her head.

'Hello, Emily,' she said happily.

'Hello, Ashley,' Baxter replied. She had always been terrible at speaking to children. It was as if they could smell her fear of them. 'You look very pretty.'

'Thank you. You do too.'

Baxter doubted that was true but smiled wearily at her.

'I just wanted to check that you still want me to come and tell you if I see anybody outside?'

'Yes please,' said Baxter as enthusiastically as she could muster. 'I'm waiting for a friend,' she lied.

'OK!'

Baxter had expected the little girl to run back upstairs but instead she just stood there giggling.

'What?'

'What?' laughed Ashley.

'What is this?' Baxter's patience was waning.

'What you asked me to do! I'm telling you that there is somebody in the back garden!'

Baxter's forced smile dropped. She grabbed Ashley and rushed her into the lounge while gesturing to her alarmed parents.

'Go upstairs and lock the door,' she whispered, thrusting their daughter into their arms.

As the three of them thudded overhead, Baxter ran back into the kitchen and removed the gun from her bag. She froze when there was a scraping noise from the side of the property. She crept over to the back windows but could not see anything out there.

There was a thump against the front door.

Baxter darted into the hallway and stepped into the bathroom. She raised the gun as she heard metal against the door lock. The front door creaked open and she saw a large shadow spill across the threshold. She held her breath and waited for the figure to pass the bathroom doorway before stepping out and pushing the end of the gun's metal slide against the hooded head, causing the intruder to drop a bag full of razorblades, sharp scissors and disposable gloves over the floor.

'Police,' said Baxter, glancing down at the assortment of ominous implements at her feet. 'Who are you?'

'Tia. Alex's fiancée. I live here.'

Baxter leaned round to see the obvious bump beneath the pregnant woman's top.

'Jesus! I am so sorry,' she said, lowering the weapon. 'I'm Emily – Emily Baxter. Nice to finally meet you.'

The head of security at Dubai International had already spoken to Wolf by the time Ashley disembarked the plane. He was a terrifying man, who barked orders at anyone and everyone in his vicinity, so it should have come as no surprise to learn that he had forced the airline to rearrange the seating for her flight to Melbourne.

Ashley felt terrible. She could see her fellow passengers crammed into every last available seat further down the cabin while she was surrounded by four empty rows. The clock on the entertainment system had adjusted to reflect the changing time zones. It was now officially Sunday morning, but she was not safe yet. She checked her unadjusted watch, knowing that she could not let her guard down until it was midnight back in England.

Ever since Wolf first told her his plan she had had reservations about boarding a plane full of innocent people. The seemingly ubiquitous killer appeared to have no bounds, and she could not help but wonder whether crashing a passenger jet might still fall within the realm of his extensive capabilities. She had been gripping the armrest for hours, expecting to fall out of the sky. She had refused all food and drink on Wolf's orders and watched warily every time that anybody got out of their seat to visit the facilities.

The dimmed lights flickered all around her and Ashley looked up alertly. The cabin crew appeared oblivious as they tiptoed between the sleeping passengers. The armrest started to tremble and then to shake beneath her hand, and an unfittingly cheery ping accompanied the illuminated seat-belt signs.

He had found her.

The entire plane began to vibrate violently, waking people from their sleep. Ashley saw the concerned expressions on the cabin crew's faces as they dished out reassurances while scurrying back to the safety of their seats. The lights went out. Ashley felt for the window beside her but could see only darkness. It was as though she was already dead . . .

The shaking gradually subsided and then the lights returned at full brightness. Nervous laughter filled the cabin and, shortly after, the seat-belt signs went dark once more. The captain's voice buzzed over the intercom, apologising for the turbulence and making a joke about everyone getting a massage chair on his airline, not just first class.

As people started dropping back off to sleep, Ashley counted the seconds in her head, ticking off the minutes until they landed.

Andrea gave her now signature sign-off. The Death Clock read: +16:59:56 as the 'On Air' light went out. She had enjoyed the day, full of positivity and people wishing Ashley Lochlan well or bestowing advice as she attempted to outrun the previously infallible killer. The vile countdown, having passed midnight and now into positive numbers, had been renamed the 'Life Clock' by one caller and, for the first time, symbolised hope rather than despair, counting up the hours to the killer's failure.

But Andrea's mood quickly dampened when she walked back into the newsroom and spotted Elijah waiting for her up on his narrow walkway. With a gesture dripping with arrogance he summoned her up and then strode into his office.

Andrea refused to rush. She stopped at her desk and took a moment to steady her nerves, trying not to think about the gravity of the decision that she was about to make, that she had already made. She crossed the chaotic room, took a deep breath and climbed the metal staircase.

Wolf was watching the news in the cheap bed and breakfast that he had paid for in cash. He had been on edge for hours and dived across the dirty room when his Pay As You Go phone went off shortly after midnight. He opened the text from the unfamiliar number and slumped back against the bed in relief as he read:

STILL HERE! L X

She was safe.

He removed the sim card from the phone and snapped it in half then crawled over to switch off the television, pausing when he realised that Andrea's news channel had already reset the Death Clock. He watched three minutes of his life disappear as though they were seconds before pushing the power button:

-23:54:23

CHAPTER 32

Sunday 13 July 2014
6.20 a.m.

Vanita and Simmons had stayed on until 7.30 p.m. and 9 p.m. respectively while Edmunds and Finlay settled in for a long night at the office. Baxter had joined them a little before 1 a.m. after sending the Lochlan family home at midnight with a police escort.

Edmunds had been expecting a series of fuming texts and phone calls from Tia for having turned their modest home into a bed and breakfast for complete strangers, however, the mum-to-be had spent the entire day playing with nine-year-old Ashley and had been fast asleep when Baxter left their maisonette.

When Baxter arrived at the office, Finlay had taken over the gargantuan task of working through the list of discharged servicemen. Edmunds, meanwhile, had emptied the archived evidence across the meeting room floor and been busy meticulously sorting through the mess.

She always found it a strange atmosphere in the office at night-time. Even though New Scotland Yard was still teeming with caffeine-fuelled employees, the night workers seemed to carry out their duties in a hushed murmur. The oppressive lighting felt a little warmer as it diffused into vacant rooms and dark corridors, and the phones that had to fight so hard to make themselves heard during the day were set to a polite hum.

At 6.20 a.m. Finlay was asleep in his chair, snoring gently beside Baxter, who had now inherited his laborious task. Based on Edmunds' profile and the overwhelming number of people that could be eliminated due to the severity of their physical injuries, they had, so far, compiled a list of just twenty-six names from the first thousand people they had assessed.

Someone cleared their throat.

Baxter looked up to find a scruffy man in a cap standing over her.

'Got some files for Alex Edmunds,' he said, gesturing to the flatbed trolley behind him, where seven more archived boxes were neatly stacked.

'Yeah, he's actually just in—'

Baxter saw Edmunds throw a box of evidence across the meeting room in a temper.

'Know what? Why don't you leave these with me?' she smiled.

A file of paperwork showered down over her head as she closed the glass door behind her.

'I can't see whatever the hell it was *he* saw!' shouted Edmunds in frustration. 'What did he find?'

He scrunched up a fistful of documents off the floor and thrust them at Baxter.

'No prints, no witnesses, no connection between the victims – nothing!'

'OK, calm down. We don't even know if what Wolf found is still here,' said Baxter.

'And we have no way of verifying that, because he outsourced the forensic testing and it's bloody Sunday so no one's at work.' Edmunds slumped down onto the floor. He looked drained and his black eyes were showing worse than ever. He smacked himself on the side of the head. 'We don't have time for me to be dim-witted.'

Baxter started to realise that her colleague's, already, impressive contribution to the case had not been driven by egocentric one-upmanship or proving himself to the team, but by the unreasonable amount of pressure that he placed upon himself, a borderline obsessiveness and dogged refusal to relinquish control to anybody else. Under the circumstances, she supposed that it would be an inopportune moment to tell him just how much he reminded her of Wolf.

'Some boxes arrived for you,' said Baxter.

Edmunds looked up at her in confusion.

'Well, why didn't you say so?' he said, getting back to his feet before rushing out of the room.

The light drizzle had gradually soaked through Wolf's clothing during the hour that he had been standing at the bus stop on Coventry Street. He had not taken his eyes off the door to the scruffy Internet café that, like the countless souvenir shops selling London-branded tat, somehow managed to survive nestled among the world's biggest brands along one of the capital's busiest and most expensive thoroughfares.

He had followed the man here, keeping his distance as he boarded the train, weaved through the crowds amassing around the street performers in Covent Garden and then entered the grotty café just a few hundred metres down from Piccadilly Circus.

The temperature had dropped with the break in the weather and his quarry had camouflaged himself in standard London attire: a long black coat, immaculately polished shoes and freshly pressed shirt and trousers, all capped off with the regulation black umbrella.

He had struggled to keep pace at times as the imposing man marched briskly through the meandering crowds. Wolf had watched a number of people coming into contact with him, pushing past from the other direction, begging him for spare change, attempting to hand him glossy fliers, not one of them aware of the monster walking among them: a wolf in sheep's clothing.

Shortly after leaving Covent Garden the man had taken a shortcut. Wolf followed him down the quiet side street and quickened his pace, seizing a rare moment of solitude in the ever-watchful city. His hurried walk turned into a jog as he chased down his unsuspecting target, but when a taxi turned the corner and pulled up a little further down the road, Wolf reluctantly slowed his pace and followed his prey back out onto the busy high street.

As the drizzle built into rain, Wolf pulled the collar of his own long black coat up around his neck and hunched over to keep warm. He watched the colourful numbers on the neon clock in the café window steadily distort in the wet glass, a reminder that this was his last day, his last chance.

He was wasting time.

Isobel Platt was being given a crash course in studio broadcasting. It apparently took five eager members of the technical team to explain to the intimidatingly attractive reporter which camera to look at and when. She had dressed in her most conservative outfit for this unexpected development in her fledgling career, much to the displeasure of Elijah, who had relayed down the message for her to 'lose the top three buttons'.

While the format of her maiden studio appearance was relatively simple: a one-on-one interview with only two VTs interrupting proceedings, it was expected that tens of millions of people would be tuning in to watch the half-hour show from all over the planet. Isobel thought she might be sick again.

She had never wanted this. She had never even really wanted the reporter job in the first place and had been as surprised as everyone else when it had been offered to her despite a total lack of experience or qualifications. She and her boyfriend had argued about her applying for other jobs, but she hated working there and was determined to get out.

Everybody at the newsroom either thought that she was thick, a tart or a thick tart. She was not deaf to the whispering behind her back. Isobel would be the first to admit that she was no genius, but where other averagely educated people were forgiven for their mispronunciations and naivety, she was ridiculed endlessly.

She smiled along with the awkward men and laughed at their obvious jokes. She pretended to be excited about the honour that had been bestowed upon her, but in reality she just wished that Andrea was in her place, negotiating the complicated camera movements and intricate timings of the programme.

'I think I could get used to this,' she laughed as one of the men wheeled her and her chair into position.

'Don't get too comfortable,' called Andrea as she crossed the studio en route to make-up, admirably early for her first official day in her new job. 'You're only here because I can't really interview myself, can I?'

'I've got something!' yelled Edmunds from the meeting room.

Finlay, Vanita, and Simmons were already inside by the time Baxter crunched across the floor of discarded paperwork and closed the door behind her. Simmons looked torn, clearly deciding whether or not to reprimand Edmunds for making such a mess.

Edmunds reached into an archive box and handed out the documents.

'Right,' he started breathlessly. 'You'll have to bear with me. It's a bit muddled up. Wait, not those.'

He snatched the papers out of Simmons' hand and tossed them onto the floor behind him.

'You'll have to share,' smiled Edmunds. 'This was one of the cases Wolf booked out of the archives – Stephen Shearman, fifty-nine, CEO of a failing electronics manufacturer. His son was a director of the company and committed suicide after a merger went bad or something . . . It's not important.'

'And this is relevant how?' asked Vanita.

'That's what I thought as well,' Edmunds enthused. 'But guess who was responsible for that merger falling apart – Gabriel Poole Junior.'

'Who?' asked Baxter, speaking for the group.

'He was the heir to the electronics corporation who disappeared from his hotel suite – puddle of blood, no body.'

'Oh,' said Baxter in feigned interest.

They all had far more important things to be doing.

'This one,' said Edmunds, unpacking another cardboard box. 'His daughter was killed by a bomb . . .' He pointed to another box. '. . . planted by this man, who managed to suffocate inside a locked cell.'

Everybody looked blank.

'Don't you see?' asked Edmunds. 'They're Faustian murders!'

Everybody looked blanker.

'It's an urban myth,' groaned Finlay.

'They're all connected,' said Edmunds. 'All of them! Revenge murders followed by a sacrifice. We never understood how Wolf fitted into a list of his enemies. Now it all makes sense.'

'This is absurd,' said Simmons.

'It *is* one hell of a leap,' said Vanita.

Edmunds rummaged through another box and removed a report.

'Joel Shepard,' he said. 'Died six months ago, questionable suicide. Convicted of three revenge murders, convinced that the Devil was coming to collect his soul. He was in a mental hospital.'

'Well, there's your answer,' smirked Simmons.

'St Ann's Hospital,' explained Edmunds. 'He was a patient there at the same time as Wolf. Wolf requested this box ten days ago and now a piece of evidence is missing.'

'What evidence?' asked Vanita.

'"One bloodstained page of the Bible",' Edmunds read straight from the report. 'I think Wolf found something.'

'So, what you're saying is that the Ragdoll Killer is significantly more prolific than we originally gave him credit for?' asked Vanita.

'What I'm saying is that the Faustian Killer isn't just a myth. I'm saying that the Ragdoll murders *are* Faustian murders. I'm saying that I believe Wolf has discovered the killer's identity and is out there, somewhere, hunting an individual who unequivocally believes he is, at the very least, a demon.'

The door to the café opened and a figure stepped out into the flow of people being drawn towards the bright lights of Piccadilly

Circus. Wolf took a few steps to his right for a better view, but the face was obscured by the crowds and by the umbrella that he had just opened up. He started to walk away.

Wolf needed to make a decision: stay or go?

It was him – Wolf was almost positive. He jogged across the road, shielding his face as he passed in front of a stationary police car, before following his target along the busy street. The human traffic was building with every step they took, and Wolf was fighting to keep the man in sight. As the rain intensified, everyone that had been braving the light shower either rushed for cover or searched frantically for their own umbrellas. Within seconds at least another dozen identical black canopies had filled the pavement in front of him.

In his desperation not to lose the man, Wolf stepped out into the traffic and sprinted ten metres down the road before dropping back in behind the imposing figure. As they passed the next shop window, he struggled to make out the man's face in the reflection. He had to be sure that it was him before he acted.

His erratic behaviour had sparked the interest of several people around him and it was clear that some of them had recognised this drenched version of the man from the news. He shoved his way forward to get away from them and was now only two people behind his mark as they passed the Trocadero. He grasped the handle of the six-inch hunting knife concealed inside his coat and moved in front of another person.

He could not miss.

He could not risk the killer surviving.

He had been waiting for the perfect opportunity: a quiet park, a deserted alleyway, but realised that this was so much better. He was hidden in plain view, a face in the heaving crowds, just another person retreating from the dead body lying in the middle of the road.

Wolf glimpsed the side of the man's face as they paused at the traffic lights. It was undoubtedly him. He moved into position, directly behind his target, close enough to feel the rain striking his face as it bounced off the black umbrella. He focused on the exposed skin at the base of the man's skull into which he would sink the knife. He pulled out the blade, keeping it close to his chest, and took a deep breath to steady his hands. He only needed to push forwards . . .

Something across the road distracted him: both his and Andrea's names were scrolling across the curved glass wall that separated the statues of the Horses of Helios below, from his three golden daughters, diving gracefully from the rooftop, above. It took him a moment to work out that the inverted letters were a reflection of the LG billboard above his head. He glanced up to read the news ticker that was running across the bottom of the advertisement:

. . . in world exclusive interview – 13:00 BST – Andrea Hall/ Fawkes to tell all in world exclusive interview – 13:00 BST – Andrea Hall/Fawkes . . .

Wolf was ejected from his thoughts as the herd of people behind began shoving past him to cross the road. The traffic had stopped, and he had lost sight of the killer in the crowds. Pulling the knife up into his sleeve, he barged forward, searching desperately for a face in a sea of black umbrellas. Suddenly the heavens opened. The shrieks of ill-prepared tourists and the hollow thud of water pelting fabric filled the crowded street.

Just as Wolf reached the famous intersection, another wave of people crashed around him. As he stood in the glow of the infamous screens, burning bright under the dark sky overhead, he realised just how exposed he was. He was being shoved from every direction by the faceless crowd, one of whom was not what they seemed.

He started to panic.

He began fighting back through the crowds, knocking people to the ground in his desperation to get out. He lost his knife to the undulating floor of shoes and wheels, seeing hostile faces everywhere he looked. He broke into a run down the centre of the road, keeping pace with the slow-moving traffic, glancing back at the army still marching after him . . .

Death was coming for him.

ST ANN'S HOSPITAL

Friday 11 February 2011

7.39 a.m.

Joel knelt in prayer on the cold floor of his room, as he did every morning before breakfast. A member of staff had woken him at the normal time to unlock the door and restrain him in the handcuffs that he was now required to wear at all times when not confined to his room.

A fortnight earlier he had subjected one of the nursing staff to a vicious and unprovoked attack in a successful attempt to prolong his incarceration. The young woman had always been kind to him and he was genuinely concerned that he might have seriously injured her, but he could not leave. He knew that it was cowardly to hide from his fate.

He was a coward; he had come to terms with that a long time ago.

There was a shout from out in the corridor. Joel paused mid-prayer to listen. A pair of heavy footsteps sprinted past his door and then a wild scream somewhere in the building set his heart racing.

He got up and stepped out into the corridor where several other patients were staring anxiously in the direction of the Rec Room.

'Back in your rooms!' bellowed a heavyset man as he ran between them and headed towards the source of the disruption before another terrifying scream of anguish filled the halls.

Joel was swept along by the crowd of curious patients as they disobeyed the man's order and rushed for the double doors that led to the room where they spent the majority of their days. There was a cry of pain. This time Joel recognised Wolf's voice. He shoved his way through the pack of brightly coloured scrubs and entered the Rec Room.

Furniture lay splintered and broken everywhere and an unconscious doctor was being tended to on the other side of the room. Three large health workers were failing to restrain the crazed man while a nurse spoke frantically on the phone.

'No!' Wolf roared, startling Joel. 'I told them! I told them he'd do this!'

Joel followed Wolf's feral gaze to the large television; a reporter was standing on a run-down London high street. Two traumatised police officers held up a makeshift screen to conceal whatever was still smoking behind.

'I could have stopped this!' screamed Wolf with tears streaming down his face.

He lashed out like a wild animal as another doctor rushed into the room holding a large syringe, like a vet left with no choice but to put him down.

All became clear when the reporter reiterated what little information she had gathered.

'For viewers just joining us, eyewitness reports state that Naguib Khalid, the suspect cleared of the Cremation Killings last May, has been arrested by police. There have been unconfirmed reports of a body and, as you can see, there is still smoke pluming into the air behind me . . .'

Wolf cried out when the doctor jabbed the enormous needle deep into his left arm. As he went limp, the battered hospital staff struggled to support his weight. Just before he passed out, he looked across at Joel, who wore an expression devoid of either pity or surprise. He simply nodded in understanding and then Wolf lost consciousness.

*

When Wolf woke up, he was back in his room. Darkness had fallen over the grounds outside his window. His vision was blurred, and it took him over a minute to work out why he was unable to raise his hands up to his pounding head; he had been restrained to the bed. He fought futilely against the thick straps, the rage that had exploded out of him earlier still broiling just beneath the surface.

He recalled the news report, the smoke billowing over the tattered white sheet. He turned his head to the side and vomited onto the floor. He did not need to see; Wolf knew better than anybody what had been obscured from the cameras. He knew just how much another young girl had needlessly suffered.

He closed his eyes and tried to focus his anger, to concentrate. It was consuming him, clouding his thoughts. He stared up at the blank ceiling and whispered the names of the people he held responsible, but then he remembered something: a desperate last resort, the nonsensical ramblings of an unstable mind . . .

'Nurse!' he called loudly. 'Nurse!'

It took an hour to convince the doctors to remove his restraints and a further half-hour to obtain their permission to make a phone call. While awaiting their decision, he had retrieved the scruffy page from underneath the mattress. He had almost forgotten that it was even there.

He could barely stand and was helped out into the corridor to use the phone at the nurses' station. Once he was alone, he unfolded the creased paper, for the first time noticing the printed words bleeding through the crayon numbers: God. Devil. Soul. Hell.

He steadied himself against the wall and punched in the sequence of numbers with his free hand.

It started to ring.

There was a muffled clicking sound followed by silence.

'Hello?' asked Wolf nervously.

Silence.

'. . . Hello?'

An automated female voice finally answered him.

'State. Your. Full. Name. After. The. Tone.'

Wolf waited for his cue.

'William Oliver Layton-Fawkes.'

Another pause followed that felt as though it lasted forever. Wolf knew that it was irrational, but there was something unsettling about the computerised voice, something about the intonation, the tone. It almost sounded as though it was delighting in his desperation, as though it was laughing at him.

'In. Exchange. For?' it eventually asked.

Wolf glanced down the empty corridor. He could hear the gentle hum of voices escaping from one of the side rooms. Instinctively, he cupped his hand over the receiver to whisper into it.

He hesitated.

'In. Exchange. For?' the voice prompted again.

'Naguib Khalid . . . Mayor Raymond Turnble . . . Madeline Ayers . . . The dock security officer . . . DI Benjamin Chambers – and everybody else with that girl's blood on their hands,' spat Wolf.

Silence.

Wolf went to put the receiver down. He paused and listened for a moment longer before hanging up. In his delirium, he laughed at himself. Even in his heavily medicated state he realised how ludicrous it all was; although, he did feel a little better for saying the names out loud, for passing them on to the outside world, even if only to an unmanned answering machine.

He was halfway back down the hushed corridor when a deafeningly shrill ring filled the air around him. He dropped to his knees, holding his hands over his ears, and turned back to face the unremarkable phone, wondering whether it could possibly be that loud or whether the medication had distorted his senses.

One of the overweight health workers rushed past him, saying something indecipherable as he approached the phone. Wolf held his breath as he watched the man grasp the receiver and press it up against his ear, unreservedly afraid of whoever or whatever was occupying the other end of the line.

A broad smile cracked across the man's face.

'Hey. I know, sorry. One of the patients was on it,' he explained apologetically.

Slowly, Wolf got back to his feet and stumbled towards his room, thinking that maybe, just maybe, he might be crazy after all.

CHAPTER 33

Sunday 13 July 2014

1.10 p.m.

Finlay crossed another name off his list and treated himself to a ten-second stretch before returning to his half of the remaining four hundred discharged servicemen. He saw Baxter at her desk in the corner, head down in concentration, earphones in to drown out the noise of the office.

Edmunds had left the meeting room in an unusable state, despite now being back at Simmons' desk to access a computer program that Finlay did not even recognise. Vanita and Simmons had shut themselves away in her poky office to watch the Andrea Hall interview, no doubt on damage control, waiting with bated breath to hear what bombshell Wolf's ex-wife might expose to the world next. Although the Death Clock had vanished for the duration of the interview, none of them needed reminding of the time constraints that they were working to.

Finlay looked down at the next name on the list. He was using a combination of what little information the Ministry of Defence had permitted them access to, the Police National Computer, the Police National Database and Google to condense his pool of suspects. He would have felt more comfortable hedging their bets a little more; after all, it was still entirely possible that their killer had never been discharged from the army, that he had never even been enlisted in the first place. He tried not to think about that. This was their best shot at finding Wolf, so he and Baxter would continue to supply Edmunds with names as they found them.

Saunders came strutting up to Baxter's desk. She left her earphones in and continued working, hoping that he would get the message and go away, but it was apparent, when he waved his hand in front of her face, that he needed telling out loud.

'Piss off, Saunders,' she snapped.

'Wow! No need for that. I just came over to check on you. You know, with Andrea Hall making some pretty scandalous allegations about Wolf and an "unnamed" female colleague,' he said with a sly smile. 'I mean, we all had our suspicions but . . .'

He trailed off and took a step back when he saw Baxter's expression. He muttered something inaudible and walked away. The news had come as a shock to Baxter and she was embarrassed to admit that she was a little hurt. She had believed that she and Andrea had talked through their issues and that Andrea had finally accepted the truth that nothing ever happened between her and Wolf. On the other hand, this was the same woman who was currently on global television dishing the dirt on her ex-husband just hours before he was due to die.

Still, these minor betrayals paled in comparison to what Baxter was feeling towards Wolf.

An hour later, Finlay ham-fistedly entered the next name on the list into the computer. He was embarrassingly slow compared to Baxter, but wanted to get through as many as possible before she finished her half and came over to take more off him. The Ministry of Defence entry was typically brief:

Staff Sergeant Lethaniel Masse, D.O.B. 16/02/74, (HUMINT)
Intelligence Corps, Discharged on medical grounds – June 2007.

'Whose side are they on?' he mumbled, wondering whether they could have been any more vague if they tried. He scribbled the words *military intelligence* on a napkin left over from his working lunch.

A quick Google search produced pages of results, mostly news stories and discussion boards. He opened the link at the top of the page:

> *. . . Staff Sergeant Masse seconded to the Royal Mercian Regiment . . . the sole survivor of the attack that left nine of his unit dead . . . their convoy encountered the roadside IED (Improvised Explosive Device) south of Hyderabad Village in Helmand Province . . . being treated for life-threatening internal injuries and 'devastating' burns to his face and chest.*

Survivor – God Complex? wrote Finlay, next to a brown sauce stain. He entered the details into the Police National Database and was pleasantly surprised to find a plethora of information, including height (six-three), marital status (unmarried), employment (unemployed), registered disabled (yes), NOK. (next of kin, none), known addresses (none in past five years).

Encouraged by the similarities to Edmunds' profile, Finlay proceeded on to the second page, where the reason for the volume of information held on Staff Sergeant Masse became apparent. Two files had been attached. The first was an incident report created by the Metropolitan Police in June 2007:

> 2874 26/06/2007
>
> Occupational Health Suite, 3rd Floor, 57 Portland Place, W1.
>
> [14:40] Attended address due to reported disturbance. A patient, Lethaniel Masse, confrontational and aggressive towards staff.
>
> On arrival at premises, raised voices heard from upstairs. Located Mr Masse (Male, 30–40yrs, 6ft+, white/British, facial scarring) sitting cross-legged on floor, staring into space and bleeding from side of face. Desk upturned, window cracked.
>
> While colleague attended to Mr Masse, I was informed that wound to head was self-inflicted and nobody else injured. Dr James Bariclough advised patient suffering from PTSD and outburst prompted by news that he could not return to army due to physical and mental injuries.

Neither doctor or staff wish to take matter further. No cause for arrest or continued police involvement. Ambulance requested due to head wound and possibility of suicide risk in current state. Will wait on scene until arrival.

[15:30] Ambulance crew on scene.

[15:40] Accompanied ambulance crew to University College Hospital.

[16:05] Clear scene.

Finlay realised that he was already standing up, eager to share their most promising suspect yet with the rest of the team. He moved his mouse over the second document and double-clicked. A photograph of a broken computer lying beside an upturned desk appeared. He scrolled to the next picture: a large cracked window. Disinterested, he brought up the final photograph and felt a chill run up his spine.

The photograph had been taken beside an open doorway with the fearful staff watching anxiously in the background. It showed the deep laceration to Lethaniel Masse's severely scarred face; however, it was not the extent of his terrible injuries that had troubled Finlay. It was his eyes: pale, dead, calculating.

Finlay had come into contact with more monsters than he could remember and had found that those who committed the most atrocious crimes shared a common trait, a look: the same detached, cold, stare gazing back at him from his computer screen now.

'Emily! Alex!' he bellowed across the office.

Lethaniel Masse was a killer, of that he had no doubt. Whether he was the Ragdoll Killer, the Faustian Killer or both, Finlay could not care less. Edmunds could worry about gathering the evidence.

All he and Baxter needed to worry about was finding him.

Wolf was on edge. He had been watching the rain pour over the high street for hours, periodically wiping condensation off the claustrophobic flat's lone window, praying that he might spot Masse returning home at any moment, more than aware that he might have missed his one opportunity to finish what he had set in motion years earlier.

He would just have to adapt, to improvise. He supposed that he was beyond redemption now anyway. He could never have anticipated having to play his part under such omnipresent media scrutiny or for Masse to have appointed Andrea, of all people, to act as his messenger. Had events unfolded differently, he would have been walking into New Scotland Yard a hero on Tuesday morning, merely another innocent target of the disturbed ex-soldier that Wolf had inadvertently killed in self-defence. Any proof of his involvement would have died with Masse. He still had the carefully chosen selection of newspaper clippings, which he had intended to plant in Masse's flat, on him.

Most of the articles were related to the Cremation Killer trial, damning accounts of the failures, with several names highlighted, that led to the needless death of schoolgirl Annabelle Adams. Others were stories regarding the military's attempts to conceal the number of Afghan civilian casualties, especially children, during skirmishes with Masse's former regiment. Wolf had been confident that this simple theme would have been considered a plausible trigger to Masse's clinically unstable mind and that the circumstances surrounding his miraculous escape from the IED attack would only add further weight to the story.

It was irrelevant now. Instead, Wolf had released a sadistic predator into the city, and any hope he might have had of returning to a normal life had disintegrated along with the plan. Elizabeth Tate and her daughter should never have been involved. It had been reckless of him to abscond with Ashley. Crucially, though, he had not expected Edmunds.

The young detective had been hounding him from the very beginning and had found at least one of Masse's earlier, less accomplished murders. Wolf knew that it was only a matter of time before he connected the dots. If he had not, so foolishly, lashed out at Edmunds, he would know exactly how much his colleagues had discovered.

None of this mattered to him quite as much as Baxter learning of what he had done, what he still had to do. He knew that she would never be able to understand it, no matter how hard she might try. Despite all evidence to the contrary, she still believed in the law, in justice, in the system that rewarded the liars and the corrupt as they operated blatantly within a culture of apathy. She would see him as her enemy – as being no better than Masse.

He could not bear to think about it.

There was a loud slam from downstairs as the main door to the neglected building swung shut. Wolf grabbed the heavy hammer that he had found beneath the sink and listened against the flimsy door. A few moments later there was another slam as someone entered the flat below and then the sound of the television reverberated up through the walls. Wolf relaxed and returned to the windowsill and the uninspiring view over the closed-up Shepherd's Bush Market and the train tracks beyond.

He had been somewhat underwhelmed by the lair of the world's most famous murderous sociopath. It felt like peering behind the curtain of a magic trick. He had expected grotesque artwork drawn in blood, sinister religious scrawling across the walls, grisly photographs or keepsakes from his accumulating list of victims, but there was nothing. And yet there was something quietly unsettling about the whitewashed room.

There was no television, no computer, no mirrors anywhere. Six sets of identical clothing were either folded neatly into drawers or hanging up in the wardrobe. The refrigerator only contained a pint of milk and there was no bed, only a thin mat on the floor, a common practice for soldiers returning home, superficially in one piece and yet changed forever. A wall of books had been organised, apparently according to colour: *On War and Morality*, *The Accidental Species: Misunderstandings of Human Evolution*, *Encyclopaedia of Explosives*, *Medical Biochemistry* . . .

Wolf wiped away the condensation again and noticed a car loitering at the entrance to the narrow service road. He could hear the engine idling through the flat's ill-fitting window. He could not make the car out clearly but could tell that it looked far too expensive to belong to any of the building's residents. He got to his feet, sensing that something was wrong.

Suddenly, the car accelerated aggressively along the driveway, pursued closely by two marked Armed Response Vehicles, which skidded to a halt on the grass and stones below his second-storey window.

'Oh shit!' said Wolf, already running for the door.

He stepped out into the gloomy corridor, letting the door to Masse's flat click shut behind him. The tired staircase at the end of the hallway was already creaking in protest beneath the weight of the first wave of armed officers.

He had nowhere to run.

Heavy boots were thundering up the stairs towards him. There was no fire exit, no windows, only the scuffed and peeling door to the flat across the hall.

Wolf kicked at it; it stood fast.

He kicked again; a crack appeared in the wood.

He threw himself against it in desperation. The lock splintered away from the wood, and he fell into the empty room just as the officers reached the top of the stairs. He pushed the door to. Seconds later, there were heavy thuds against Masse's door.

'Police! Open up!'

After another moment, there was a huge bang as the officers used an Enforcer ram to gain entry to the tiny flat. Wolf's heart was racing. He lay on the floor listening to the intimidating sounds of the raid taking place just metres away.

'It's one bloody room!' he heard a familiar voice say as they argued with someone on the stairs. 'If they haven't found him by now, they're probably not going to.'

Wolf climbed back to his feet and peered through the fisheye peephole as Baxter and Finlay stepped into view. While they were waiting impatiently out in the corridor, Baxter stared directly at him and, for a moment, Wolf was sure that she could see him. She looked down at the broken lock.

'Nice place,' she remarked to Finlay.

She gave the door a gentle push. It opened half an inch before hitting Wolf's foot. He glanced back at the empty room and the low rooftop of the adjoining building, which he would be able to reach from the window.

'All clear!' someone bellowed out in the corridor as the lead officer came out of Masse's flat holding something.

'Found this inside the mattress. One of yours, I believe,' he said accusingly, handing Baxter the laptop tagged with a Homicide and Serious Crime ID. Bloody fingerprints decorated the silver casing, black and dirty in the dusty light of the corridor. She opened it up warily before handing it to Finlay as if she could not even bear to look at it.

'It's Chambers',' she explained, removing the gloves she had used to handle it.

'How can you tell?'

'The password.'

Finlay read the bloody scrap of paper tucked between the screen and the keyboard:

'Eve2014.'

He tapped a key. The sleeping computer booted back up. He carefully typed in the password and was confronted with the familiar home screen of the Met's secure server. A short email had been left open, dated 7 July:

> You are receiving this because you were recently removed from the mail group Homicide&Serious_Crime_Command. If you believe this to have been actioned in error or still require access, please contact the helpdesk.
> Regards,
> IT Support Team

Finlay turned the screen to show Baxter.

'He's been logged on to our server the entire time,' she groaned. '*That's* why he's always been one step ahead of us! Edmunds is full of shit. Wolf wasn't leaking information!'

'I know you want to believe that. I do too. But we don't know for sure.'

She looked annoyed with him and moved away.

'Thank you, thank you . . . Much obliged . . . Come again,' said Baxter as she hurried the armed officers out through the door.

Wolf rushed to the window, climbed out onto the rooftop and descended the first fire escape that he came to. He tried to conceal his face as he passed the officers guarding the entrance to the service road and heard the tinny tapping of rain striking the market's metal shutters fade away as he climbed the stairs of Goldhawk Road Station. He boarded a train just as the doors were closing and watched the flashing blue lights pass beneath him as it pulled away and rattled over the bridge.

He had just lost his advantage.

CHAPTER 34

Monday 14 July 2014

5.14 a.m.

Baxter was woken by the sound of rain hammering against her apartment windows. As her eyes flickered open, a gentle rumble of thunder rolled across the sky somewhere in the distance. She was lying on her sofa in the cosy glow cast by the kitchen spotlights, her cordless phone pressing uncomfortably into her cheek where she had fallen asleep on it.

Part of her had expected Wolf to call. How could he not? As angry and betrayed as she felt, too many things had been left unresolved – or did she really mean so little to him? She was not even sure what she would want out of their final conversation: an apology? An explanation? Perhaps confirmation that Wolf had completely lost his mind and that her friend was, in fact, sick rather than evil.

She reached for her mobile phone on the coffee table to find no missed calls or new messages. As she sat up and swung her legs off the sofa, she sent an empty wine bottle rolling loudly across the wooden floor and hoped that she had not woken her neighbour downstairs. She went over to the window and looked out over the glistening rooftops. The angry clouds above looked a dozen different shades of charcoal every time the blanket lightning lit up the sky.

Whatever happened, she was going to lose something forever before the day was out.

She only wished she knew how much.

Edmunds had worked through the night analysing the incriminating monetary trails zigzagging across the city like numeric breadcrumbs. Combined with being in possession of Chambers' laptop, it amounted to irrefutable proof of Lethaniel Masse's guilt and, incredibly, that the Ragdoll and Faustian murders were one and the same. He felt a little disappointed that he would not be there to apprehend this fascinating and imaginative serial killer himself, although, there was no doubt that the revelation of Wolf's involvement was significantly more shocking than whatever monster he had been conjuring up in his head.

He wondered whether the world would ever really know.

Edmunds was tired and was struggling to concentrate as he finished up his work. He had received a text message from Tia's mother at around 4 a.m. and had immediately phoned her back. Tia had had a very minor bleed during the night and the maternity ward had asked her to come in as a precaution, to ensure that everything was all right with the baby. They had taken themselves down to the hospital and been told that everything was fine and that there was no need to worry. They just wanted to monitor her for a few hours.

When Edmunds asked, furiously, why she had not thought to phone him earlier, she explained that Tia had not wanted to worry him on such an important day, that she would be livid when she found out that they had spoken. The idea of Tia going through this scare in secret upset him and, after getting off the phone, he could not think about anything else other than how much he wanted to be there with her.

At 6.05 a.m. Vanita walked into the office dressed in an attention-grabbing trouser suit in anticipation of a day in front of the cameras. Her dripping umbrella marked her route from the doorway, abruptly changing course on spotting Edmunds at his desk.

'Morning, Edmunds,' she greeted him. 'You have got to hand it to the press – they're determined. It's apocalyptic out there!'

'They started setting up just before midnight,' said Edmunds.

'You've been here all night again?' she asked, more impressed than surprised.

'It's not a habit I intend to continue.'

'None of us ever do, and yet . . .' She smiled at him. 'You're going places, Edmunds. Keep up the good work.'

He handed her the completed financial report that he had spent the night compiling. She flicked through the stack of paperwork.

'Airtight?' she asked.

'Completely. The studio flat at Goldhawk Road is owned by a charity that provides housing for injured soldiers, hence why it was harder to find. He just pays them a heavily discounted rent. It's all on page twelve.'

'Excellent work.'

Edmunds picked up an envelope off his desk and handed it to her.

'Is this related to the case?' she asked as she started ripping it open.

'In a way,' said Edmunds.

She paused on hearing his tone, frowned at him, and then walked away towards her office.

Baxter arrived at the office at 7.20 a.m. after being asked to leave the Central Forensic Image Team in peace. In truth, she was relieved to get out of the darkened room. She had no idea how the CFIT officers endured their hours confined to the headache-inducing room, where they oversaw feeds from CCTV cameras from all over the city.

A team of super-recognisers, chosen for their unrivalled ability to pick out and identify individual facial structures in large crowds, had been working through the night alongside the facial recognition software in search of Wolf and Masse. Baxter knew that it was like looking for two needles in a haystack, but that did not soothe her frustration when they, unsurprisingly, failed to find either of them.

She had chided a member of staff when he returned from his break two minutes late, holding a coffee. The supervisor had taken exception to this and made a show of dressing Baxter down in front of everyone before instructing her to leave. She stormed back to Homicide and Serious Crime Command and approached Edmunds, who was midway through composing a text to Tia.

'Any progress in the camera room?' he asked as he finished typing and put his phone away.

'I got kicked out,' said Baxter. It spoke volumes that Edmunds merely shrugged; he did not even bother to ask the reason why. 'It's a waste of time anyway. They don't know where to look. They're watching the area around Wolf's flat, which he obviously isn't going back to, and Masse's flat, which I can't see him going back to either.'

'What about facial recognition?'

'You're joking right?' laughed Baxter. 'So far, it's flagged Wolf up three times. One was an old Chinese woman, the second was a puddle, and the third was a poster of Justin Bieber!'

Despite the immense pressure that they were under and the severe consequences of CFIT's failure to locate either man, they both smirked at the preposterous list of matches.

'I need to talk to you about something,' said Edmunds.

Baxter dropped her bag to the floor with a heavy thud and perched on the desk to listen.

'DC Edmunds,' Vanita called from the doorway of her office. She was holding a folded piece of paper in her hand. 'A moment?'

'Uh-oh,' said Baxter teasingly as he got up and walked towards the office.

Edmunds closed the door behind him and took a seat at the desk, where the letter he had typed at 4.30 a.m. that morning lay open.

'I must say that I am surprised,' she said. 'Especially today, of all days.'

'I feel that I have contributed everything that I possibly can to the case,' he said, gesturing to the hefty file sitting beside the letter.

'And what a contribution it has been.'

'Thank you.'

'You *are* sure about this?'

'I am.'

She sighed: 'I really do see a bright future for you.'

'So do I. Just not here, unfortunately.'

'Very well, I'll submit the transfer paperwork.'

'Thank you, Commander.'

Edmunds and Vanita shook hands and then he left the room. Baxter had been watching the brief exchange from where she had been loitering beside the photocopier, attempting to eavesdrop. Edmunds collected his jacket and wandered over to her.

'Going somewhere?' she asked.

'Hospital. Tia was admitted overnight.'

'Is she . . .? Is the baby . . .?'

'I think they're both OK, but I need to be there.'

He could tell that Baxter was struggling to balance her compassion for him and his family with her disbelief that he would abandon the team, abandon her, at such a critical time.

'You don't need me here,' he assured her.

'Has she,' Baxter nodded towards Vanita's office, 'signed off on this?'

'To be quite honest, I don't really care. I just handed in a transfer request to return to Fraud.'

'You did what?'

'Marriage. Detective. Divorce,' said Edmunds.

'I didn't mean . . . It's not the case for everyone.'

'I've got a baby on the way. I'm not going to make it.'

Baxter smiled, remembering her ruthless reaction to the news of his pregnant fiancée.

'Then why don't you stop wasting my time and just go back to Fraud?' she recited with a sad smile.

To Edmunds' surprise, she embraced him tightly.

'Come on, I couldn't stay if I wanted to,' he told her. 'Everyone in here hates me. You don't turn on your own, even when they're as guilty as sin, apparently. I'll be on the phone if you need me for anything today,' he said before reiterating sincerely: '*Anything.*'

Baxter nodded and released him.

'I'll be back at work tomorrow,' he laughed.

'I know.'

Edmunds smiled fondly at her, put on his jacket and left the office.

Wolf binned the kitchen knife that he had stolen from the bed and breakfast as he turned off Ludgate Hill. He could barely make out the clock tower of St Paul's Cathedral through the lashing rain, which eased as he walked along Old Bailey, the street that gave the Central Criminal Court its famous nickname, the tall buildings providing a little shelter from the storm.

He was not sure why he had chosen the courtrooms when there were several other locations that held just as much significance to him: Annabelle Adams' grave, the spot where they had found Naguib Khalid standing over her burning body, St Ann's Hospital. For some reason the courts had felt right, the place where it had all started, a place where he had already come face to face with a demon and survived to tell the tale.

Wolf had let his dark beard grow out over the week and had donned a pair of glasses. The unrelenting rain had flattened his thick hair, which only enhanced the simple but effective, disguise. He reached the visitors' entrance to the old courtrooms and joined the back of the long, sodden queue of people. From what he could gather from the loud American tourist in front, there was a high-profile murder trial taking place in Court Two. As the queue slowly grew behind him, he overheard several conversations involving his name and excited predictions on how the Ragdoll murders would end.

When the doors finally opened, the crowd shuffled obediently out of the rain and through the X-ray machines and security checks. A court official ushered the first group, which included Wolf, along the hushed hallways and deposited them outside the entrance to Court Two. Wolf had no option but to ask whether he could sit in on Court One instead. He had not wanted to draw attention to himself and was concerned for a moment that the official, surprised by the request, had recognised him, but she shrugged and escorted him to the appropriate door. She instructed him to stand with the other four people waiting outside the public viewing gallery. They all appeared to know each other and eyed him suspiciously.

After a short wait the doors were opened and the familiar smells of polished wood and leather wafted out from the room that Wolf had not set foot in since being dragged out, wrist shattered, covered in blood. He followed the others inside and took a seat in the front row, looking down over the courtroom.

The various staff, lawyers, witnesses and jurors filtered into the room beneath him. When the defendant was escorted into the dock, he heard movement behind him as his fellow spectators waved and gestured to the heavily tattooed man that Wolf could confidently predict was guilty of whatever he was being accused of just by looking at him. The room then got to its feet as the judge entered the court and took his lonely seat on the elevated bench.

Vanita had released photographs of Masse to the press after confirming that Edmunds' evidence was accurate. His unmistakable ruined face was now being paraded on every news channel in the world. Usually the PR team had to beg the television studios to broadcast even a three-second glance at their photofits, so Vanita had wasted no time in capitalising on the unprecedented level of exposure. She smiled at the cliché: the killer's own lust for notoriety precipitating his downfall.

Despite clear instructions to the public, the call takers had been inundated with hundreds of phone calls giving sightings of Masse dating back as far as 2007. Baxter had taken the job of checking through the updates every ten minutes and liaising with the CFIT officers. She was growing increasingly frustrated as time wore on.

'Don't these people bloody listen!' she yelled, scrunching the latest printout into a ball. 'Why would I give a toss whether he was in Sainsbury's five years ago or not? I need to know where he is *now*!'

Finlay dared not say a word. An alert on Baxter's computer went off.

'Great, here comes another lot.'

Slumping back into her chair, she opened the email from the call centre. She skimmed the list of irrelevant dates until she came across one from 11.05 a.m. that morning. She traced her finger across the screen to read the rest of the details. The call had been made by an investment banker, who immediately struck Baxter as being more reliable than the psychics and intoxicated homeless who constituted three quarters of the calls. The location: Ludgate Hill.

Baxter leapt to her feet and sprinted past Finlay before he could even ask her what she had found. She tore down the stairs towards the CFIT control room.

Wolf found it strange to witness such a relaxed and civilised affair in comparison to his experience on the Khalid trial. He gathered that the accused had pleaded guilty to manslaughter but not to murder. The trial was into its third day, not to determine the man's guilt, only to decide just how guilty he was.

Ninety minutes into the proceedings, two of the people behind Wolf in the gallery crept out, disturbing everybody in the subdued courtroom as the door closed heavily behind them. The defence lawyer had just settled back into his speech when the first fire alarm went off in a distant part of the building. Like dominoes, other alarms triggered one by one, the wailing sound approaching like a wave until it flooded the quiet courtroom.

'No, no, no! Out!' ordered the same supervisor who had already kicked Baxter out once that morning.

'Ludgate Hill. 11.05 a.m.,' she said, out of breath.

The officer at the control board looked to his supervisor for instructions. When he reluctantly nodded, the man switched the screens to the current feed from the nearest CCTV cameras in order to access the recorded data.

'Wait!' shouted Baxter. 'Wait! What's happening?'

The screens were filled with crowds of people milling around aimlessly. Most were dressed in smart suits, and one woman was wearing a black gown and a wig. The officer typed hastily on another computer.

'Fire alarm at the Central Criminal Court,' he read seconds later.

Baxter's eyes lit up, and she ran back out of the room without another word. The officer at the computer looked back to his supervisor in confusion.

'Am I still doing this or not?' he asked politely.

Baxter sprinted back up the stairs but slowed as she reached the door to the office. She walked calmly over to Finlay's desk and knelt down to speak to him privately.

'I know where Wolf is,' she whispered.

'That's great!' said Finlay, wondering why they were whispering about it.

'He's at the Old Bailey. They both are. It makes perfect sense.'

'Don't you think you should be telling someone more important than me?'

'We both know what's going to happen if I tell anyone Wolf and Masse are in the same building together. They're gonna send every armed officer in London there.'

'And so they should,' said Finlay, already sensing where this was going.

'Do you think Wolf's gonna let anyone lock him back up?'

Finlay sighed.

'My thoughts exactly,' said Baxter.

'So?'

'So, we need to get in there first. We need to talk him down.'

Finlay sighed even more heavily.

'I'm sorry, lass. I'm not going to do that.'

'What?'

'Emily, I . . . You know I don't want anything to happen to Will, but he's made his choices. I've got my retirement to think about . . . and Maggie. I cannae jeopardiase that. Not now. Not for him.'

Baxter looked hurt.

'And if you think I'm letting you go in there alone—'

'I am.'

'No.'

'I just need a few minutes with him and then I'll call for backup. I swear.'

Finlay considered it for a moment.

'I'm going to call it in,' he said.

Baxter looked crushed.

'. . . in fifteen minutes,' he added.

Baxter smiled. 'I need thirty.'

'I'll give you twenty. Be careful.'

Baxter gave him a kiss on the cheek and grabbed her bag off her desk. Finlay felt sick with worry as he started the timer on his watch. He watched her stroll past Vanita's office before breaking into a run the moment she was clear of the doorway.

Wolf remained seated as the people behind and below gathered their belongings and evacuated in an orderly fashion. The man in the dock looked tempted to make a break for it but he was too indecisive and two security officers hurried inside to usher him out. After a straggling lawyer ran back to collect his laptop, Wolf was left alone in the famous courtroom. Even over the alarms, he could hear doors slamming and people being directed to their nearest fire exit.

Wolf wished that it was only a fire but suspected that it was something far more dangerous.

CHAPTER 35

Monday 14 July 2014

11.57 a.m.

After twenty solid minutes the alarms had ceased abruptly but survived as the ghosts of echoes reverberating endlessly around the Great Hall's domed ceiling. As the ringing in Wolf's ears slowly subsided, and the courtroom returned to an appropriate hush, a new sound grew out of the silence: a lone set of uneven footsteps approaching the courtroom doors. Wolf remained seated up in the gallery. He had to fight to keep his breathing steady, his knuckles blanching as he clenched his fists.

A hazy memory had chosen an inopportune moment to return: the glaring overhead lights illuminating a long corridor, the deafening ring of a phone, somebody answering. A patient? A nurse? He vaguely remembered them holding the receiver up to their ear. He wanted to call out to them, to warn them, despite himself, surrendering to the irrational, even if only for a moment.

It was the same fear that had taken him now.

He found himself straining to listen as the unhurried footsteps grew louder and jumped when a thunderous bang rattled the old doors violently against their frames.

There was a short pause in which Wolf did not dare breathe.

A worn hinge creaked somewhere below him and then he felt the vibration of a door swinging closed. Wolf watched the empty room with wide eyes as the footsteps returned and an imposing figure, dressed all in black, materialised from beneath the gallery. The deep hood of its long coat was pulled over its head. In his impressionable state, Wolf's imagination ran rife: it was as if the Recording Angel herself had torn free of the building's grand entranceway, amidst a shower of rubble and dust, to pass judgement upon him.

'I must say,' began Masse. Each syllable sounded as though it had to be ripped out of him. Spittle glistened in the artificial light as he spat his mutated words across the room. It was as if he had forgotten how to speak. 'I am very impressed that you stayed.'

He passed between the benches, running his skeletal-white fingers along the polished surfaces and the assortment of items abandoned during the evacuation. Wolf found it deeply unsettling that Masse had not looked up at him, yet appeared to know precisely where he was. Wolf had chosen the courtrooms but began to worry that he was exactly where Masse wanted him.

'"Any coward can fight a battle when he's sure of winning; but give me the man who has pluck to fight when he's sure of losing",' recited Masse as he ascended the steps up to the judge's bench.

Wolf's heart sank as the hooded man lifted the Sword of Justice off the wall. He wrapped his long fingers round the golden hilt and slowly unsheathed the weapon to the scrape of metal on metal. He paused to admire the long blade for a moment.

'George Eliot said that,' he continued thoughtfully as spots of reflected light flickered in and out of existence across the dark wood panels. 'I believe that she would have liked you.'

Masse raised the priceless piece of history above his head and then swung it down into the desk in the centre. Although blunted, the weighty length of metal embedded itself deep into the wood, quivering gently as he took a seat.

Wolf's nerve was wavering the longer he spent in Masse's presence. He knew that, beneath the hood, Masse was just a man: a proficient, ruthless and ingenious killer, no doubt, but a man all the same, yet it was impossible to ignore the fact that he was the terrifying truth at the heart of whispered urban legends, to ignore the universal enthralment that his latest work had demanded from a chronically apathetic world.

Masse was no demon, but Wolf had no doubt that he was the closest thing to one he would ever encounter.

'A real sword,' Masse gestured to the weapon. 'Hung above the judges' heads in a room guaranteed to contain at least one suspected murderer at any given time.' He raised a hand to his throat, suggesting that the monologue was taking its toll on him. 'You have got to love the British. Even after what you yourself did within these very walls, they regard pomp and tradition far more highly than they do security and common sense.'

Masse broke into a fit of painful rattling coughs.

Wolf used the break in proceedings to unthread his shoelaces, hoping that he would never find himself within close enough proximity to Masse for them to come in useful. He was just coiling the loose laces around his hand when he froze; Masse was sliding the heavy hood away from his scarred scalp.

He had seen photographs, read the medical reports, but none had fully captured the devastating extent of Masse's injuries. Rivers of scars meandered over a deathly white surface, narrow tributaries flooding or drying up with his changes of expression. He finally looked up into the gallery.

Wolf had learned from his own investigation that Masse had come from money – public school, family crest, sailing clubs. He had even been quite handsome once. There was still a hint of his upper-class diction mutilated somewhere within his graceless delivery, and yet it was nothing short of bizarre watching this scarred, merciless killer addressing him so eloquently and quoting Victorian novelists.

It started to dawn on Wolf why Masse had isolated himself, why he could never go back to his family's life of fundraisers and golf clubs, why he had been so desperate to return to the army; there was no place for him back in the real world.

A brilliant mind trapped within a broken body.

He wondered whether Masse would merely have been another normal member of society had events unfolded differently, or if he had simply lost the protection of his aristocratic facade in that bomb blast.

'Tell me William, is it all that you hoped it would be?' asked Masse. 'Can little Annabelle Adams finally rest easy in the knowledge that she has been avenged?'

Wolf did not answer.

A lopsided grin cut across Masse's face:

'Did you bask in the heat as the mayor went up in flames?'

Subconsciously, Wolf shook his head.

'No?'

'I never wanted this,' murmured Wolf, unable to help himself.

'Oh, but you did,' smirked Masse. '*You* did this to them.'

'I was sick! I was angry. I didn't know what I was doing!' Wolf was furious with himself. He knew that he was letting Masse get to him.

Masse sighed heavily.

'I will be so very disappointed if you turn out to be one of those: "I didn't mean it", "I need to go back on our arrangement" or my personal favourite: "I found God". Although, if by chance you have, I would sincerely love to know where the little prick is hiding.'

Masse's wheezy laughter erupted into another bout of tearing coughs, giving Wolf time to compose himself:

'And I'll be disappointed if you turn out to be one of those freaks—'

'I am not a freak!' Masse interrupted, leaping to his feet, screaming louder than Wolf even thought possible.

The sound of sirens approaching pierced the tense atmosphere.

Frothy blood foamed on the courtroom floor as Masse panted in rage, his terrifying loss of control only encouraging Wolf.

'. . . who blames all his darkness and perversions on the voices in his head. You kill for the same mundane reason as everybody else – it makes the weak feel powerful.'

'Must we pretend that you don't know who I am? *What* I am?'

'I know exactly what you are, Lethaniel. You are a deluded narcissistic psychopath, soon to be nothing more special than another *freak* in a boiler suit.'

The look that Masse shot Wolf scared him. He remained unsettlingly quiet as he considered his reply.

'I am constant, eternal, forever,' said Masse with utter self-belief.

'You don't look particularly constant, eternal, or forever from where I'm sitting,' said Wolf in feigned confidence. 'In fact, you look as though a mild head cold might take you out before I get the chance.'

Masse ran a self-conscious hand over the deep valleys running through his skin.

'These belonged to Lethaniel Masse,' he said quietly, remembering. 'He was weak, frail, and as he burned in the fire, I claimed the vessel he left behind.'

Prising the ceremonial sword from the wooden desk, he walked back out onto the courtroom floor.

The sirens were right on top of them now.

'You're attempting to antagonise me? This is why I like you, William! You are defiant, determined. If the courts say you need evidence, you fake it. Should the jury declare someone innocent, you take it upon yourself to beat them within an inch of their life. They fire you, they rehire you. And even when you come face to face with death you cling devotedly to life. It's admirable. Really.'

'If you're such a big fan . . .' quipped Wolf.

'Let you go?' asked Masse, as though the idea was entirely new to him. 'You know that is not how this works.'

The sirens had gone quiet, meaning that the building would be flooded with armed officers at any moment.

'They're here, Masse,' said Wolf. 'There's nothing you can tell them they don't already know. It's over.'

Wolf got up to leave.

'Fate . . . destiny. It is all so cruel,' said Masse. 'Even now you believe that you won't die in this courtroom – and why would you? All you have to do is leave through that door and not come back. You should. You really should.'

'Goodbye, Lethaniel.'

'It is so sad to see you like this: muzzled, kicked into submission. This . . .' Masse gestured up at Wolf, 'this isn't the real William Fawkes, weighing up his options, making sensible decisions, actually showing some sense of self-preservation. The real William Fawkes is all fire and wrath, the man that they had to lock away, the man who came to me for vengeance, the man who tried to stamp a killer into this very floor. The real William Fawkes would *choose* to come down here to die.'

Wolf was unsettled. He did not understand what Masse was trying to achieve. Cautiously, he made his way to the exit.

'Ronald Everett was quite a large man,' said Masse conversationally as Wolf pushed against the door. 'Thirteen pints of blood maybe? More? He accepted that he was going to die with gentlemanly dignity. I punctured a small hole in his femoral artery and he talked to me about his life as he bled out onto the floor.

'It was nice . . . calm.

'Approximately five minutes in, he began to show the first signs of hypovolaemic shock. I would hazard a guess at twenty to twenty-five per cent total blood loss. At nine and a half minutes he lost consciousness, and by eleven minutes his exsanguinated heart had stopped beating.'

Wolf paused when he heard Masse hauling something across the floor.

'I only mention this,' he called up to Wolf from somewhere below the gallery, 'because she's already been bleeding for eight.'

Wolf slowly turned back round. A smear of bright red blood painted their route across the courtroom floor as Masse dragged Baxter behind him, pulling her along by a fistful of her hair. He had gagged her with the silk summer scarf that she always kept in her bag and her own handcuffs bound her hands together.

She looked weak and startlingly pale.

'I must admit, I'm improvising here,' Masse called up to Wolf as he heaved her further into the room. 'I had other plans for you. Who would ever have thought she would come looking for us alone? But she did, and I now see that this is the only way it could have ended.'

Masse dropped her to the floor and looked back up at Wolf, whose expression had turned dark, in anticipation. Any apprehensions that he had harboured regarding the faux demon or the weighty weapon that he wielded had dissipated.

'Ah!' said Masse, pointing the sword up at Wolf. 'Finally! There you are.'

Wolf burst out through the doors and towards the stairs.

Masse knelt down over Baxter. Up close, the scar tissue pulled taut and wrinkled as he moved. She tried to fight him off as he took hold of her arm. She could smell his foul breath on the air and the concoction of medicines and ointments that he had slathered on to soothe his angry skin. He replaced her elbow just to the right of her groin and pressed down until the bleeding slowed.

'Just like before. Keep the pressure on.' He dribbled over her as he spoke. 'We don't want you running out too quickly.'

Masse stood back up and watched the doors:

'And so our hero comes to die.'

CHAPTER 36

Monday 14 July 2014

12.06 p.m.

Wolf could hear voices in a distant part of the building: the firefighters being pulled out ahead of the Armed Response Unit's search of the premises. He leapt down the final three stairs and ran across the magnificent hall, already feeling a tightness in his chest and the stab of a painful stitch in his side. He focused on the courtroom door, trying desperately to ignore the churchlike setting: a white-robed Moses looked down on him from his seat at the foot of Mount Sinai; carved cherubs were frozen in flight, scattered around stained-glass windows and the likenesses of archbishops, cardinals and rabbis preaching the word of God, corroborating Masse's claims.

There is a God. There is a Devil. Demons walk among us.

Wolf stepped in the shallow crimson puddle seeping out from beneath the doors as he burst through into the courtroom. Baxter was still at the far end, below the dock, bleeding into wood already saturated with Khalid. He made a movement towards her but Masse stepped between them, sword raised.

'That's far enough,' he said.

His distorted grin was repulsive.

Baxter felt lethargic. Her damp trousers were cold where they clung against her skin. She was struggling to keep pressure on the artery and felt as though she might fall asleep every time she blinked. She had cut deep scratches into her face while attempting to remove the gag that Masse had tied so tightly round her head and knew that she could not spare the blood to try again.

She could feel the gun pressing into the small of her back, just out of her handcuffed reach. Masse had missed it. She went for it once more but as she tentatively lifted her elbow away from her leg, the constant trickle of blood began to pump frighteningly in time to her racing heart.

She reached around to the right, but her left arm restricted her movement. Her fingertips brushed tantalisingly against the metal. She arched her back, willing her arm to dislocate, to break, anything to gain a few millimetres more.

The puddle that she was sitting in had grown to twice the size in just a few seconds. She cried out in frustration and then replaced her elbow to stem the bleeding, having just traded seven seconds of fruitless exertion for several minutes of life.

Masse had draped his long coat over one of the benches. Beneath it, he wore the same shirt, trouser and shoe set that Wolf had discovered in Goldhawk Road: his camouflage. Wolf was still breathing heavily as the two substantial men came face to face for the second time. What little advantage he gained in height and bulk, Masse more than made up for in muscle.

In their haste to evacuate, somebody had left an expensive-looking fountain pen on top of a stack of papers. Wolf shifted position, covertly picking up the makeshift metal weapon as Masse continued.

'I knew you were there yesterday, in Piccadilly Circus.'

Wolf's anger gave way to surprise.

'I wanted to see whether you could do it,' said Masse. 'But you are weak, William. You were weak yesterday. You were weak the day you failed to finish Naguib Khalid, and you are weak now. I can see it in you.'

'Believe me, if you hadn't moved—'

'I didn't,' interrupted Masse. 'I watched you panic. I watched you run past me. I wonder, did you really fail to see me standing directly in front of you or do you think that perhaps you just didn't want to?'

Wolf shook his head. He tried to remember the moment that he had lost sight of Masse in the crowds. He *would* have had the courage to finish him. Masse was manipulating him, making him doubt himself.

'So, you must see the futility in this?' Masse continued softly. He paused. 'Because I like you – and sincerely, I do – I am going to offer you a choice that wasn't made available to any of your counterparts: you can get on your knees, and you have my word I'll make it clean. You won't feel a thing. Or we can fight this out and things will inevitably turn . . . unpleasant.'

Wolf adopted the same hungry look that Masse wore so well.

'Predictable as ever,' sighed Masse, raising his sword.

Baxter needed to stop the bleeding. She had not dared try while Masse had been watching. As things stood, she was at least able to control it. Had he realised her intentions, he would have ensured that there was no way to stem the blood loss.

Without moving her elbow out of position, she was able to unbuckle her belt with her shackled hands. Taking a deep breath, she pulled the material out from under her and wrapped it around her leg, just above the wound. She pulled it tighter and tighter, the pain excruciating, until the bleeding was no more than a trickle once more.

She was still losing blood, but now she had regained the use of her hands.

Masse took a step towards Wolf. Wolf stepped back. Another. Wolf unscrewed the surprisingly weighty lid from the fountain pen, placing his thumb just below the nib, holding it out in front of him as if wielding a knife.

Masse surged forward, swinging the lethal antique wildly. Wolf stumbled backwards as it struck the wall beside him and Masse swung again, the blade slicing through the air just inches from Wolf's face, the force of his own swing knocking him off balance. Wolf risked a fleeting step forward and jabbed the pen in and out of Masse's upper arm before retreating back to a safe distance.

Masse cried out and assessed the damage, calmly prodding the fresh puncture wound in fascination.

This moment of composure passed like the eye of a storm as, incensed, he swung again. Wolf backed into the corner, instinctively turning his body away from the attack; however, the glancing blow was agonising where it connected with his left shoulder. Throwing himself at Masse, he stabbed at him repeatedly, sinking the metal deeper and deeper into his sword arm until a weakened blow knocked him to the floor. He heard the pen drop and disappear out of sight.

Both men paused for a moment. Wolf was on the floor, holding his dropped shoulder in pain, while Masse watched in fascination as a stream of dark red blood trickled out from under the cuff of his shirt. He showed no sign of fear or pain, only surprise at the amount of damage that his unworthy opponent had managed to inflict. He attempted to lift the heavy weapon again but could barely raise it off the floor and was forced to seize it with his left hand instead.

'Get on your knees, Lethaniel,' said Wolf with a smirk as he struggled back to his feet. 'You have my word I'll make it clean.'

Wolf saw Masse's expression twitch with the insult. He stole a glance towards Baxter, as did Masse.

'I wonder, would you fight quite so hard to save her if you knew?'

Wolf ignored the baiting comment and took a step closer to her before Masse blocked his path again.

'If you knew that her name was far more deserving of a place on our list than most,' Masse continued.

Wolf was confused.

'Detective Inspector Chambers was not a brave man. He begged. He whimpered. He pleaded as he proclaimed his innocence.'

When Masse shot Baxter a taunting smile, Wolf saw an opening and lunged at him. Masse blocked the attack but stumbled backwards into one of the benches.

Baxter watched as Masse's long coat slid off the bench, spilling the contents of her workbag over the floor with it. Her eyes flicked from the bloodstained nail scissors, which Masse had used to incapacitate her, to her mobile phone and then to the small set of keys sitting beside the table leg.

'It transpires that, for Emily's sake,' continued Masse, 'in order to preserve your friendship, he had allowed you to think that *he* had sent the letter to Professional Standards . . .'

Wolf looked uneasy.

'. . . the letter that brought down your entire case against Khalid.' Masse watched with eager amusement as Wolf stared at Baxter in disbelief. 'I'm afraid we killed the wrong person.'

Baxter could not meet his eye. But suddenly, she looked up and let out a muffled cry.

He saw Masse approaching too late. With no other option, Wolf charged towards him, blocking his wild swing, bringing them both down heavily onto the hard floor. The sword slid beneath one of the benches as Wolf mercilessly struck Masse time and time again, the damage that he was inflicting masked by the man's already devastating injuries.

When Masse reached up in desperation and grasped Wolf's shattered shoulder, feeling the broken bone grating beneath the skin, it only enraged him further, feeding the attack against him. Wolf cried out in hatred and fury, the roar deafening to the ears of his floundering enemy. He drove his head down into Masse's ruined face with brutal force, shattering his nose and robbing his thrashing limbs of fight.

Masse stared up helplessly, incapacitated by the ferocity of the onslaught. His eyes were wide, pleading – afraid.

*

Baxter had crawled across the courtroom floor, staining the wood behind her. She reached for the scissors and cut the painful gag off her face. Weakening by the second, she clawed her way towards the keys.

Wolf reached into his pocket and removed the shoelaces. He doubled them up for extra strength, yanked his defeated opponent's head up off the floor and wrapped them tightly around his throat. In a final flurry of adrenaline, Masse kicked out viciously and pulled his head away.

'You're only making this harder on yourself,' Wolf told the writhing man.

He spotted the fountain pen beneath a table and got to his feet to collect it.

'So tell me,' said Wolf, spitting a mouthful of Masse's blood onto the floor as he calmly returned with the bloodied weapon, 'if you're the Devil, what does that make me?'

Masse's feeble attempts to drag himself away were thwarted when Wolf crouched over him and, without hesitation, drove the pen through his right leg, mirroring the wound that he had dared inflict on Baxter. He silenced Masse's cries of pain by wrapping the laces back around his neck and pulling them as taut as his injured shoulder could endure.

Relishing the sound of the desperate splutters, he felt the pathetic attempts to fight him off grow weaker. He watched the blood vessels bursting in the whites of Masse's eyes and pulled tighter still, until his arms were shaking with the effort.

'Wolf!' shouted Baxter, struggling with the keys as she lost the dexterity in her fingers. The room was spinning. 'Wolf! Stop!'

He could not even hear her through his rage. He looked back down at Masse. The life was draining from his eyes. This was no longer self-defence – this was an execution.

'That's enough!'

There was a sharp click as Baxter raised the gun and pointed it at his chest. He stared at her in bewilderment and then looked down at the bloodied heap beneath him as if seeing it for the first time.

'I said, that's enough.'

CHAPTER 37

Monday 14 July 2014

12.12 p.m.

Baxter knew that she was on the verge of passing out. Her skin felt clammy and cold, while the nausea worsened with every passing second. She had propped herself up against the witness stand and kept the gun trained on Wolf, unsure whether she could trust anything that she thought she knew about him any more. As Wolf stepped away from Masse, he stared down at the broken man at his feet, as if surprised by the extent of his own brutality.

Baxter could see that Masse was unconscious but still alive. From where she was sitting, she could just make out the rise and fall of his chest as he gasped for air through his ruined face and could hear the crackle of blood fouling each hard-earned breath. As much as he deserved to suffer, it was impossible not to feel a little sympathy for the discarded body lying face up on the courtroom floor.

The fight had been over well before Wolf had finished with him.

There were shouts close by, snapping Wolf out of his daze. He rushed over to Baxter.

'Don't touch me!' she screamed.

She looked terrified of him and he saw her finger twitch over the trigger.

He raised his arms as best he could.

'I can help,' he told her, surprised by her reaction.

'Stay away from me.'

Wolf realised that his sleeves were sodden with dark red blood.

'You're afraid of me?' His voice cracked as he asked the question.

'Yes.'

'This . . . it isn't my blood,' he assured her.

'And you think that makes it better?' asked Baxter in disbelief. She was beginning to slur her words. 'Look at what you've done!' She gestured towards the man dying in the corner. 'You are a monster,' she whispered.

Wolf wiped some of Masse's blood out of his eyes.

'Only when I have to be,' he said sadly. His eyes were glistening as he fought to keep his arms raised. 'I would never hurt you.'

Baxter laughed bitterly at that. 'You already have.'

Wolf looked wounded and she could feel her resolve weaken.

There was a loud bang somewhere in the building as the Armed Response Unit continued their search.

'In here!' she shouted, desperate for it all to be over. Her eyelids fluttered as she struggled to focus. 'I need the truth, Wolf. Did you do this? Did you set Masse on these people?'

Wolf hesitated.

'Yes.'

The admission seemed to knock the air out of Baxter.

'The day Annabelle Adams died,' he continued. 'After I was reinstated, I started looking into the stories but I didn't think it was real! Not really. Not until I saw that list two weeks ago.' He met Baxter's eye. 'I made a terrible, terrible mistake, but I've been trying *so* hard to make it right. I never wanted any of this.'

Baxter had slouched lower to the floor. Her breathing rate had increased dramatically.

'You could have said something.' Her voice was slowing as the gun grew heavy. Her arm swayed as she battled to support the weight. 'You could have come to me.'

'How could I? How am I supposed to tell you that I did this?' Wolf looked every bit as damaged as he had in his infamous photograph beside Elizabeth Tate. 'That I did this to those people, to our friends.' He looked physically sickened by the puddle of blood that Baxter was sitting in. 'That I did this to you?'

A reluctant tear escaped Baxter's eye and rolled down her cheek. She did not have the strength to hide it from him and let it drop to the bloody floor.

'I would've been taken off the case,' said Wolf, 'probably suspended. I thought I'd be more use to the team, and I *knew* I could find him.' He gestured to Masse. 'I'd already done all the groundwork.'

'I want to believe you – but . . .'

Baxter's body finally surrendered. The gun dropped into her lap and she slumped to the side.

There were more shouts from out in the Great Hall and the reverberating roar of an unseen enemy approaching. Wolf looked longingly at the door behind the witness stand, aware that a future of captivity was bearing down on him while his escape route stood unguarded . . .

He gently lowered Baxter's head to the floor and folded Masse's crumpled coat underneath her feet to raise her legs above her exhausted heart. She suddenly regained consciousness when Wolf pulled the makeshift tourniquet tighter, crying out as something shifted inside his injured shoulder. It felt as though her leg was going to burst as it throbbed sluggishly in time to her faltering heart. Wolf was kneeling above her, holding pressure over the wound.

'No,' whined Baxter, trying to push him away as she attempted to sit up.

'Stay still,' he told her. He helped her gently back to the floor. 'You fainted.'

The words took a moment to sink in. Her eyes darted around as she tried to ascertain exactly where she was, noting that the gun was still on the floor beside her head. To Wolf's surprise, she held an unsteady hand out to him. He took hold of it, squeezing as tenderly as his cumbersome hands were able.

A clicking sound accompanied the sensation of cold metal around his wrist.

'You're under arrest,' whispered Baxter.

He automatically pulled his hand away to find that Baxter's followed, dangling limply below it. He smiled down at her fondly, not in the least bit surprised that she would refuse to let something as trivial as a near-death experience interrupt her day. He sat down on the floor beside her, keeping both hands pressed over the source of the bleeding.

'That letter . . .' Baxter started. Despite everything that had happened, she felt she owed him an explanation.

'It doesn't matter now.'

'Me and Andrea were so worried about you. We were trying to help.'

Masse made a guttural groan on the other side of the room before his strained breathing ceased altogether. Baxter glanced over anxiously while Wolf wore a hopeful expression.

A few moments later, Masse spluttered loudly and his breathing resumed.

'Bollocks,' whispered Wolf.

Baxter gave him a disapproving look.

'What were you thinking, coming here on your own?' asked Wolf. His voice was a mixture of concern, anger, and just a hint of admiration.

'Trying to save you,' whispered Baxter. 'Thought I might bring you in before you got yourself killed.'

'And how's that working out for you?'

'Not so good,' she laughed. She had regained a little strength since lying down.

'Clear!' a gruff voice echoed out in the Great Hall.

She could feel the thud of their boots through the floor as she watched Wolf look back impatiently at the set of open doors.

'We're in here!' he called.

It occurred to Baxter that he had not made a single attempt to justify any of his actions; neither had he tried to convince her to let him go, or asked her to back up some fictional story in support of his innocence. For the first time in his life, he was actually taking responsibility instead of looking for a way out.

'In here!' he yelled again.

She took hold of his hand once more, only this time she meant it.

'You didn't leave me,' she said with a smile.

'I nearly did,' he smirked.

'But you didn't. I knew you wouldn't.'

Wolf felt the metal slide away from his wrist. He looked down at his free hand in confusion.

'Go,' whispered Baxter.

He made no attempt to move and still had one hand pressed firmly against her leg.

The rumble of running boots was approaching like a speeding train.

'Go!' she ordered, pulling herself upright against the wood. 'Wolf, please!'

'I'm not leaving you.'

'You're not,' Baxter assured him desperately, feeling fainter again already. 'Help's here.'

Wolf opened his mouth to argue.

The noise was intensifying, the distorted crackles of radios and the clink of metal on metal growing clearer.

'There's no time! Just go!' pleaded Baxter, shoving him away from her with what little strength she had left.

Wolf looked disorientated but snatched the coat off the floor and ran to the small door behind the witness stand. He paused and looked back at her for a fleeting moment, no trace of the monster that she had witnessed ripping Masse apart in his deep blue eyes.

And then he was gone.

She glanced over at Masse, doubting that he would survive, and then remembered that she needed to hide the gun. She reached to her right, but her fingers only found the hard floor. With great effort, she turned her head to discover that it was gone.

'Bastard!' she smiled to herself.

She raised her hands in the air, holding her identification high above her head as the pack of black-clad officers stormed the room.

Wolf followed the familiar corridors away from the sound of the ongoing search. He buttoned up Masse's coat to conceal his blood-stained shirt and put his glasses back on before bursting through the first emergency exit he came to. Alarms went off all around him, but he knew that it would be impossible for anyone out on the street to hear them over the chaos in front of the building.

The rain was hammering down, lending the array of brightly coloured emergency vehicles an additional sheen, so that they appeared to glow against the dreary city and the dark clouds overhead. The press and the ever-growing crowd of curious passers-by had gathered on the other side of the road, jostling for position as they struggled to catch a glimpse of whatever everybody else was looking at.

Wolf calmly crossed the no man's land between the building and the police cordon as two paramedics rushed by. He waved his ID in the general direction of a young officer, who was far too preoccupied holding the reporters at bay to care. As he ducked beneath the police tape, he caught sight of the statue of Lady Justice watching from the rooftop, teetering ever closer to the edge, and then started weaving through the crush of people ceilinged by dark umbrellas.

As the rain intensified, he pulled the hood of the long black coat over his head and made his way towards the edge of the crowd, feeling people pushing past him, stepping over those ignorantly blocking his path and ignoring their scathing looks when he did so, not one of them aware of the monster walking among them.

A wolf in sheep's clothing.

ACKNOWLEDGEMENTS

I'm bound to forget someone and offend them, but here goes . . .

Ragdoll wouldn't exist without a long list of very nice and talented people working incredibly hard to get it out into the world.

From Orion, I'd like to thank Ben Willis, Alex Young, Katie Espiner, David Shelley, Jo Carpenter, Rachael Hum, Ruth Sharvell, Sidonie Beresford-Browne, Kati Nicholl, Jenny Page and Clare Sivell. (I haven't forgotten you, Sam – you get a special mention at the end.)

From Conville & Walsh, I'd like to thank my friends Emma, Alexandra, Alexander and Jake as well as Dorcas and Tracy, who go above and beyond to look after me.

My family – Ma, Ossie, Melo, Bob, B, and KP for all of their help and support.

A very special thank you to the 'curiously omnipresent' force of nature that is my incredible editor Sam Eades, for her relentless enthusiasm and for having such belief in something I wrote.

And an equally special thank you to my friend and confidante Sue Armstrong (she's also my agent), who picked *Ragdoll* up off the slush pile, and without whom this book would probably still be collecting dust under my bed with everything else I'd ever written until I was fortunate enough to meet her. A very special lady.

Finally, thanks to everyone else who has worked on the book in the UK and publishing teams all over the world, and everyone who has taken the time to read it when there are so many incredible books out there you could have been reading instead.

OK, I'm done.

Daniel Cole
2017

Author Q & A with Daniel Cole

RAGDOLL is a masterfully written crime thriller – have you always been a fan of the genre?
I'm more influenced by TV than anything else. As much as I love some of the UK crime shows, there's this common theme of them looking a bit drained of colour, being true-to-life gritty and unrelentingly sombre. But then the US shows often descend into cringe-worthy cheesiness and gimmicks (There's an episode of *Castle* where they wake up as 1920's detectives – I never watched it again).

So, when I started writing screenplays (of which, RAGDOLL was one), I was aiming for that perfect balance between the two – grounded escapism; cherry-picking all of my favourite aspects and trying to make them work together.

The main characters are all such distinct personalities – were they based on anyone you know? Do you have a favourite character?
I don't have a favourite character.

Wolf was a combination of all my favourite heroes/anti-heroes – he's one part Captain Mal Reynolds from *Firefly*, one part Sawyer from *Lost*. There's definitely some Rick Grimes from *Walking Dead* in there, set off against a dash of *Lethal Weapon's* Martin Riggs among others.

None of the other characters were based on anybody specific apart from Baxter, who is loosely based on my amazing sister and biggest fan, Melody.

Baxter and Fawkes are set to return in 2018. What can we expect?
Book 2 is certainly the clichéd bigger, darker, more shocking sequel that you'd expect it to be, but at the same time it's funnier, more poignant and more personal as well. Some familiar faces return. Some new faces are introduced and yes, I'm aware that this is the vaguest answer ever given . . . I can only apologise.